YE

•GUILHERME•PETRECA•

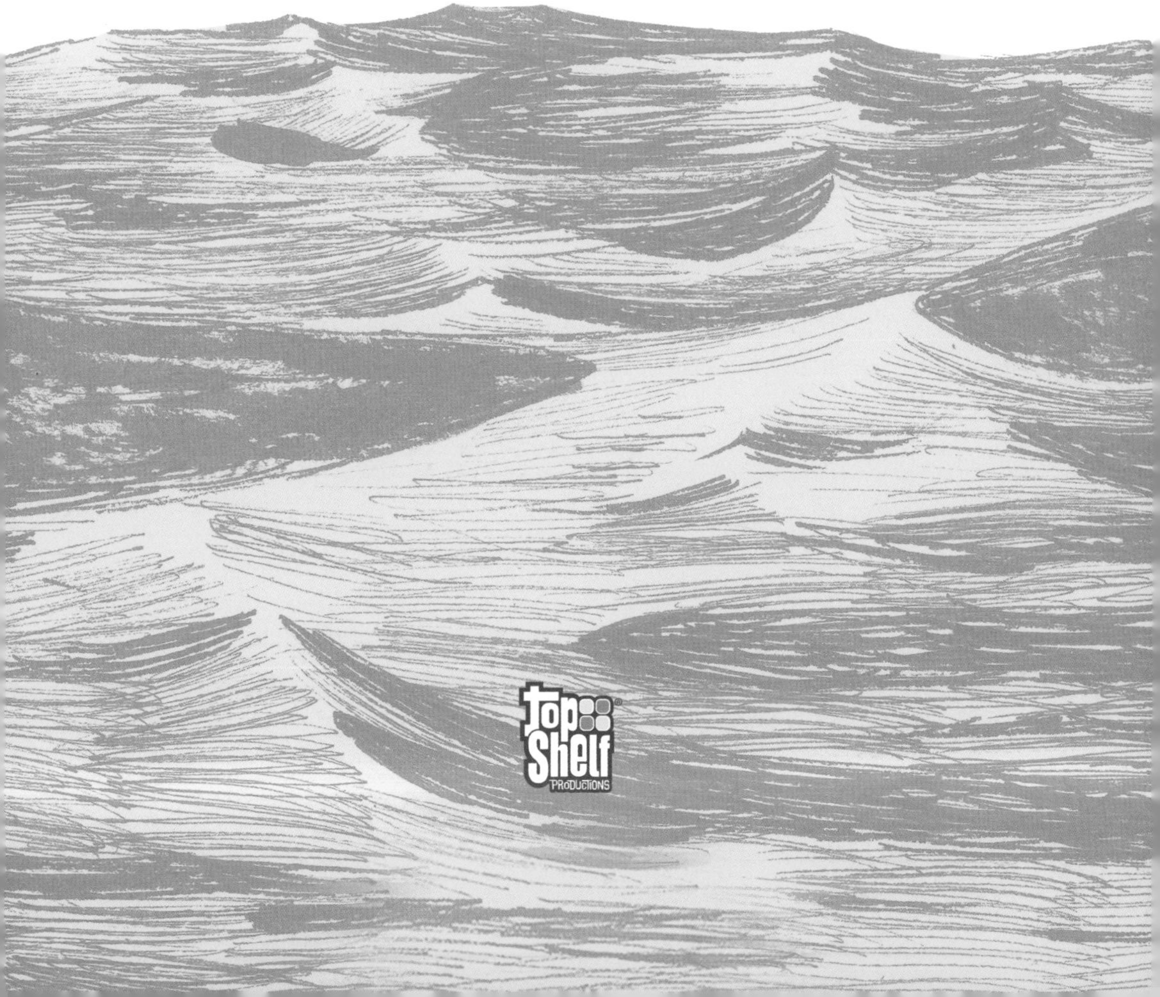

Top Shelf Productions

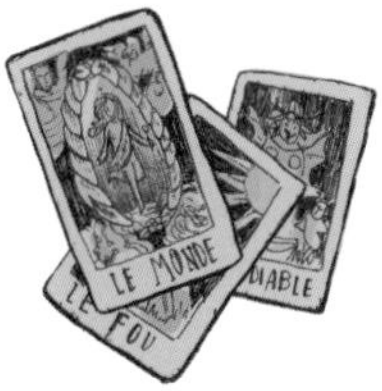
LE MONDE
LE FOU
DIABLE

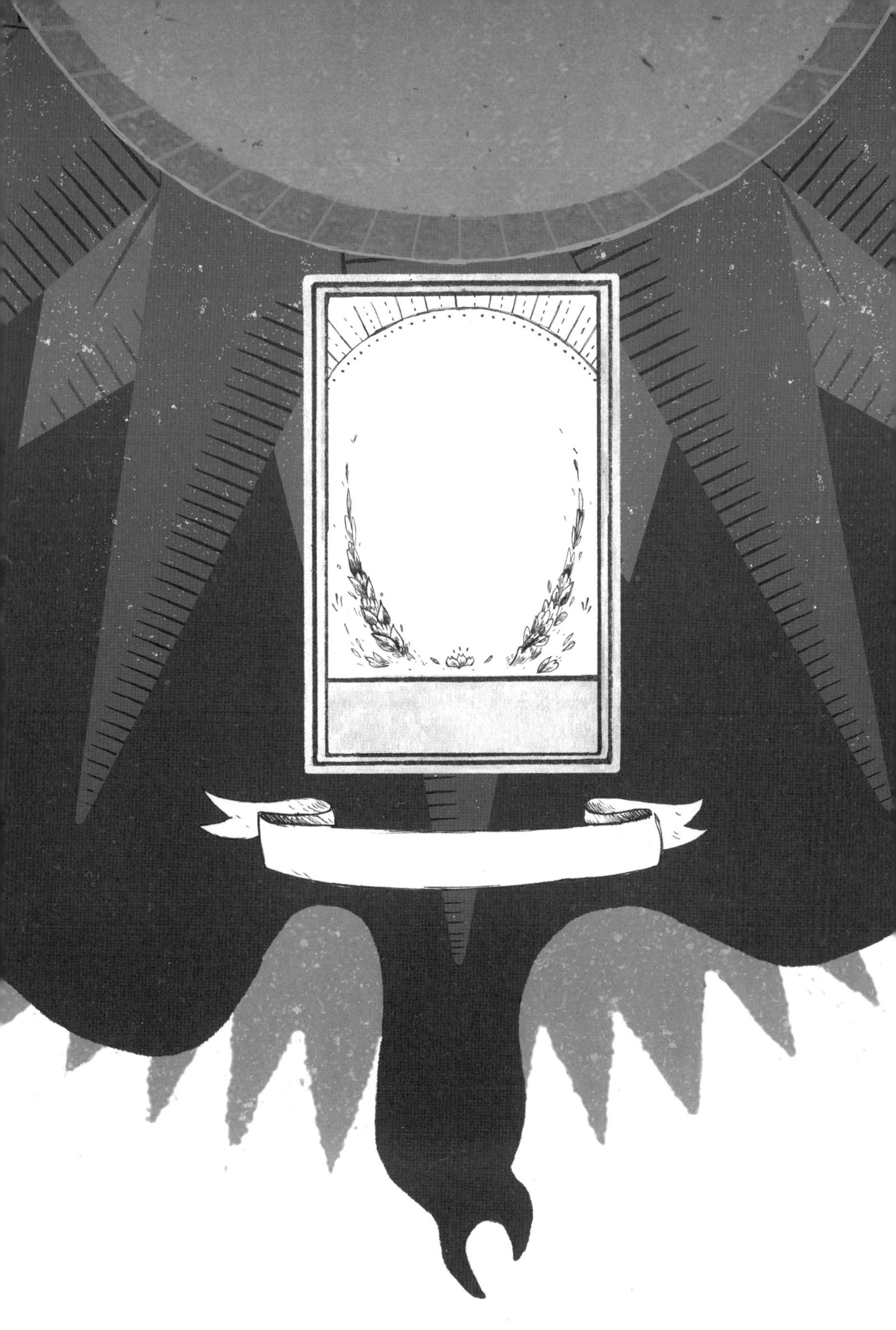

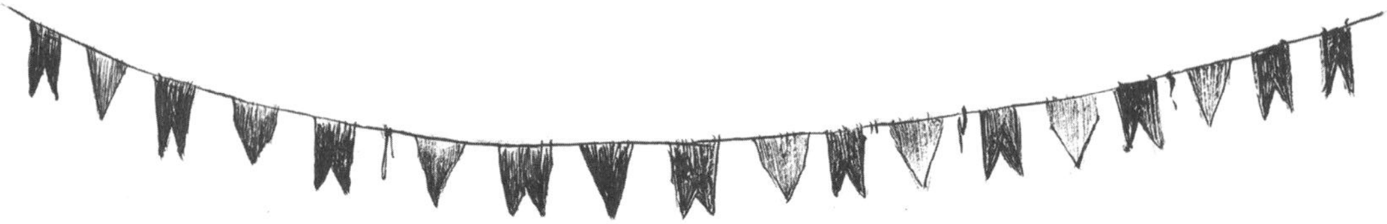

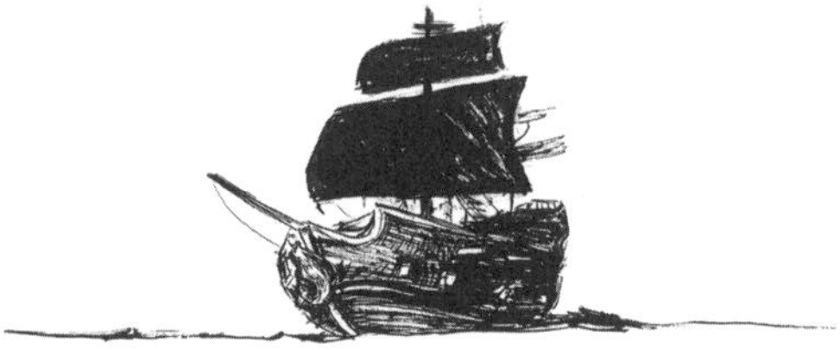

Color assistance by Juliana Adlyn and Rodrigo Otäguro.
Art assistance by Andre Rocca.

Published by Top Shelf Productions, PO Box 1282, Marietta, GA 30061-1282, USA.
Top Shelf Productions is an imprint of IDW Publishing, a division of Idea and Design Works, LLC.
Offices: 2765 Truxtun Road, San Diego, CA 92106. Top Shelf Productions®, the Top Shelf logo,
Idea and Design Works®, and the IDW logo are registered trademarks of Idea and Design Works, LLC.

Editor-in-Chief: Chris Staros.

Designed by Gilberto Lazcano.

Printed in Korea.

ISBN: 978-1-60309-440-5 23 22 21 20 19 5 4 3 2 1

Visit our online catalog at topshelfcomix.com.

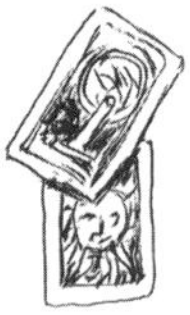

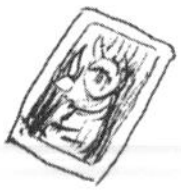

The text on posters and cards has been preserved
in French and Spanish at the author's request.

Originally published in Portuguese by Veneta.

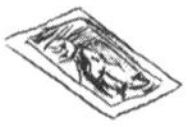

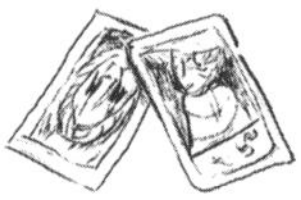

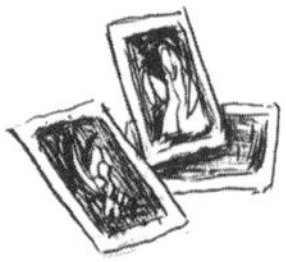

YE

•GUILHERME•PETRECA•

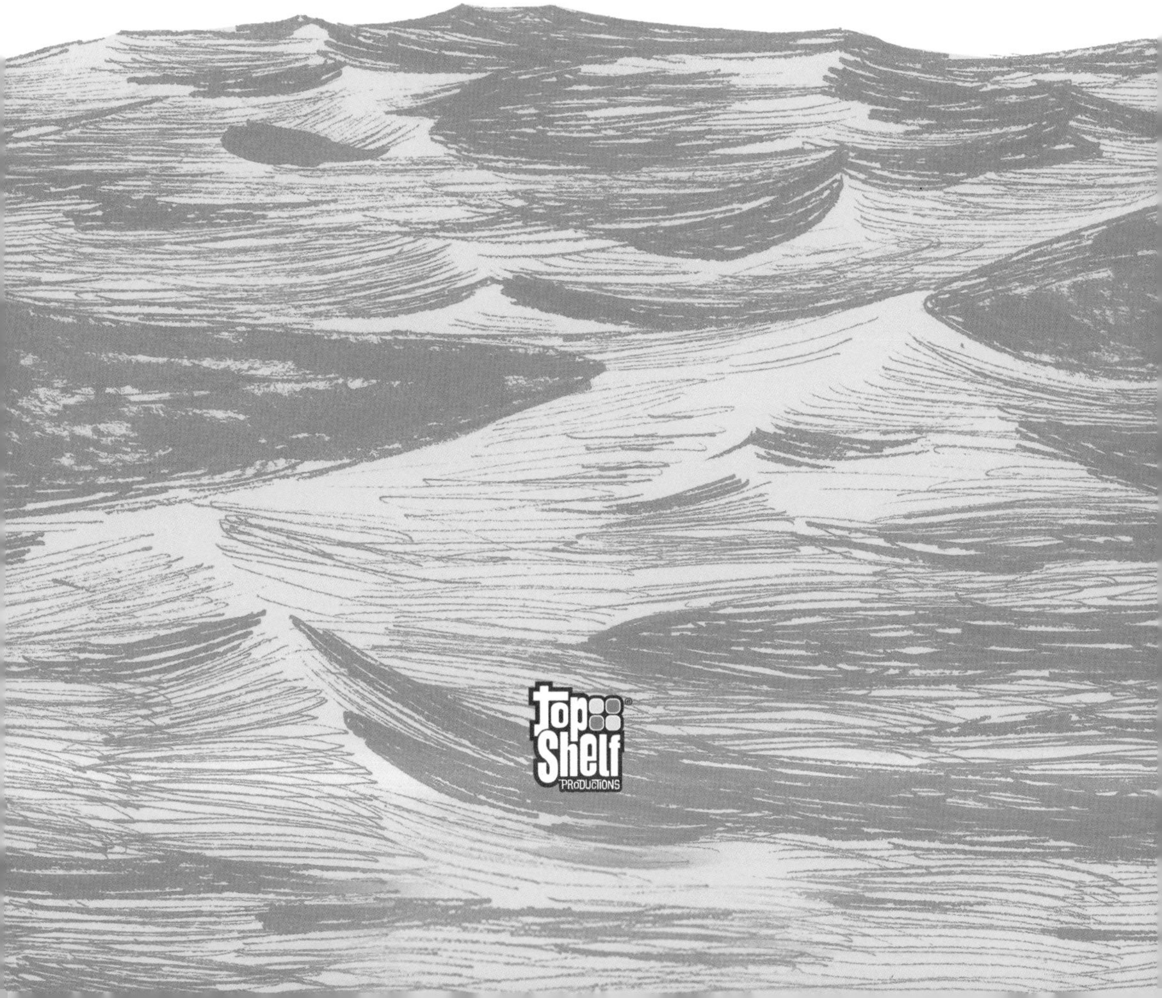
Top Shelf
PRODUCTIONS

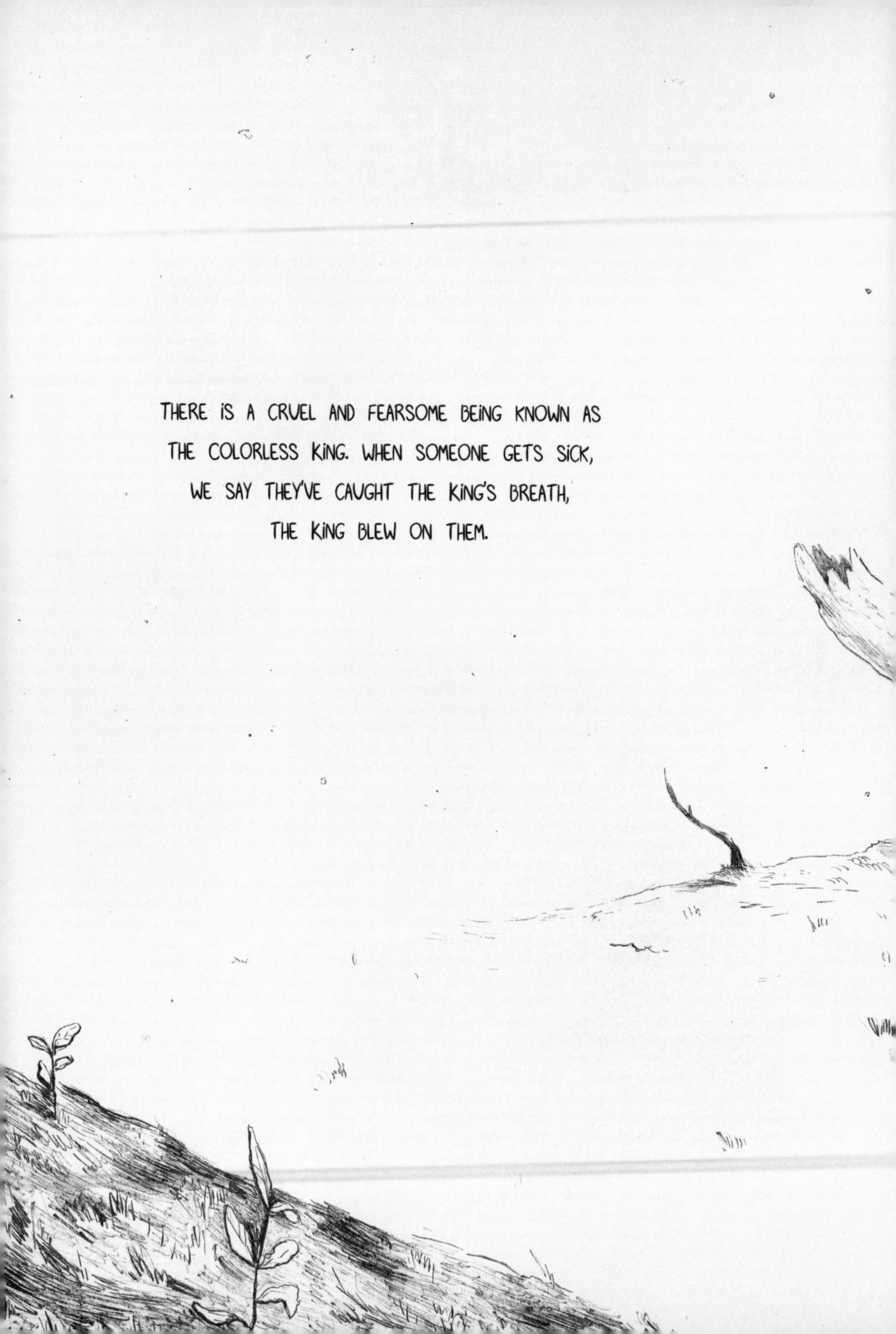
THERE IS A CRUEL AND FEARSOME BEING KNOWN AS THE COLORLESS KING. WHEN SOMEONE GETS SICK, WE SAY THEY'VE CAUGHT THE KING'S BREATH, THE KING BLEW ON THEM.

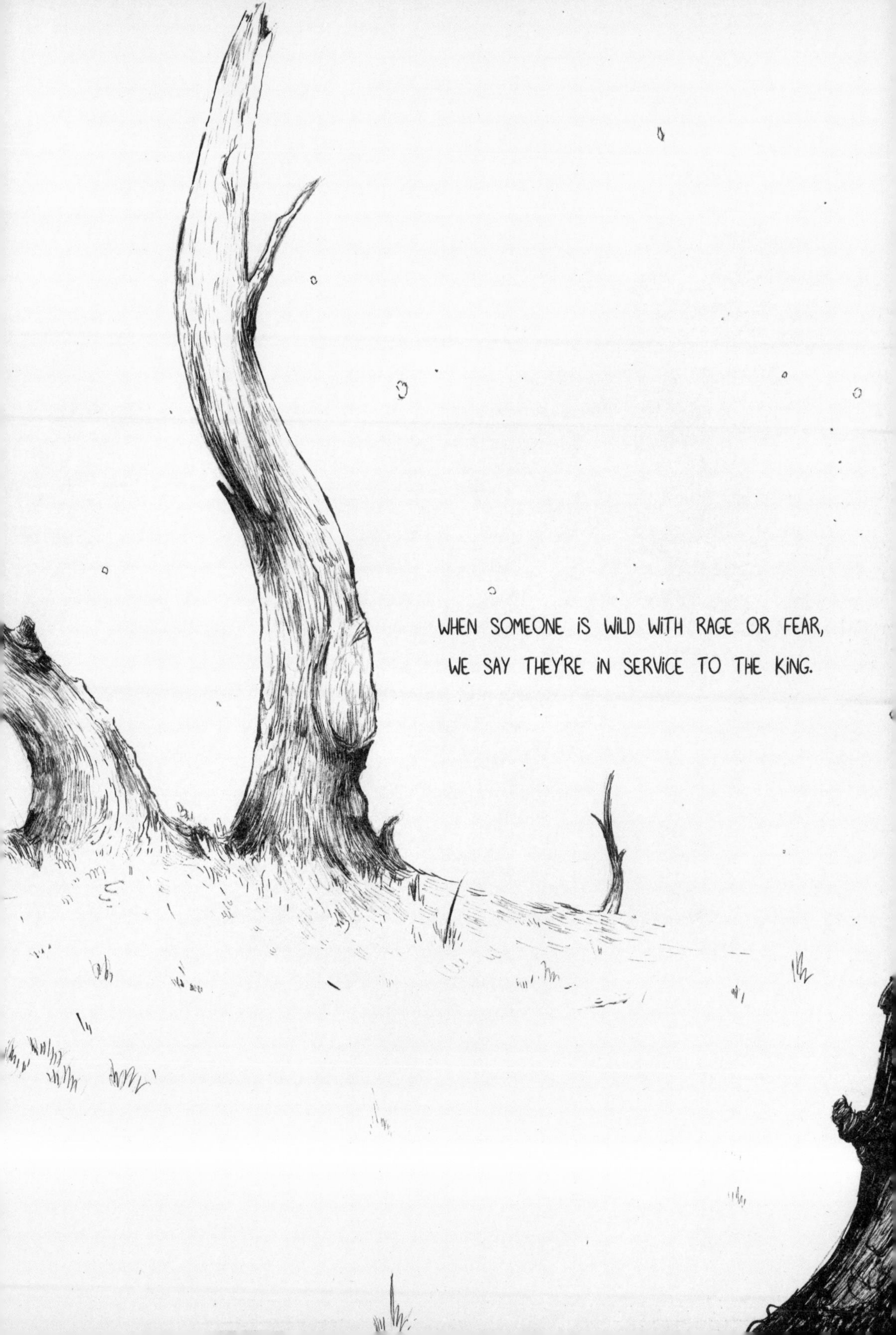
WHEN SOMEONE IS WILD WITH RAGE OR FEAR,
WE SAY THEY'RE IN SERVICE TO THE KING.

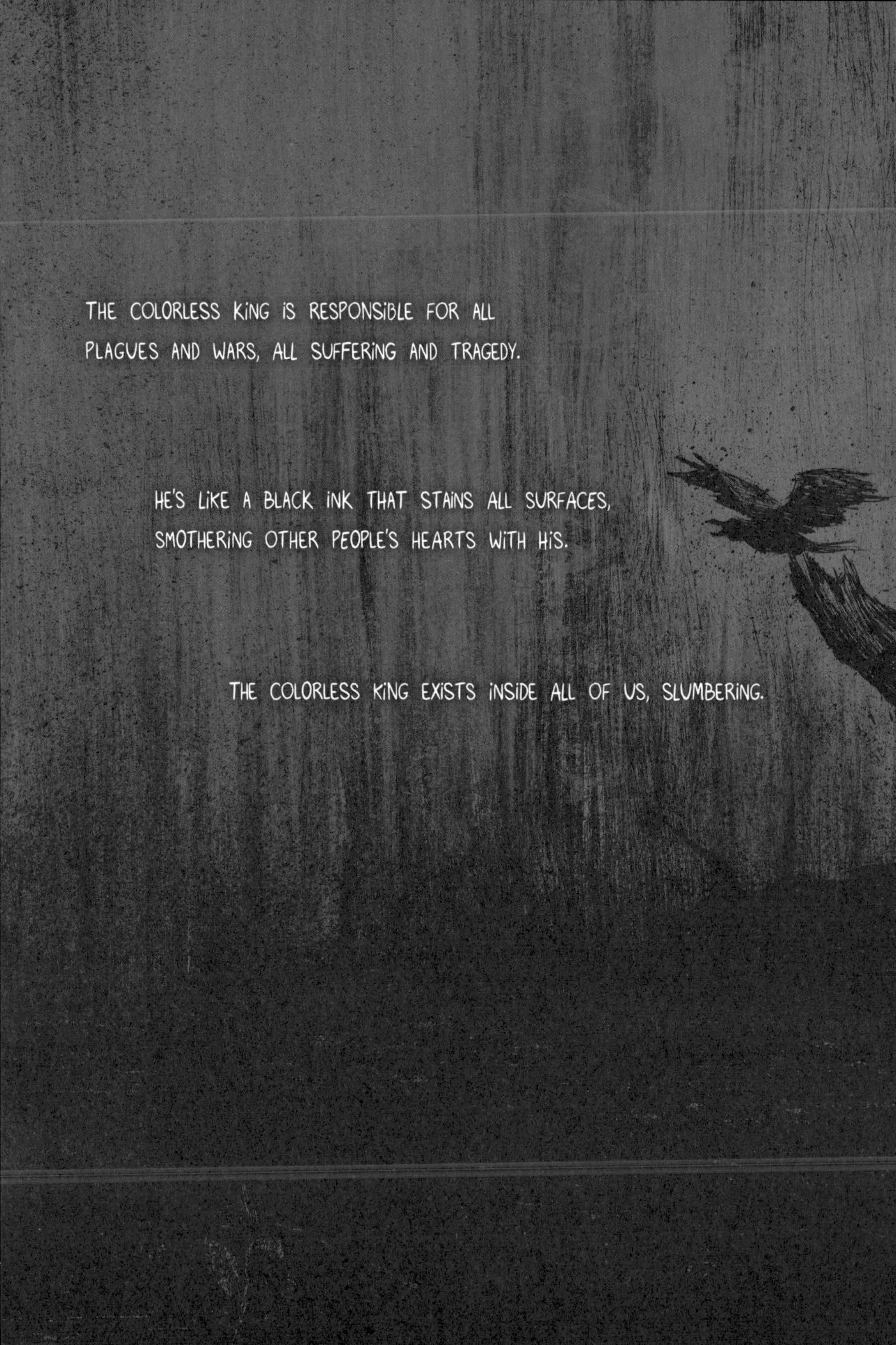
THE COLORLESS KING IS RESPONSIBLE FOR ALL PLAGUES AND WARS, ALL SUFFERING AND TRAGEDY.
HE'S LIKE A BLACK INK THAT STAINS ALL SURFACES, SMOTHERING OTHER PEOPLE'S HEARTS WITH HIS.
THE COLORLESS KING EXISTS INSIDE ALL OF US, SLUMBERING.

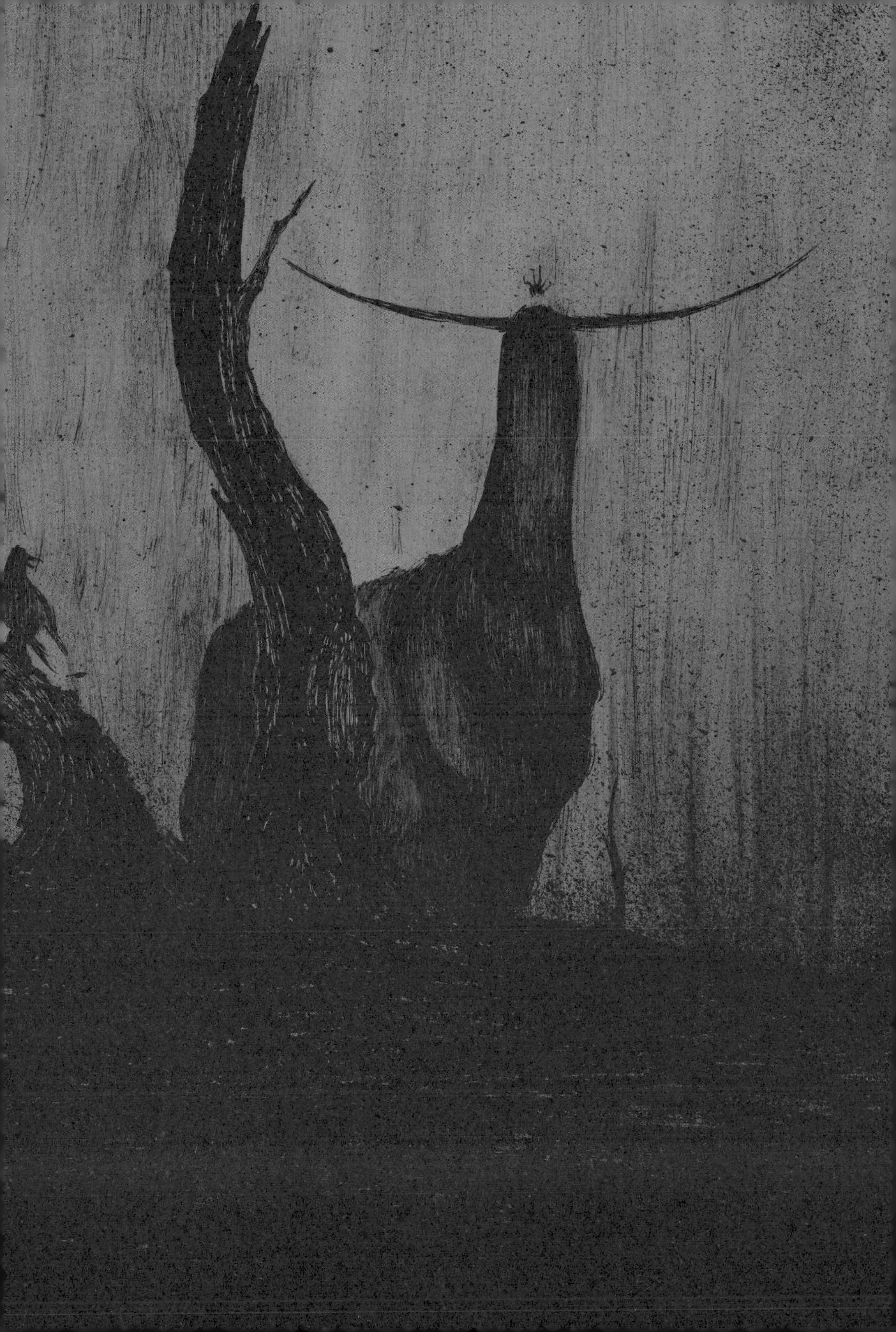

WE ARE ALL CAPABLE
OF BEING A COLORLESS KING.

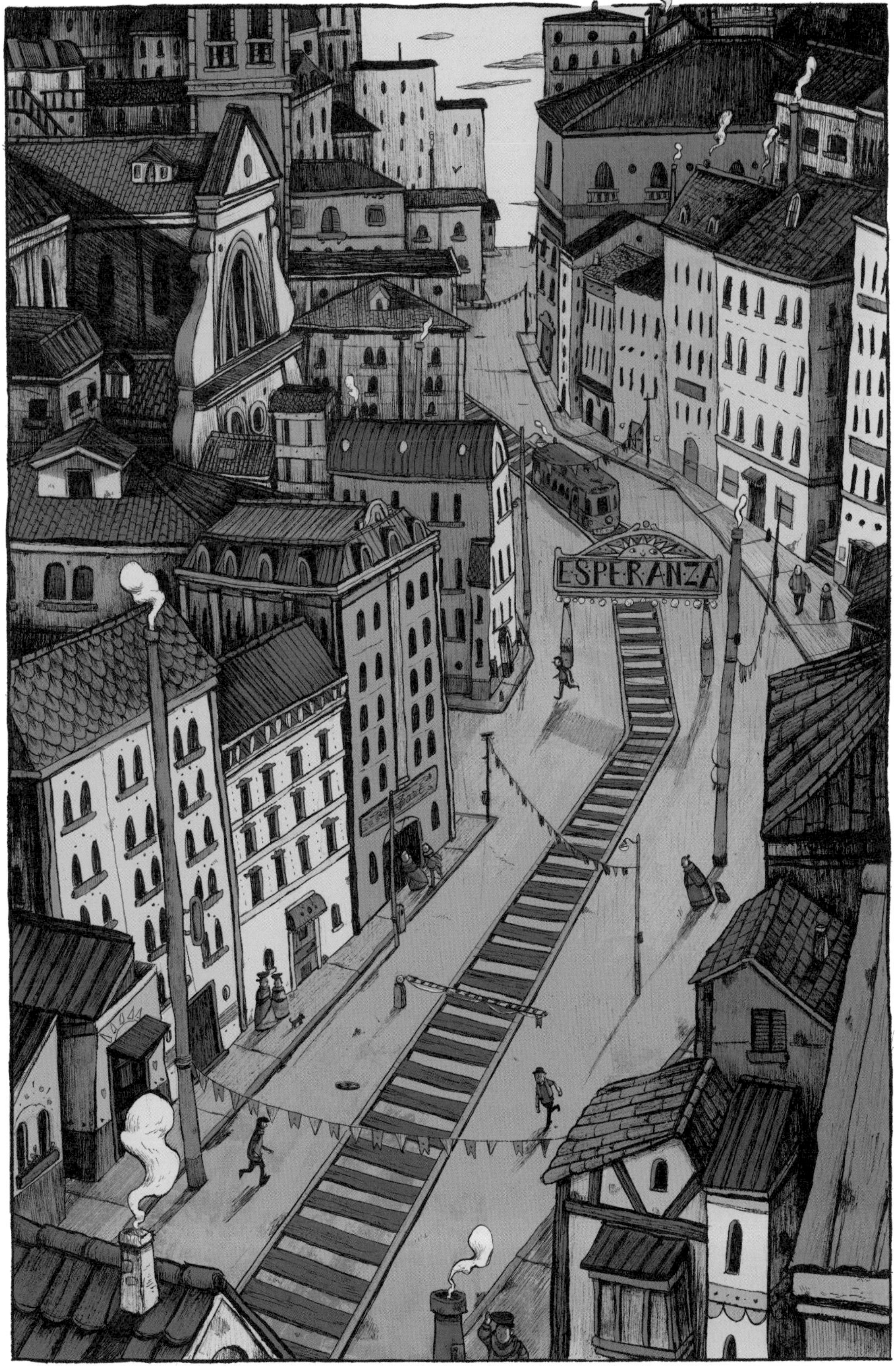
ESPERANZA

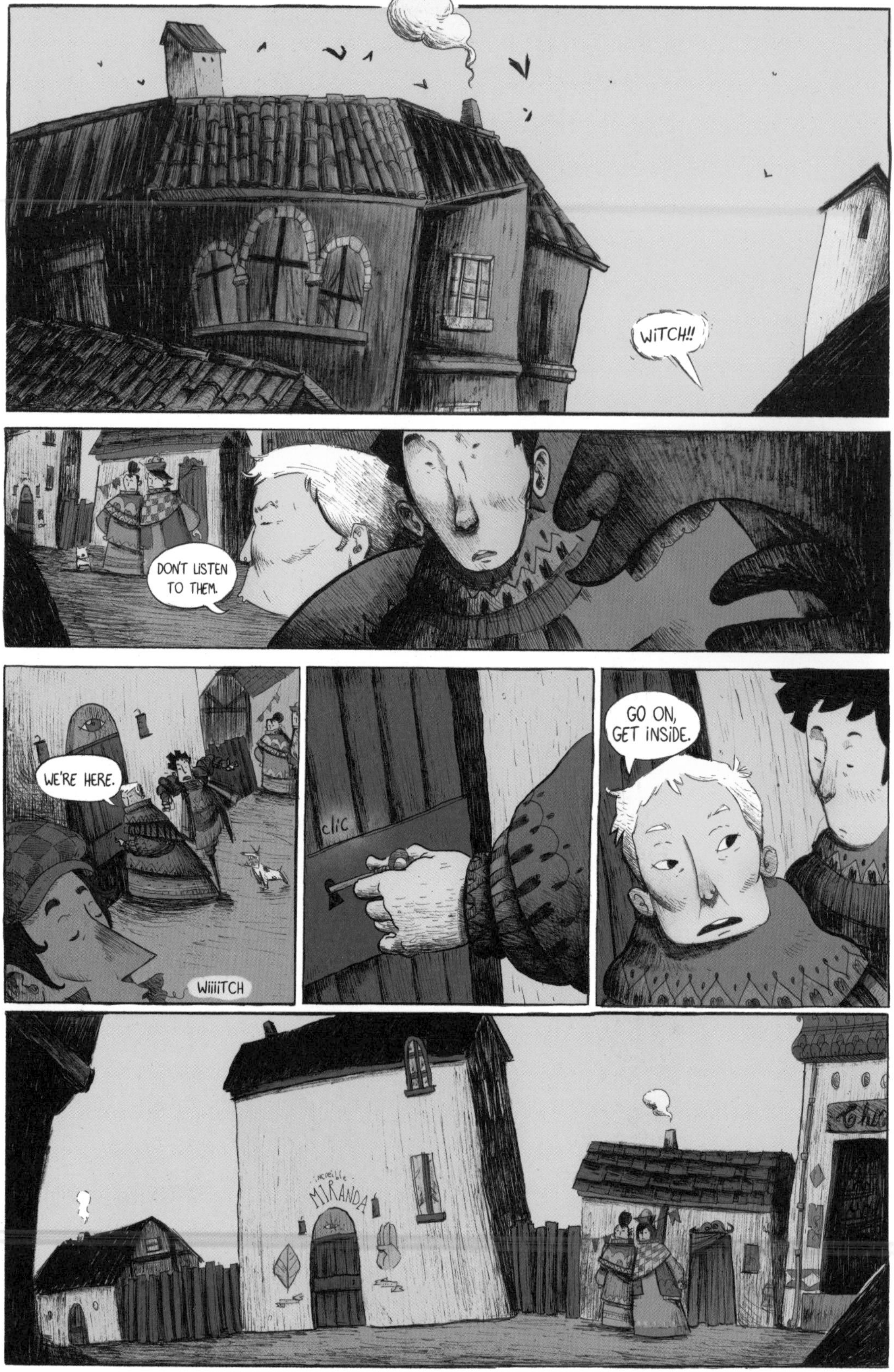
WITCH!!
DON'T LISTEN TO THEM.
WE'RE HERE.
WIIIITCH
clic
GO ON, GET INSIDE.
MIRANDA

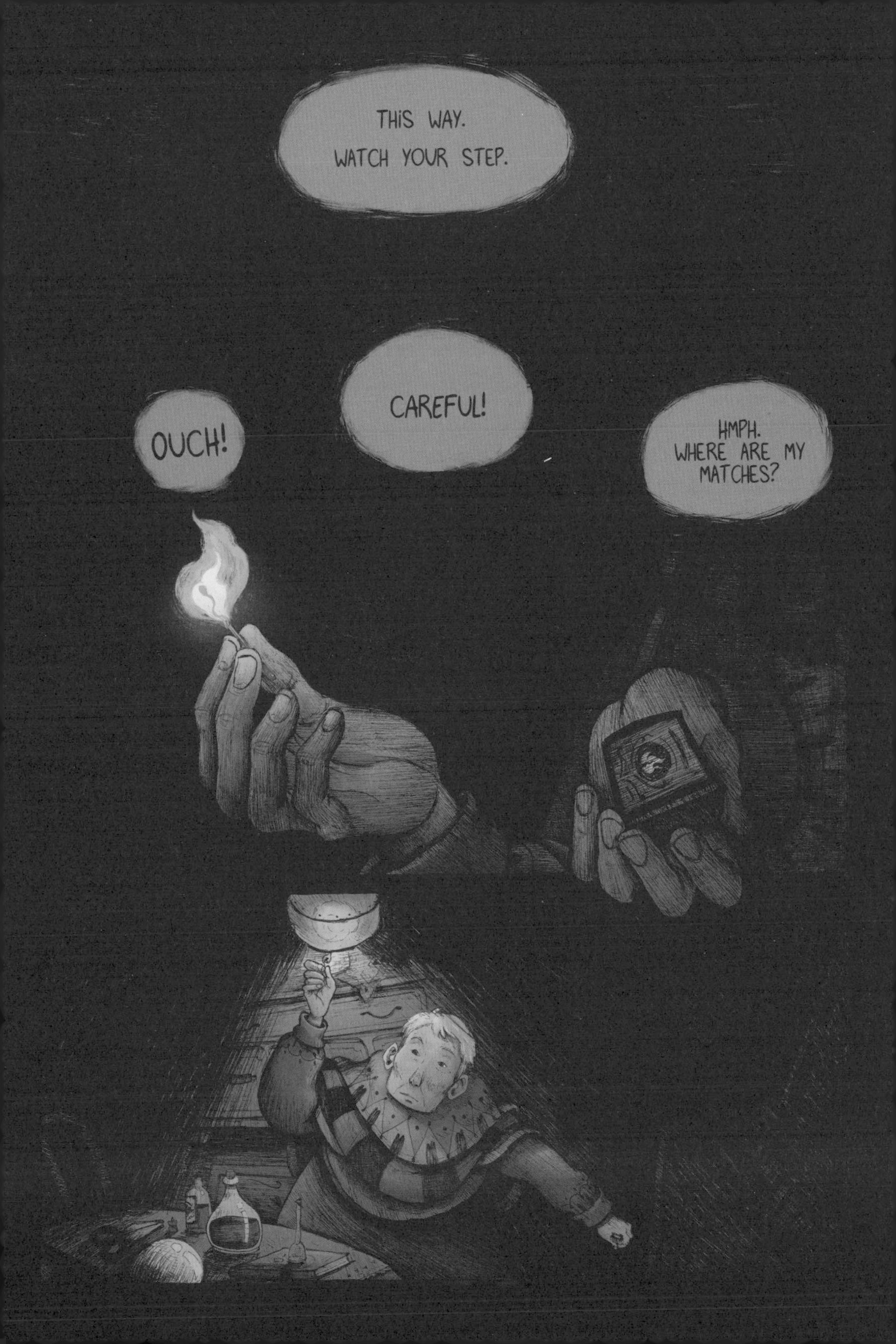
THIS WAY.
WATCH YOUR STEP.
OUCH!
CAREFUL!
HMPH.
WHERE ARE MY
MATCHES?

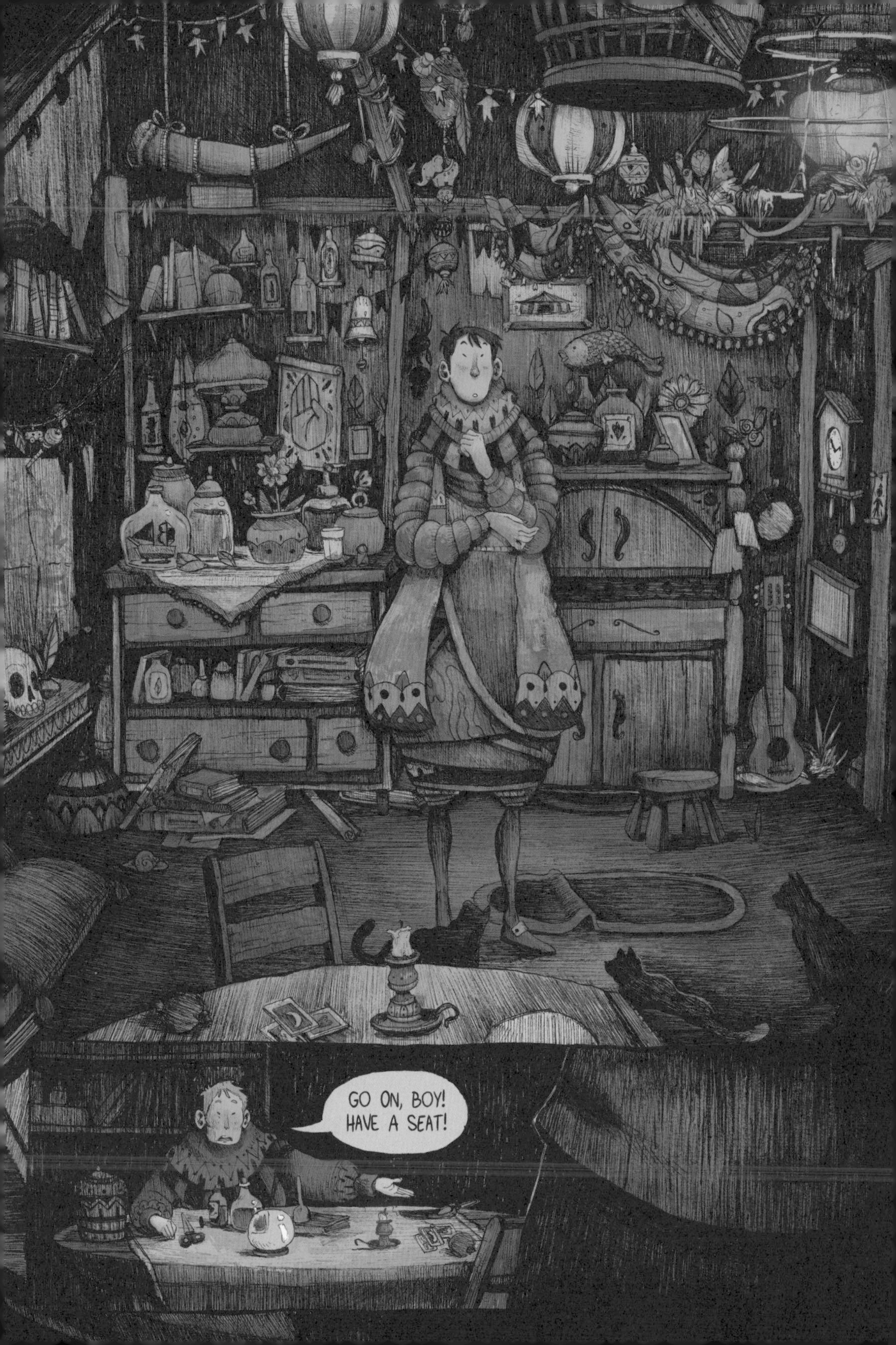
GO ON, BOY! HAVE A SEAT!

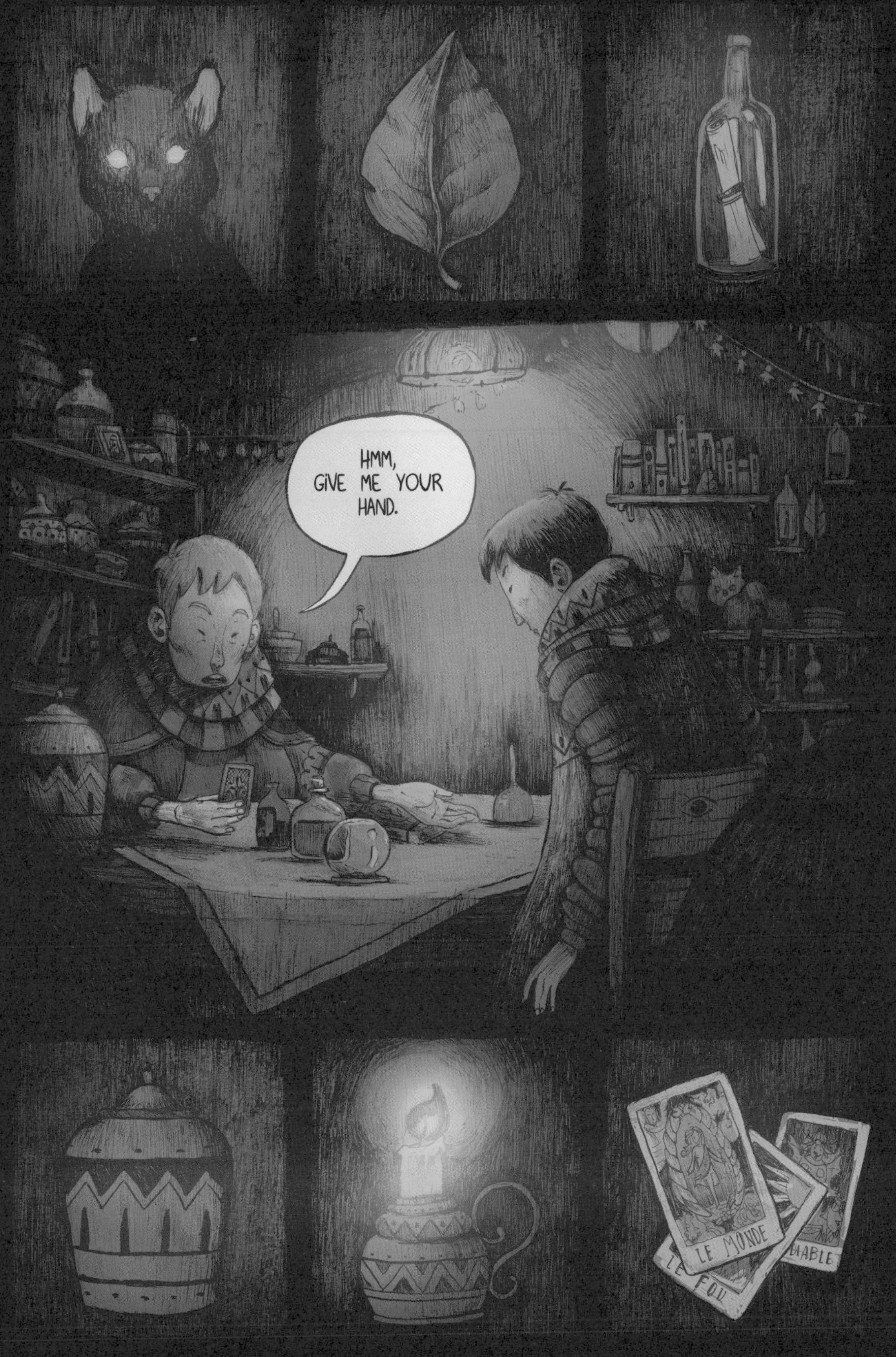
HMM, GIVE ME YOUR HAND.
LE MONDE
LE FOU
DIABLE

YOU'VE LIVED THROUGH A LOT!

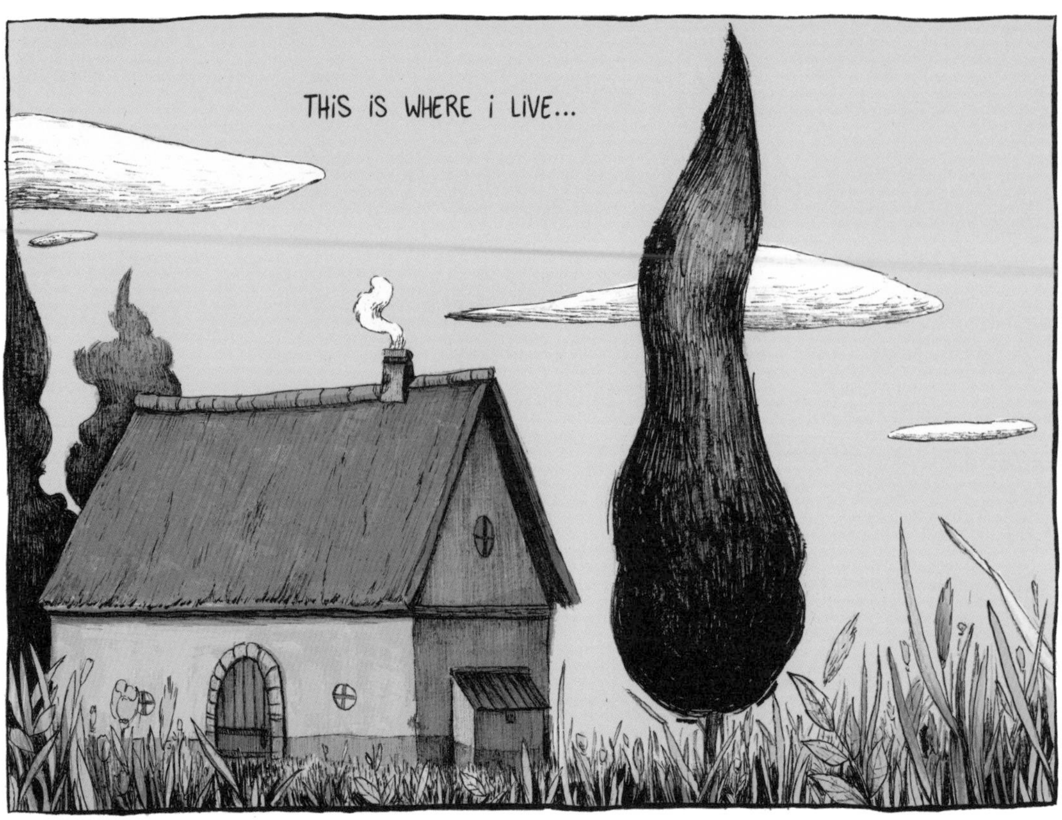
THIS IS WHERE i LIVE...

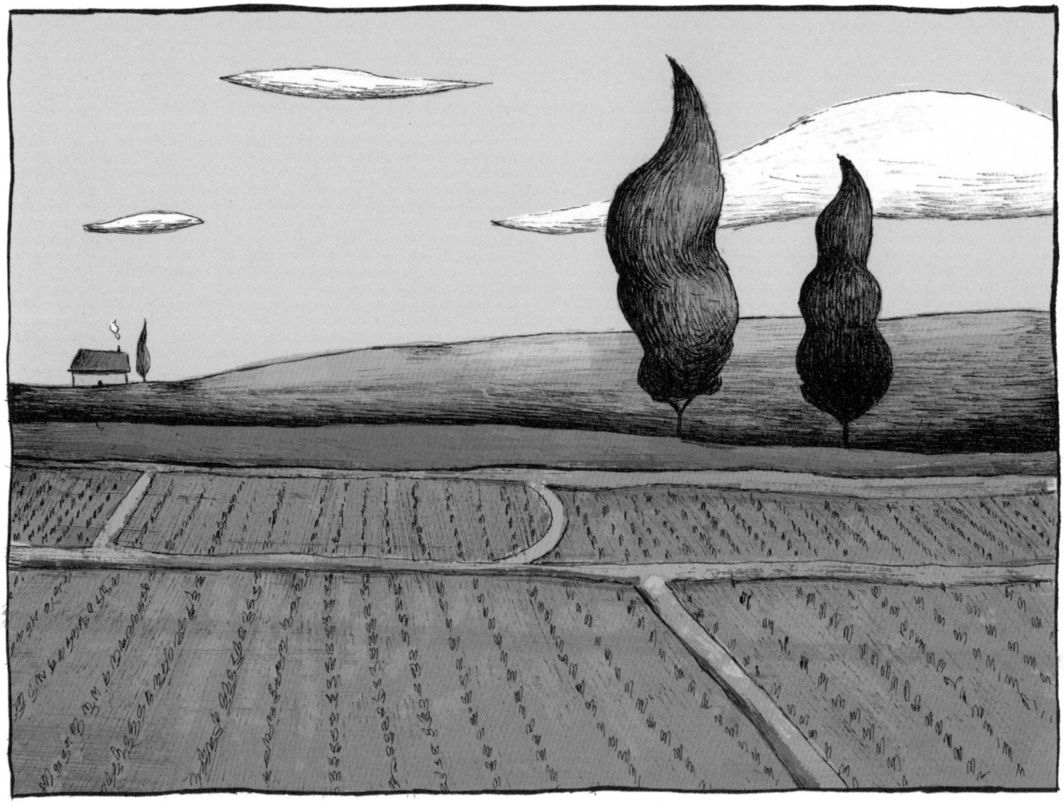

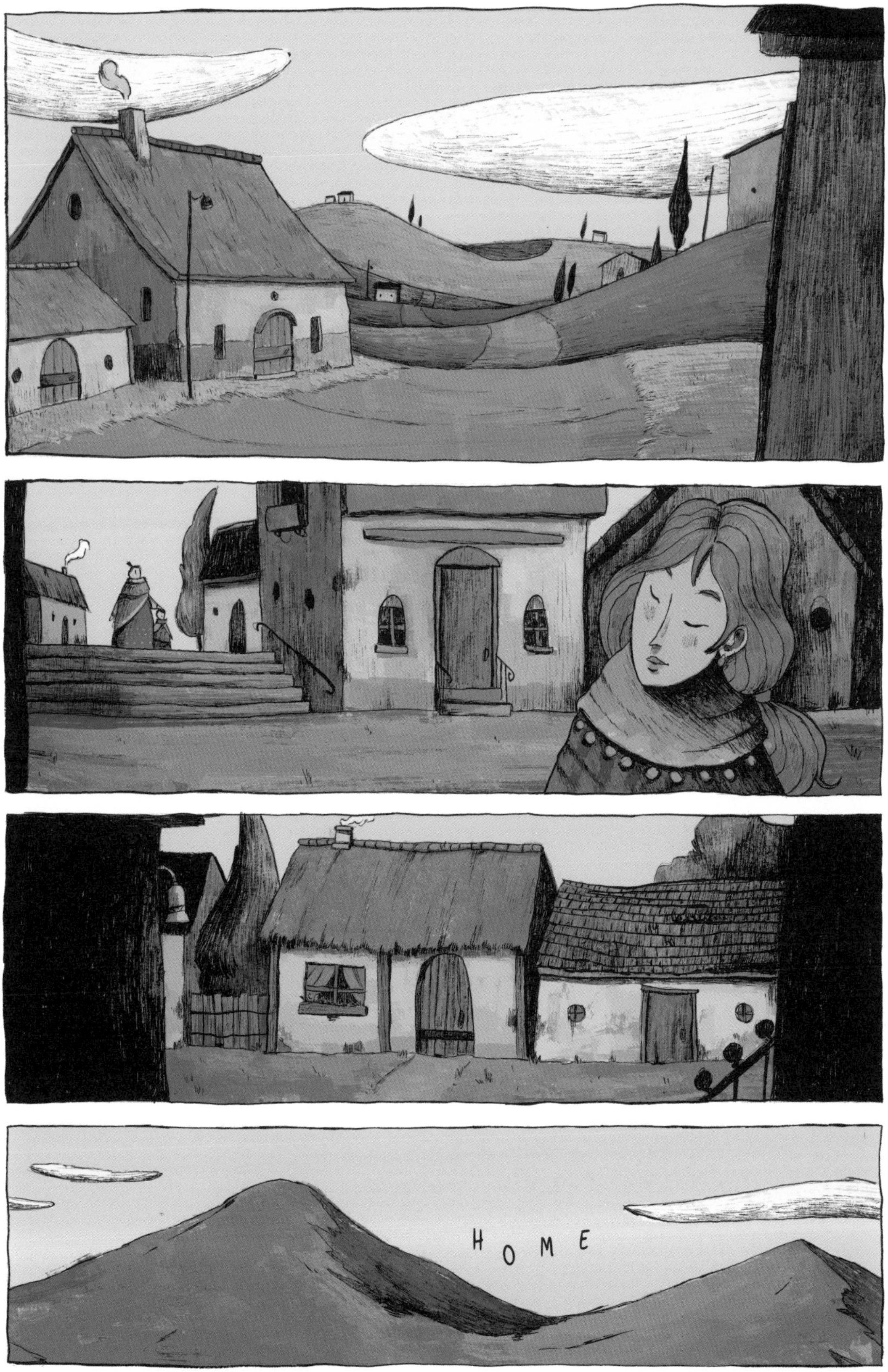
HOME

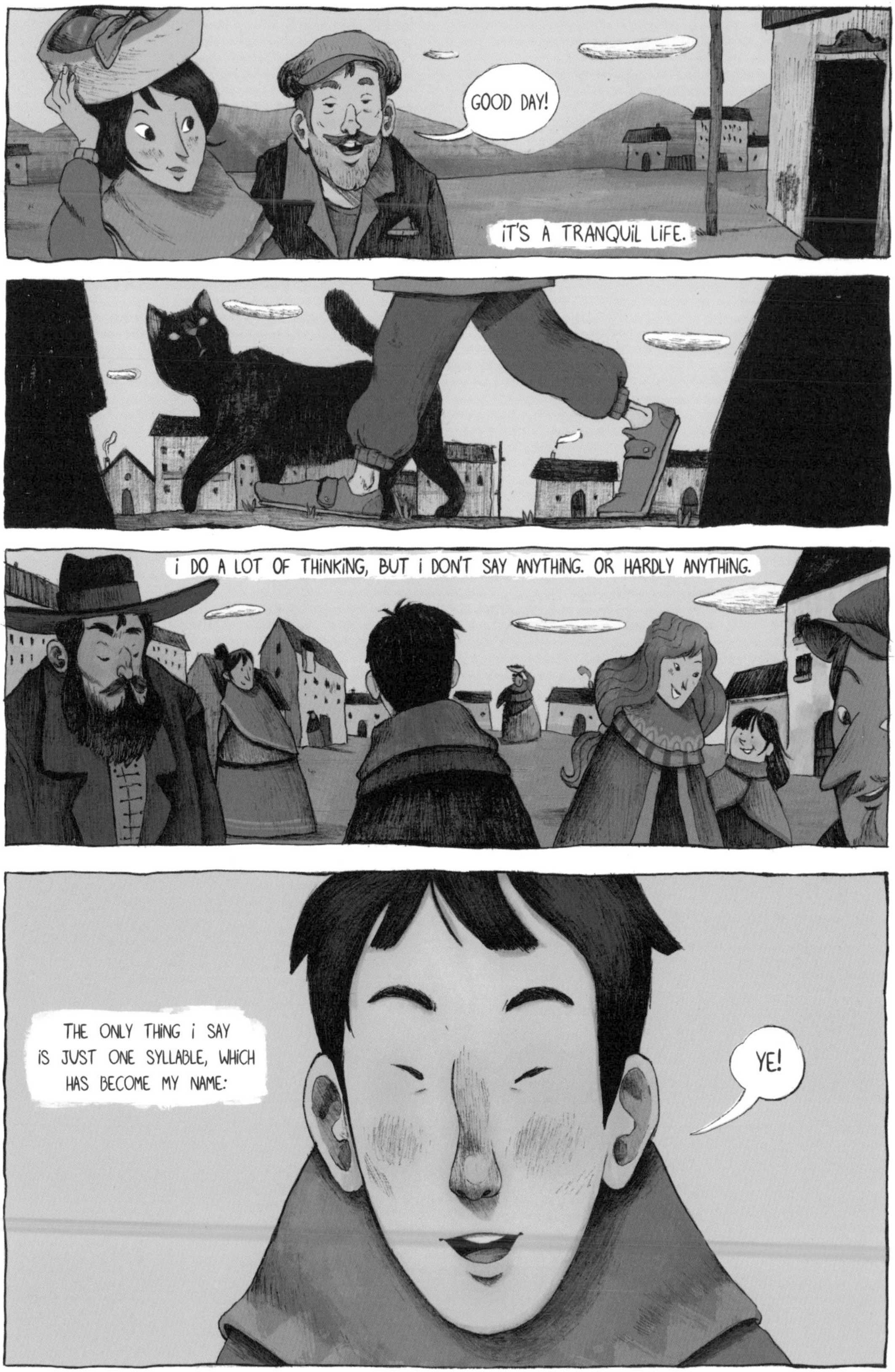
GOOD DAY!
IT'S A TRANQUIL LIFE.
I DO A LOT OF THINKING, BUT I DON'T SAY ANYTHING. OR HARDLY ANYTHING.
THE ONLY THING I SAY IS JUST ONE SYLLABLE, WHICH HAS BECOME MY NAME:
YE!

THIS IS THE STORY OF HOW THE COLORLESS
KING LEFT HIS MARK ON ME.

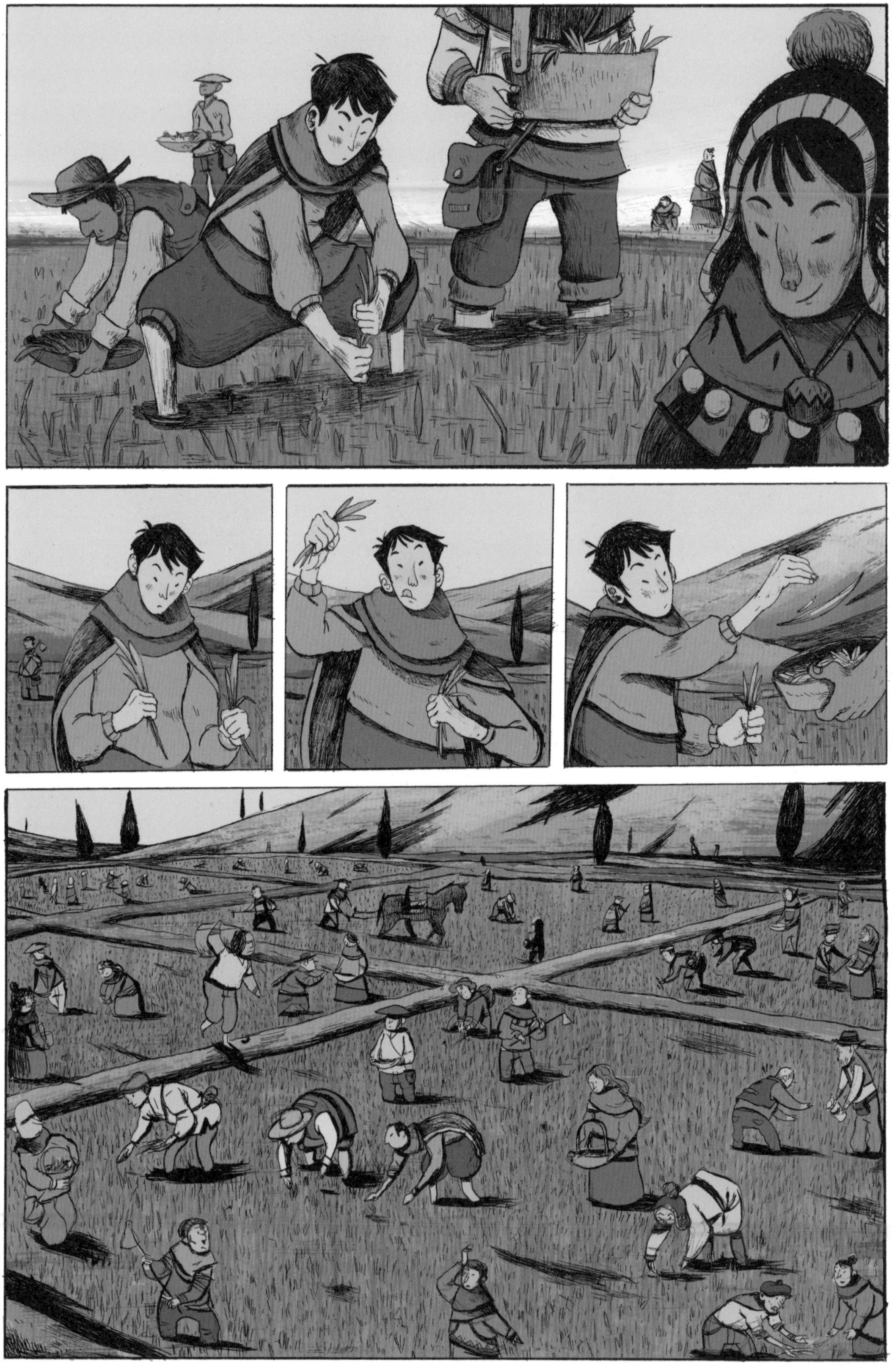

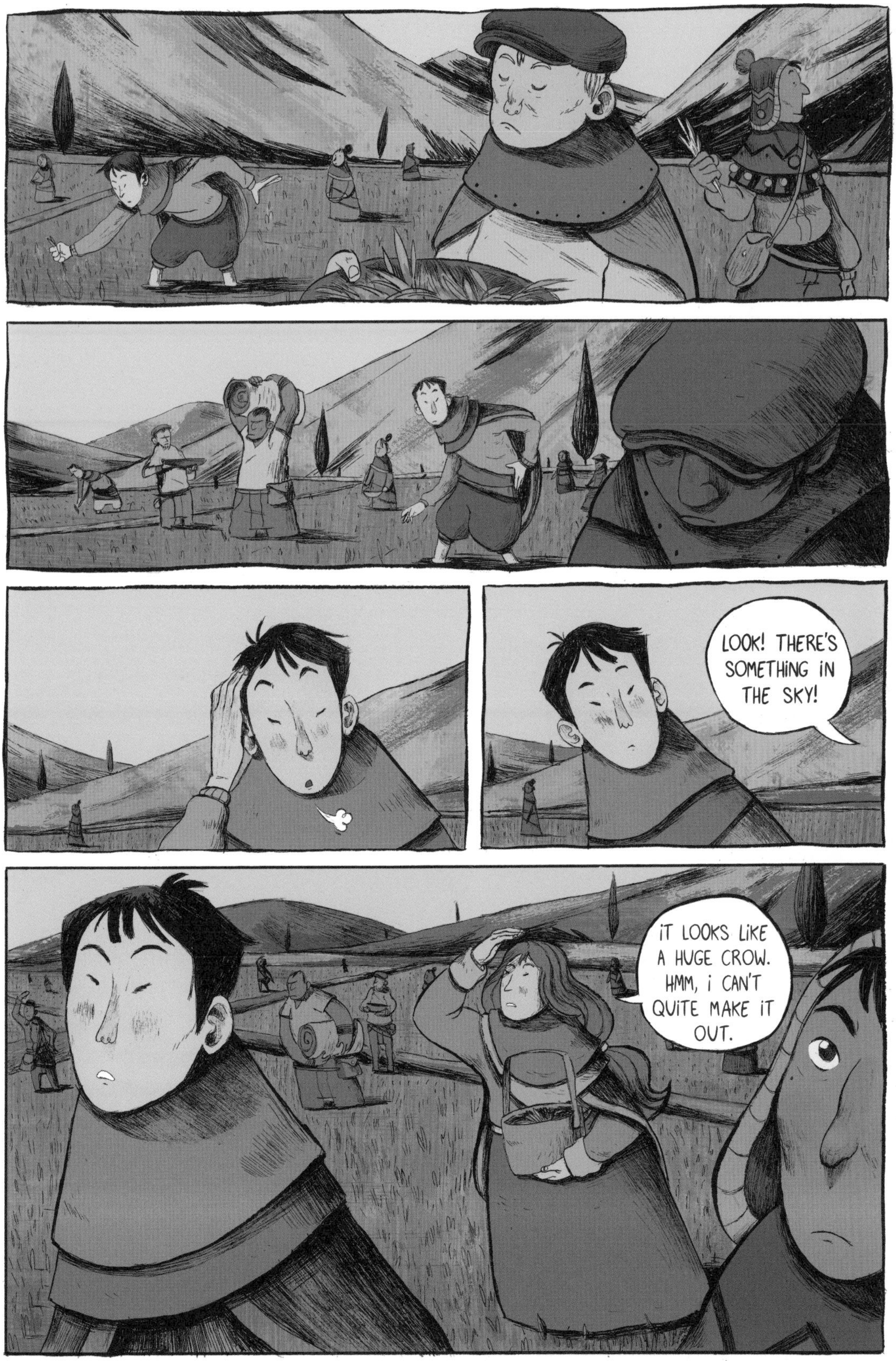
LOOK! THERE'S SOMETHING IN THE SKY!
IT LOOKS LIKE A HUGE CROW. HMM, I CAN'T QUITE MAKE IT OUT.

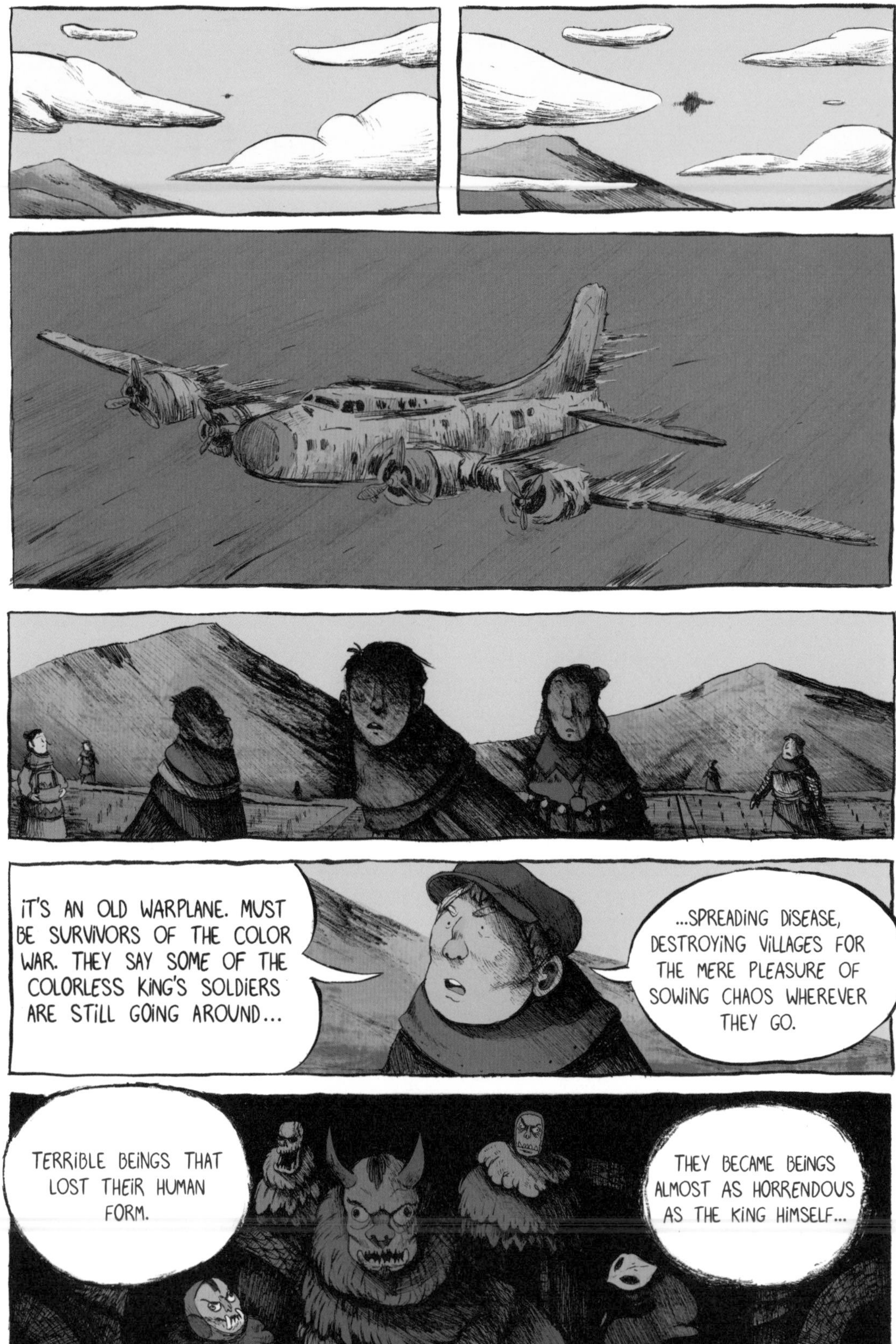
IT'S AN OLD WARPLANE. MUST BE SURVIVORS OF THE COLOR WAR. THEY SAY SOME OF THE COLORLESS KING'S SOLDIERS ARE STILL GOING AROUND...
...SPREADING DISEASE, DESTROYING VILLAGES FOR THE MERE PLEASURE OF SOWING CHAOS WHEREVER THEY GO.
TERRIBLE BEINGS THAT LOST THEIR HUMAN FORM.
THEY BECAME BEINGS ALMOST AS HORRENDOUS AS THE KING HIMSELF...

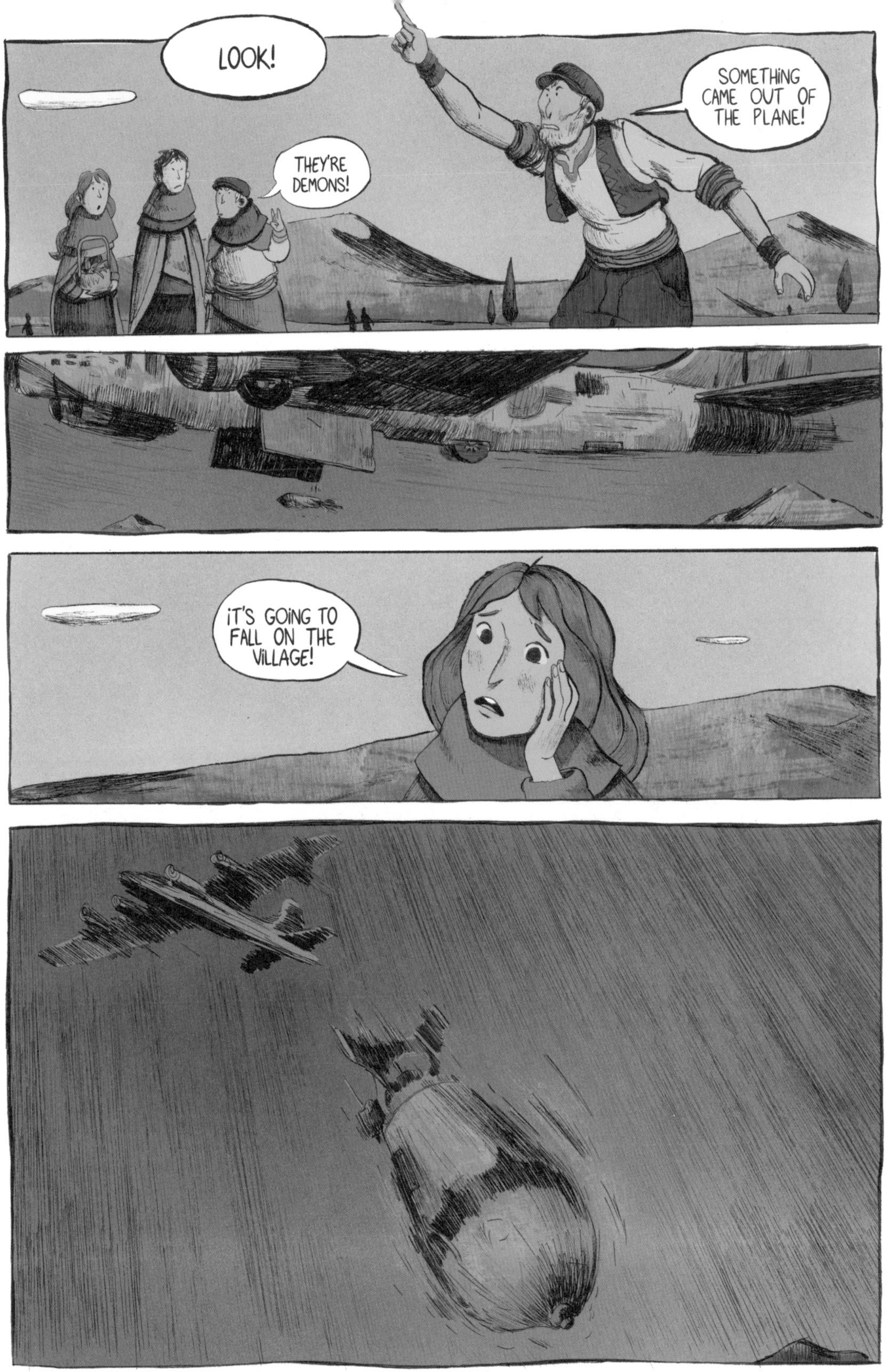
LOOK!
SOMETHING CAME OUT OF THE PLANE!
THEY'RE DEMONS!
iT'S GOING TO FALL ON THE VILLAGE!

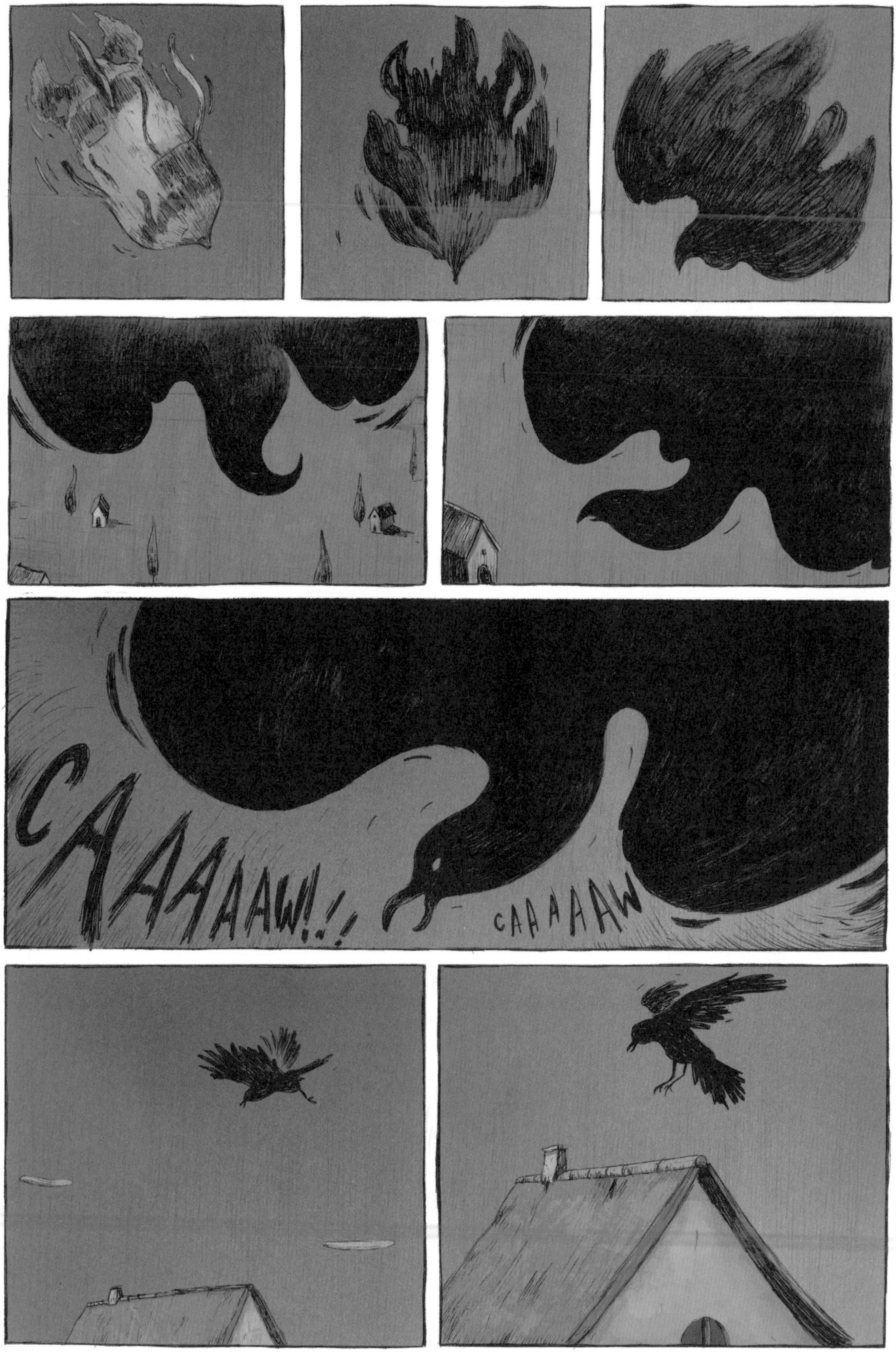
CAAAAAW!.!
CAAAAAW

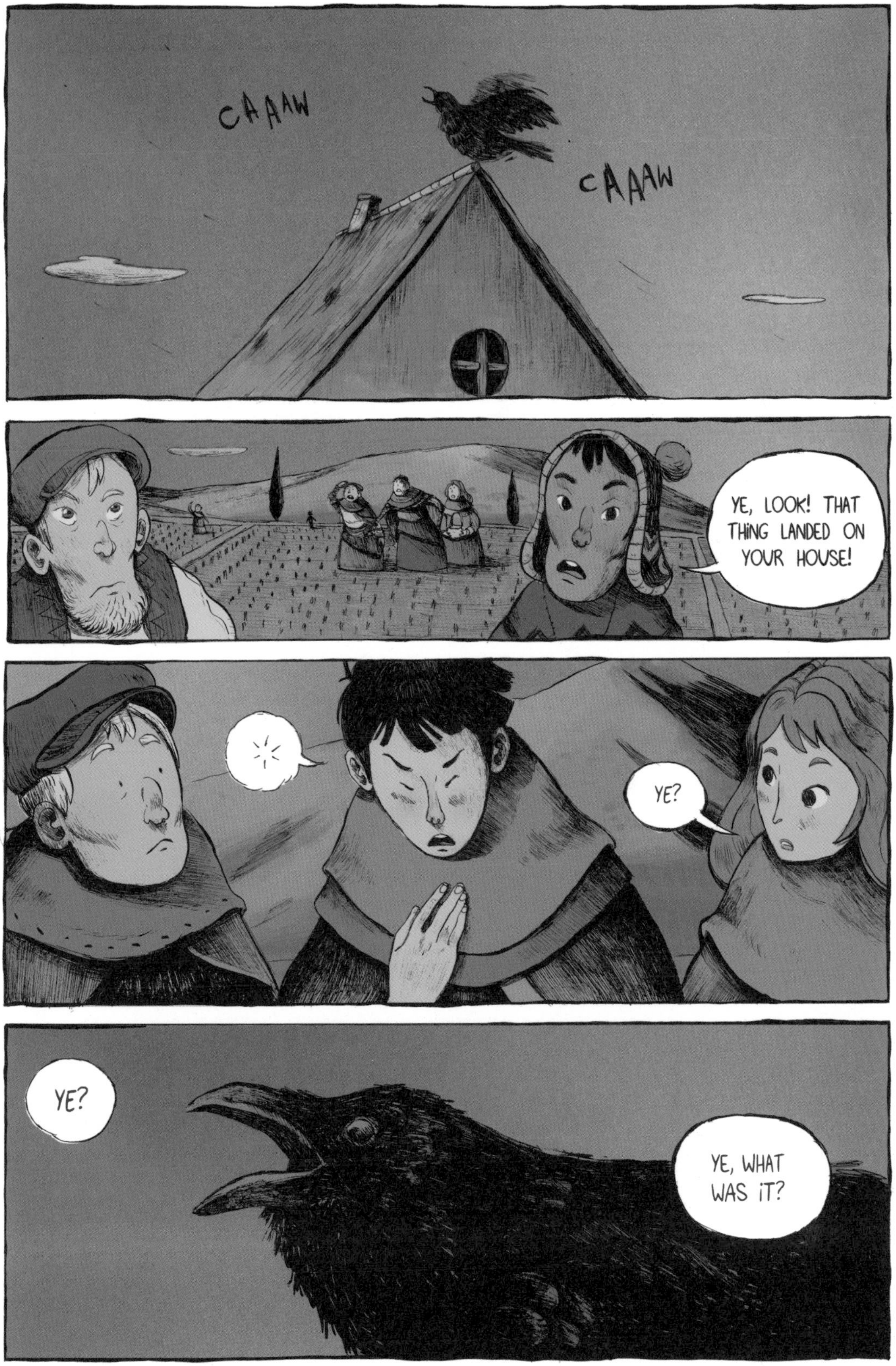
CAAAW
CAAAW
YE, LOOK! THAT THING LANDED ON YOUR HOUSE!
YE?
YE?
YE, WHAT WAS IT?

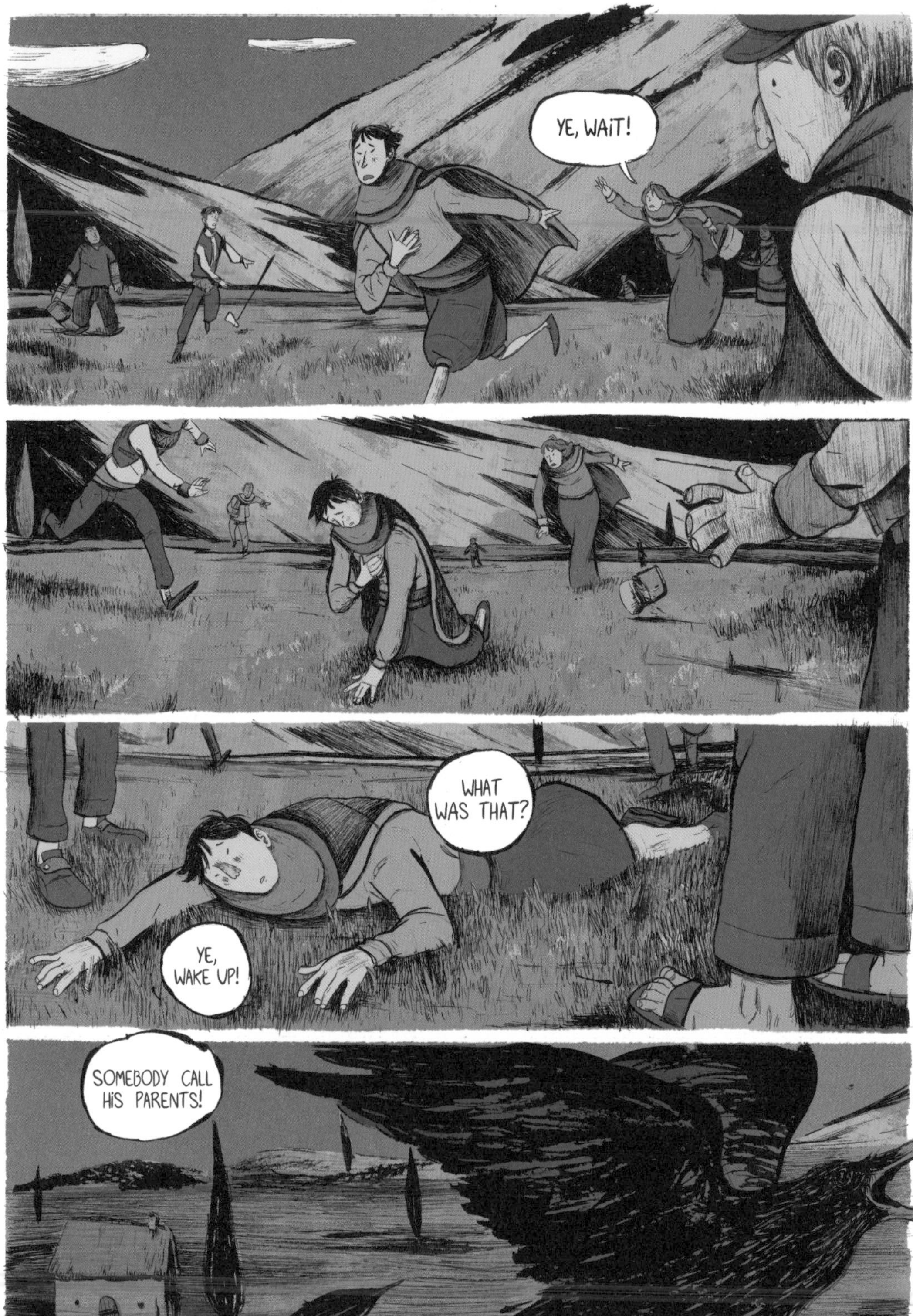
YE, WAIT!
WHAT WAS THAT?
YE, WAKE UP!
SOMEBODY CALL HIS PARENTS!

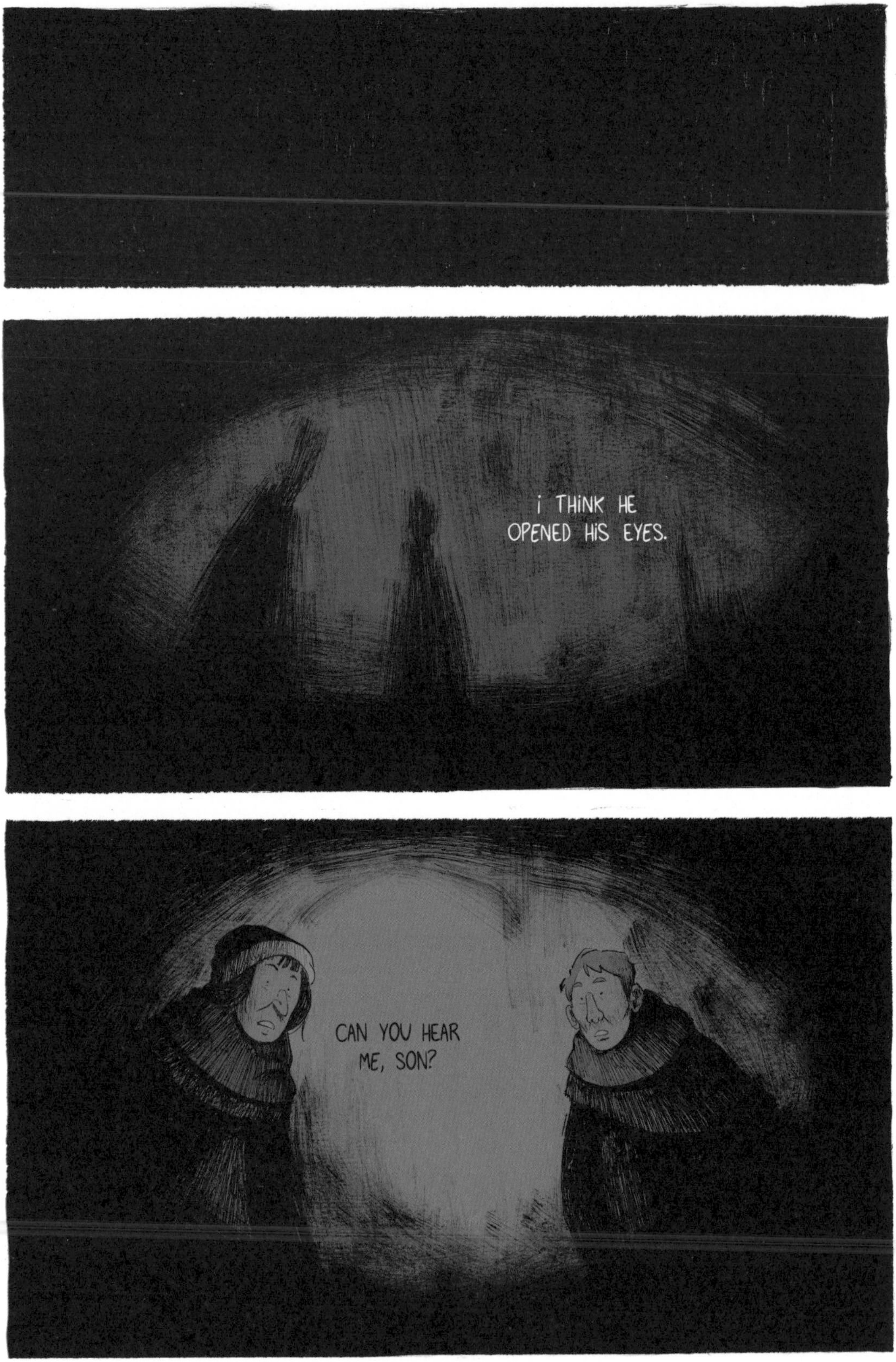
I THINK HE
OPENED HIS EYES.
CAN YOU HEAR
ME, SON?

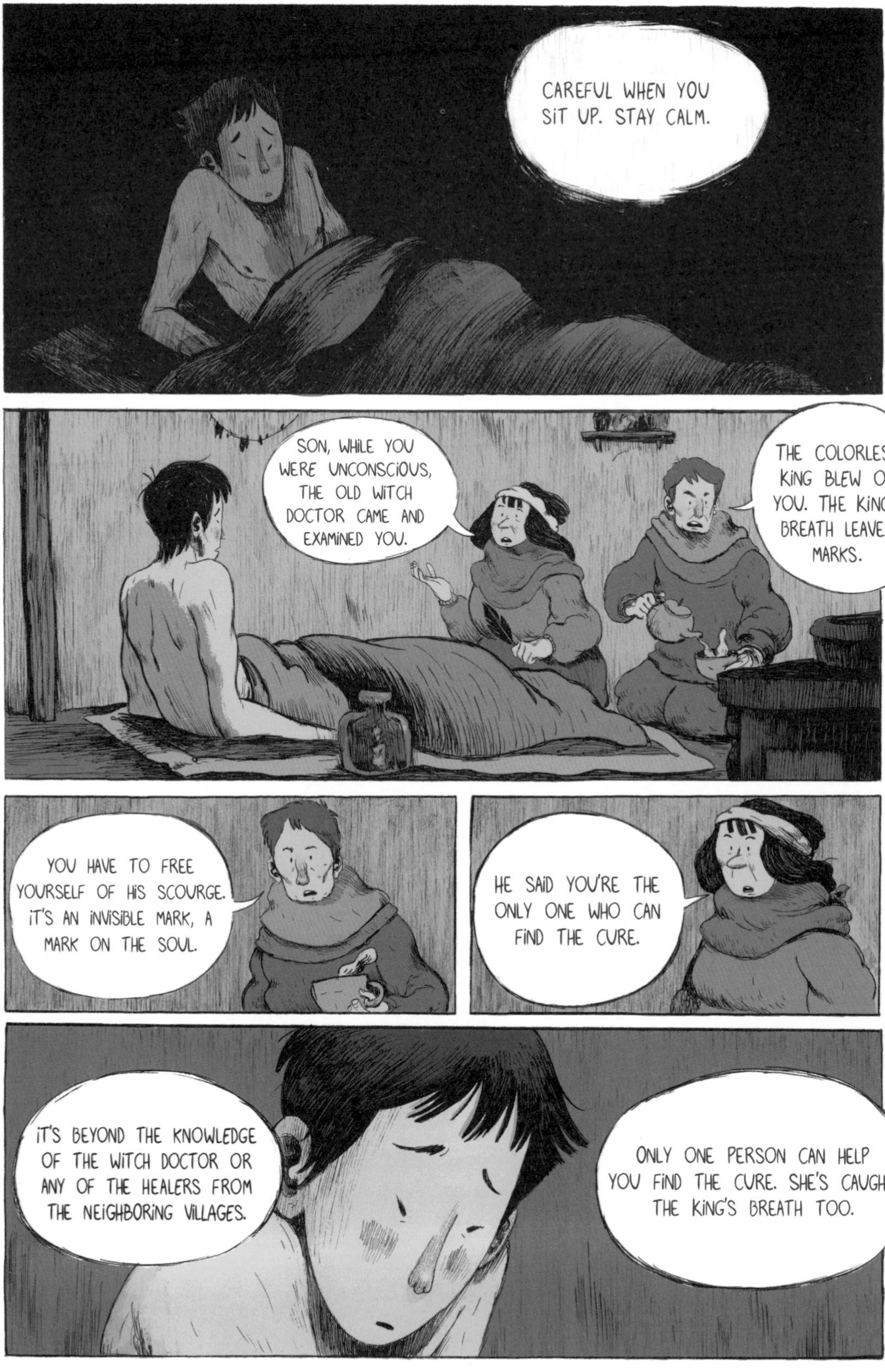
CAREFUL WHEN YOU SIT UP. STAY CALM.
SON, WHILE YOU WERE UNCONSCIOUS, THE OLD WITCH DOCTOR CAME AND EXAMINED YOU.
THE COLORLESS KING BLEW ON YOU. THE KING'S BREATH LEAVES MARKS.
YOU HAVE TO FREE YOURSELF OF HIS SCOURGE. IT'S AN INVISIBLE MARK, A MARK ON THE SOUL.
HE SAID YOU'RE THE ONLY ONE WHO CAN FIND THE CURE.
IT'S BEYOND THE KNOWLEDGE OF THE WITCH DOCTOR OR ANY OF THE HEALERS FROM THE NEIGHBORING VILLAGES.
ONLY ONE PERSON CAN HELP YOU FIND THE CURE. SHE'S CAUGHT THE KING'S BREATH TOO.

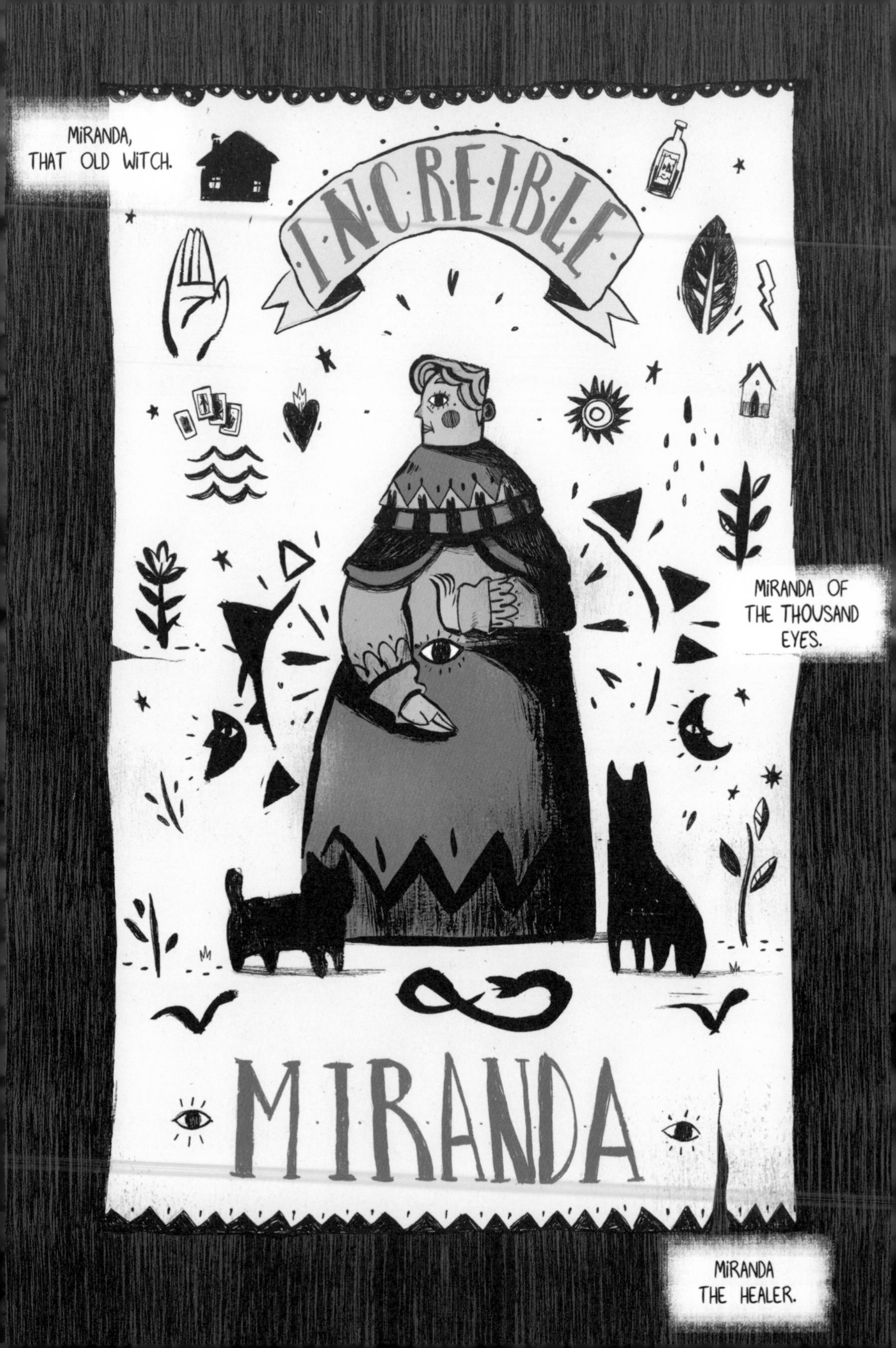
MIRANDA, THAT OLD WITCH.
INCREIBLE
MIRANDA OF THE THOUSAND EYES.
MIRANDA
MIRANDA THE HEALER.

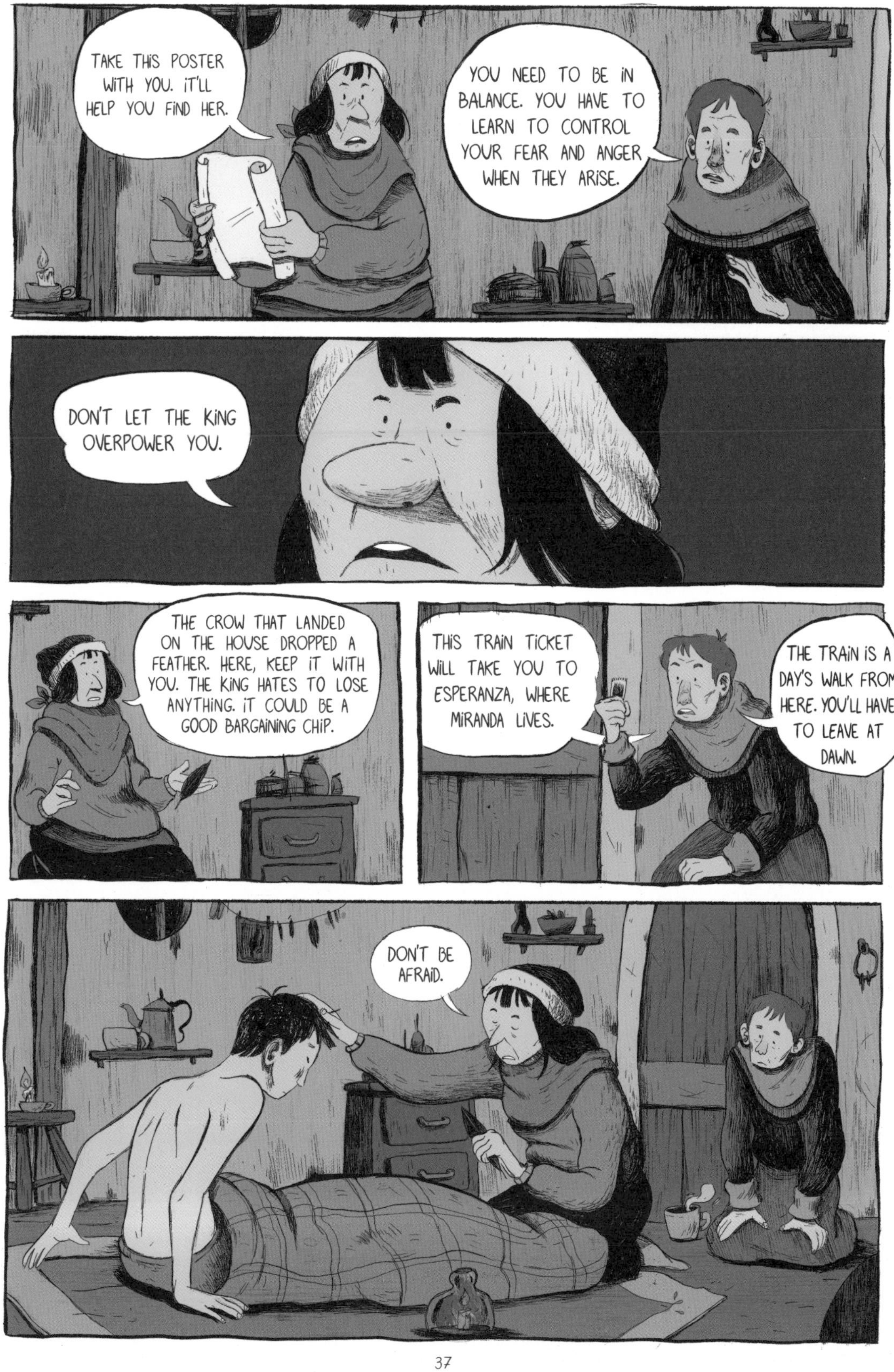
TAKE THIS POSTER WITH YOU. IT'LL HELP YOU FIND HER.
YOU NEED TO BE IN BALANCE. YOU HAVE TO LEARN TO CONTROL YOUR FEAR AND ANGER WHEN THEY ARISE.
DON'T LET THE KING OVERPOWER YOU.
THE CROW THAT LANDED ON THE HOUSE DROPPED A FEATHER. HERE, KEEP IT WITH YOU. THE KING HATES TO LOSE ANYTHING. IT COULD BE A GOOD BARGAINING CHIP.
THIS TRAIN TICKET WILL TAKE YOU TO ESPERANZA, WHERE MIRANDA LIVES.
THE TRAIN IS A DAY'S WALK FROM HERE. YOU'LL HAVE TO LEAVE AT DAWN.
DON'T BE AFRAID.

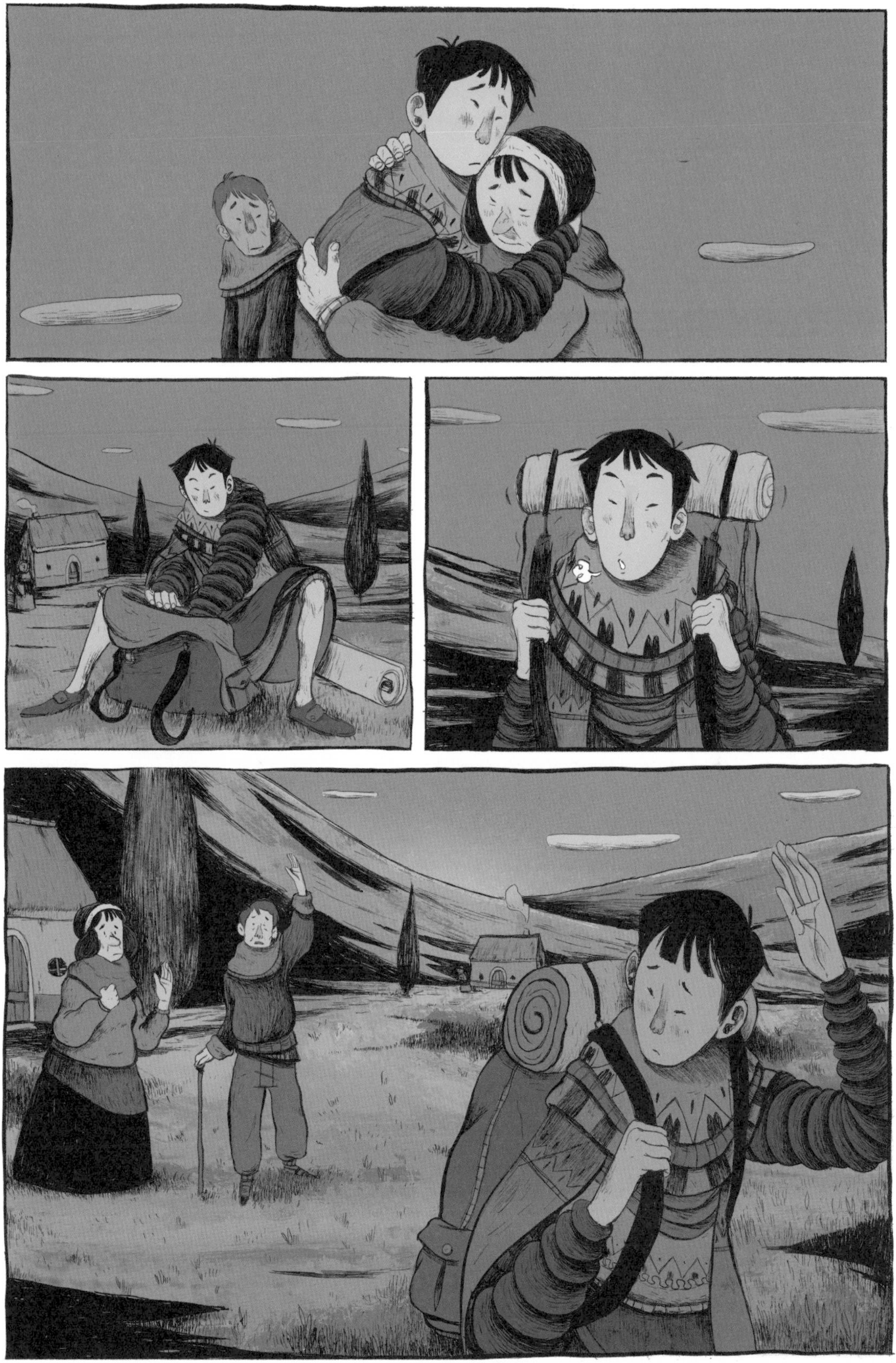

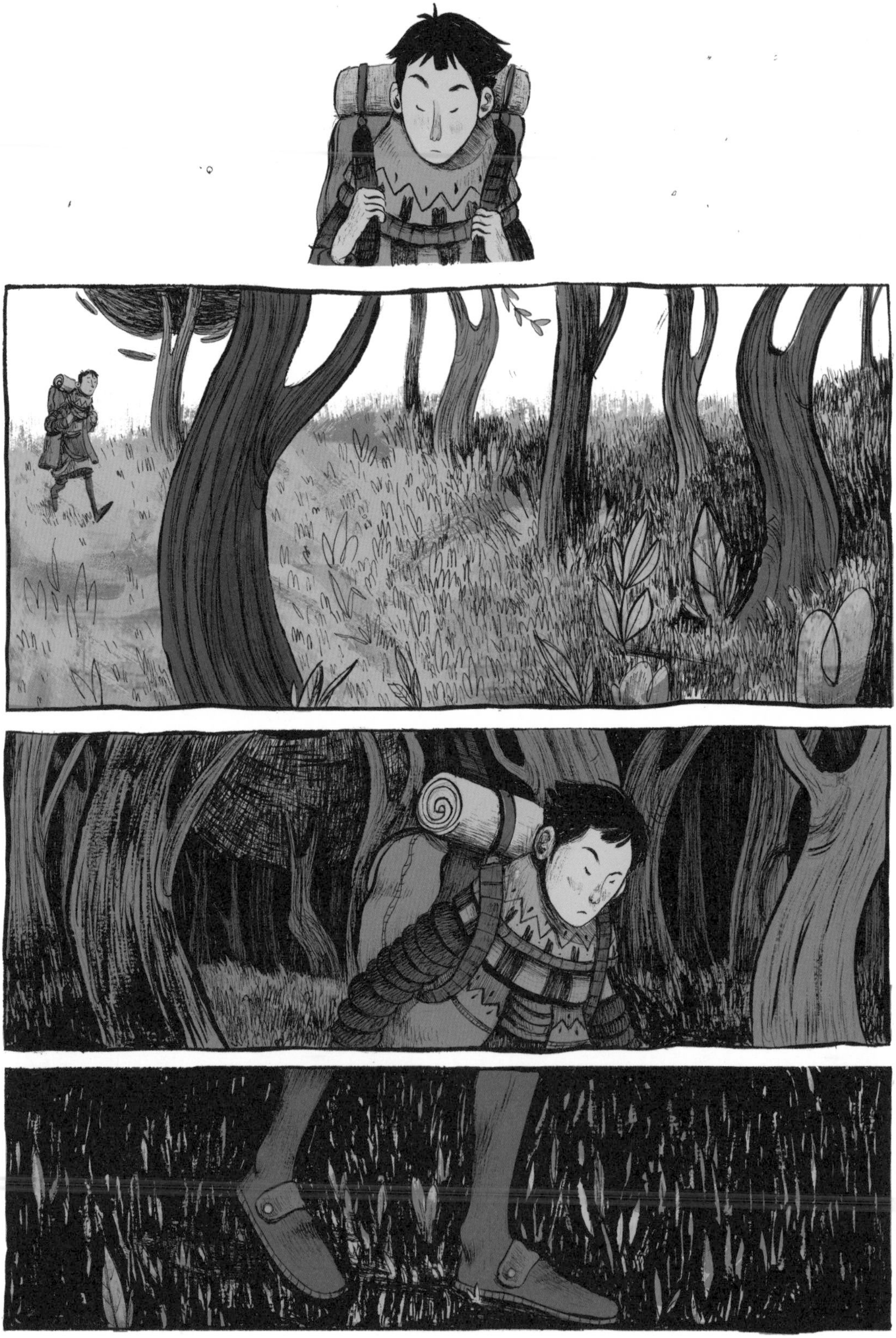

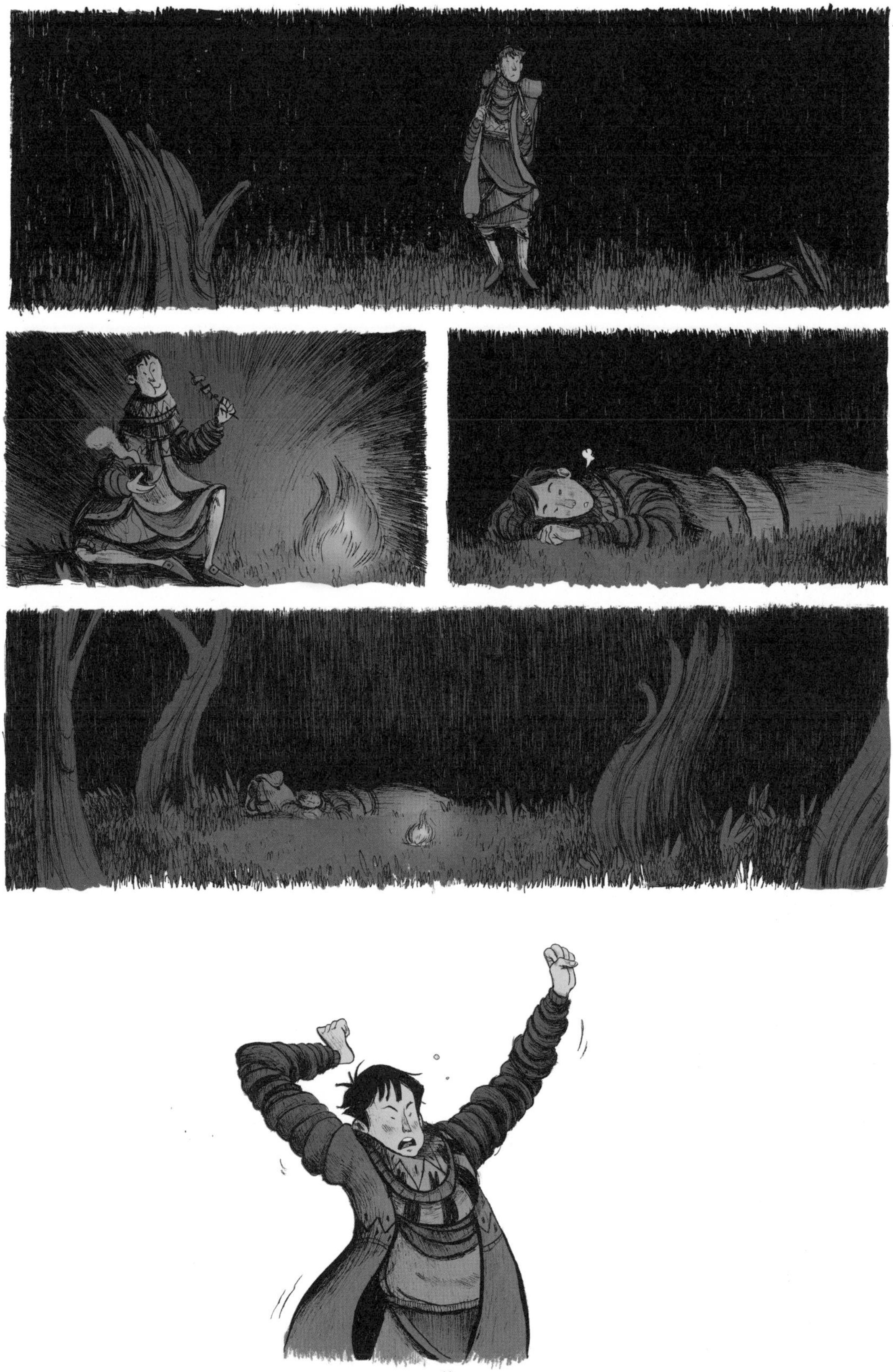

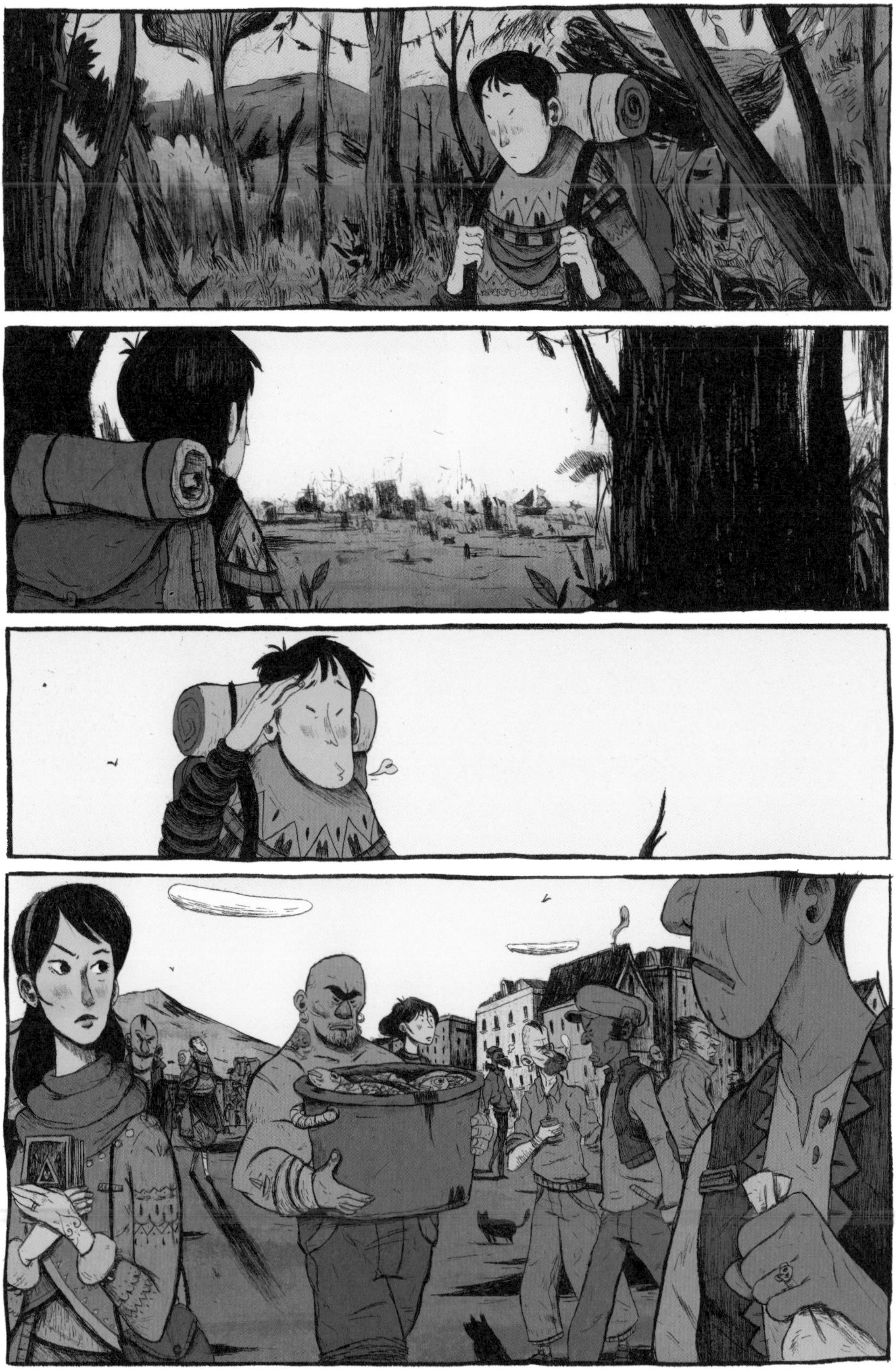

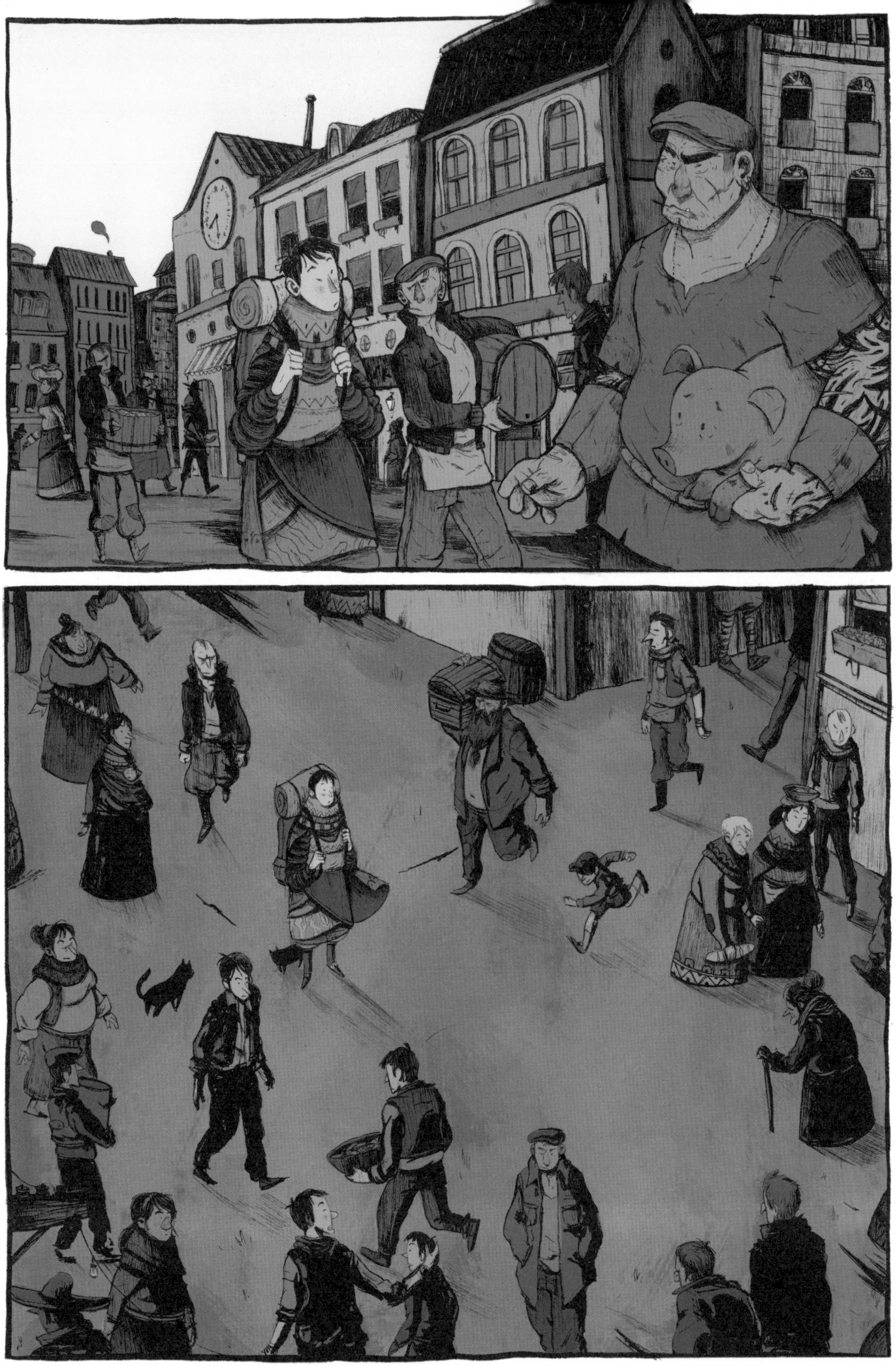

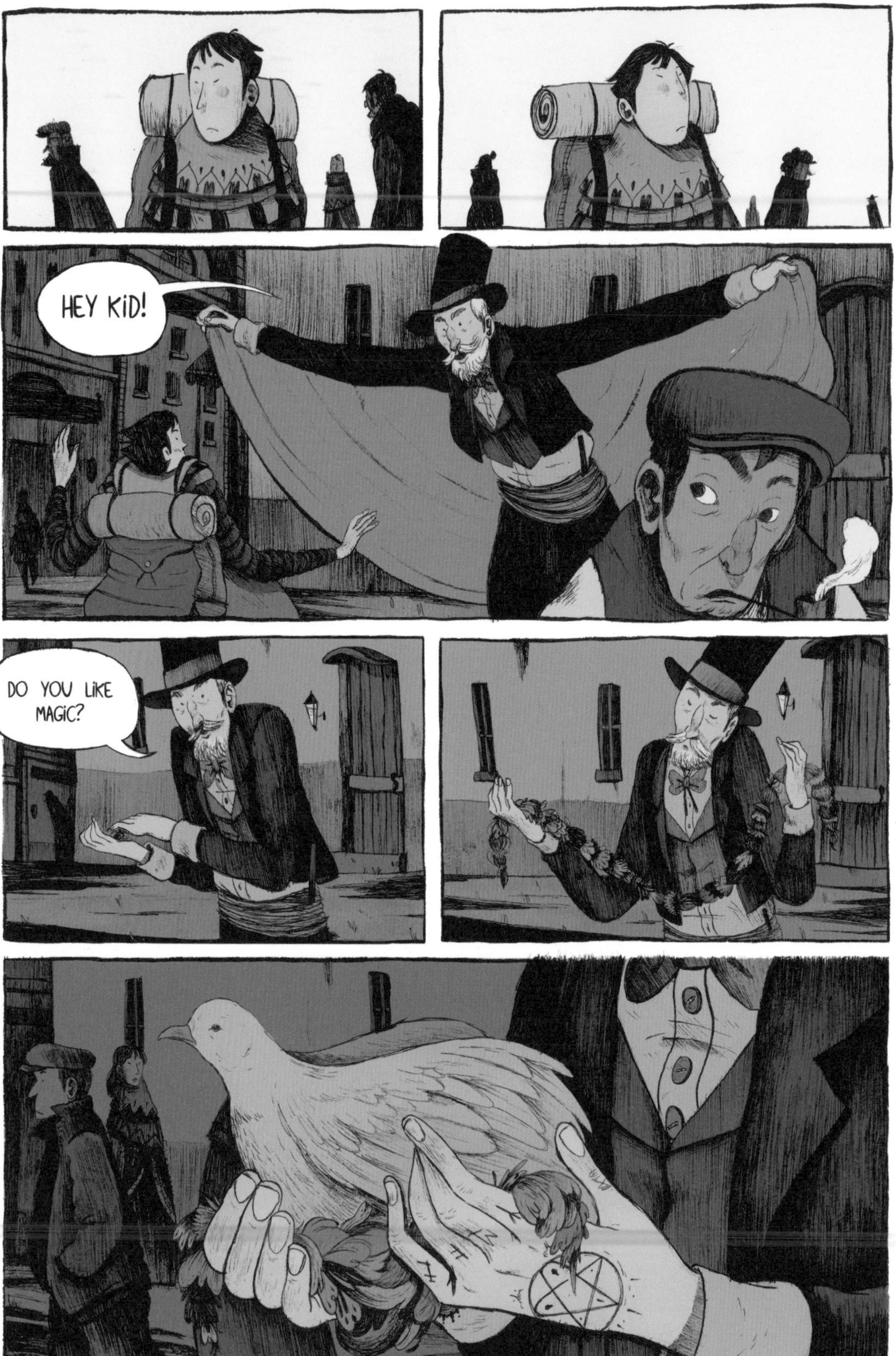
HEY KID!
DO YOU LIKE MAGIC?

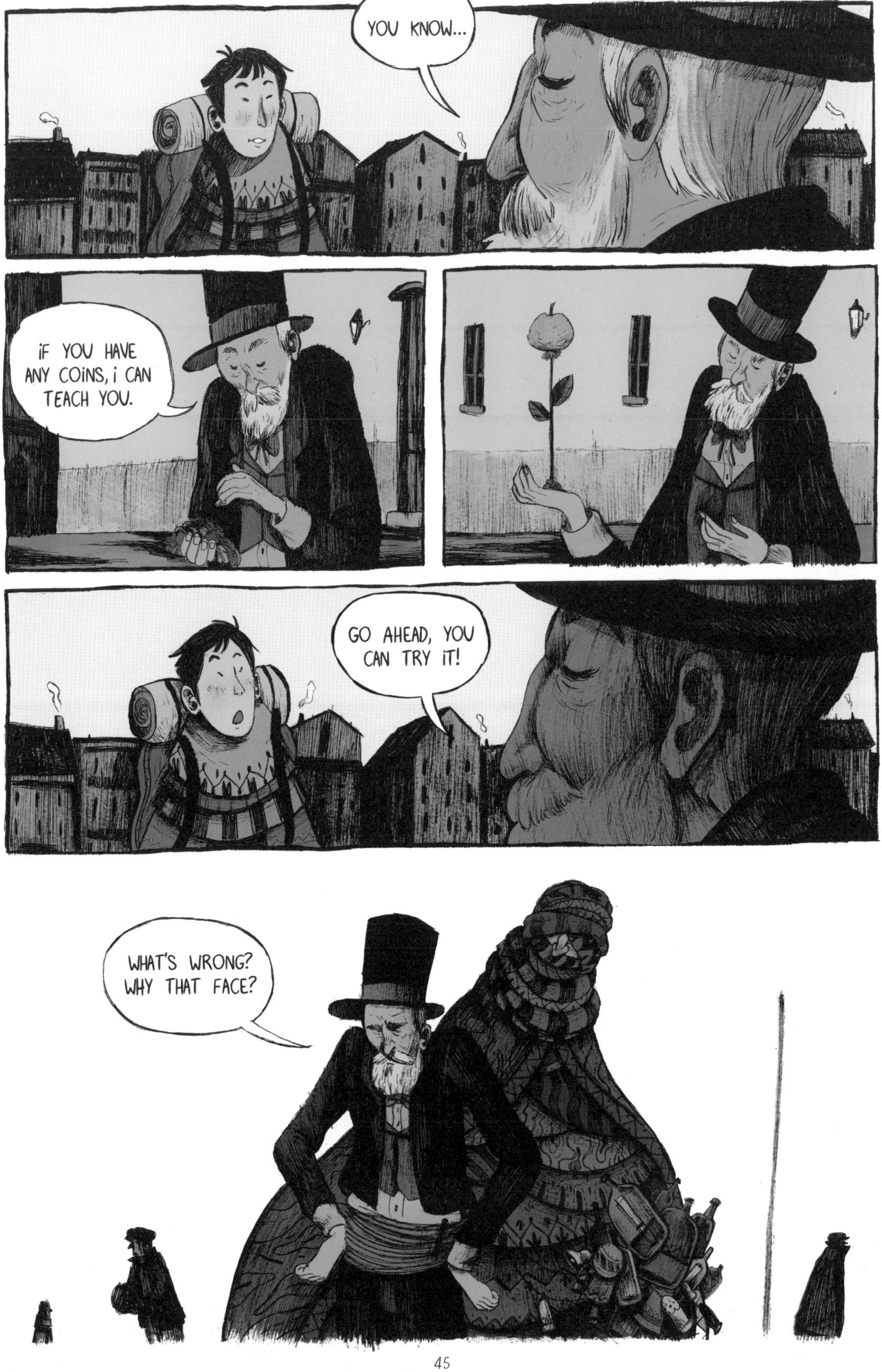
YOU KNOW...
iF YOU HAVE ANY COiNS, i CAN TEACH YOU.
GO AHEAD, YOU CAN TRY iT!
WHAT'S WRONG? WHY THAT FACE?

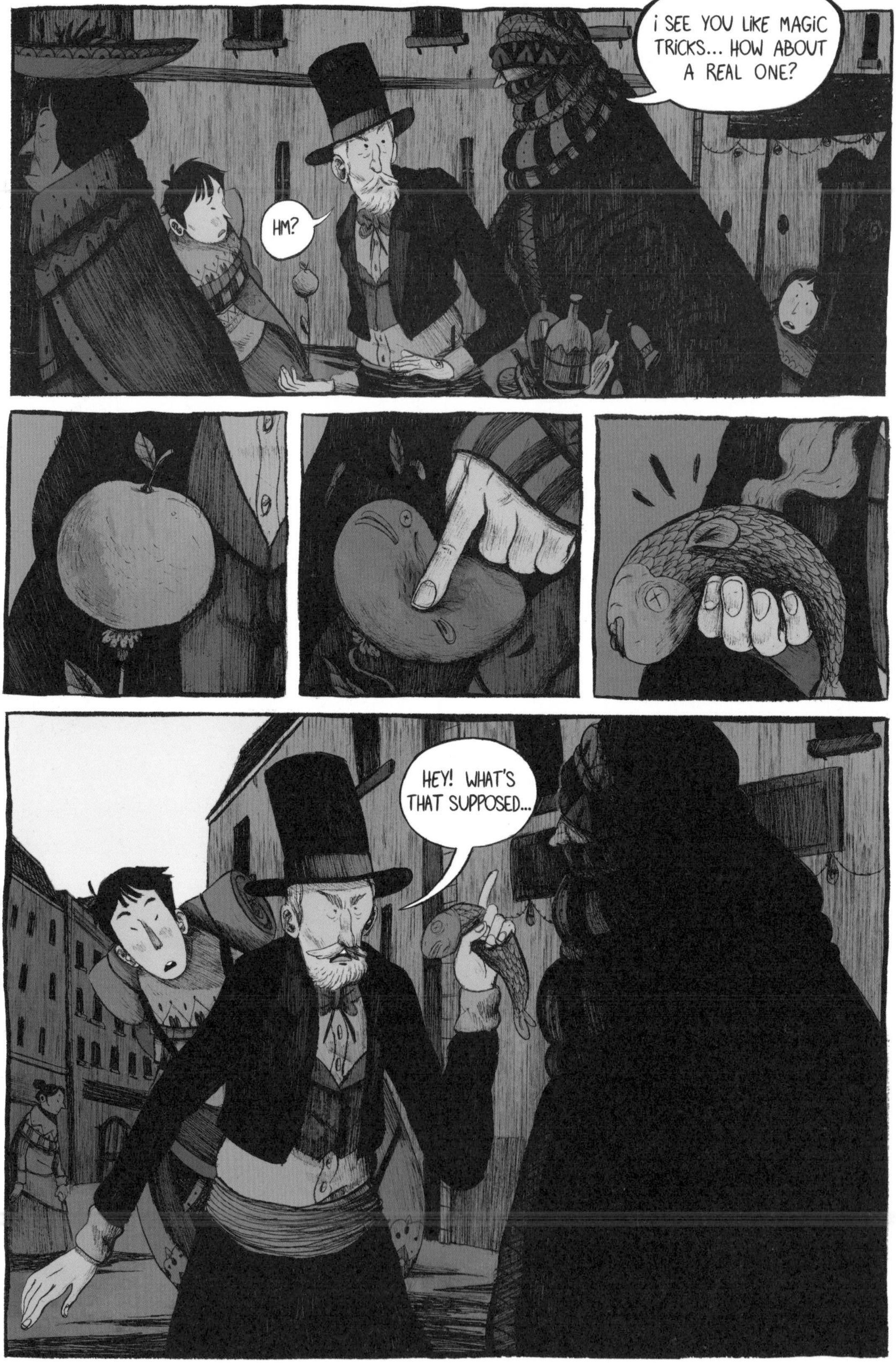

¡ SEE YOU LiKE MAGiC TRiCKS... HOW ABOUT A REAL ONE?
HM?
HEY! WHAT'S THAT SUPPOSED...

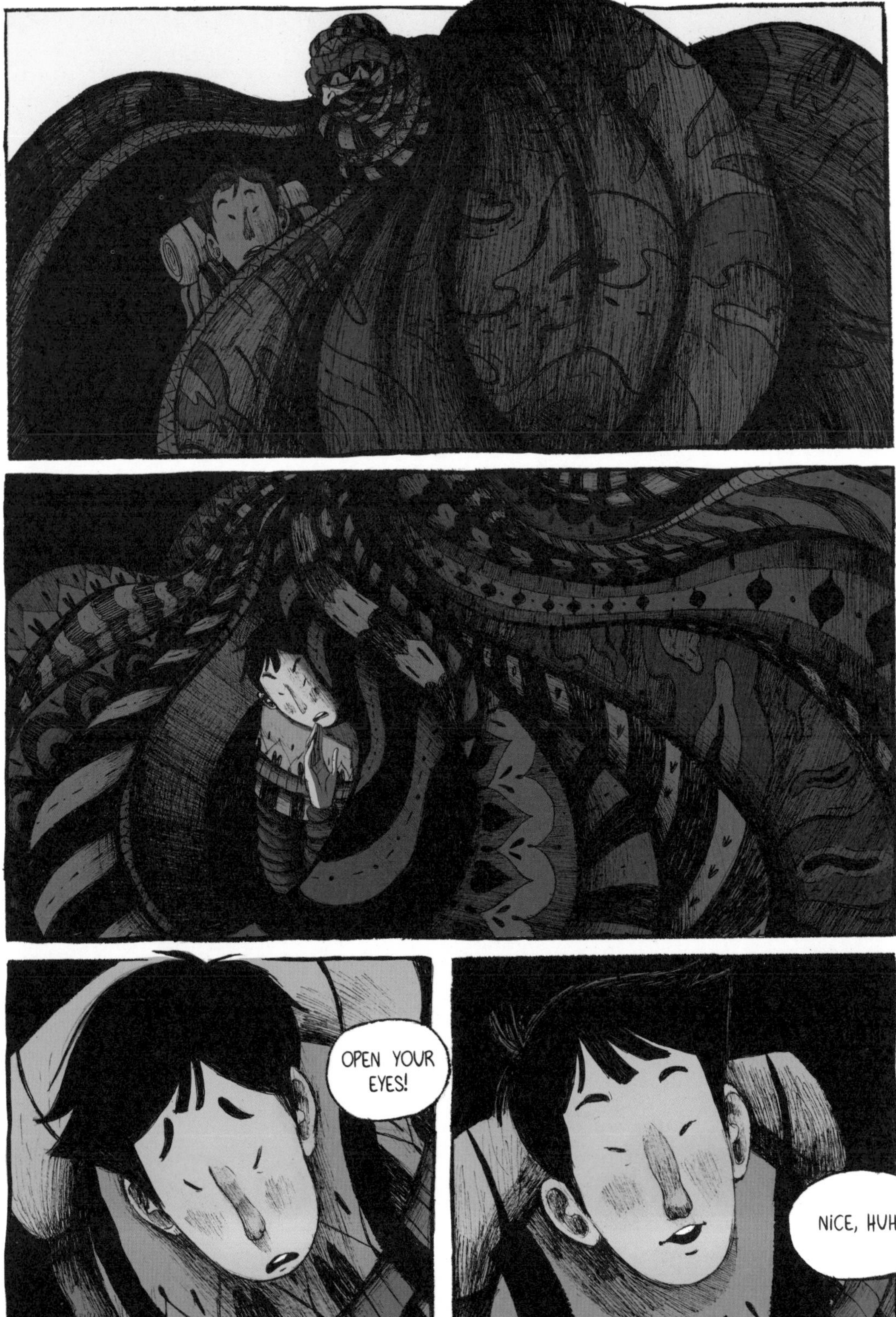
OPEN YOUR EYES!
NICE, HUH?

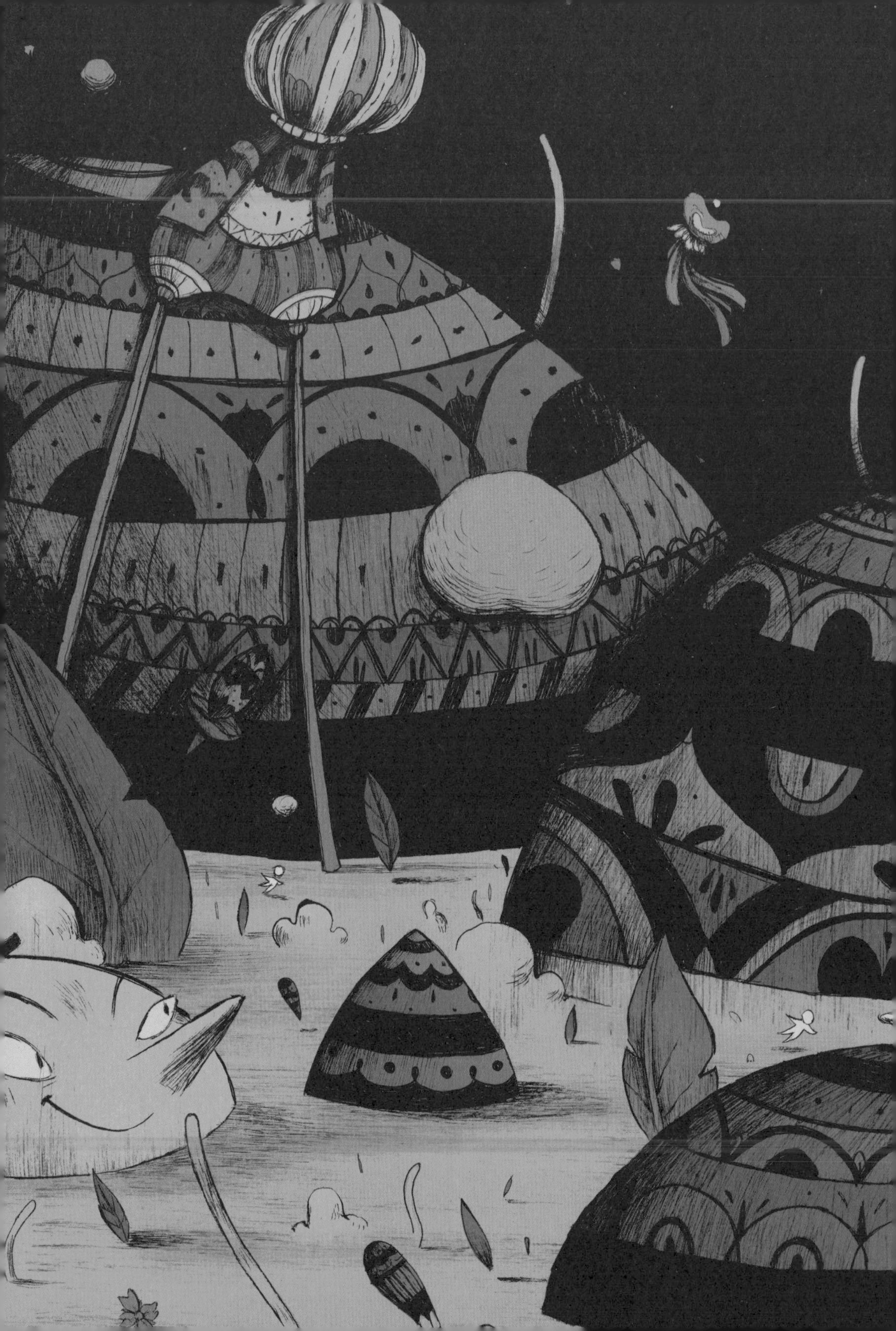

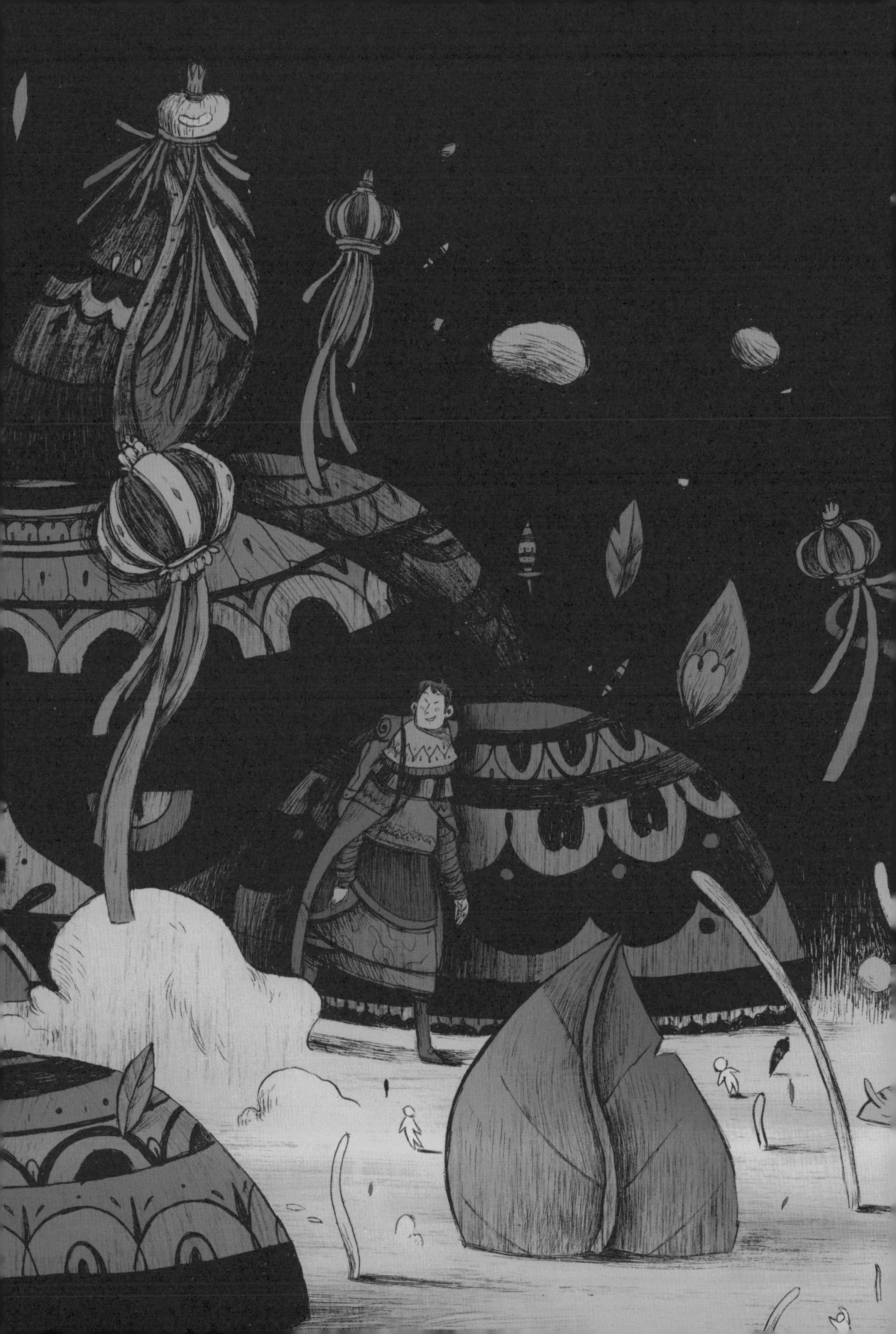

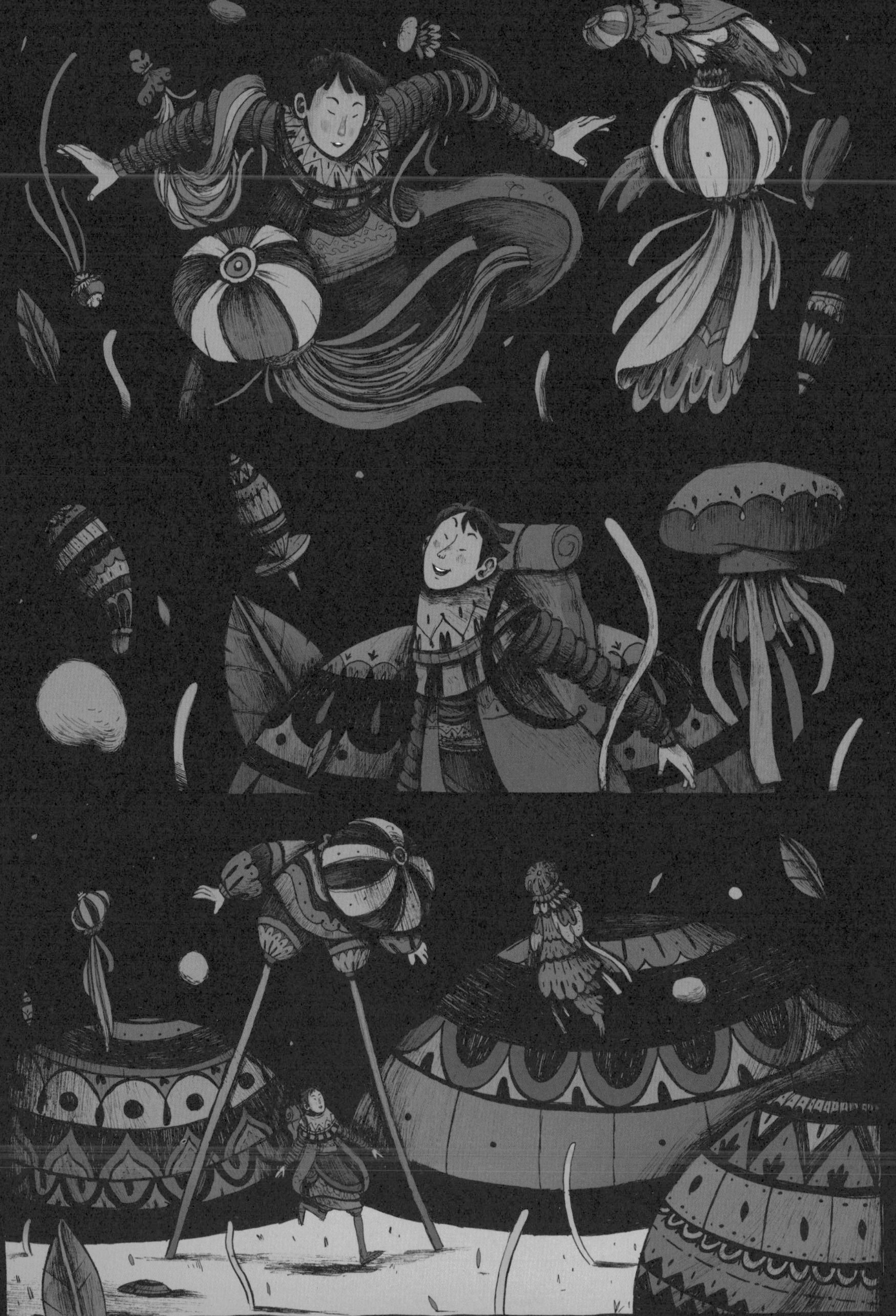

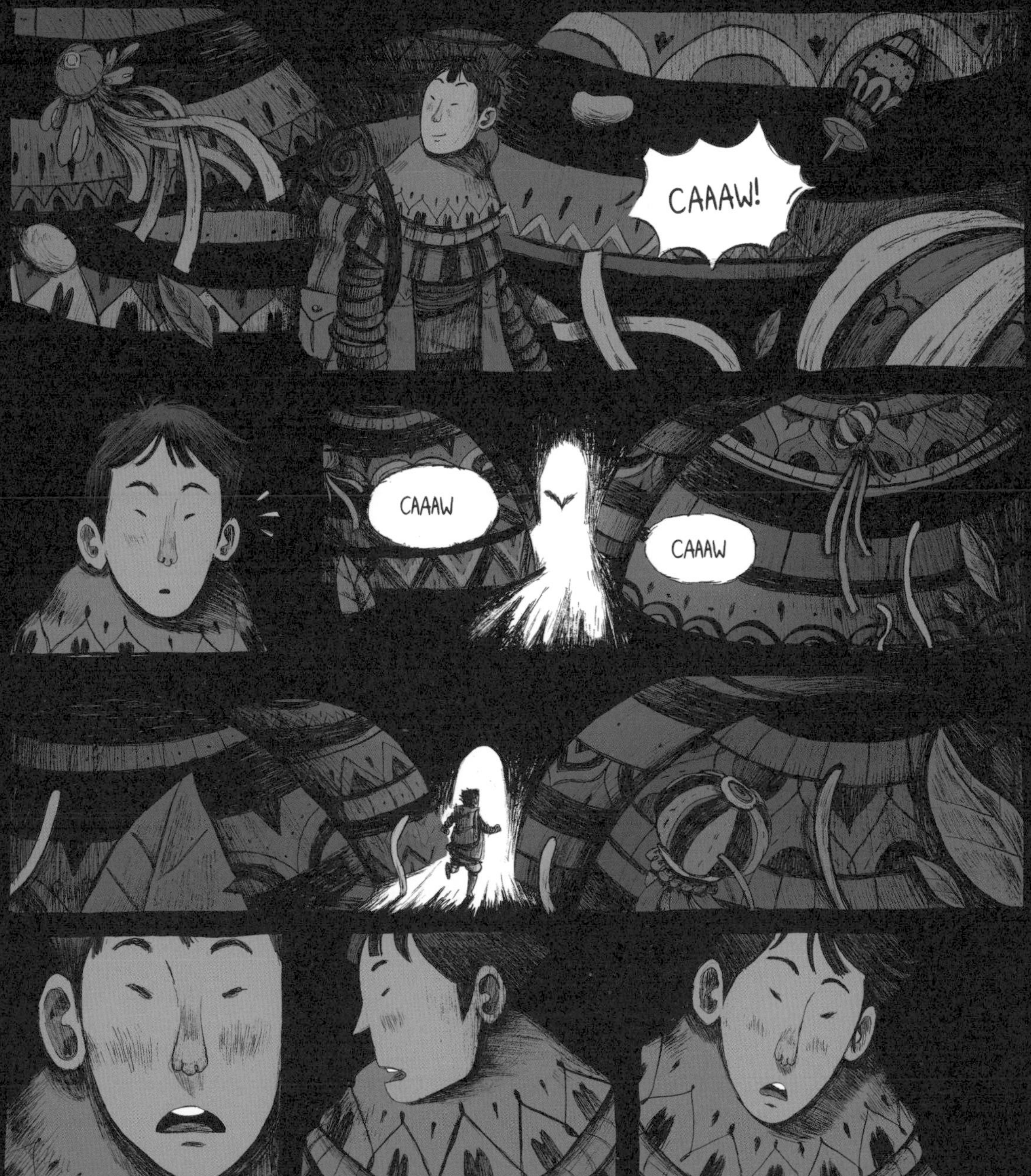
CAAAW!
CAAAW
CAAAW

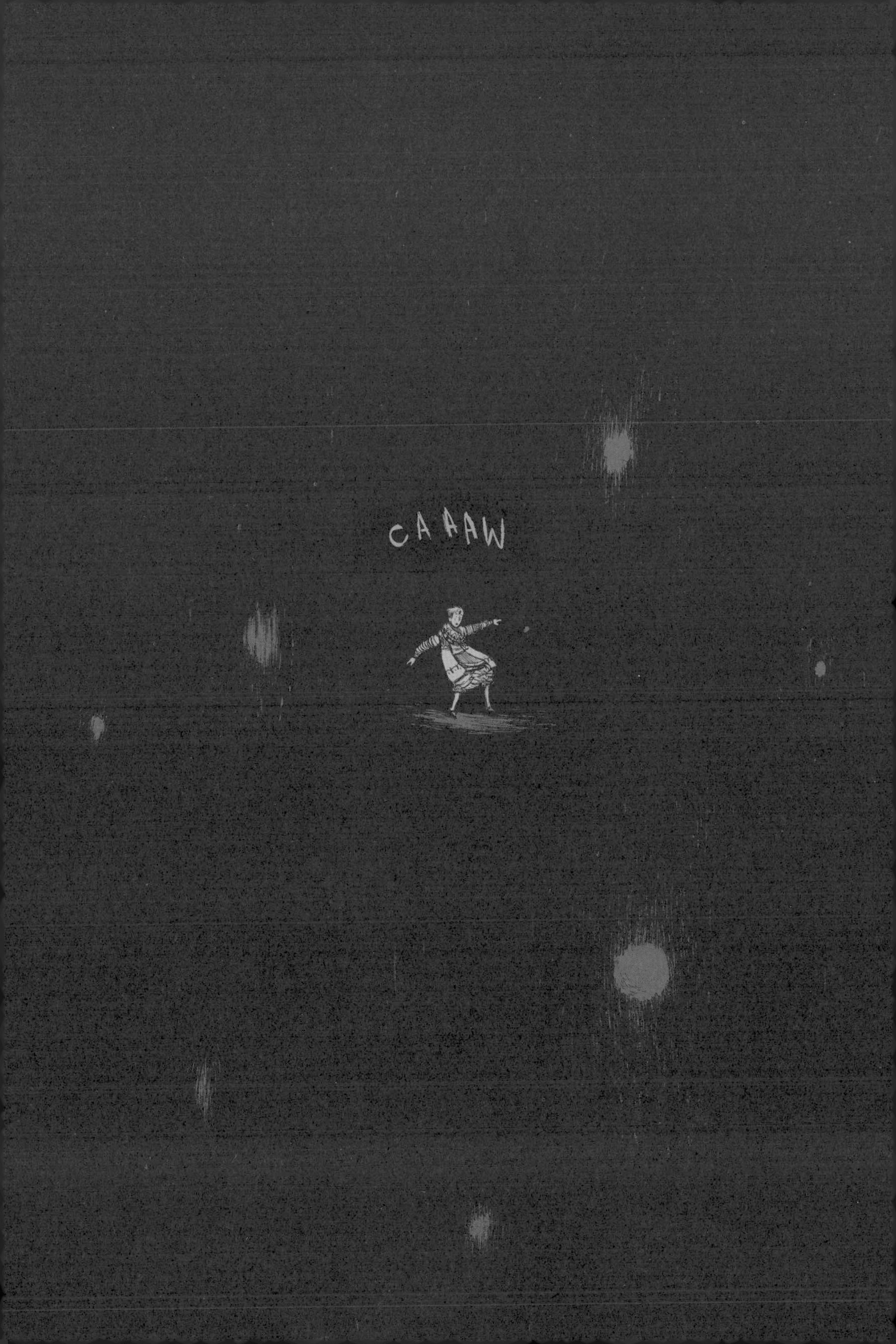
CAAAW

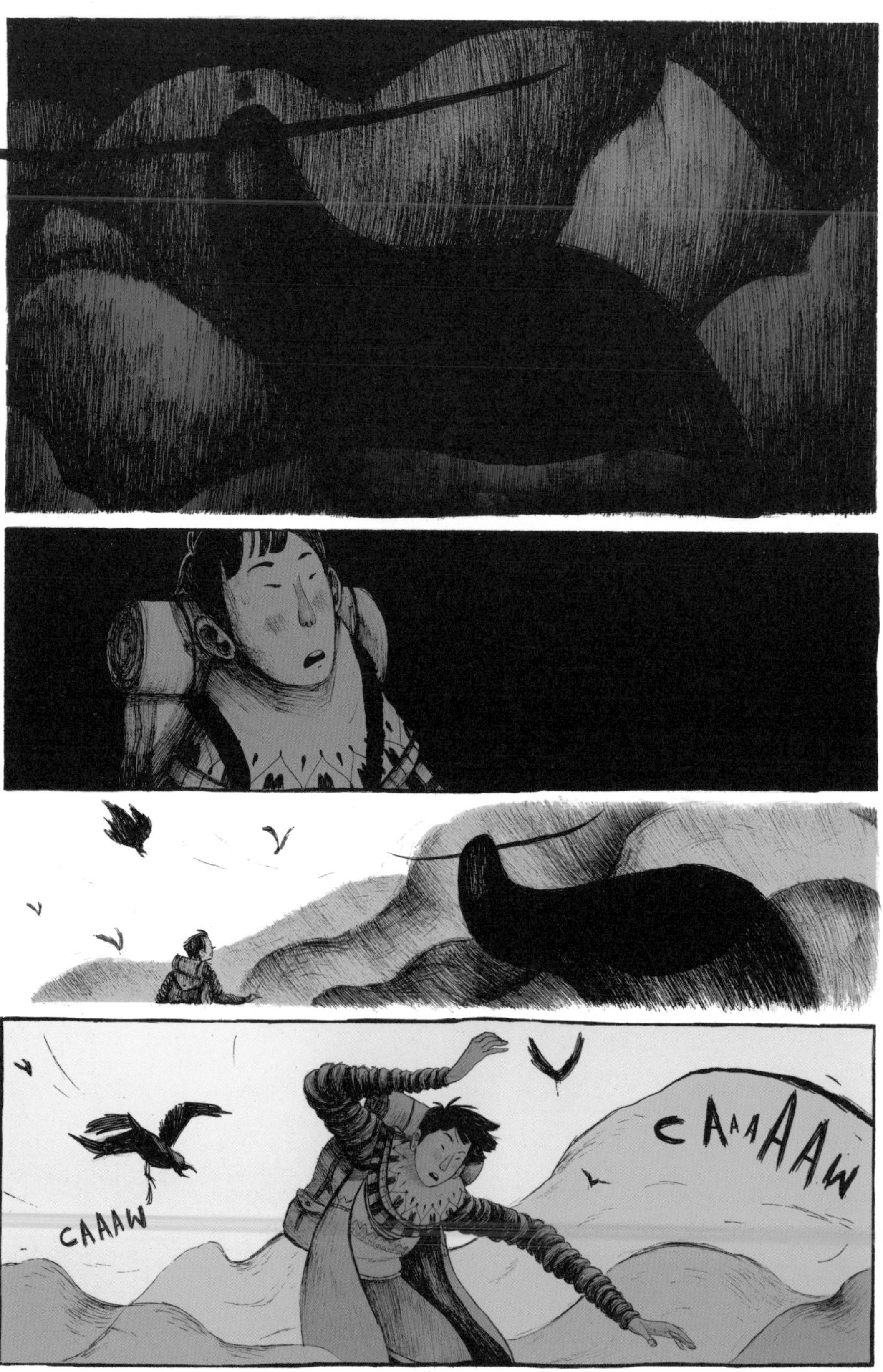
CAAAW
CAAAAAW

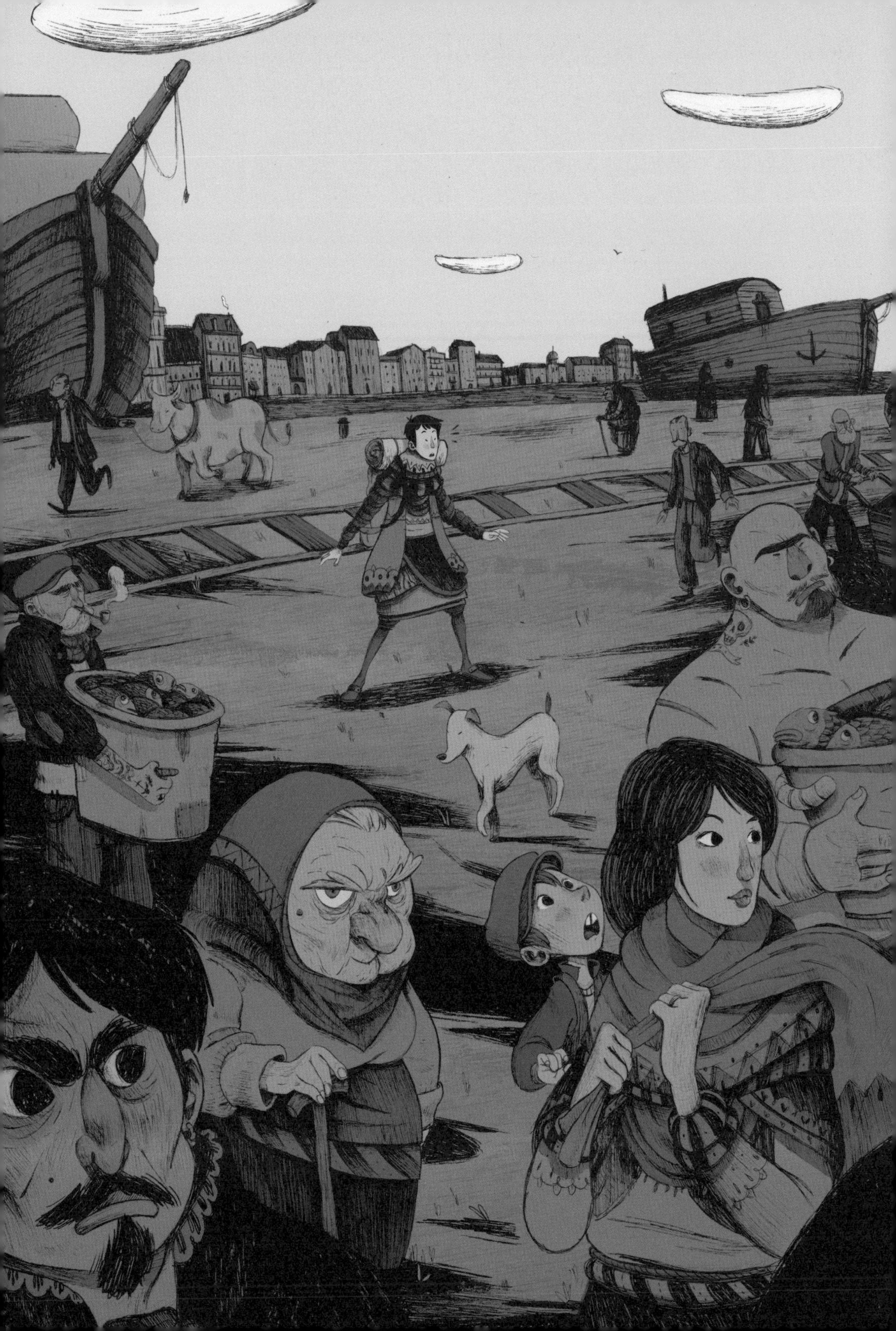

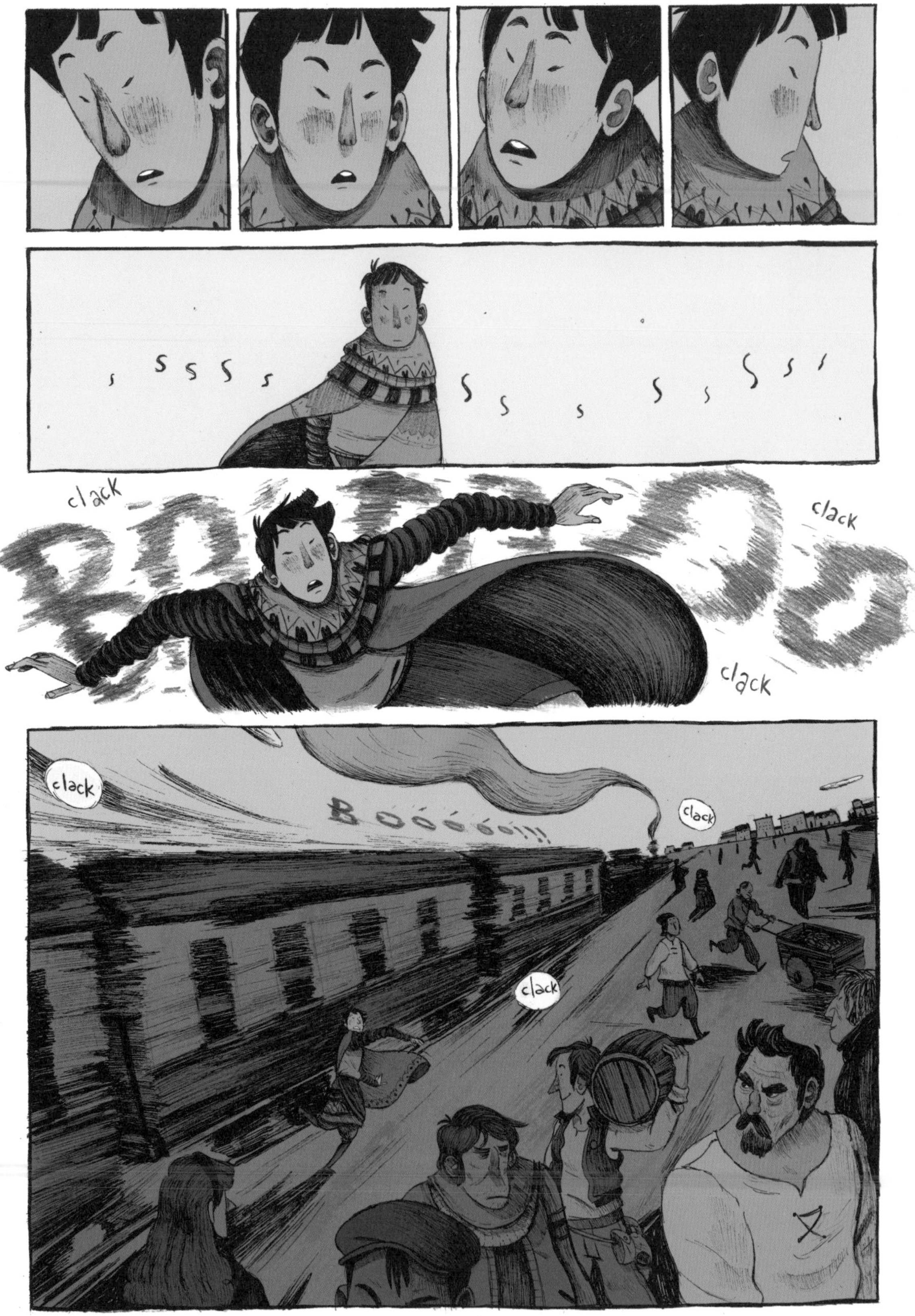
clack
clack
clack
clack
clack
clack

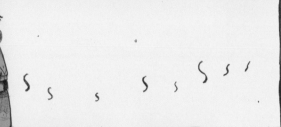

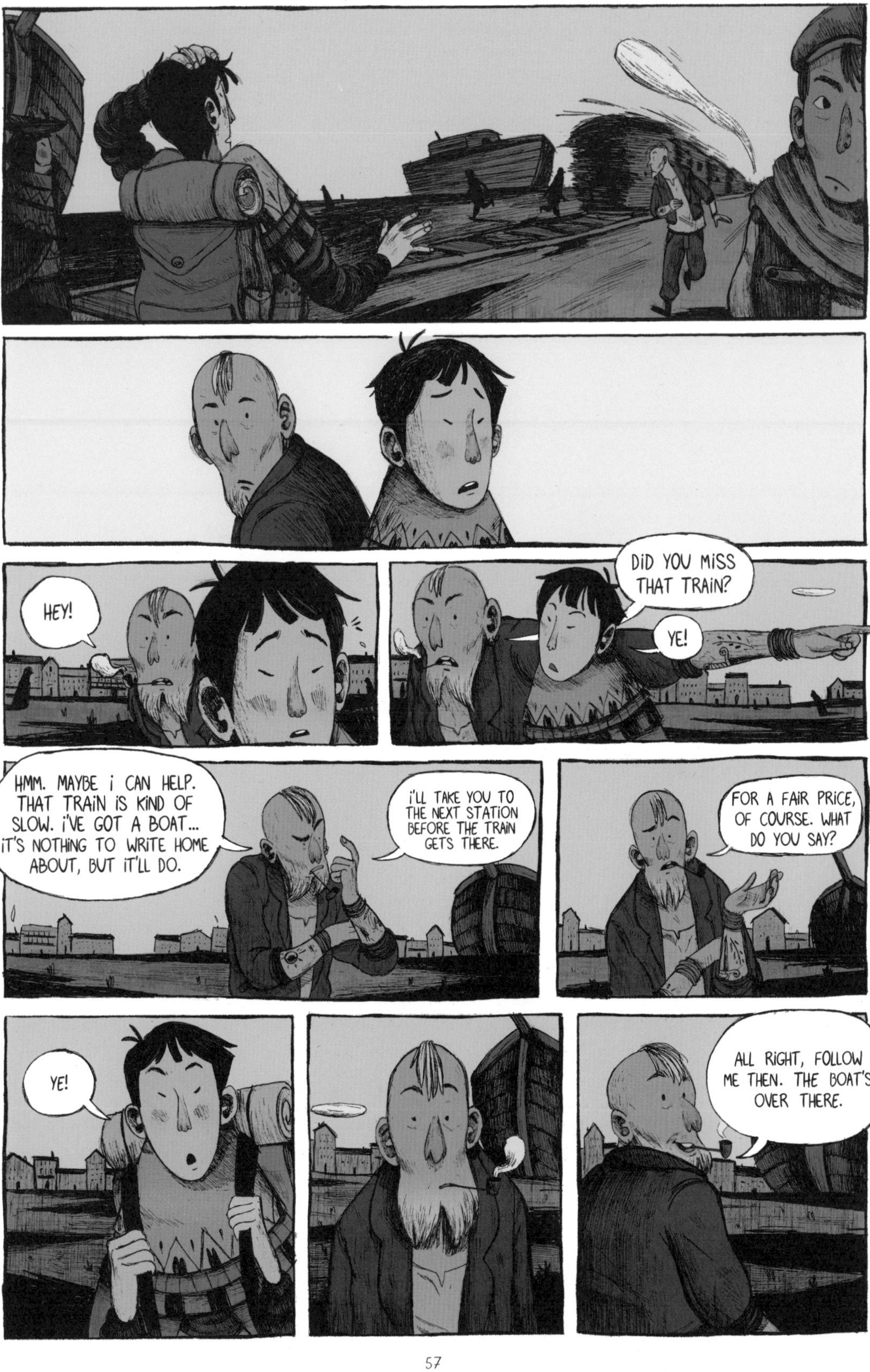
HEY!
DID YOU MISS THAT TRAIN?
YE!
HMM. MAYBE i CAN HELP. THAT TRAIN iS KIND OF SLOW. i'VE GOT A BOAT... iT'S NOTHING TO WRITE HOME ABOUT, BUT IT'LL DO.
i'LL TAKE YOU TO THE NEXT STATION BEFORE THE TRAIN GETS THERE.
FOR A FAIR PRiCE, OF COURSE. WHAT DO YOU SAY?
YE!
ALL RiGHT, FOLLOW ME THEN. THE BOAT'S OVER THERE.

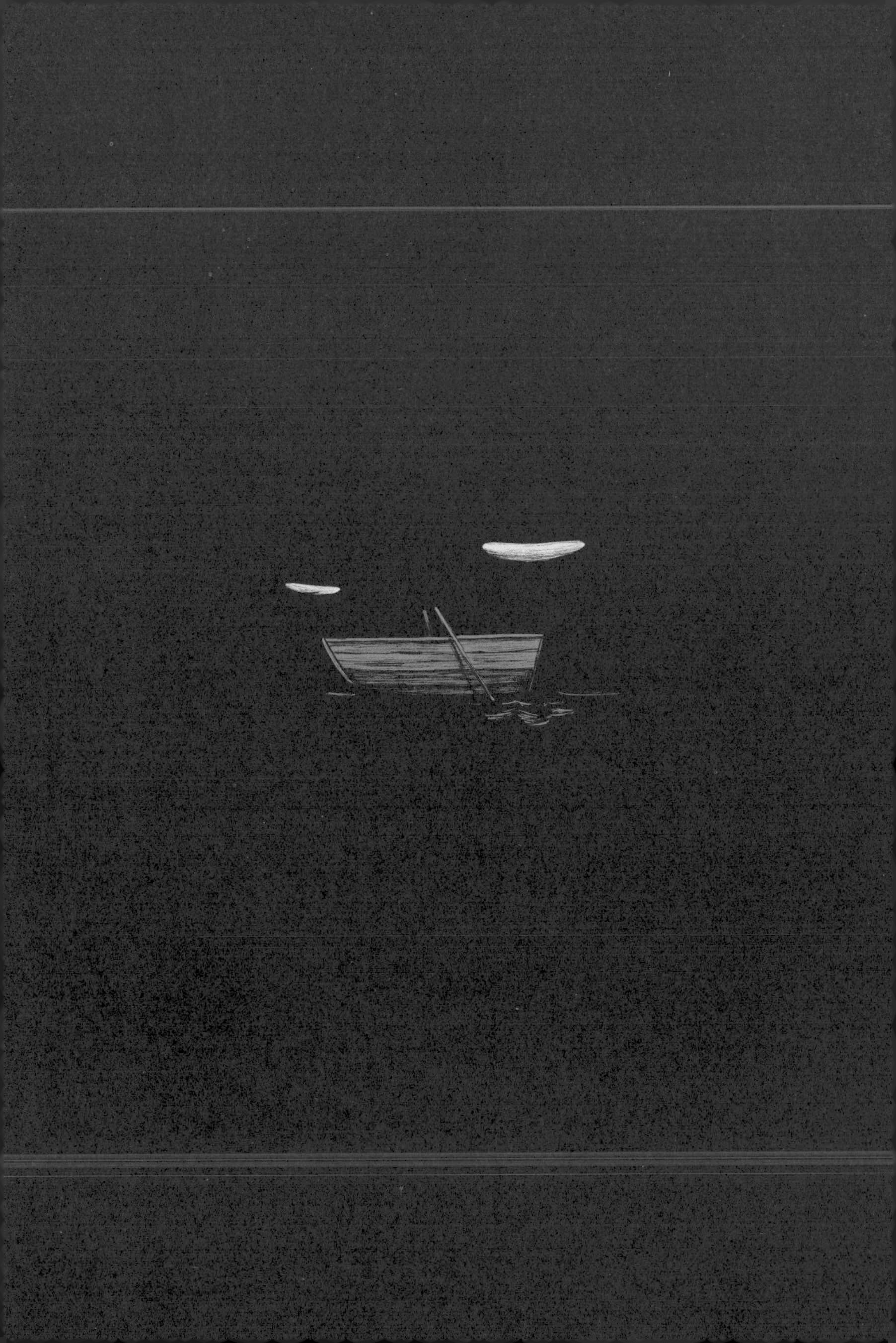

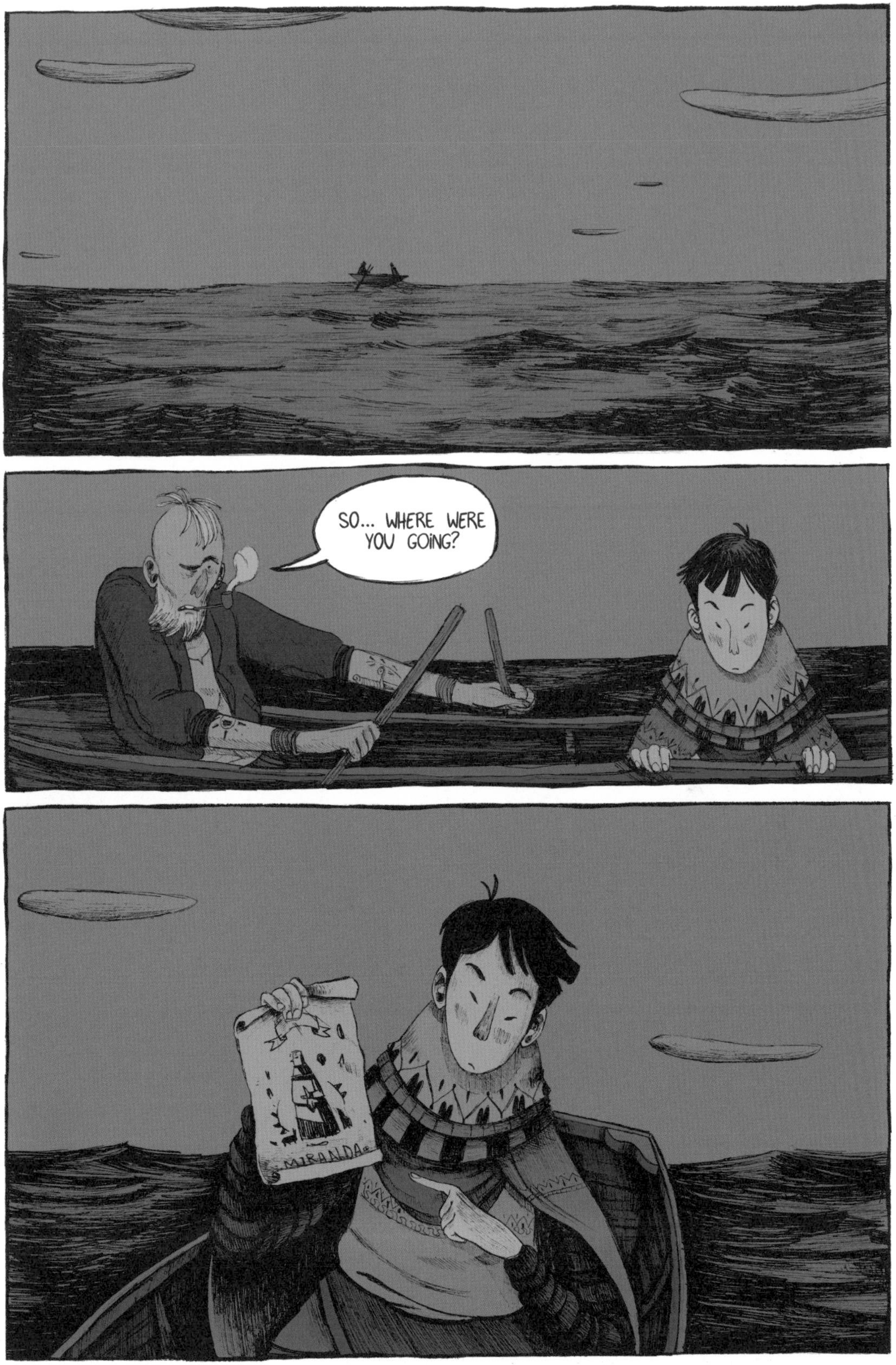
SO... WHERE WERE YOU GOING?
MIRANDA

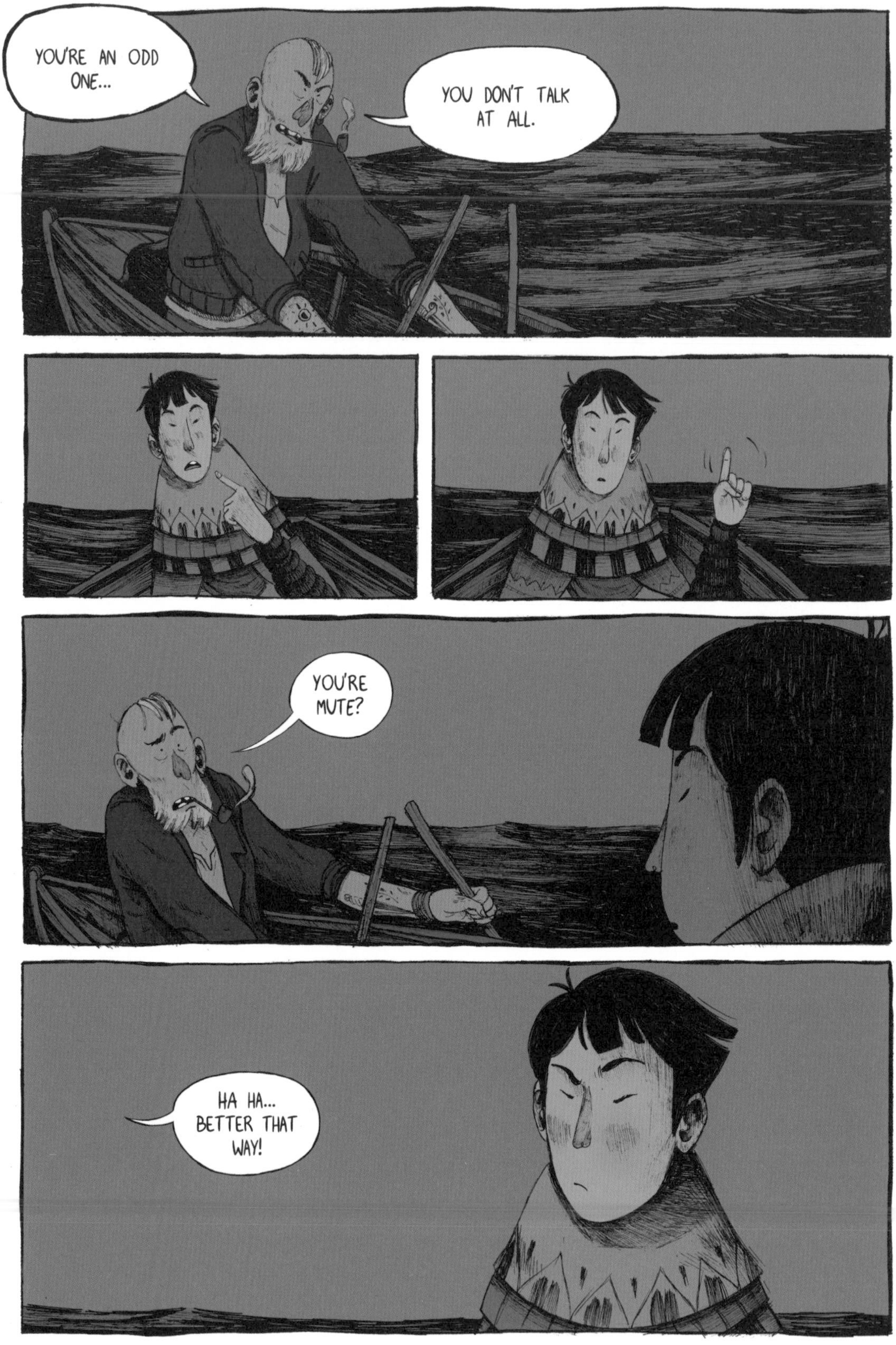
YOU'RE AN ODD ONE...
YOU DON'T TALK AT ALL.
YOU'RE MUTE?
HA HA... BETTER THAT WAY!

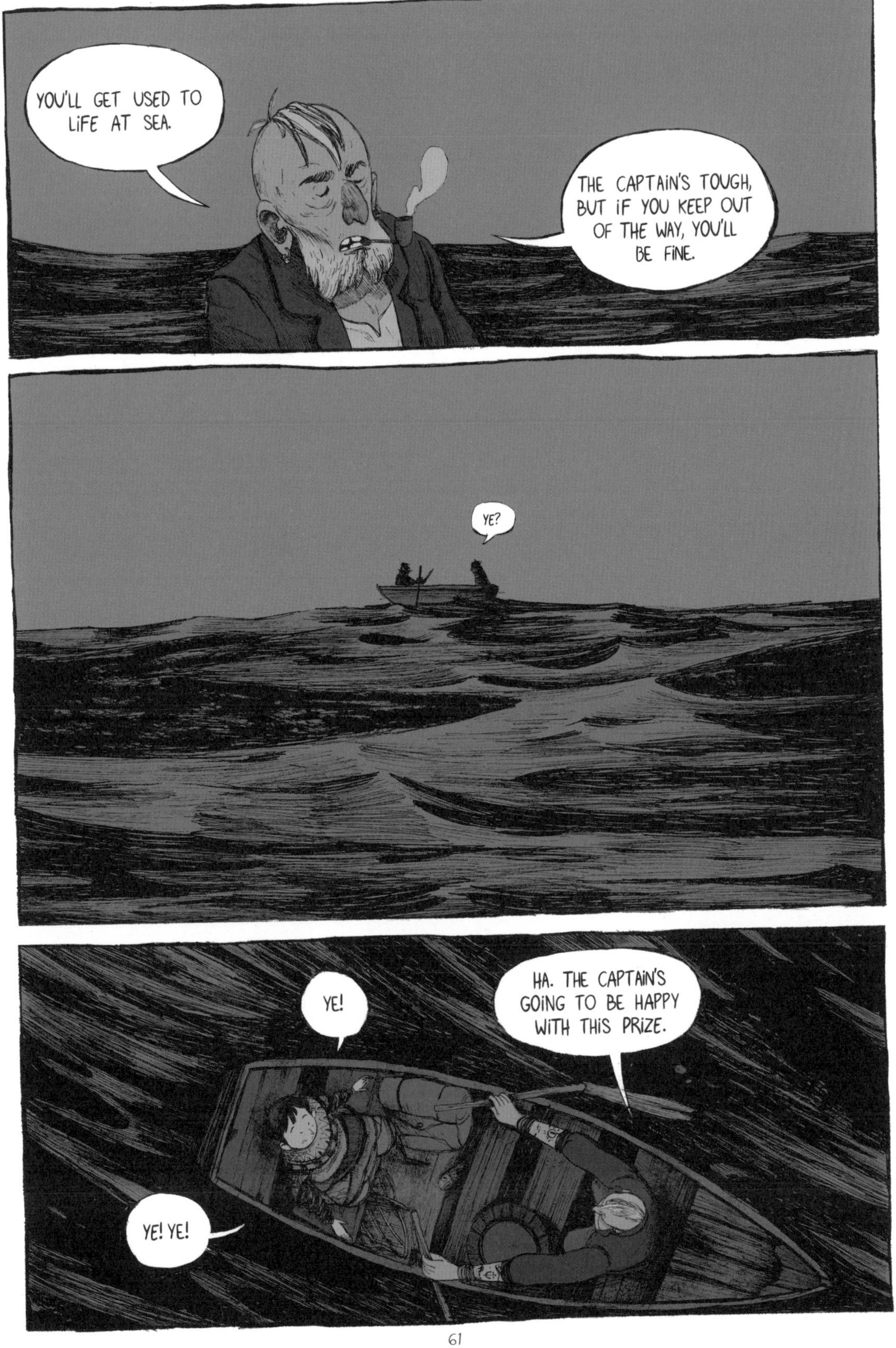
YOU'LL GET USED TO LIFE AT SEA.
THE CAPTAIN'S TOUGH, BUT IF YOU KEEP OUT OF THE WAY, YOU'LL BE FINE.
YE?
YE!
HA. THE CAPTAIN'S GOING TO BE HAPPY WITH THIS PRIZE.
YE! YE!

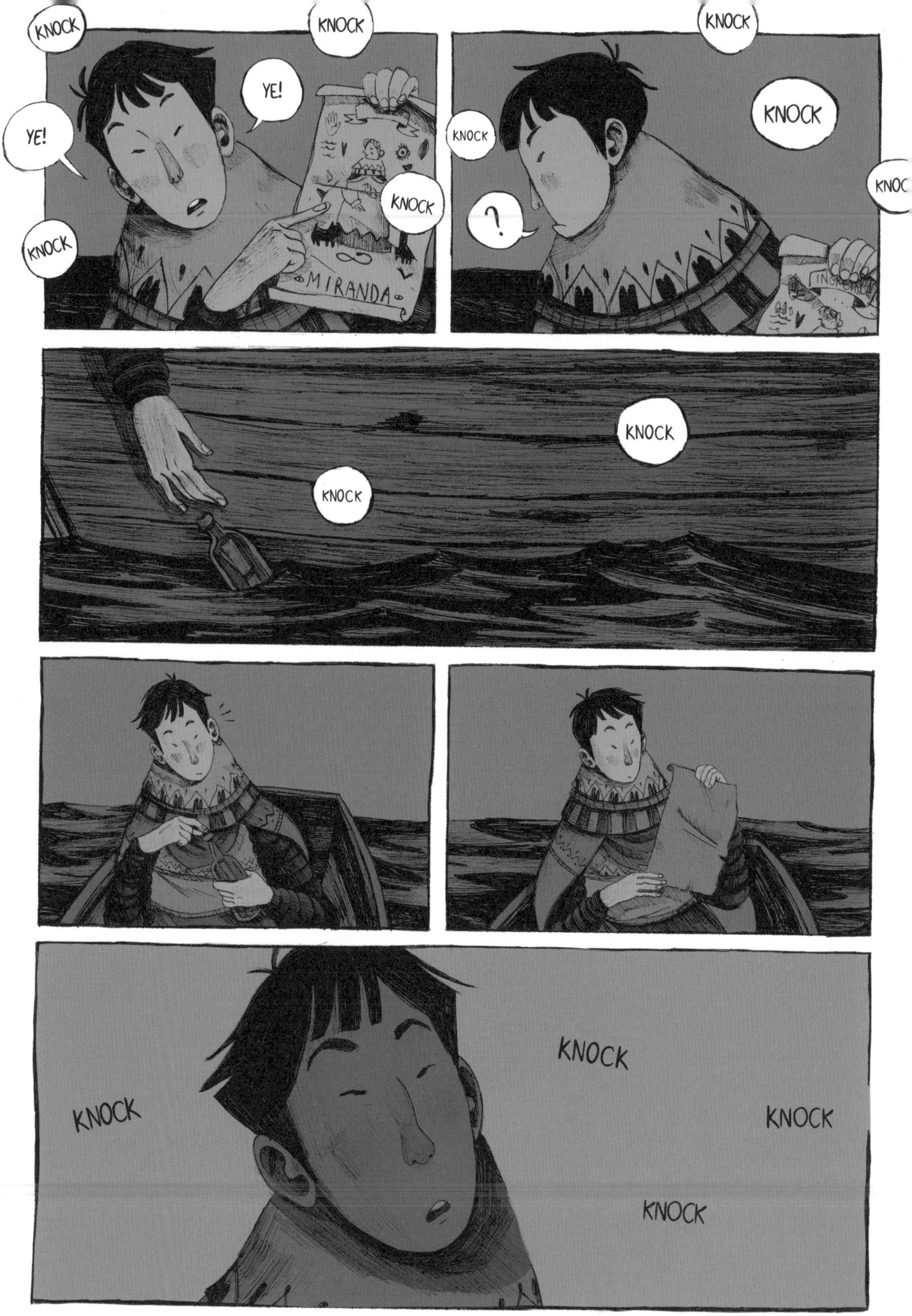
KNOCK
KNOCK
YE!
YE!
KNOCK
MIRANDA
KNOCK
KNOCK
KNOCK
KNOCK
?
KNOC
KNOCK
KNOCK
KNOCK
KNOCK
KNOCK
KNOCK

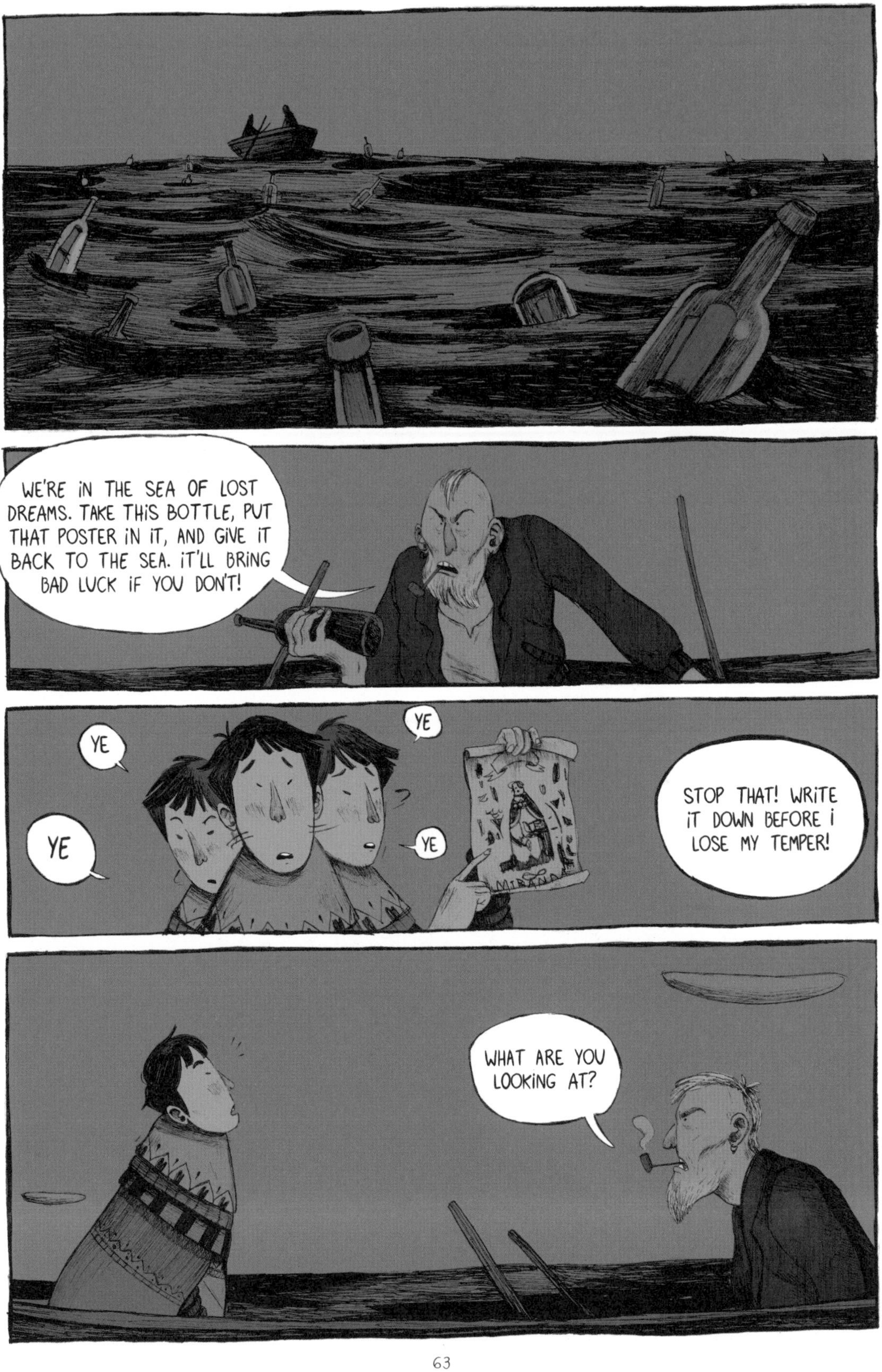
WE'RE IN THE SEA OF LOST DREAMS. TAKE THIS BOTTLE, PUT THAT POSTER IN IT, AND GIVE IT BACK TO THE SEA. IT'LL BRING BAD LUCK IF YOU DON'T!
YE
YE
YE
YE
MIRANDA
STOP THAT! WRITE IT DOWN BEFORE I LOSE MY TEMPER!
WHAT ARE YOU LOOKING AT?

HEY!

WAKE UP!

FFFFFF

FFFFFFFF

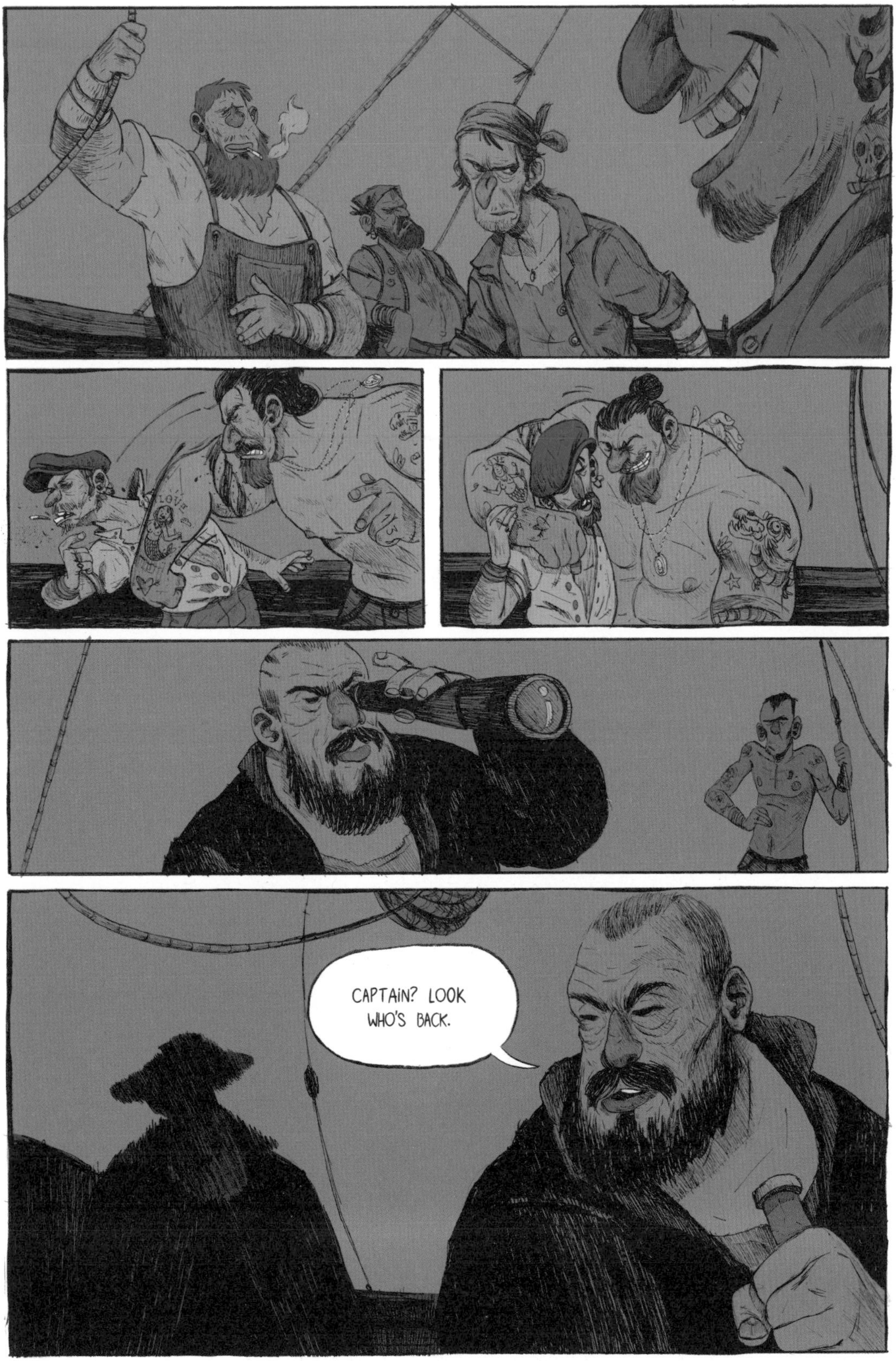
CAPTAIN? LOOK WHO'S BACK.

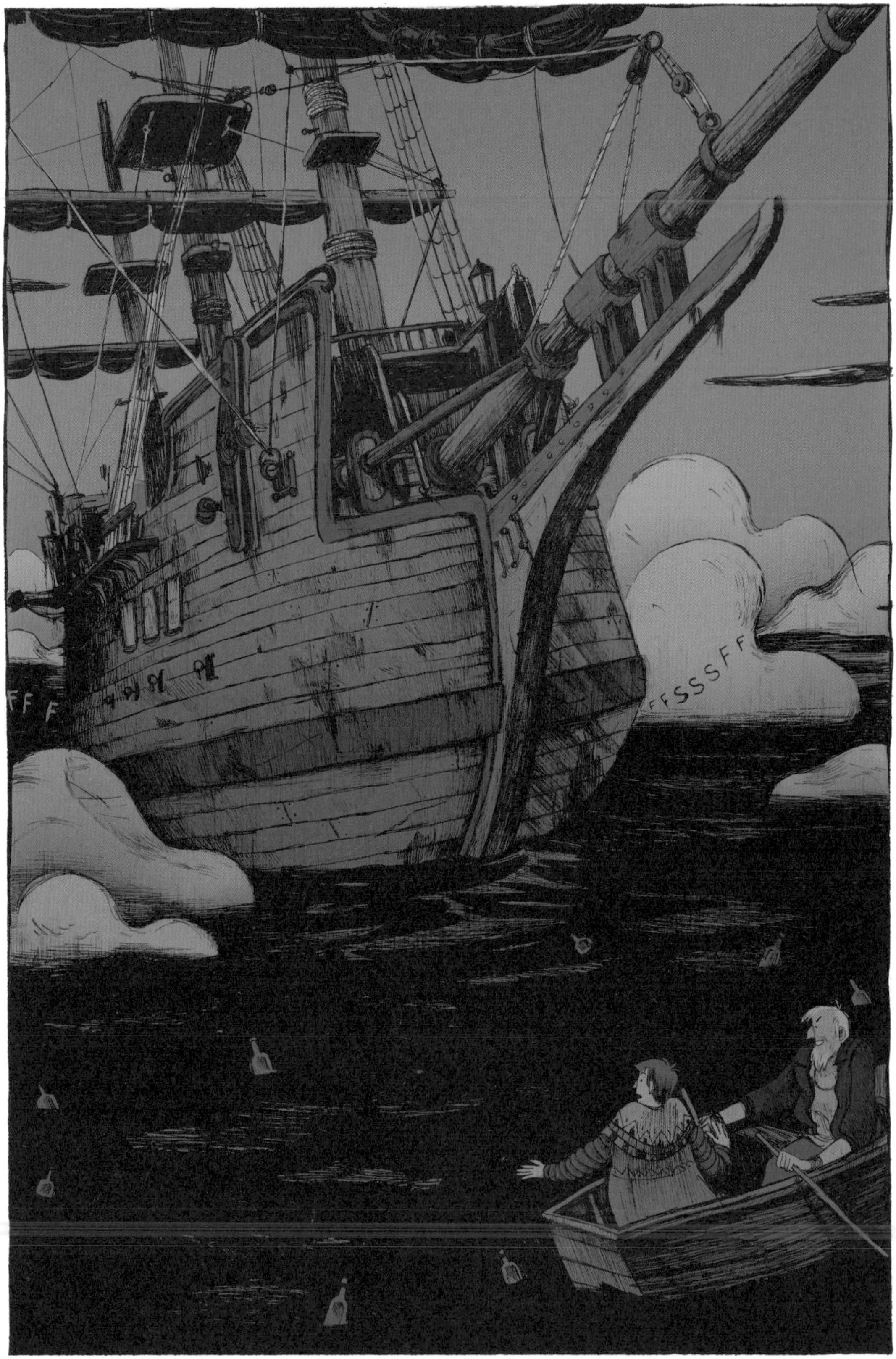
FFFFF
FFSSSFF

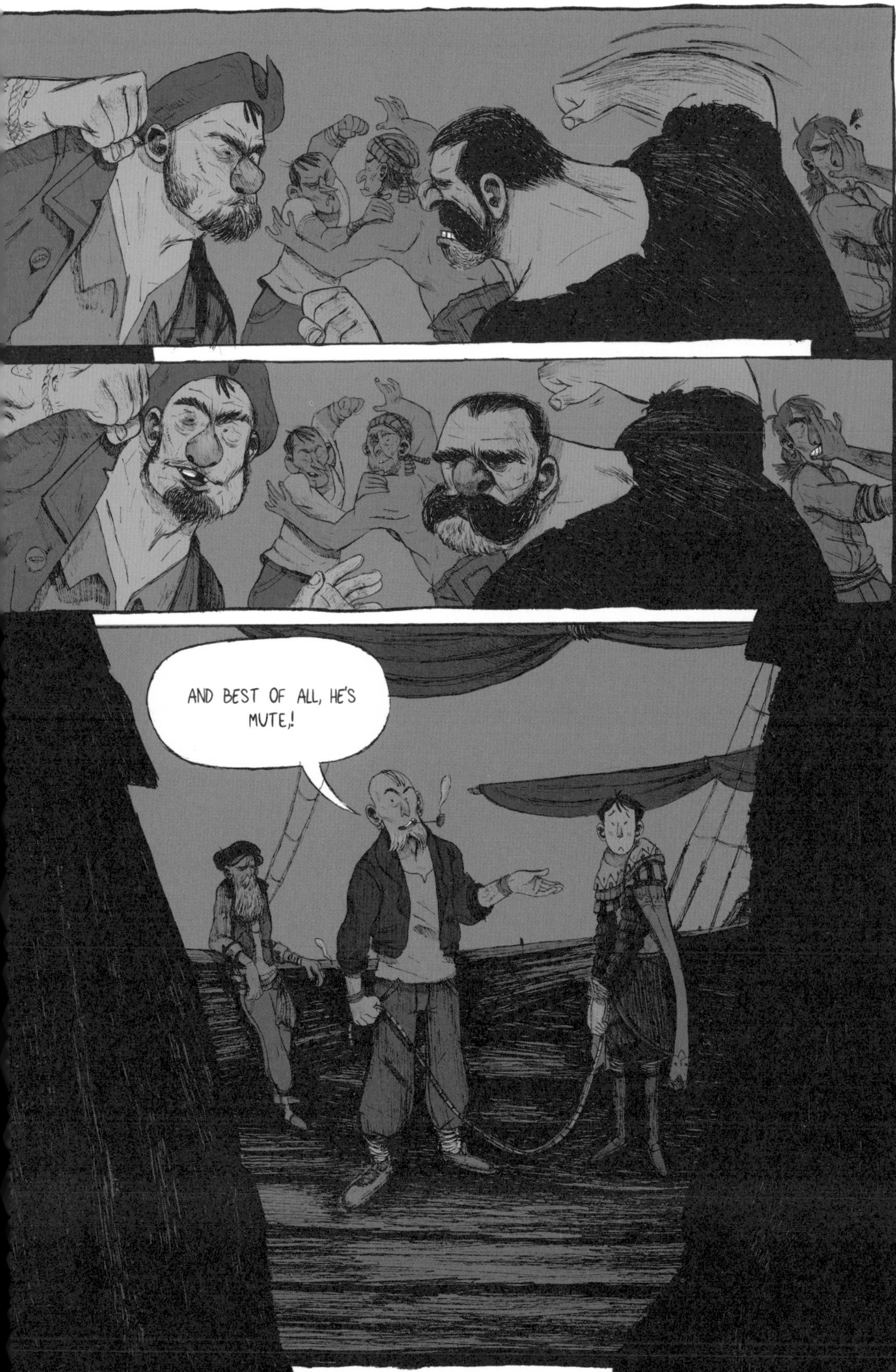
AND BEST OF ALL, HE'S MUTE,!

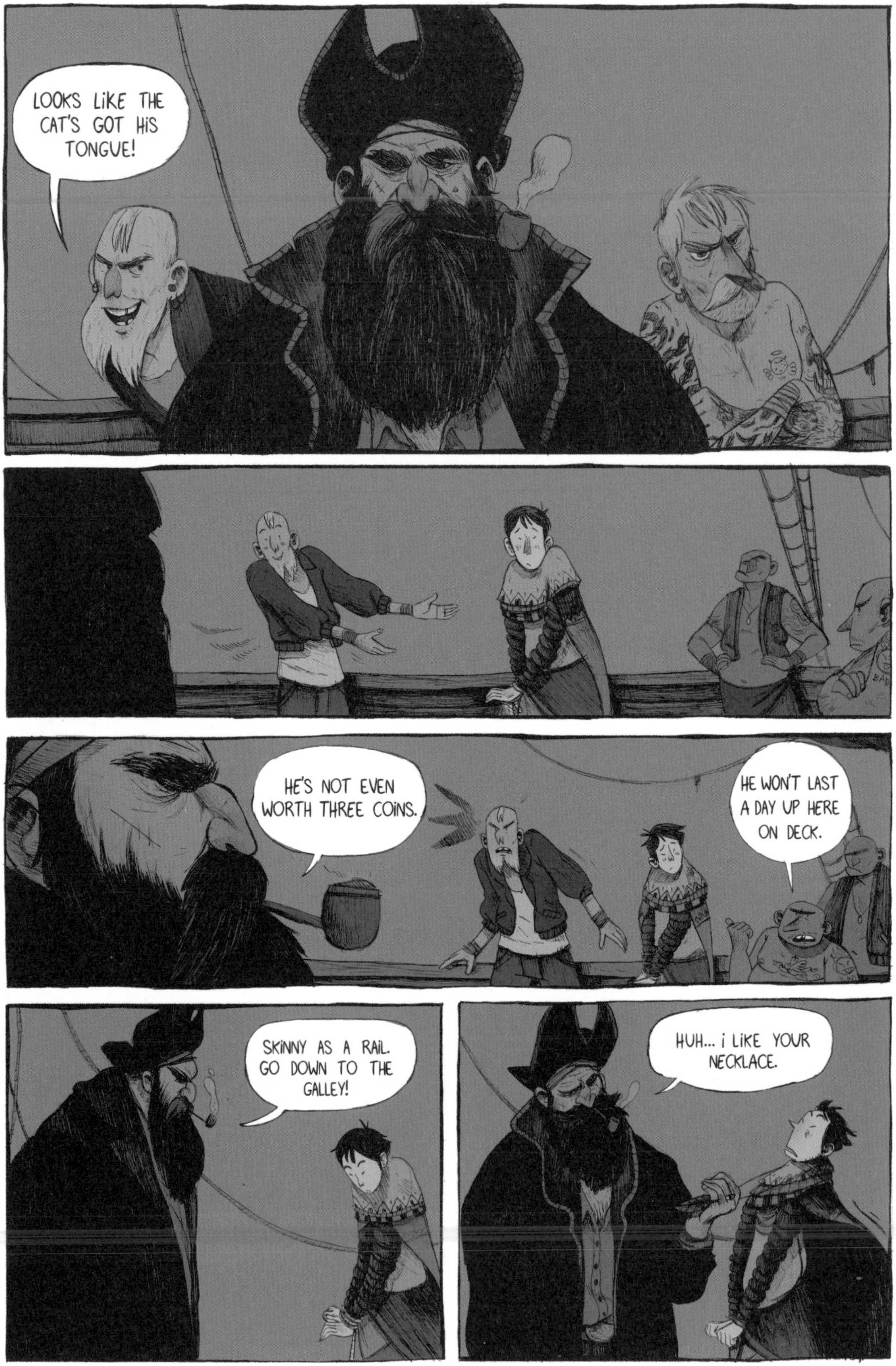
LOOKS LIKE THE CAT'S GOT HIS TONGUE!
HE'S NOT EVEN WORTH THREE COINS.
HE WON'T LAST A DAY UP HERE ON DECK.
SKINNY AS A RAIL. GO DOWN TO THE GALLEY!
HUH... I LIKE YOUR NECKLACE.

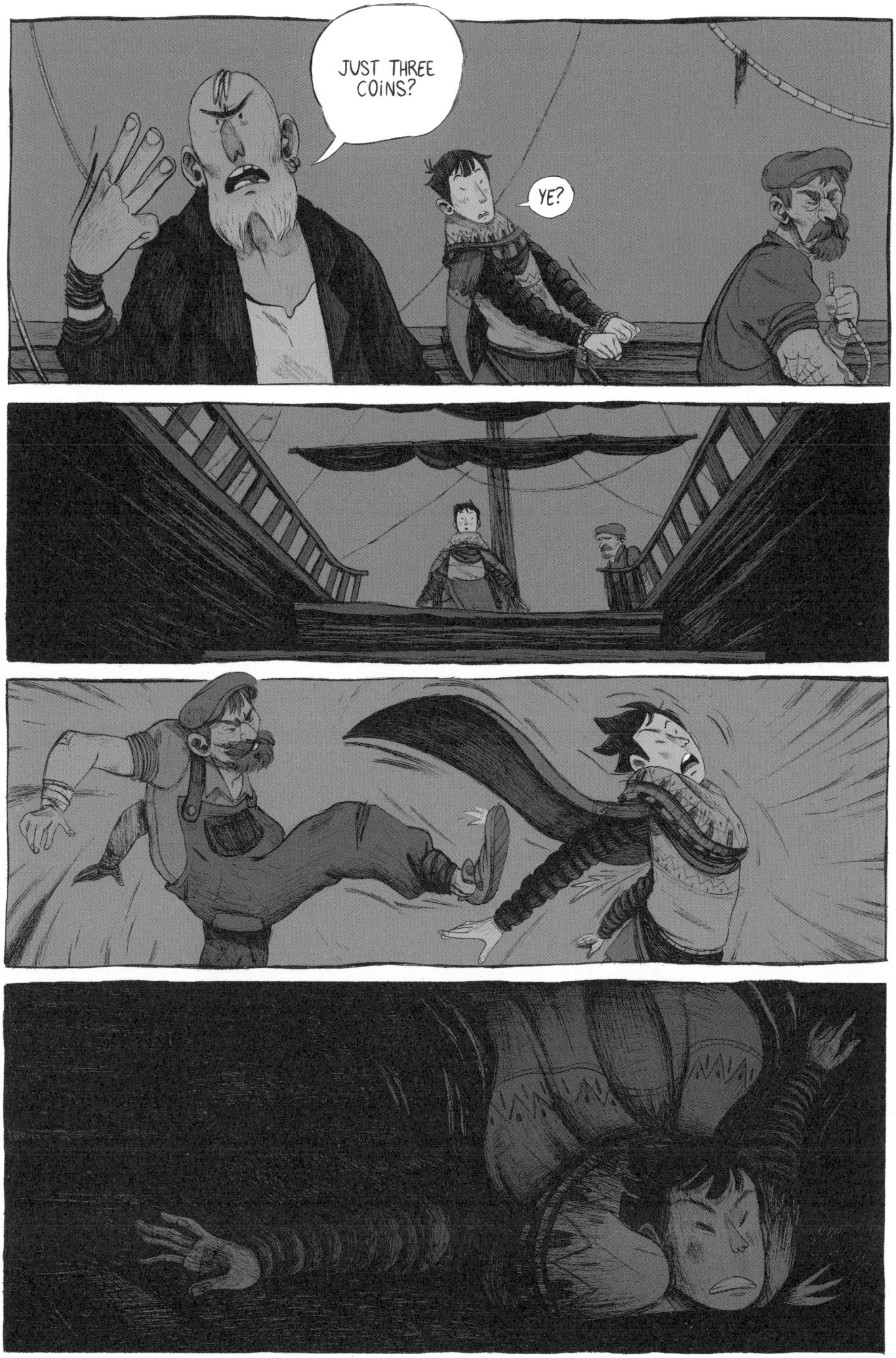
JUST THREE COINS?
YE?

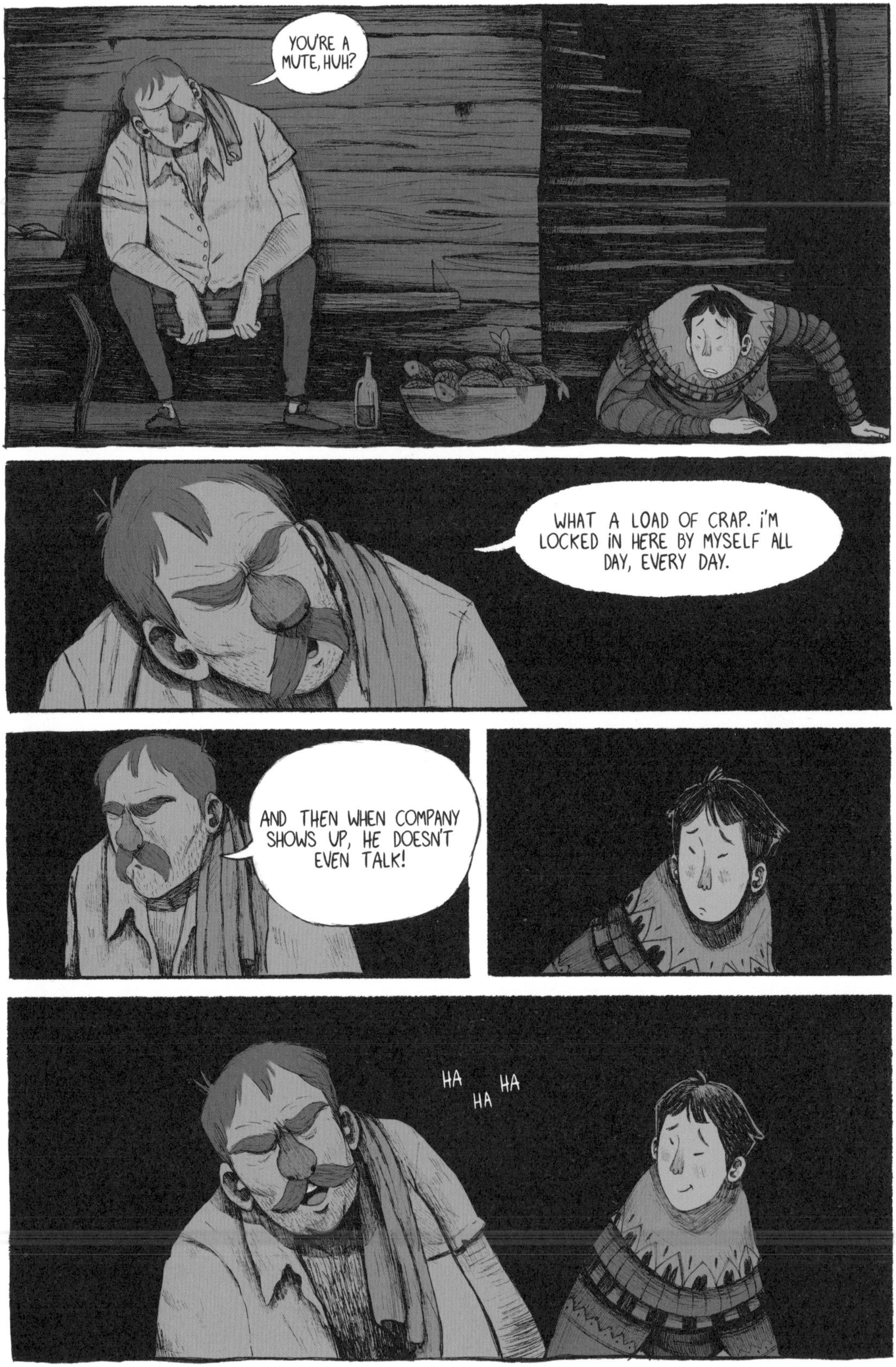
YOU'RE A MUTE, HUH?
WHAT A LOAD OF CRAP. I'M LOCKED IN HERE BY MYSELF ALL DAY, EVERY DAY.
AND THEN WHEN COMPANY SHOWS UP, HE DOESN'T EVEN TALK!
HA HA HA

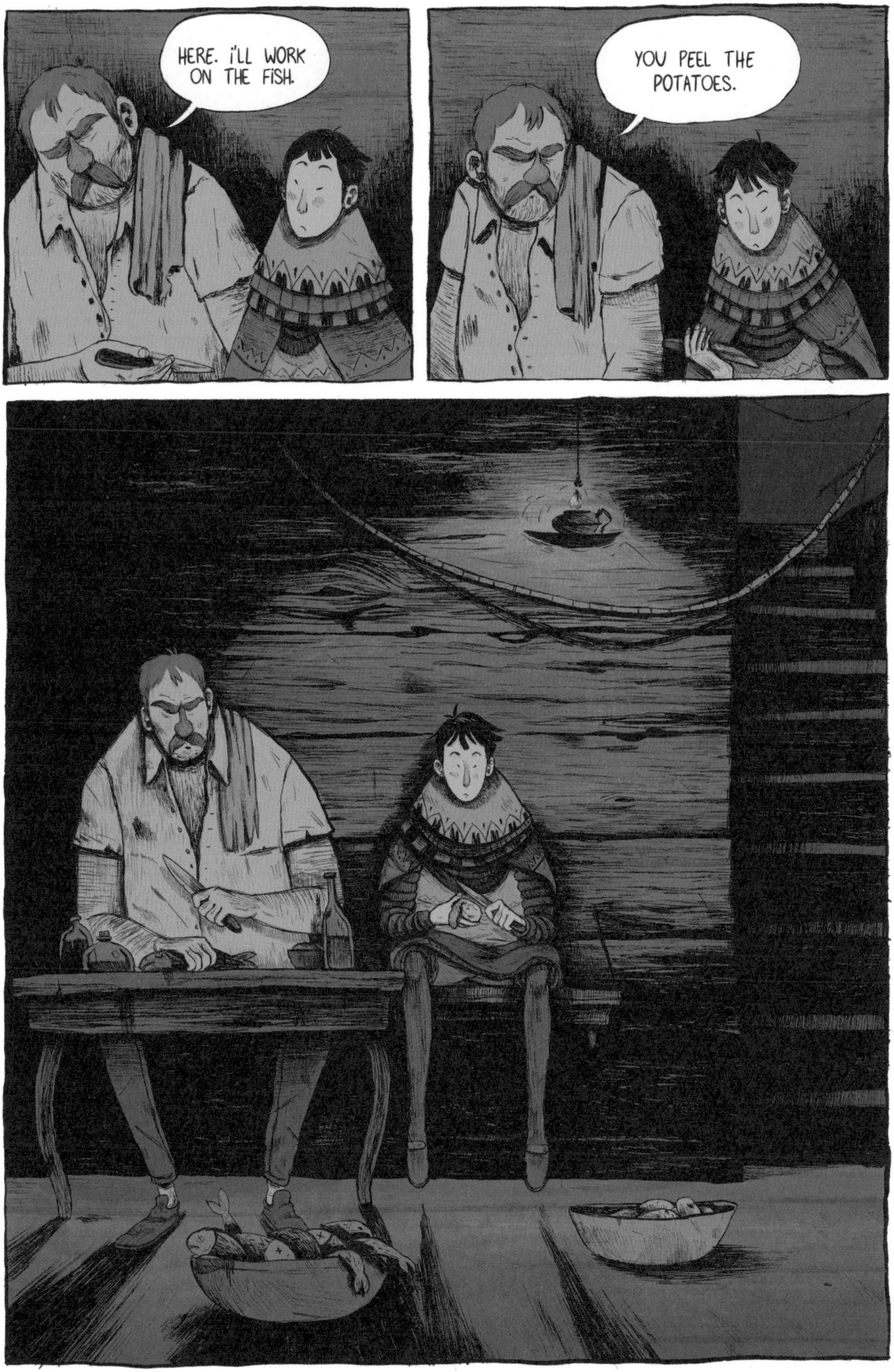
HERE. i'LL WORK ON THE FiSH.
YOU PEEL THE POTATOES.

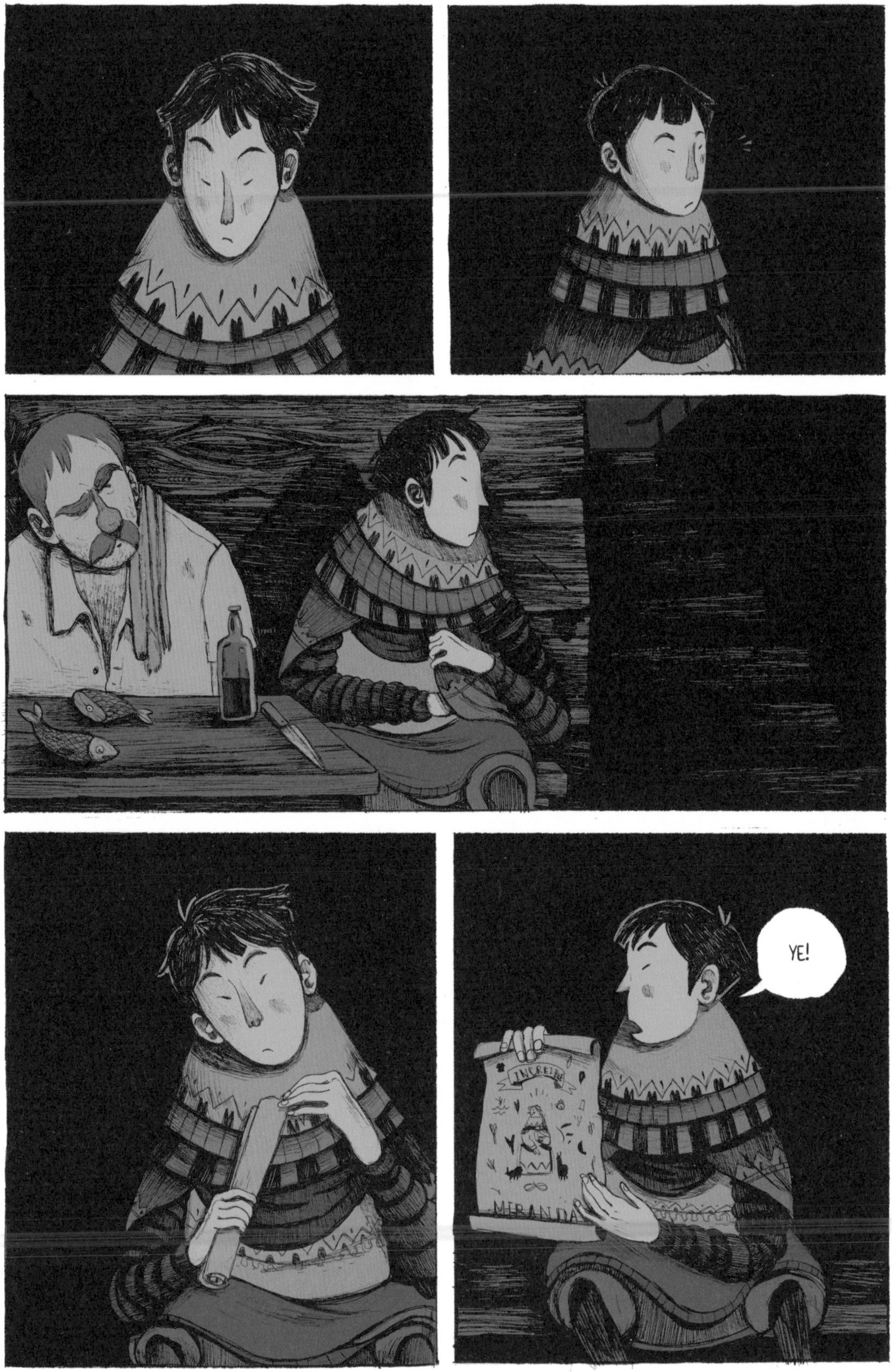
MIRANDA
YE!

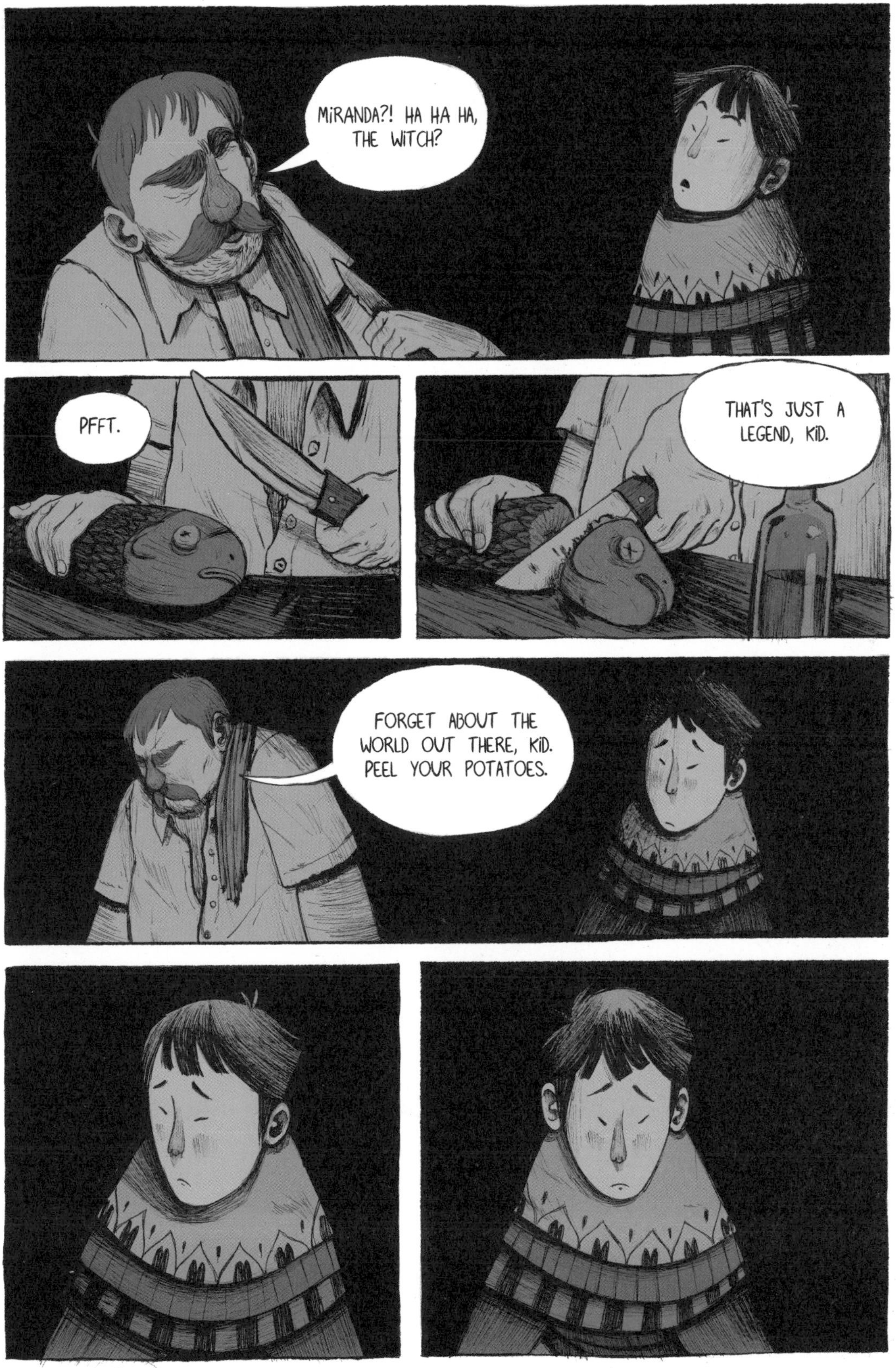
MIRANDA?! HA HA HA, THE WITCH?
PFFT.
THAT'S JUST A LEGEND, KID.
FORGET ABOUT THE WORLD OUT THERE, KID. PEEL YOUR POTATOES.

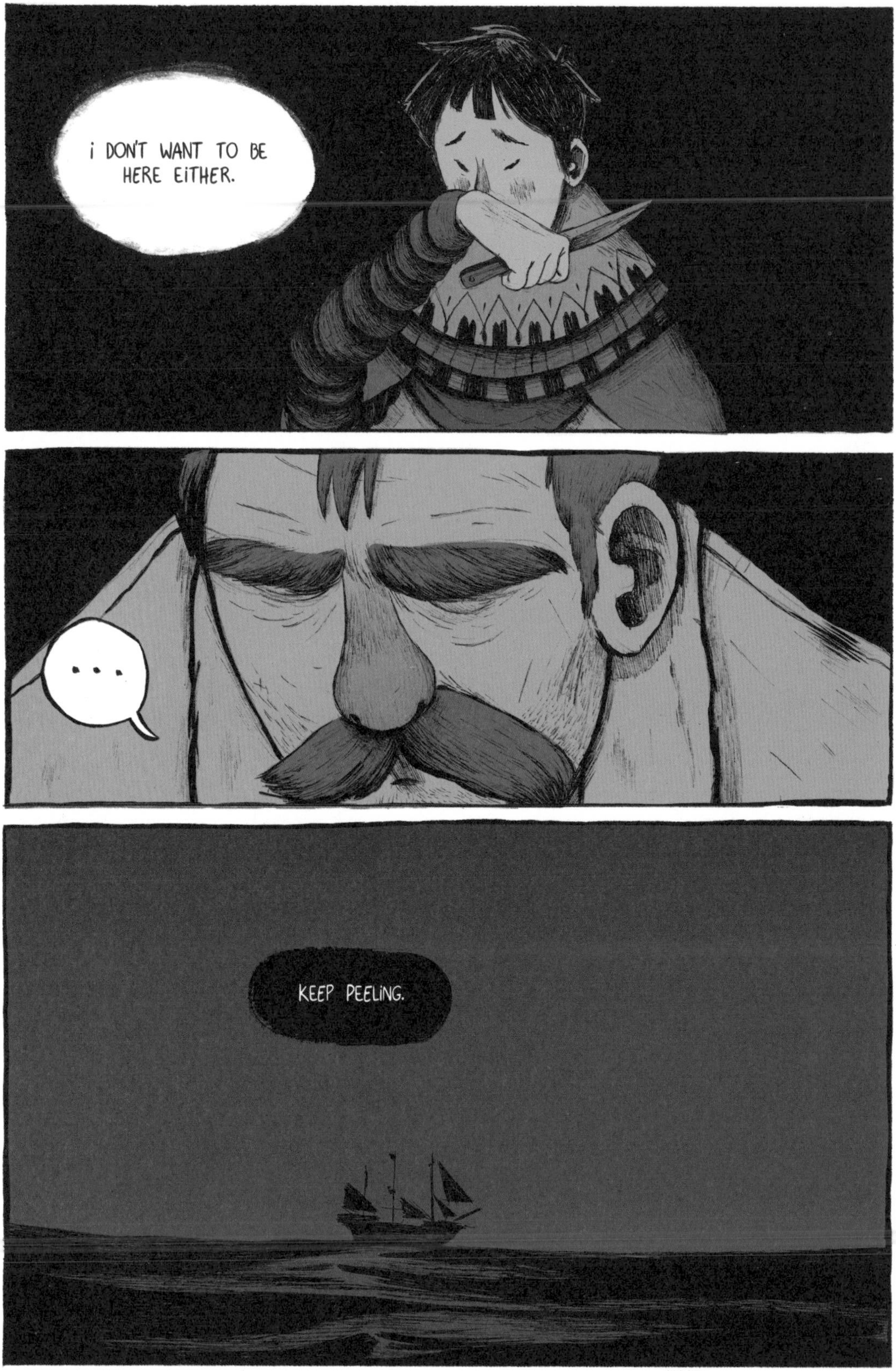
i DON'T WANT TO BE HERE EiTHER.
...
KEEP PEELiNG.

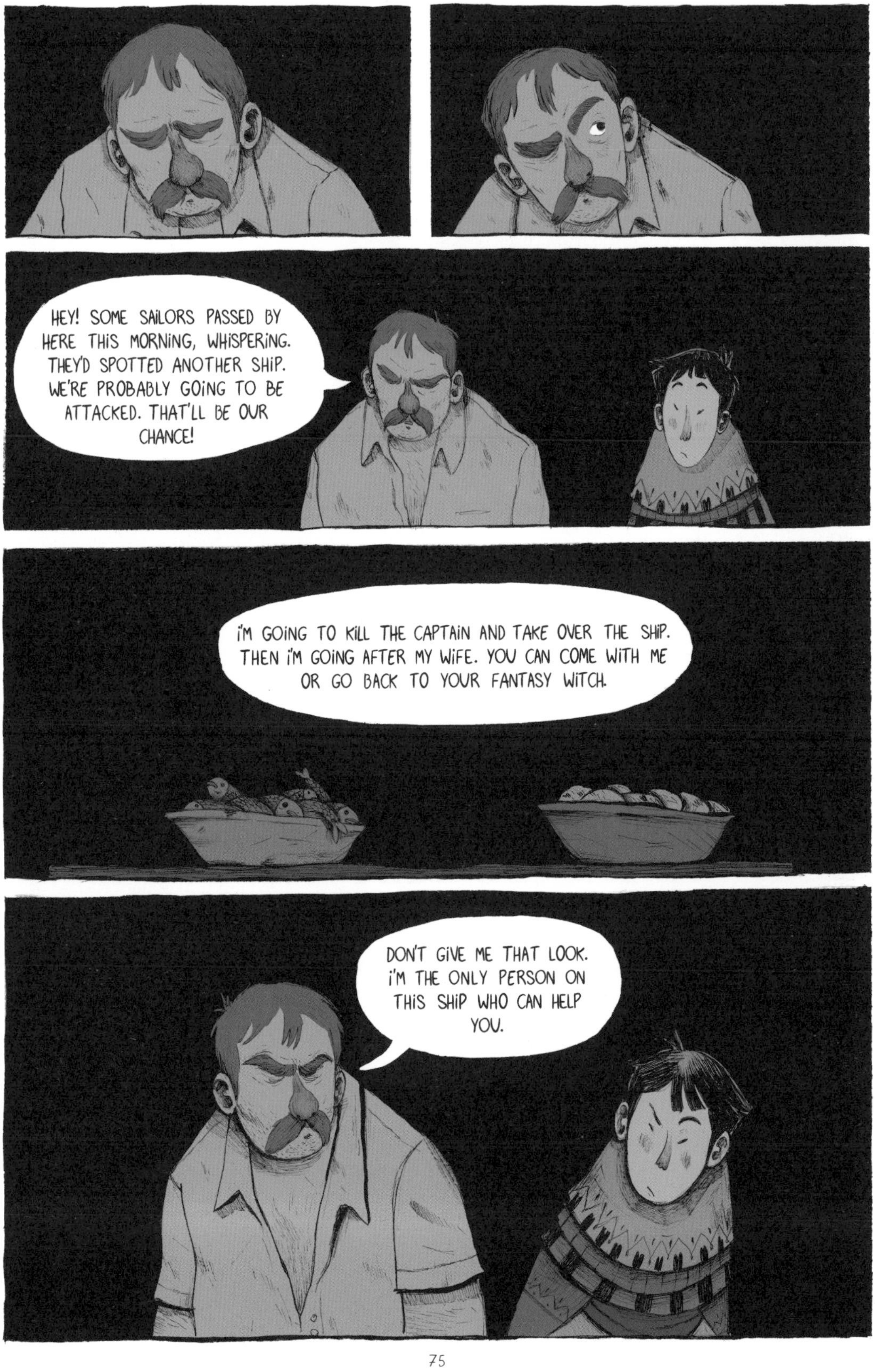
HEY! SOME SAILORS PASSED BY HERE THIS MORNING, WHISPERING. THEY'D SPOTTED ANOTHER SHIP. WE'RE PROBABLY GOING TO BE ATTACKED. THAT'LL BE OUR CHANCE!
I'M GOING TO KILL THE CAPTAIN AND TAKE OVER THE SHIP. THEN I'M GOING AFTER MY WIFE. YOU CAN COME WITH ME OR GO BACK TO YOUR FANTASY WITCH.
DON'T GIVE ME THAT LOOK. I'M THE ONLY PERSON ON THIS SHIP WHO CAN HELP YOU.

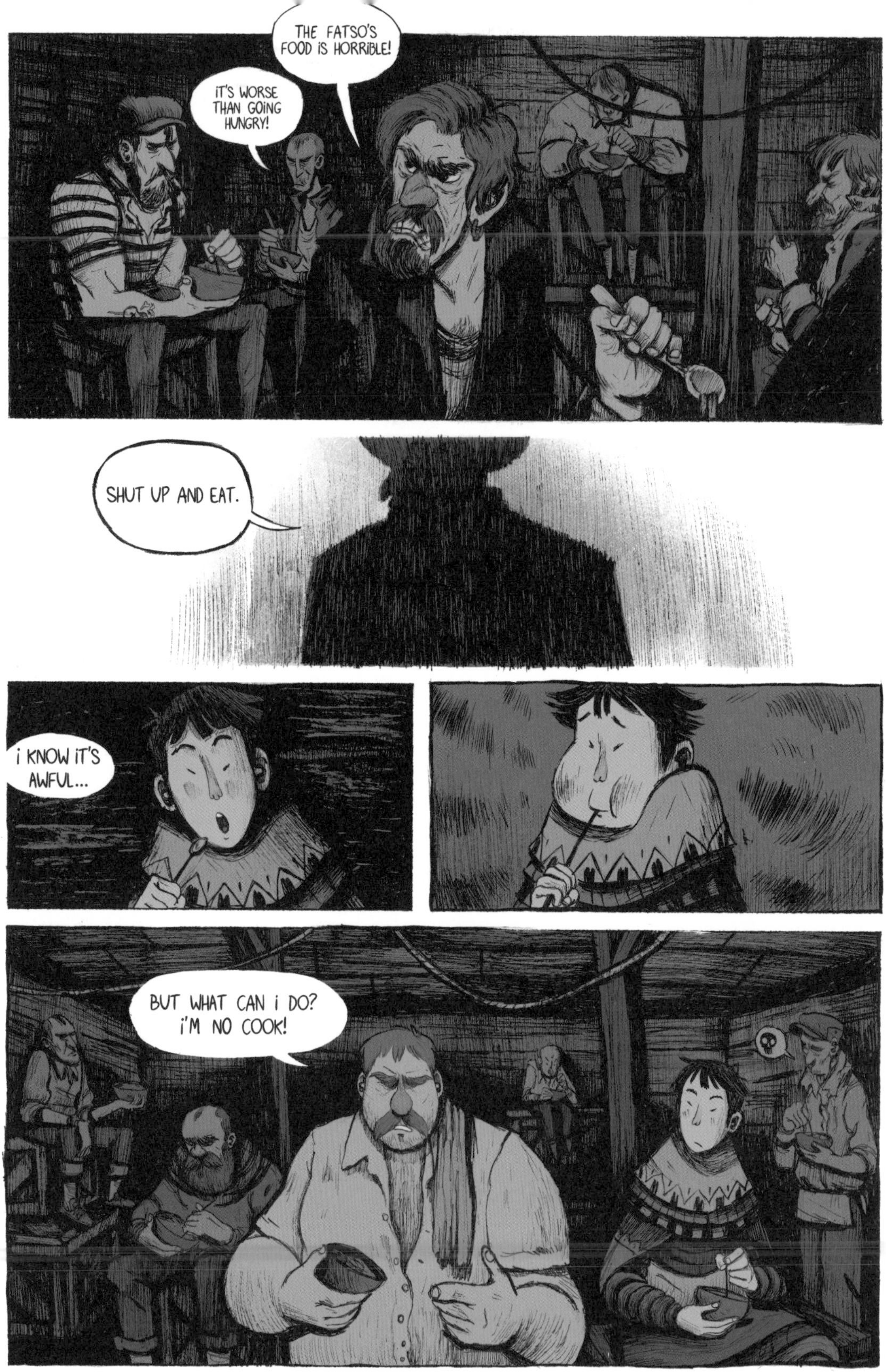
iT'S WORSE THAN GOiNG HUNGRY!
THE FATSO'S FOOD iS HORRiBLE!
SHUT UP AND EAT.
i KNOW iT'S AWFUL...
BUT WHAT CAN i DO? i'M NO COOK!

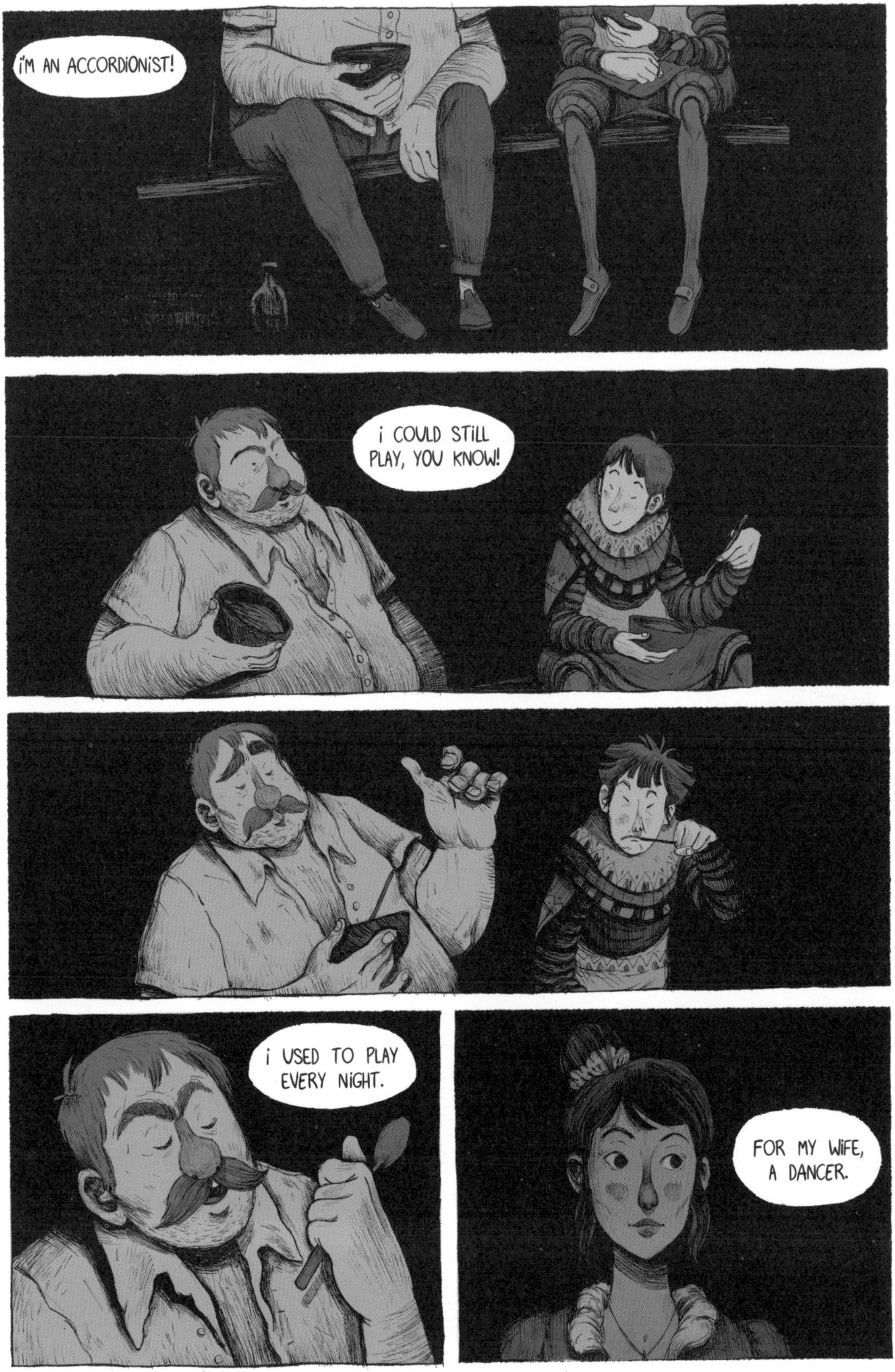
i'M AN ACCORDiONiST!
i COULD STiLL PLAY, YOU KNOW!
i USED TO PLAY EVERY NiGHT.
FOR MY WiFE, A DANCER.

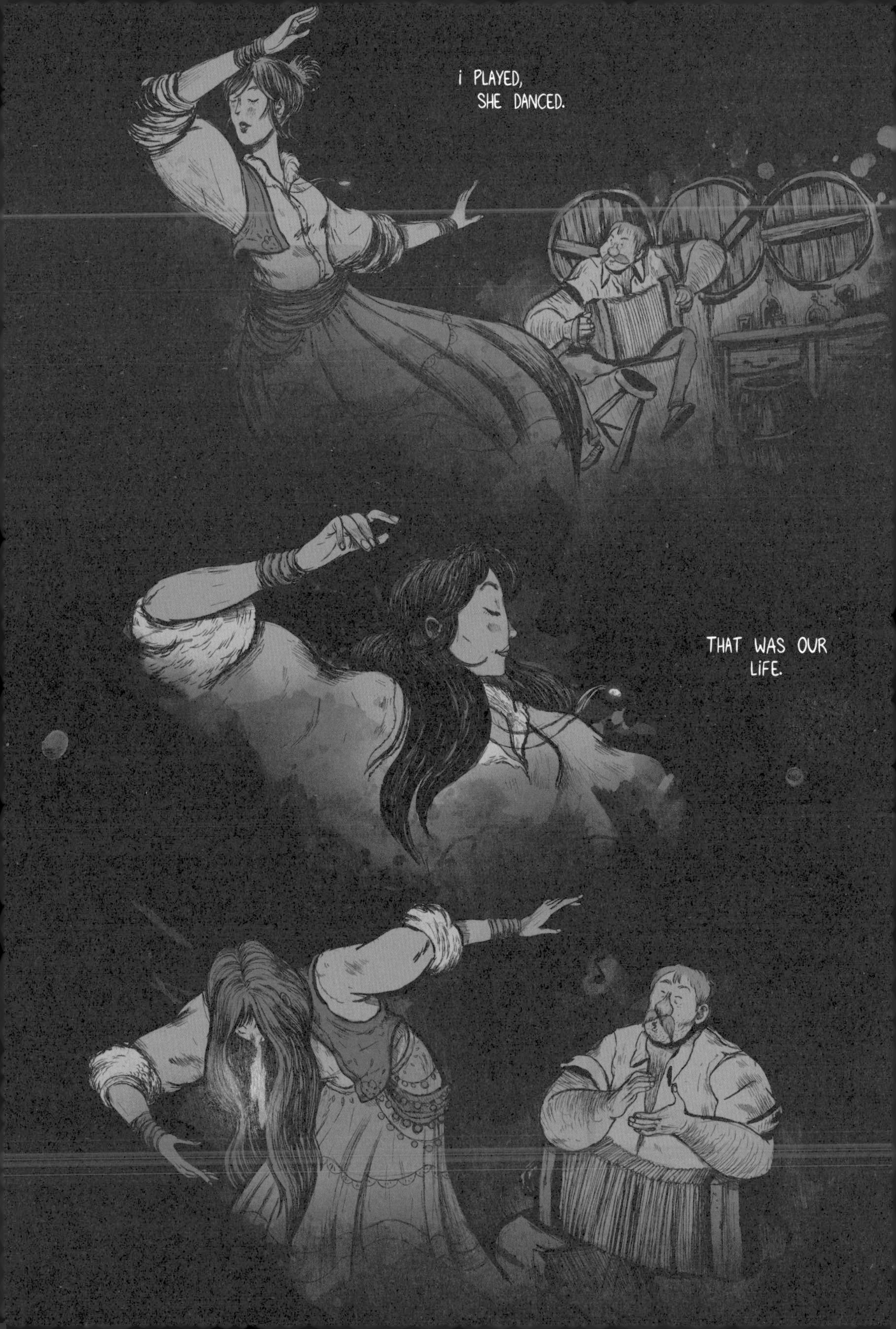
I PLAYED,
SHE DANCED.
THAT WAS OUR
LIFE.

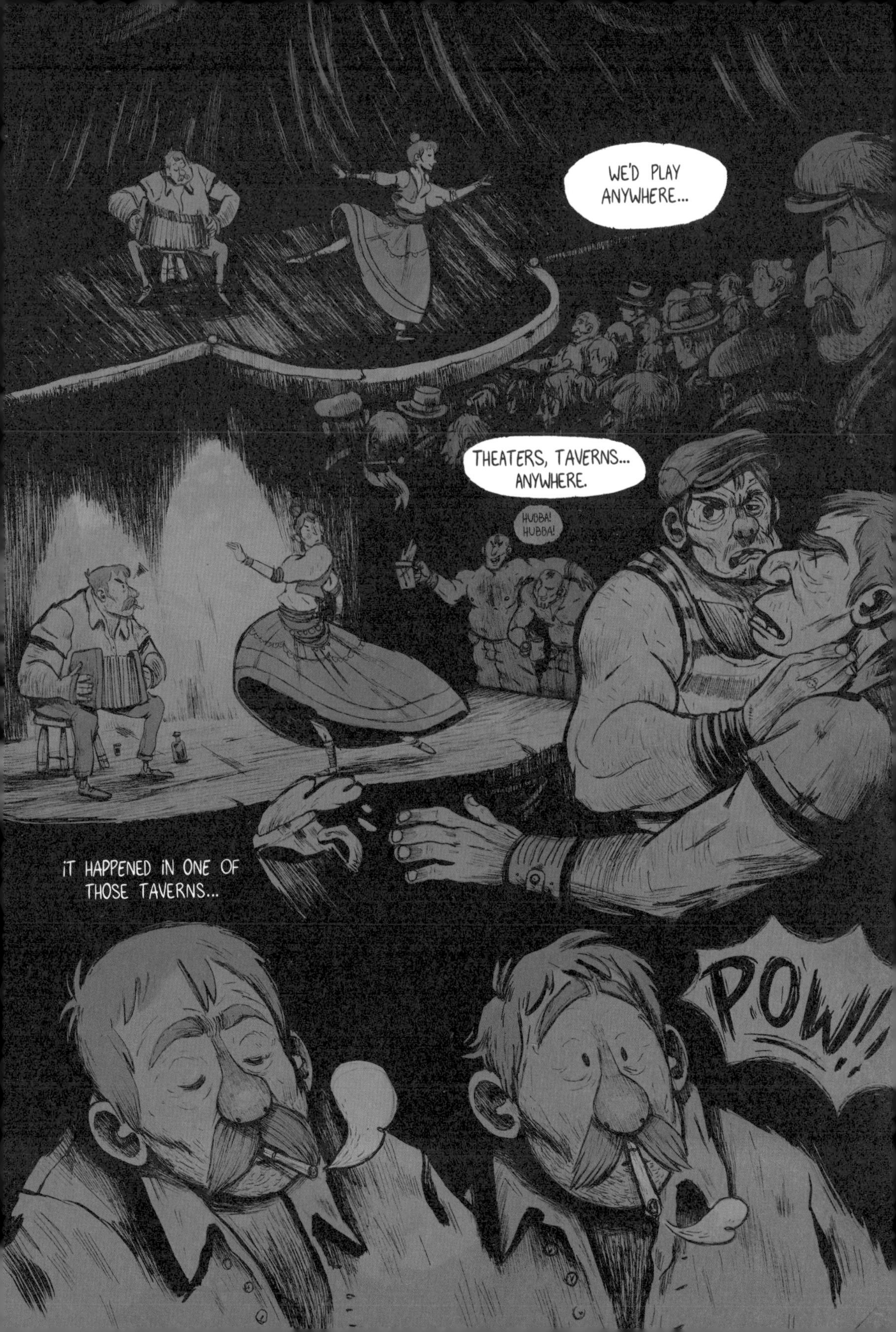
WE'D PLAY ANYWHERE...
THEATERS, TAVERNS... ANYWHERE.
HUBBA! HUBBA!
iT HAPPENED iN ONE OF THOSE TAVERNS...
POW!!

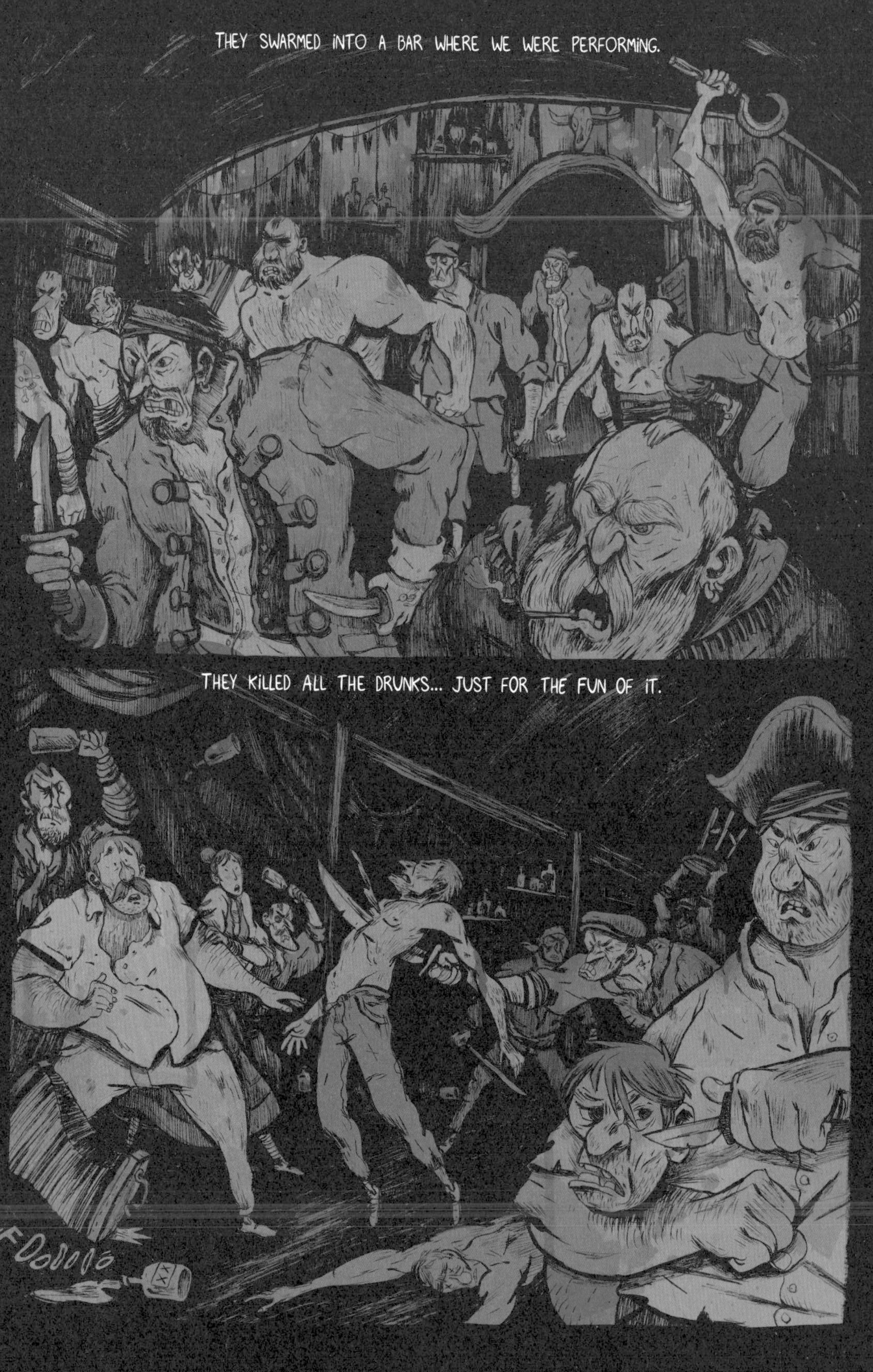
THEY SWARMED INTO A BAR WHERE WE WERE PERFORMING.
THEY KILLED ALL THE DRUNKS... JUST FOR THE FUN OF IT.

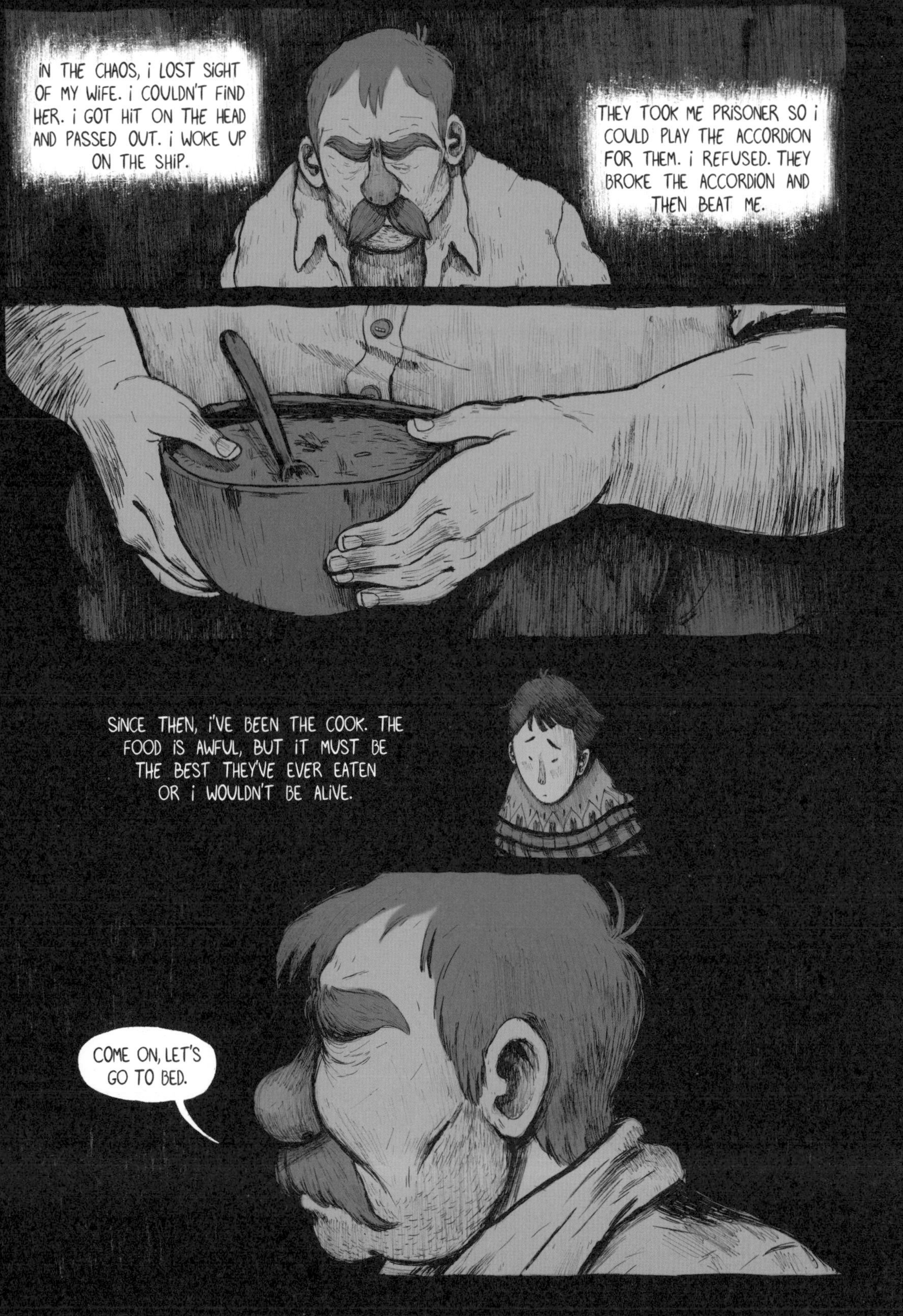
IN THE CHAOS, I LOST SIGHT OF MY WIFE. I COULDN'T FIND HER. I GOT HIT ON THE HEAD AND PASSED OUT. I WOKE UP ON THE SHIP.
THEY TOOK ME PRISONER SO I COULD PLAY THE ACCORDION FOR THEM. I REFUSED. THEY BROKE THE ACCORDION AND THEN BEAT ME.
SINCE THEN, I'VE BEEN THE COOK. THE FOOD IS AWFUL, BUT IT MUST BE THE BEST THEY'VE EVER EATEN OR I WOULDN'T BE ALIVE.
COME ON, LET'S GO TO BED.

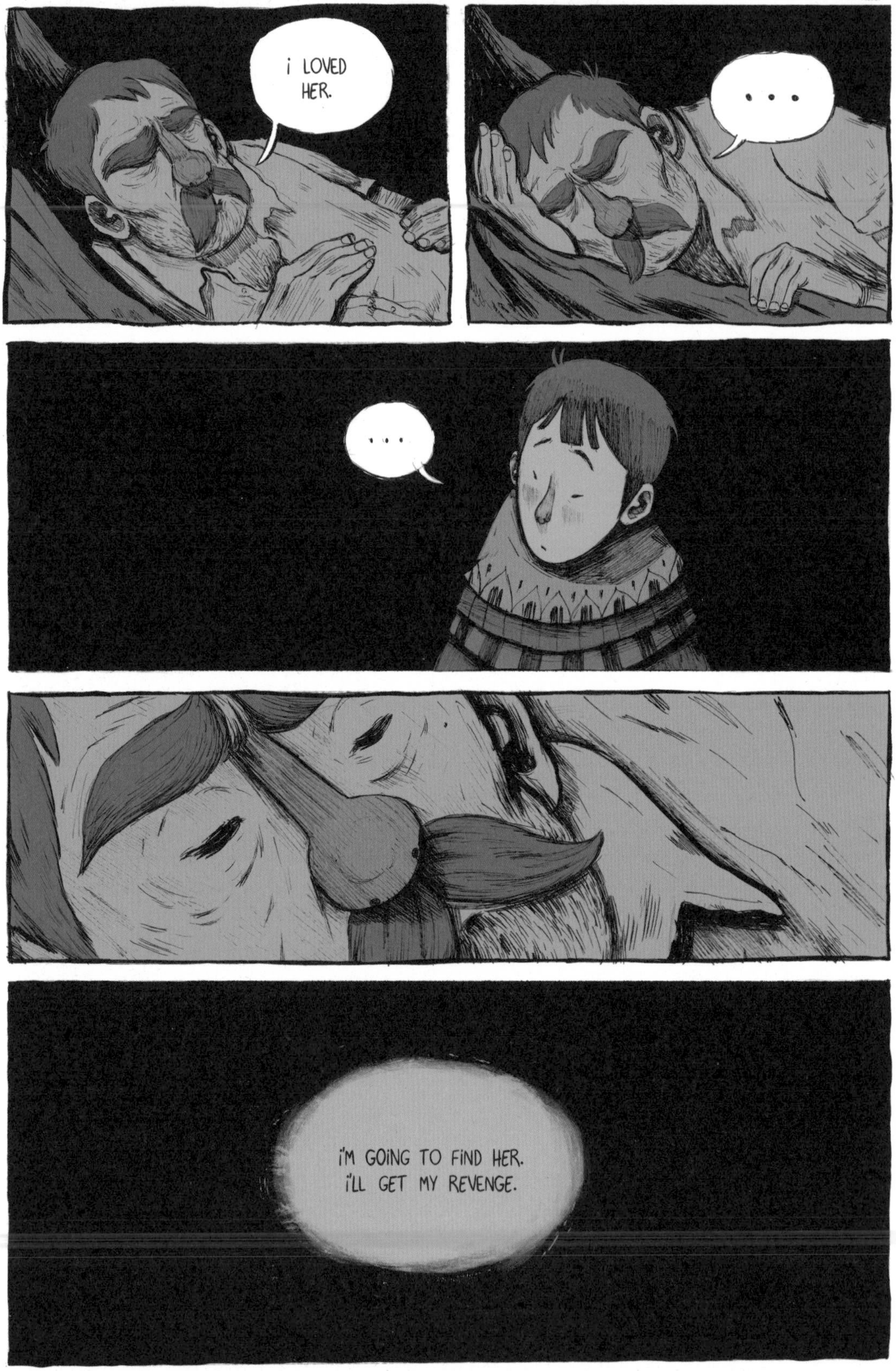
i LOVED HER.
...
...
i'M GOING TO FiND HER. i'LL GET MY REVENGE.

BOOOM

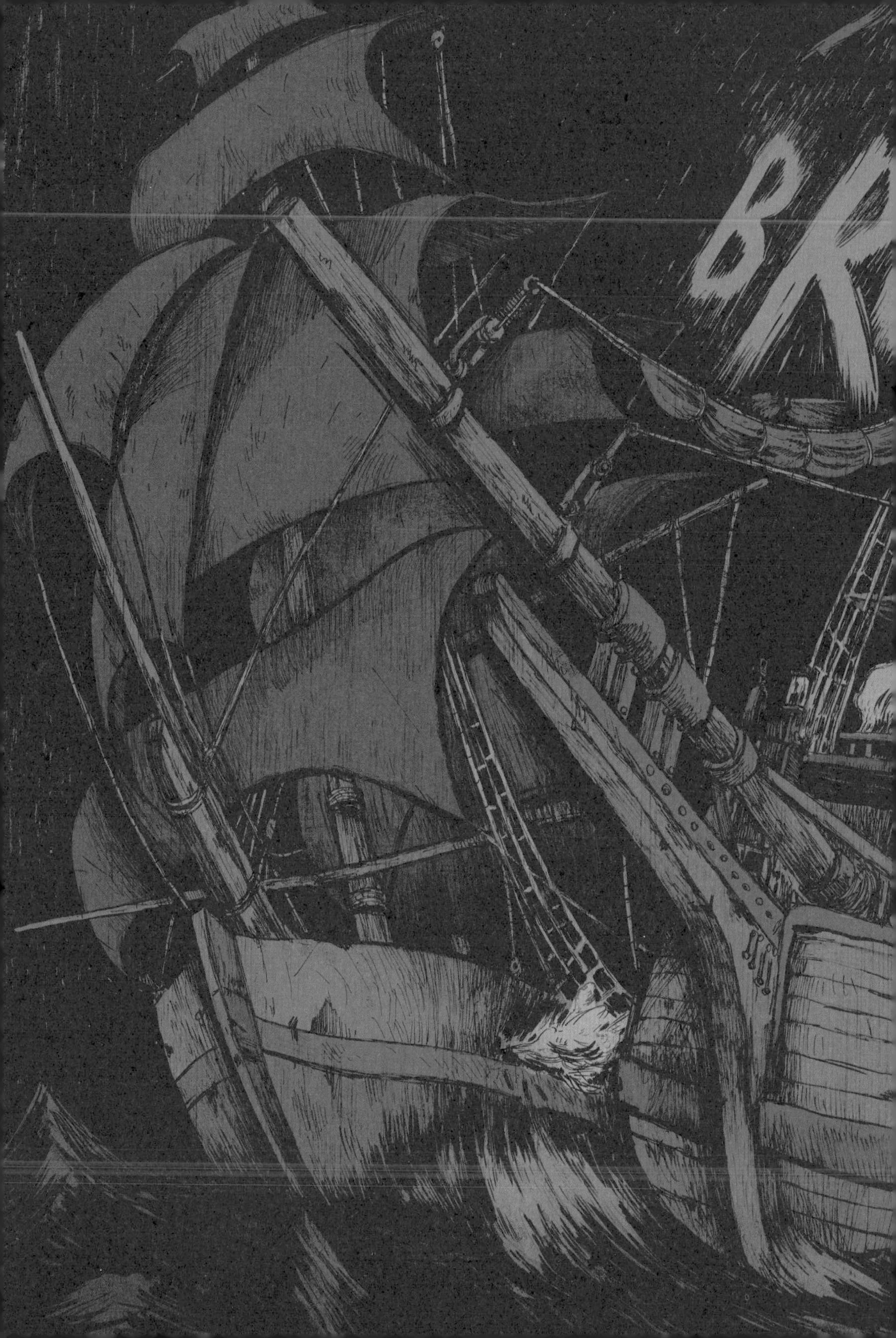
BR

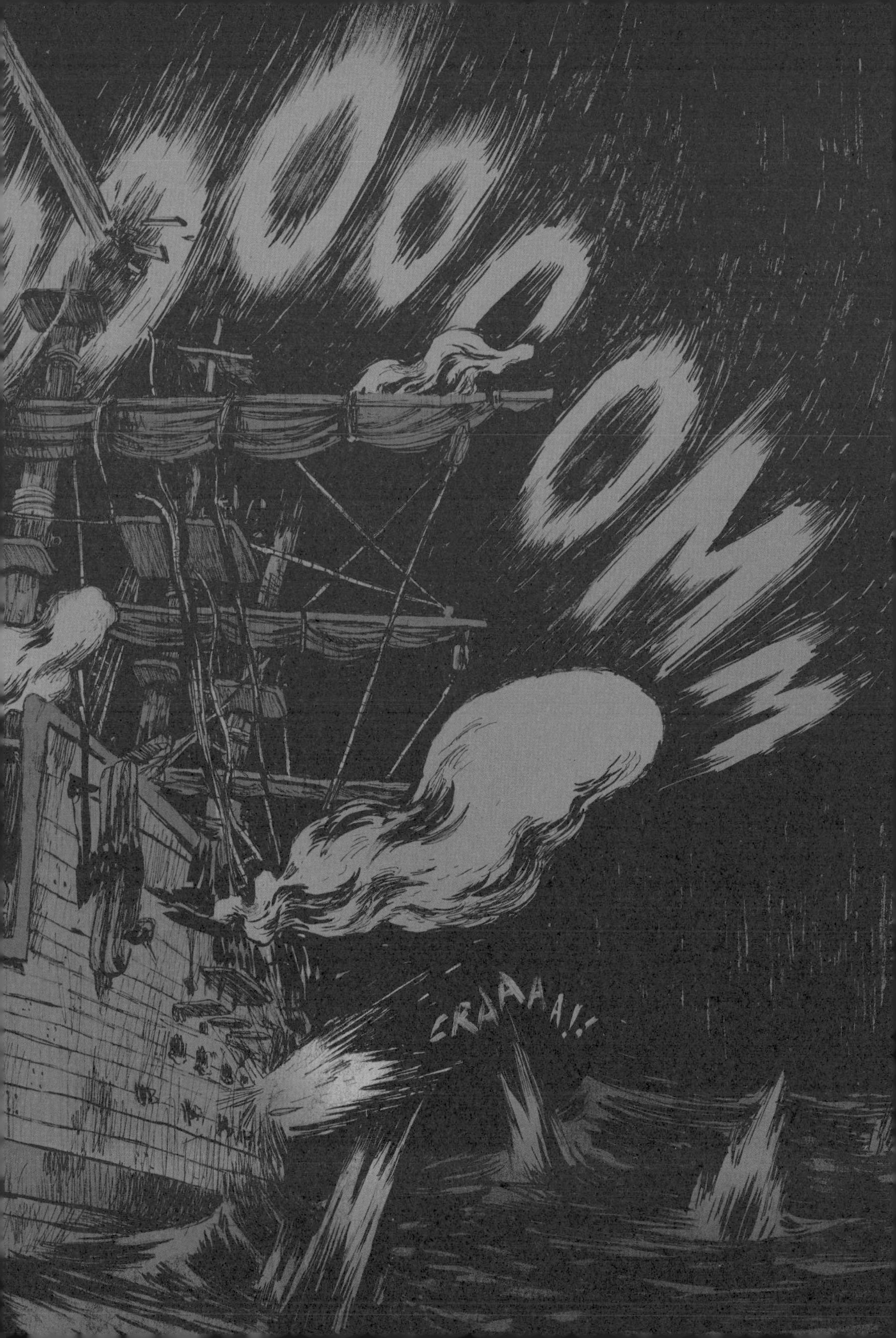
OOOOOM
CRAAAA!!

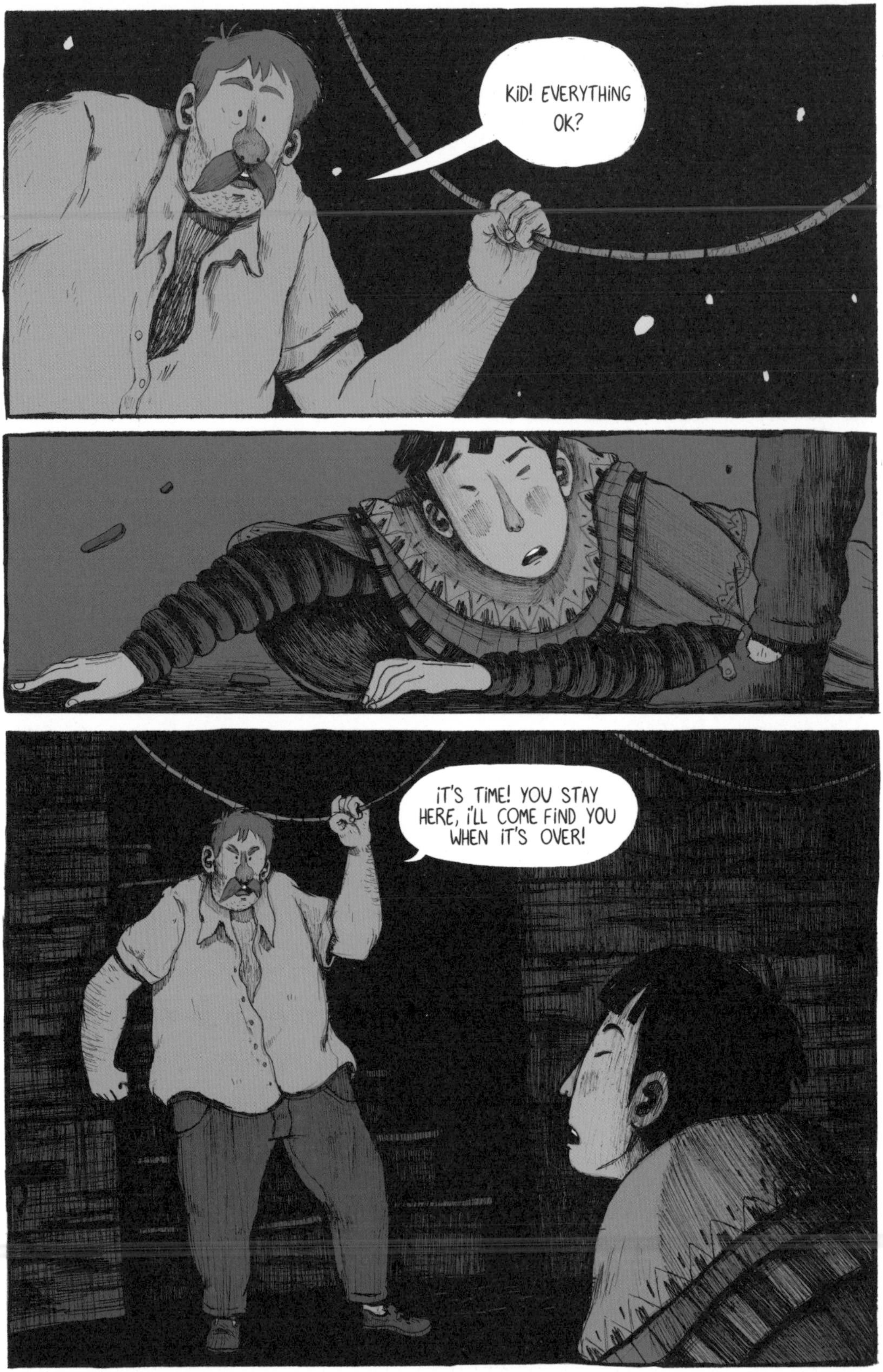
KiD! EVERYTHiNG OK?
iT'S TiME! YOU STAY HERE, i'LL COME FiND YOU WHEN iT'S OVER!

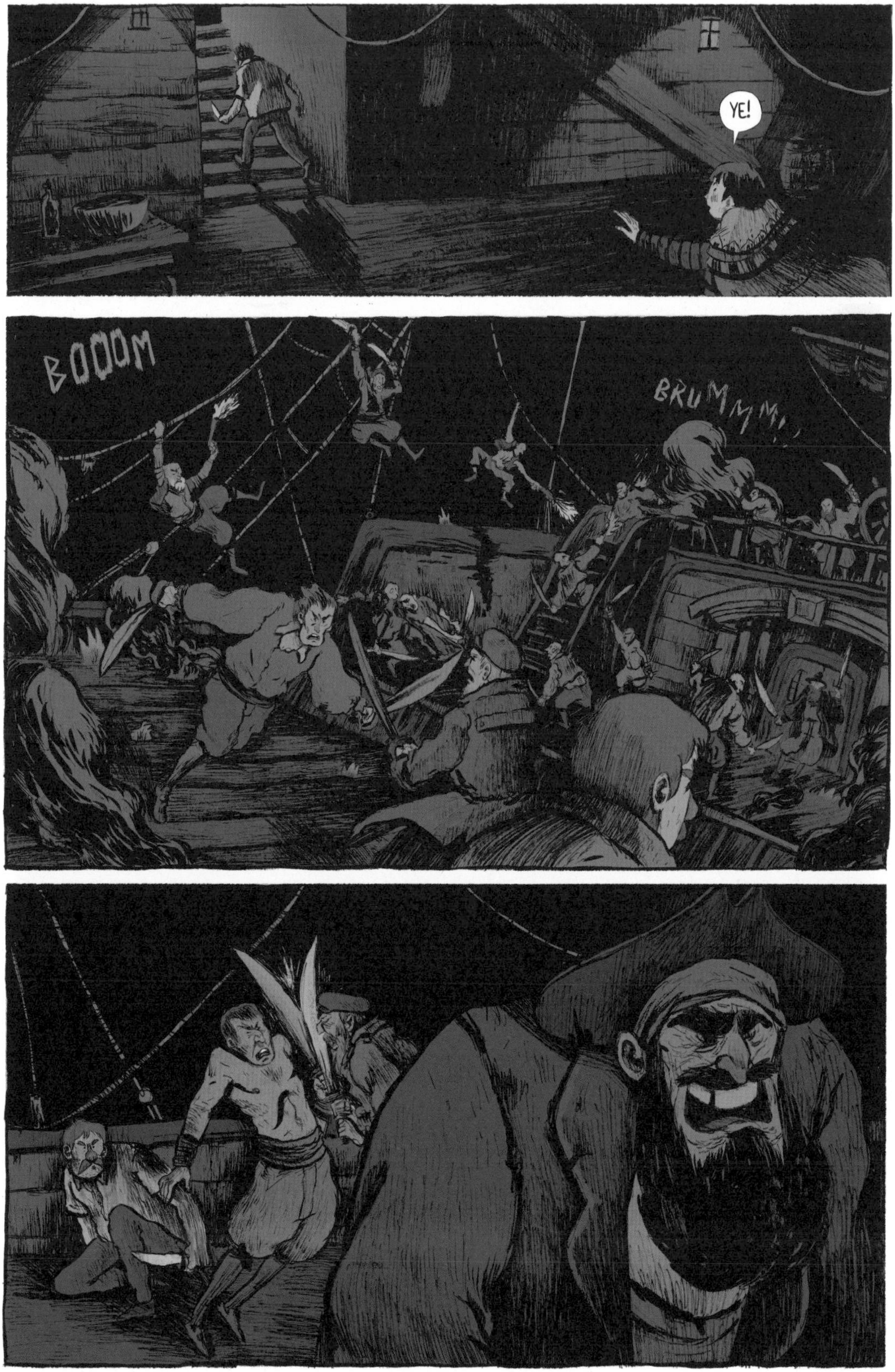
YE!
BOOOM
BRUMMM

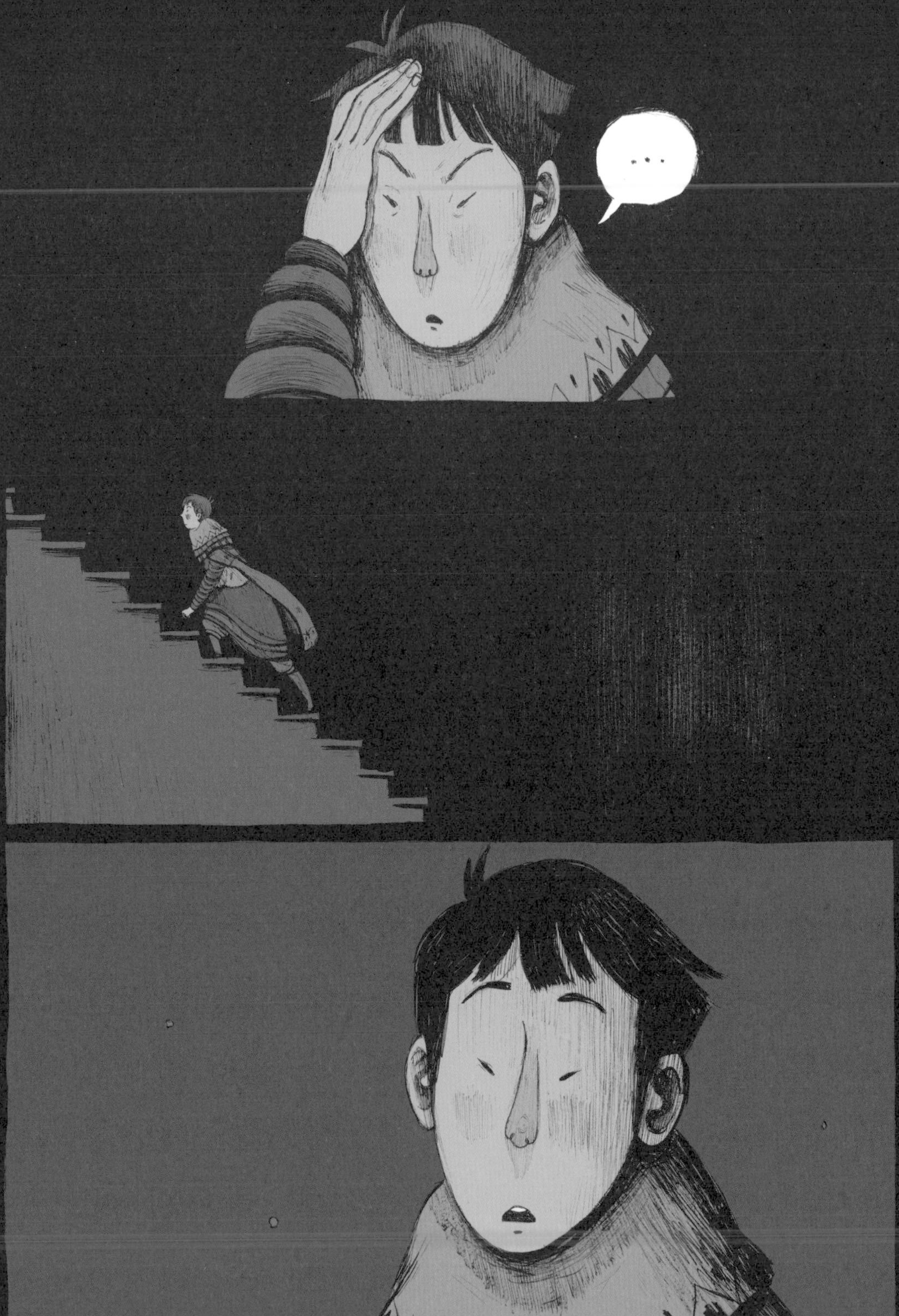
...

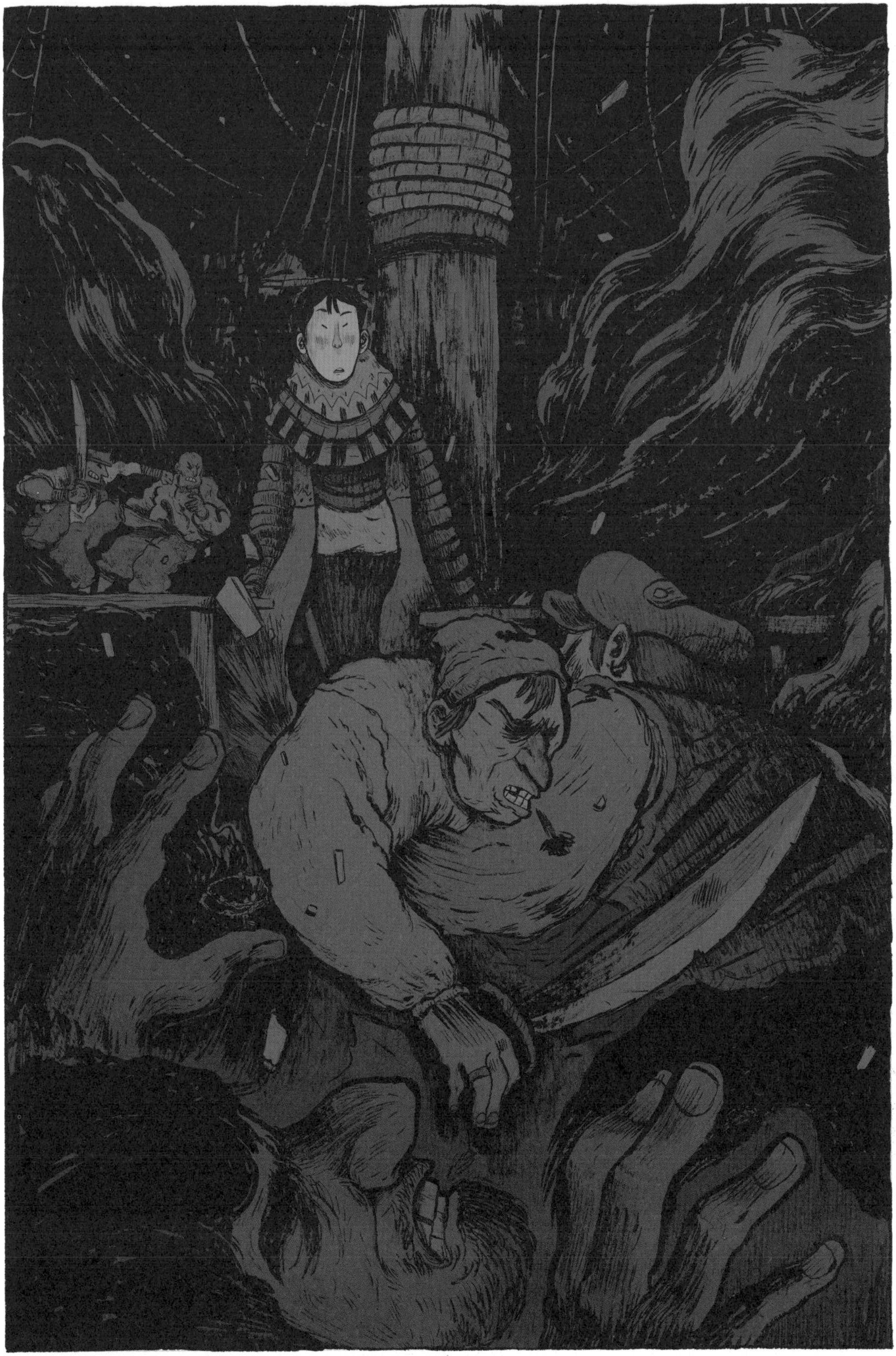

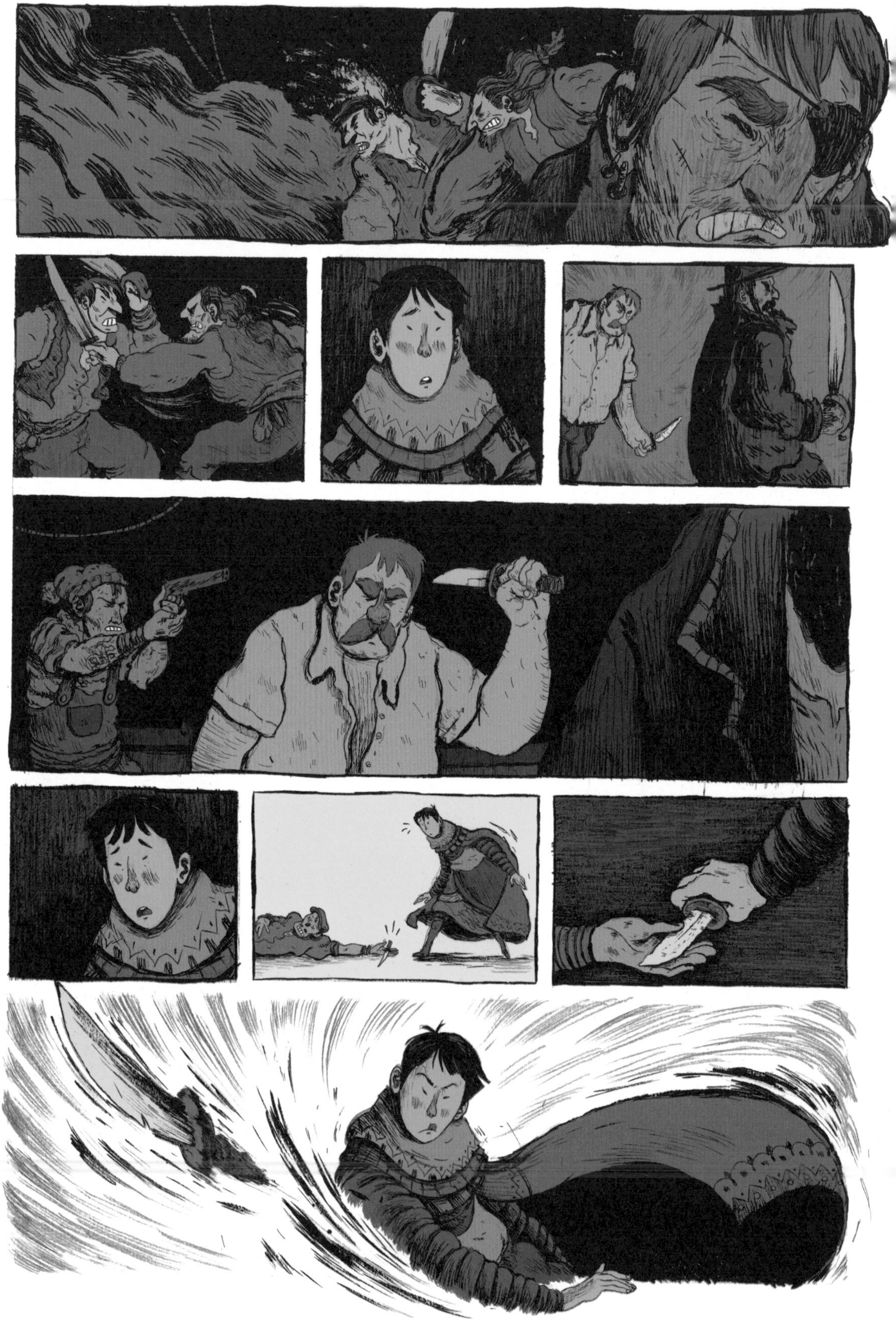

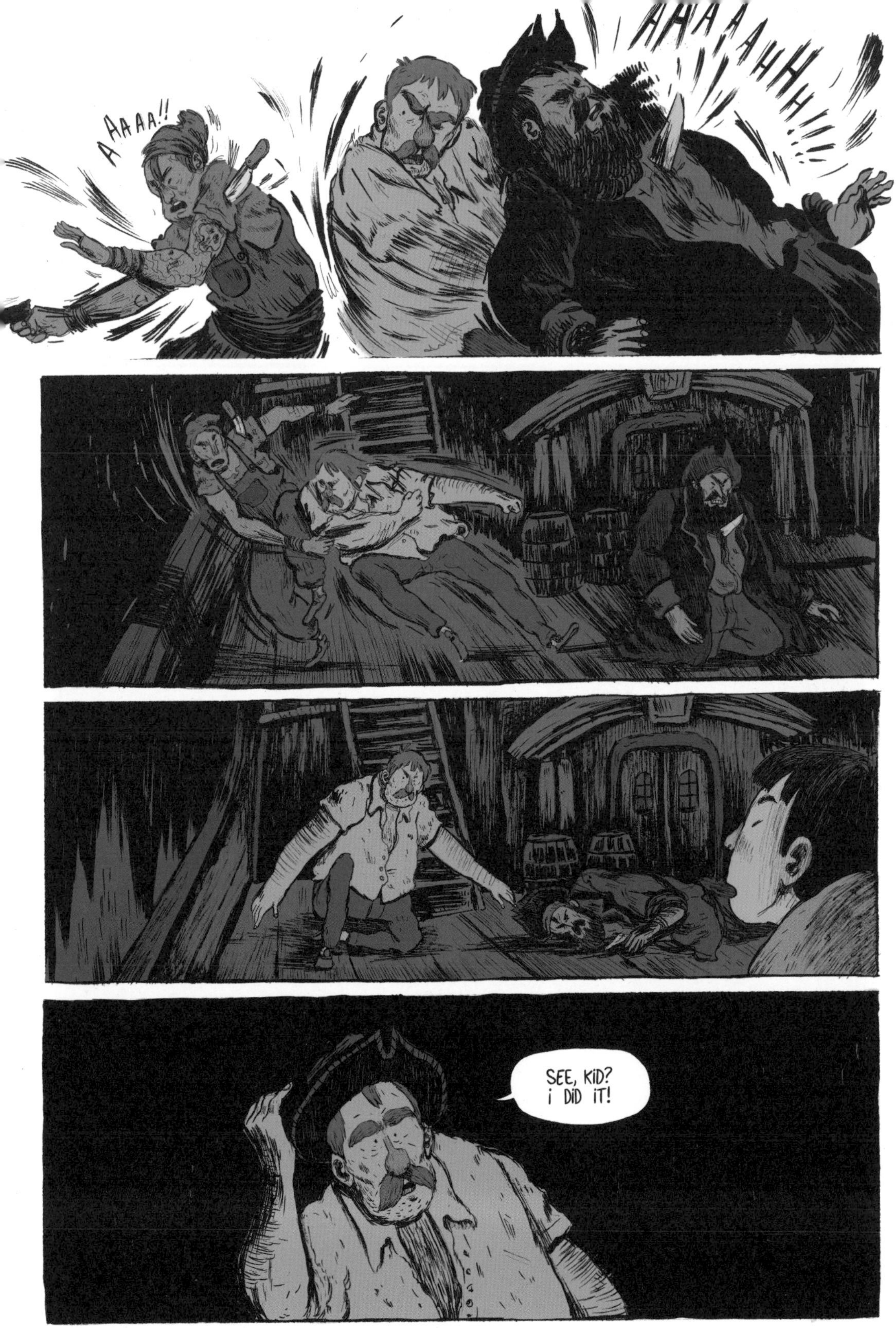
AAAAA!!
AAAAAAAHHH!!
SEE, KID?
¡ DID IT!

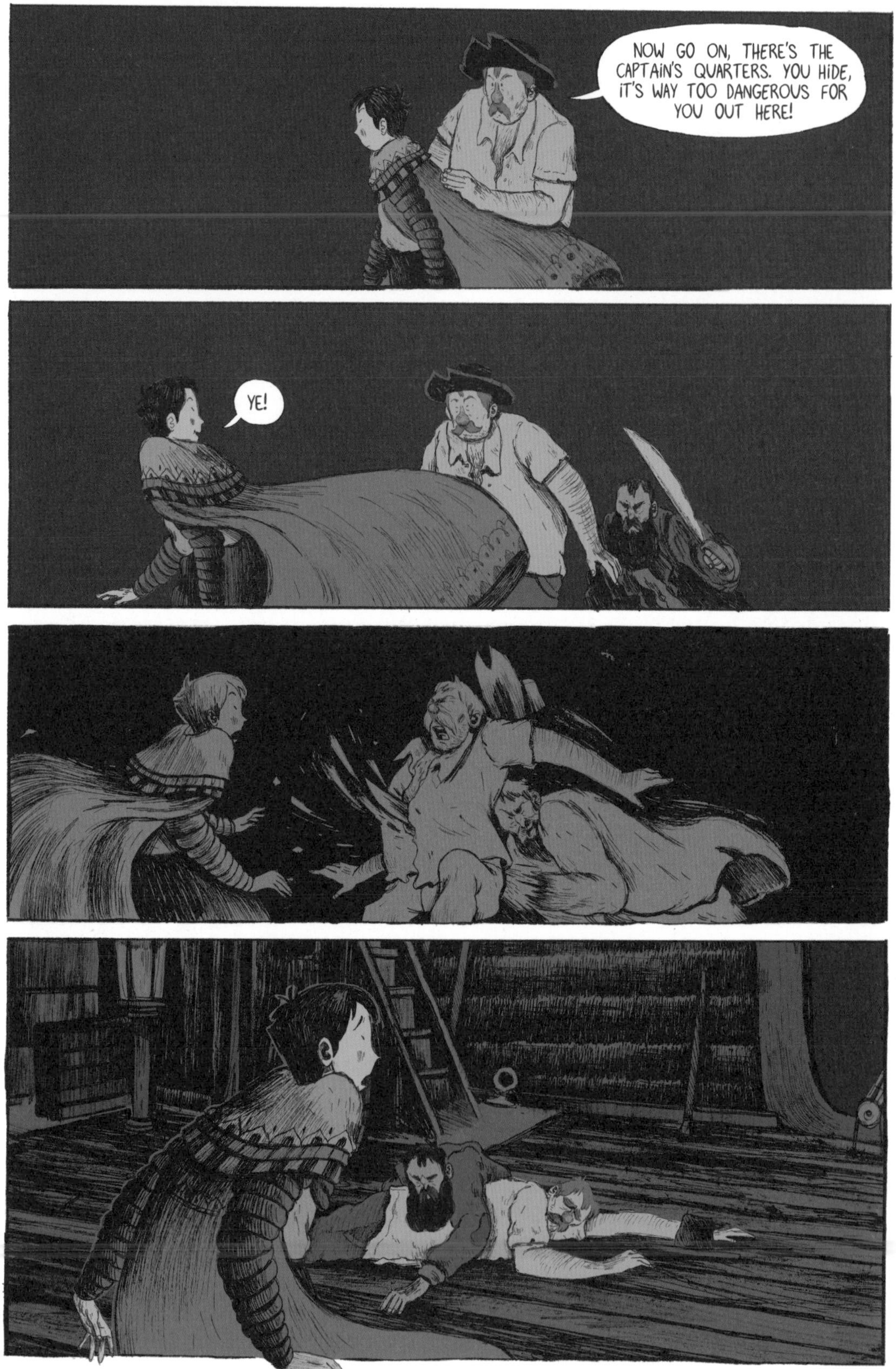
NOW GO ON, THERE'S THE CAPTAIN'S QUARTERS. YOU HIDE, IT'S WAY TOO DANGEROUS FOR YOU OUT HERE!
YE!

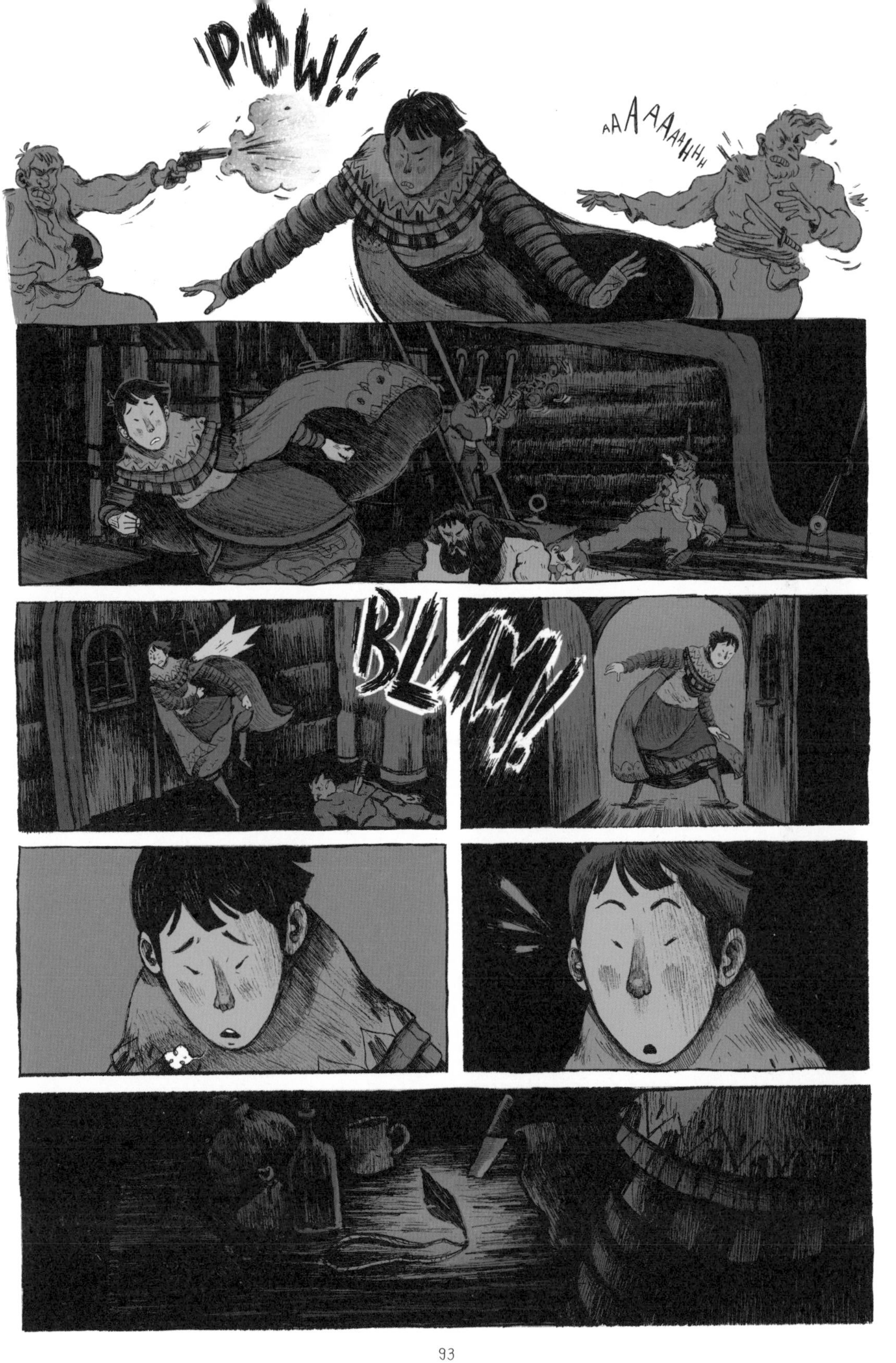
POW!!
AAAAAAAHHH
BLAM!

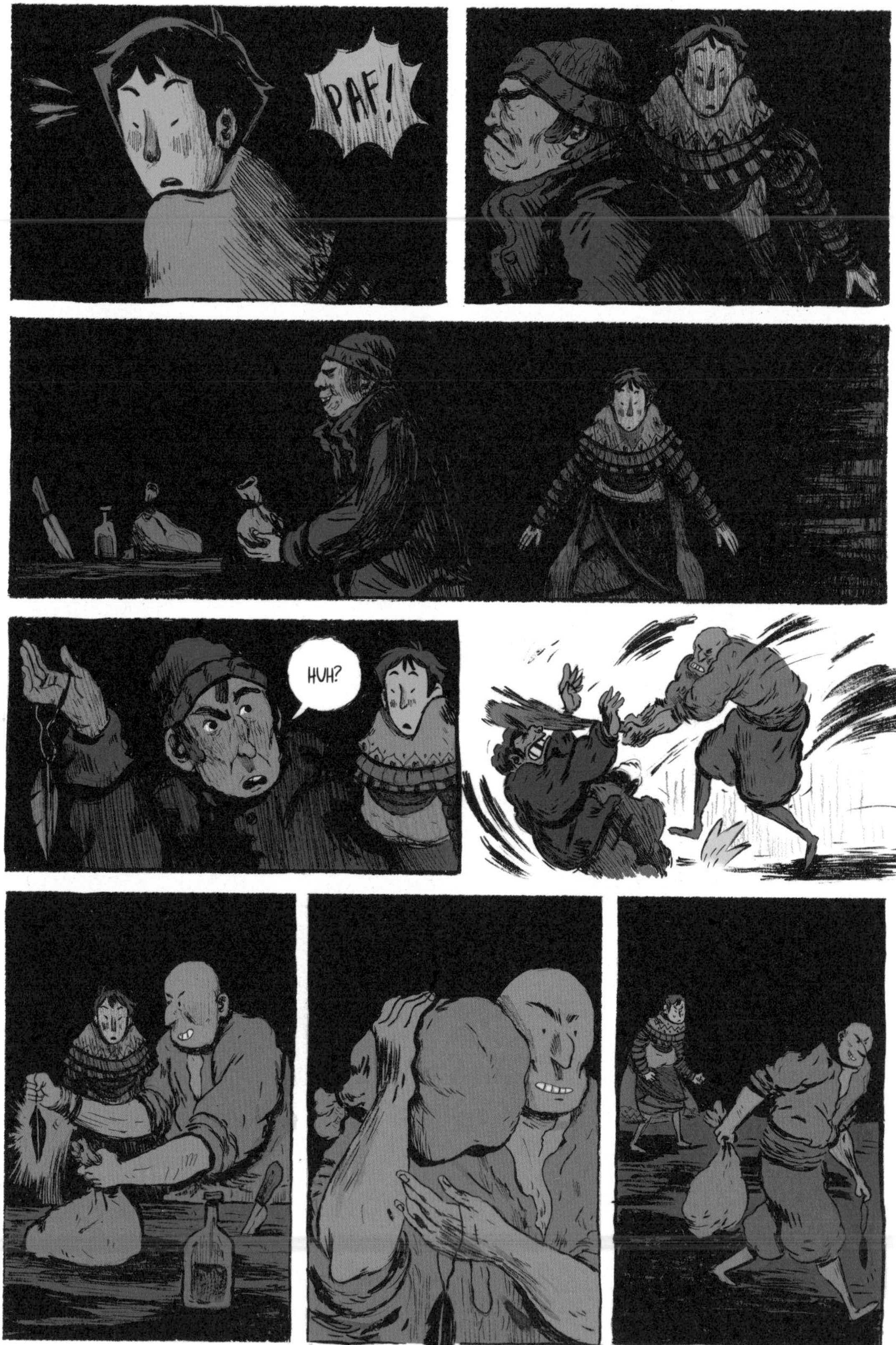
PAF!
HUH?

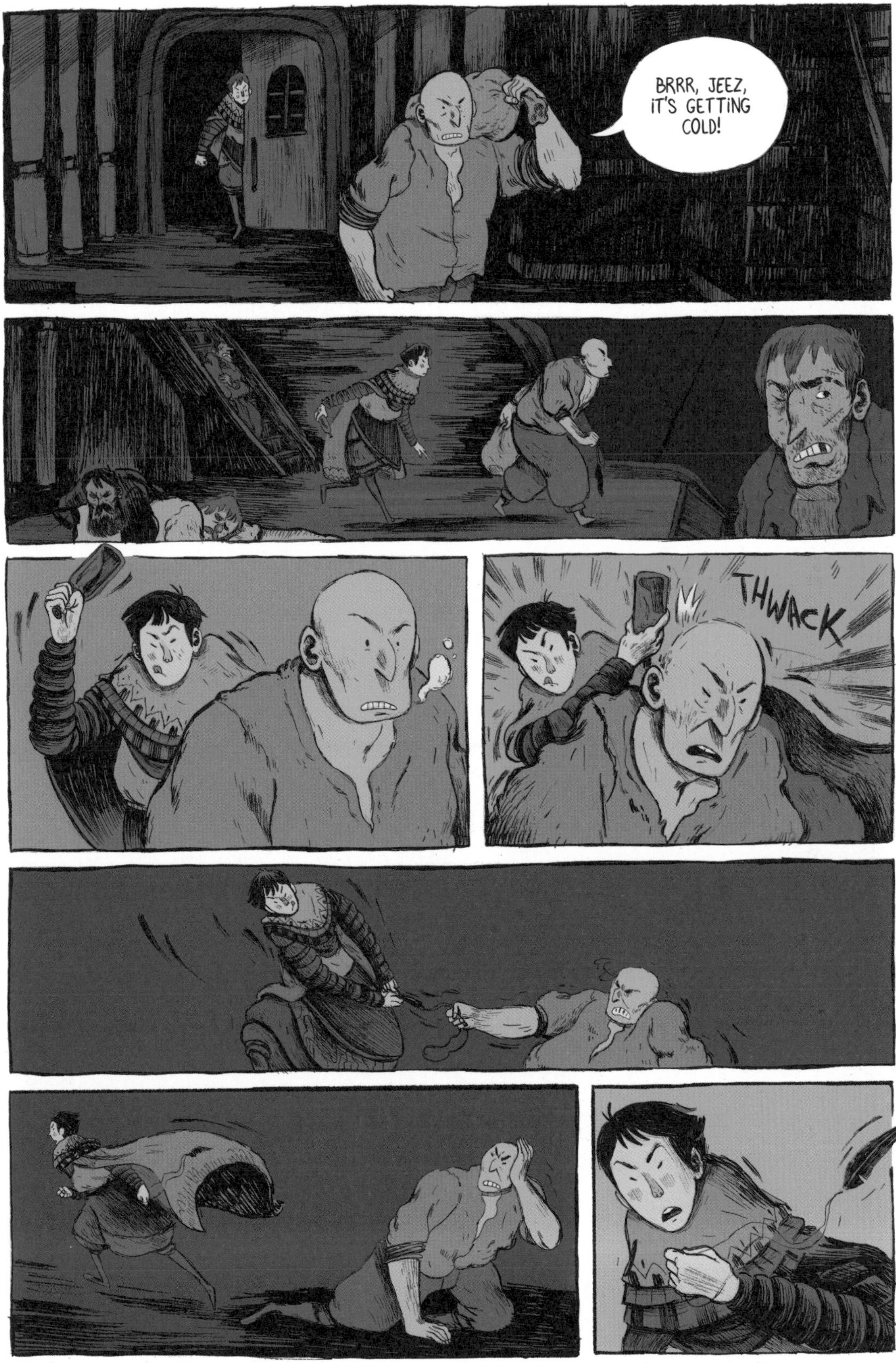
BRRR, JEEZ, iT'S GETTiNG COLD!
THWACK

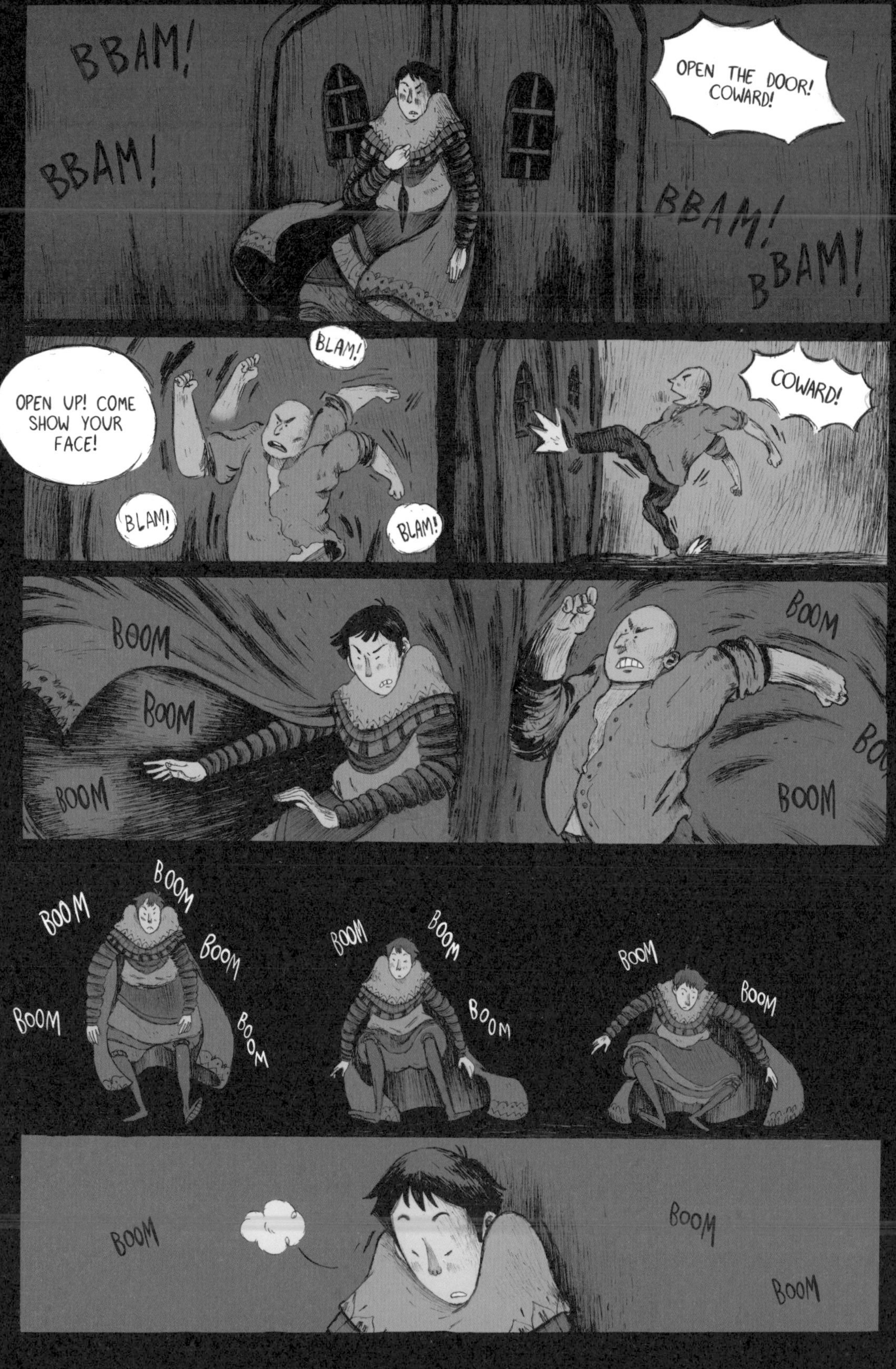
BBAM!
BBAM!
OPEN THE DOOR! COWARD!
BBAM!
BBAM!
OPEN UP! COME SHOW YOUR FACE!
BLAM!
BLAM!
BLAM!
COWARD!
BOOM
BOOM
BOOM
BOOM
BOOM
BOOM
BOOM
BOOM
BOOM
BOOM
BOOM
BOOM
BOOM
BOOM
BOOM
BOOM
BOOM

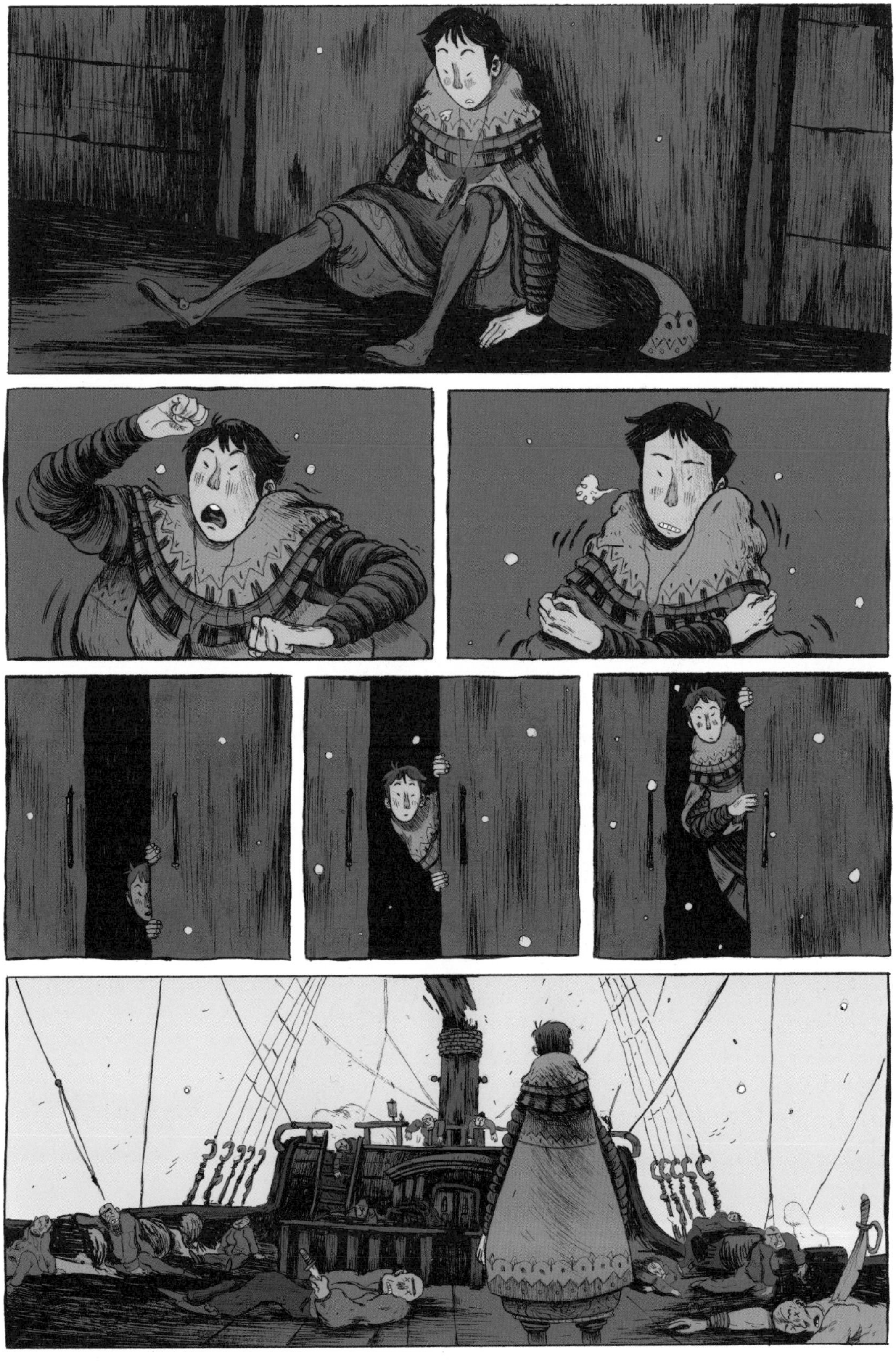

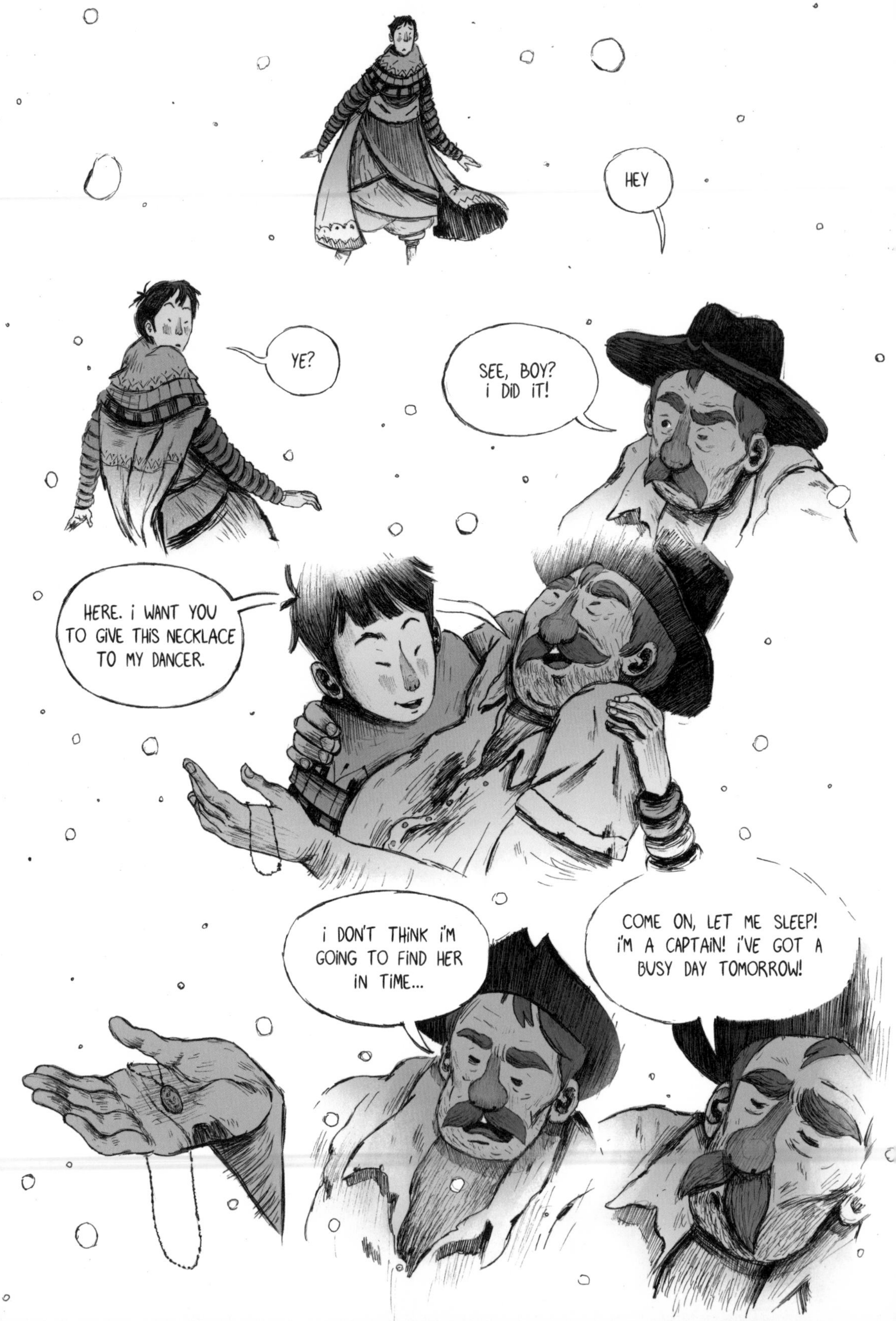
HEY
YE?
SEE, BOY? i DID iT!
HERE. i WANT YOU TO GIVE THIS NECKLACE TO MY DANCER.
i DON'T THiNK i'M GOiNG TO FiND HER iN TiME...
COME ON, LET ME SLEEP! i'M A CAPTAiN! i'VE GOT A BUSY DAY TOMORROW!

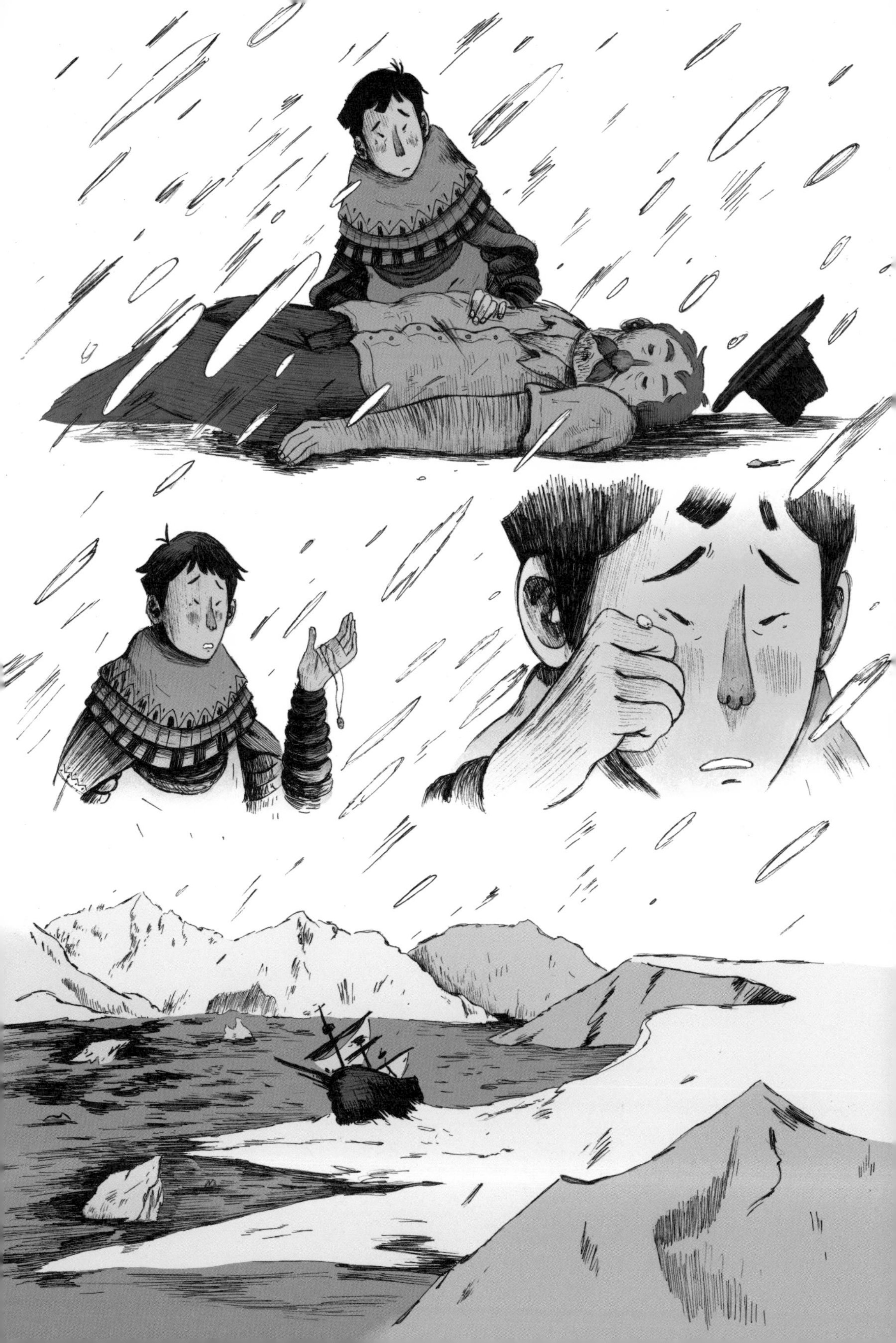

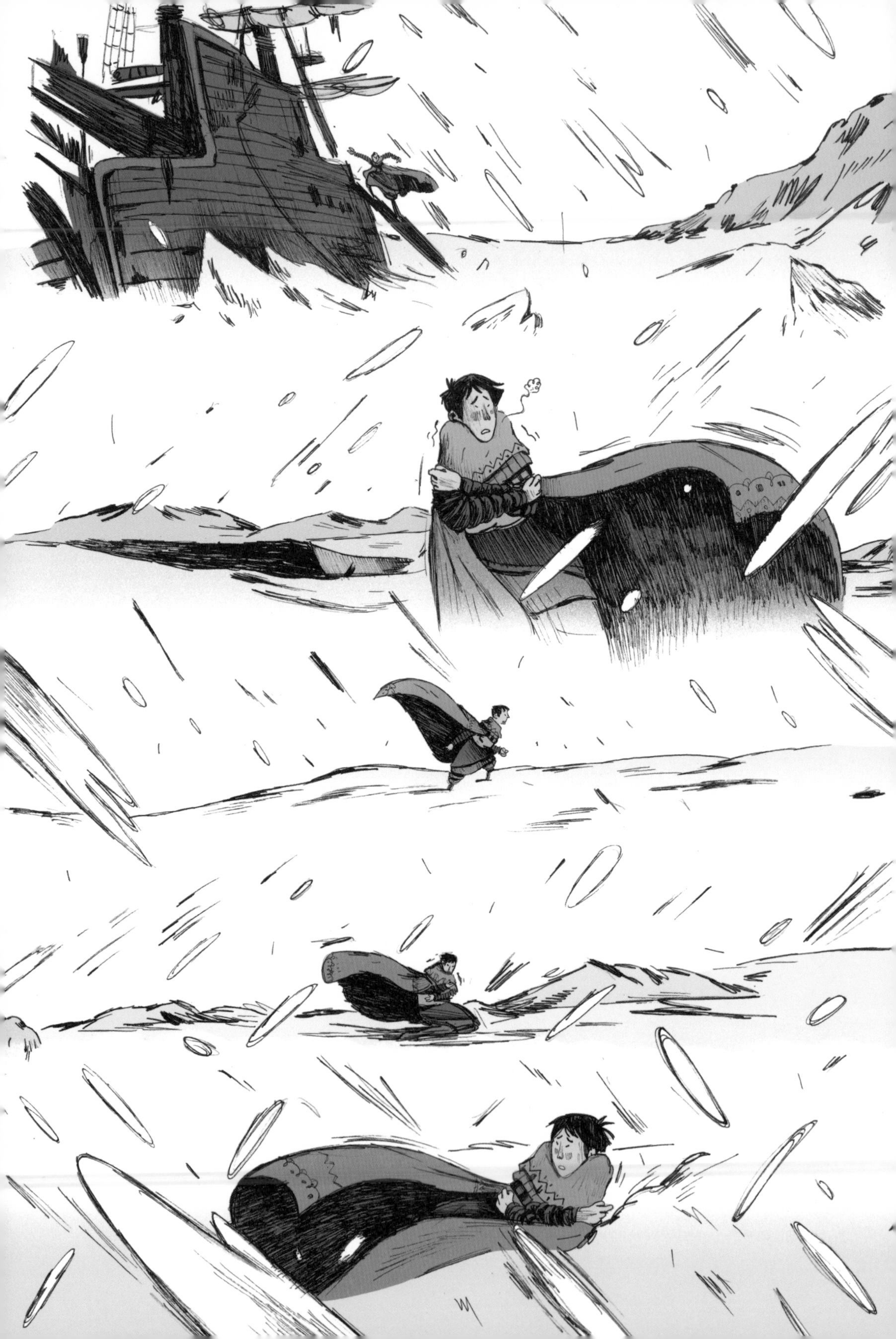

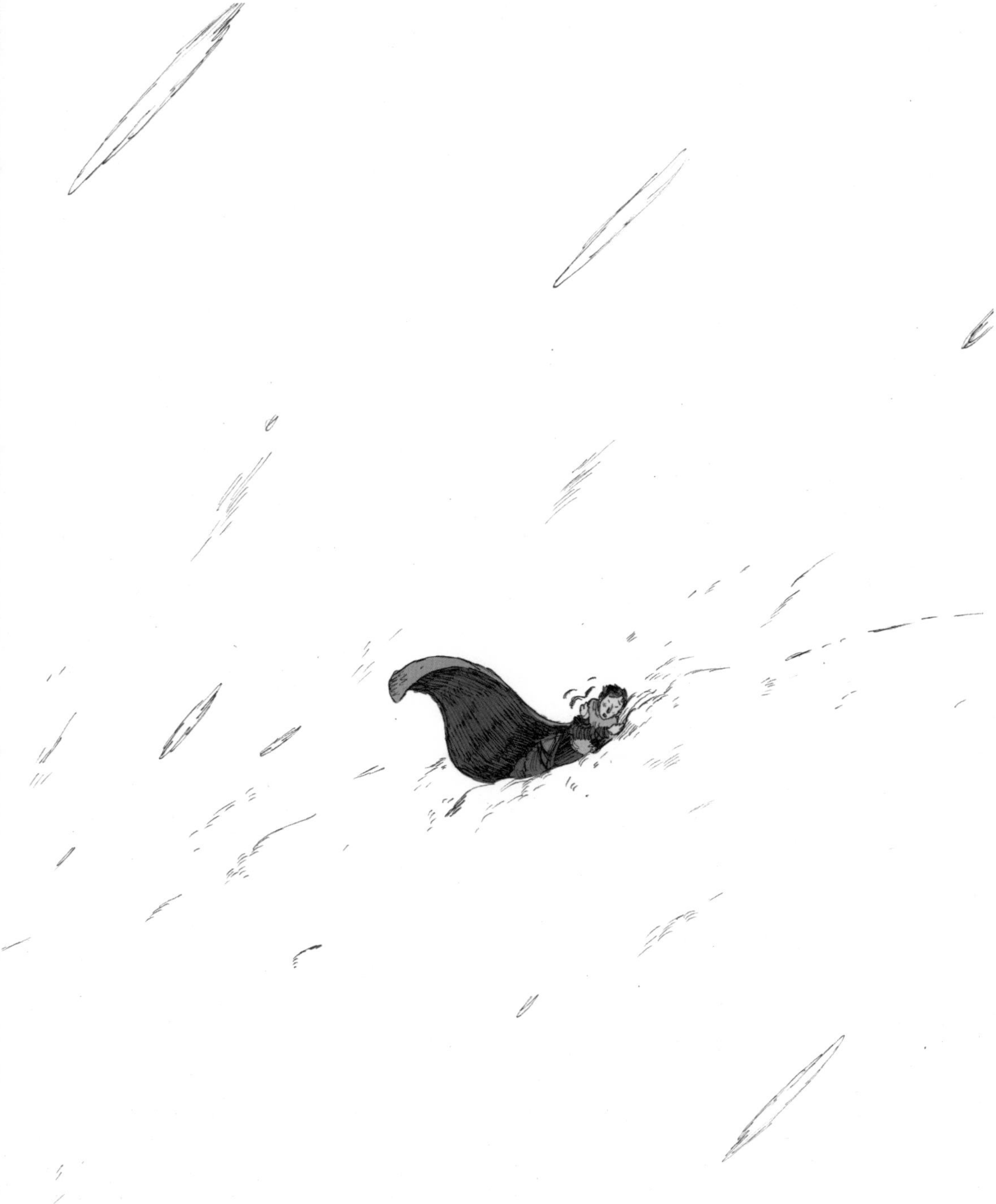

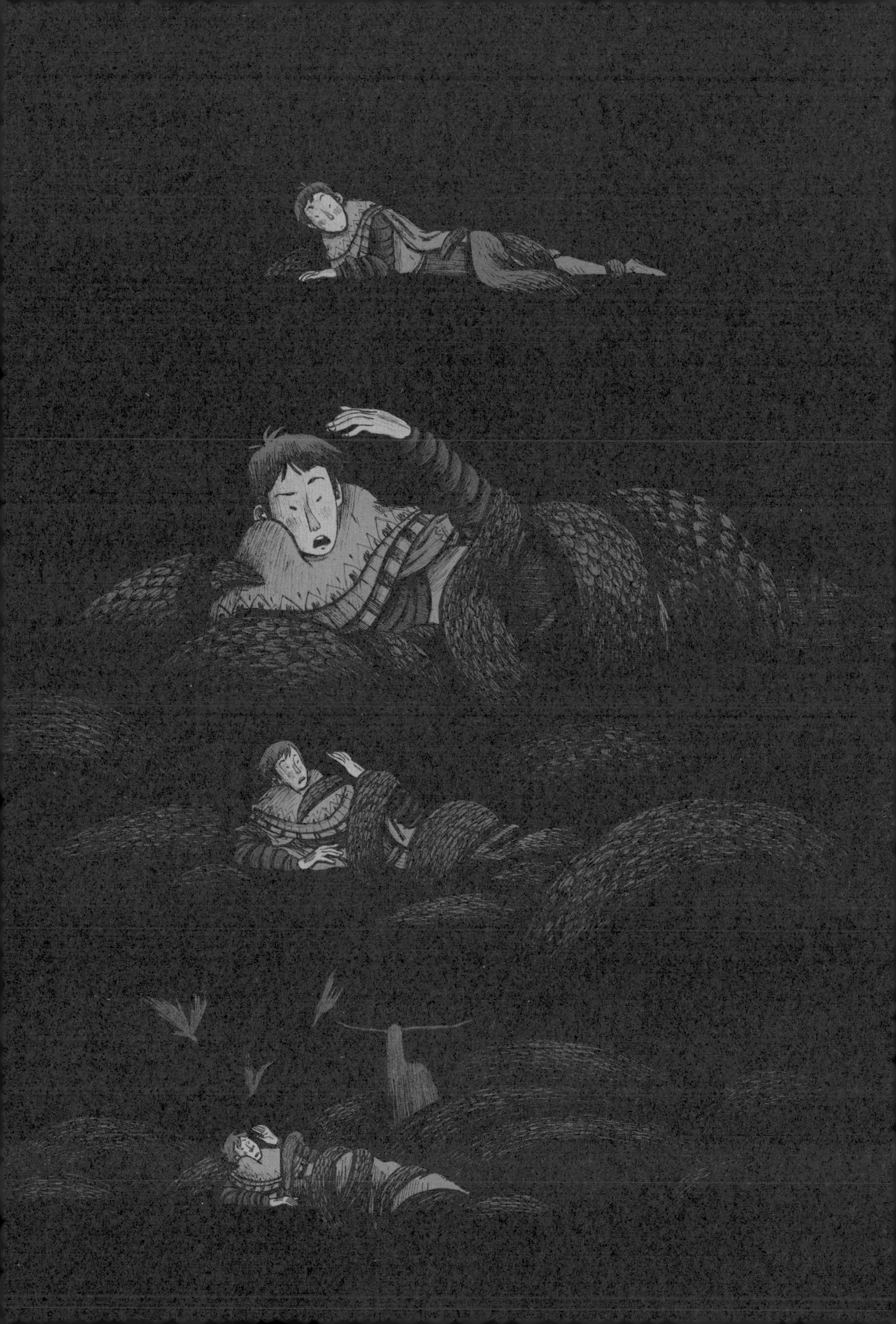

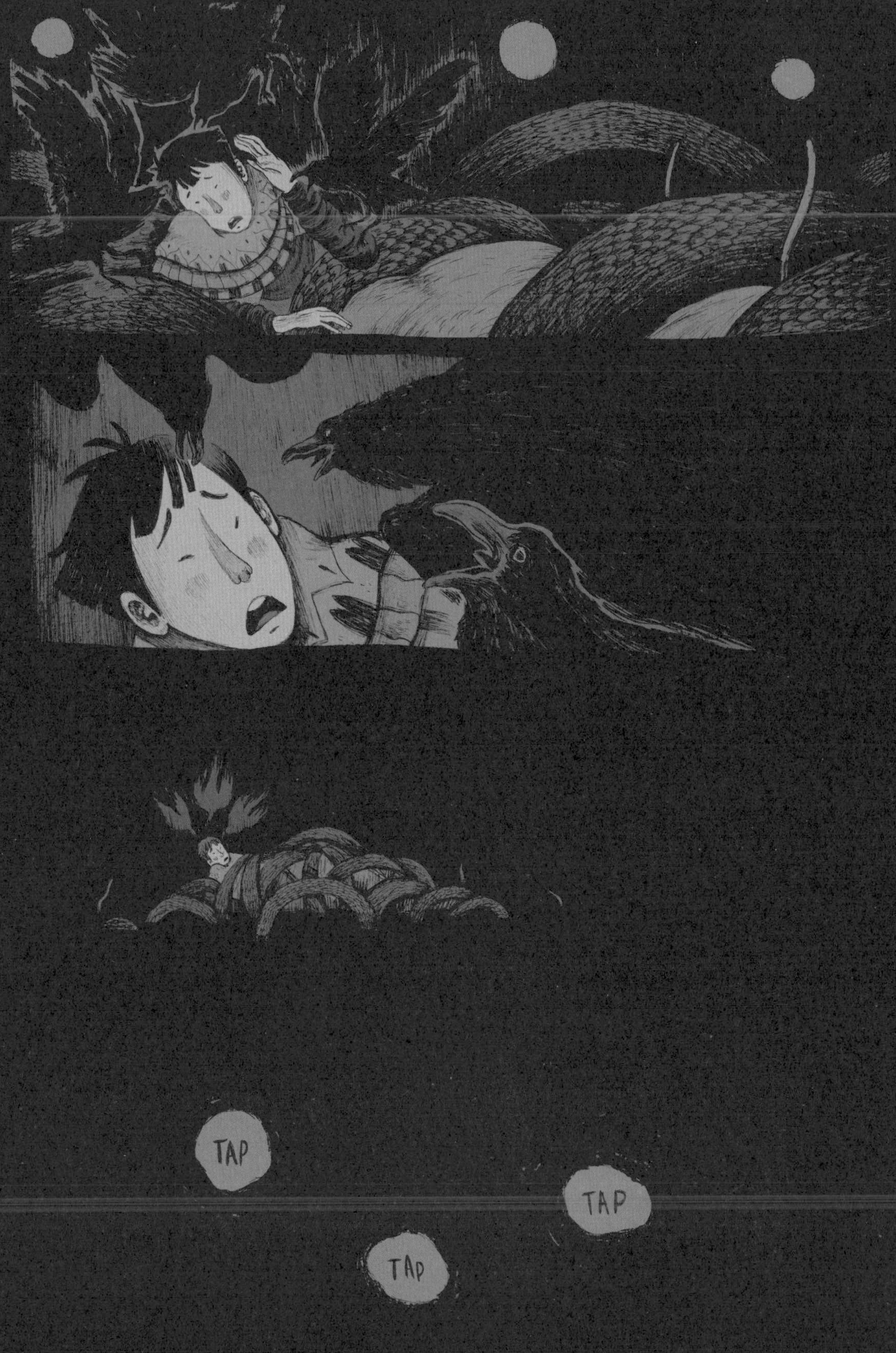
TAP
TAP
TAP

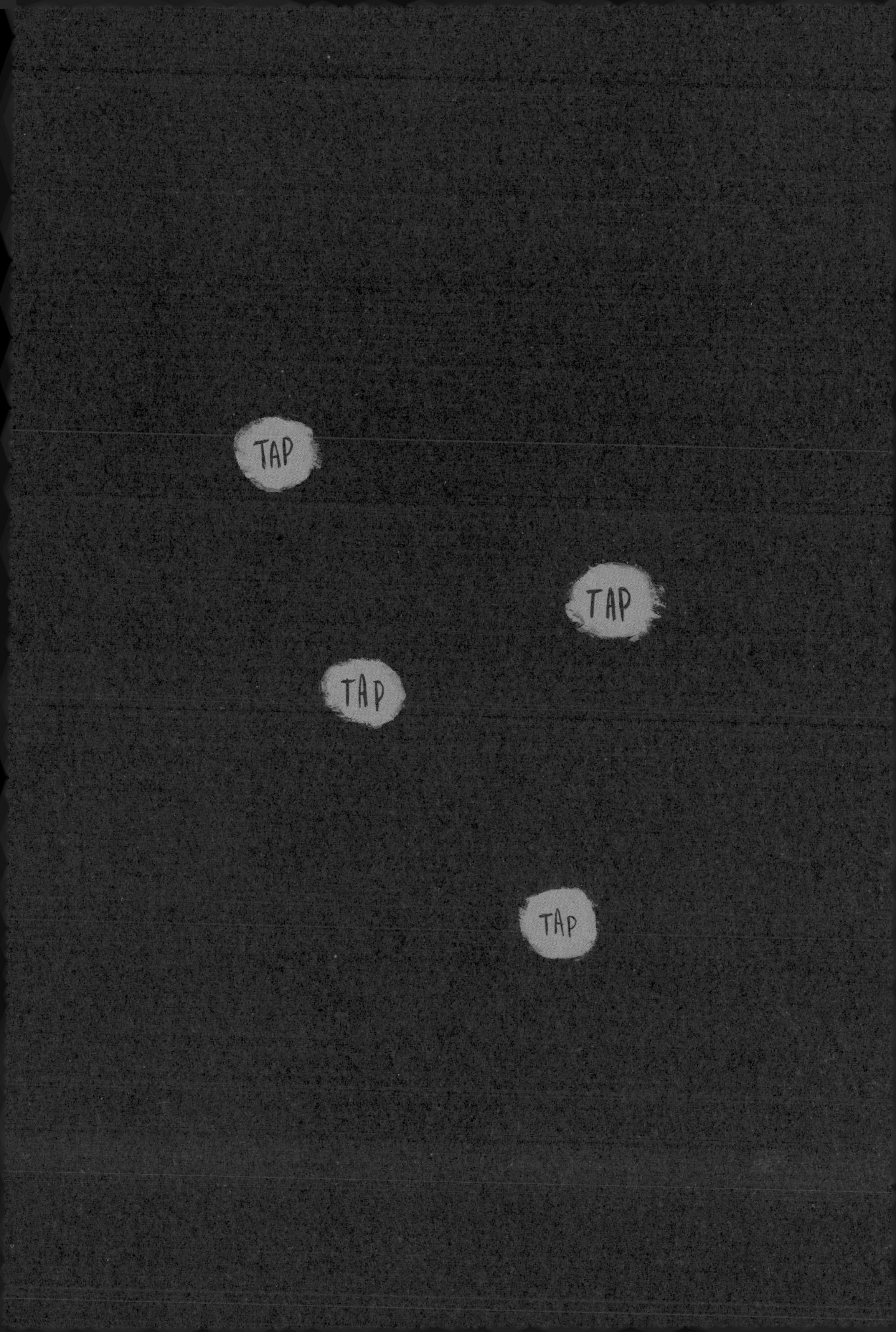
TAP
TAP
TAP
TAP

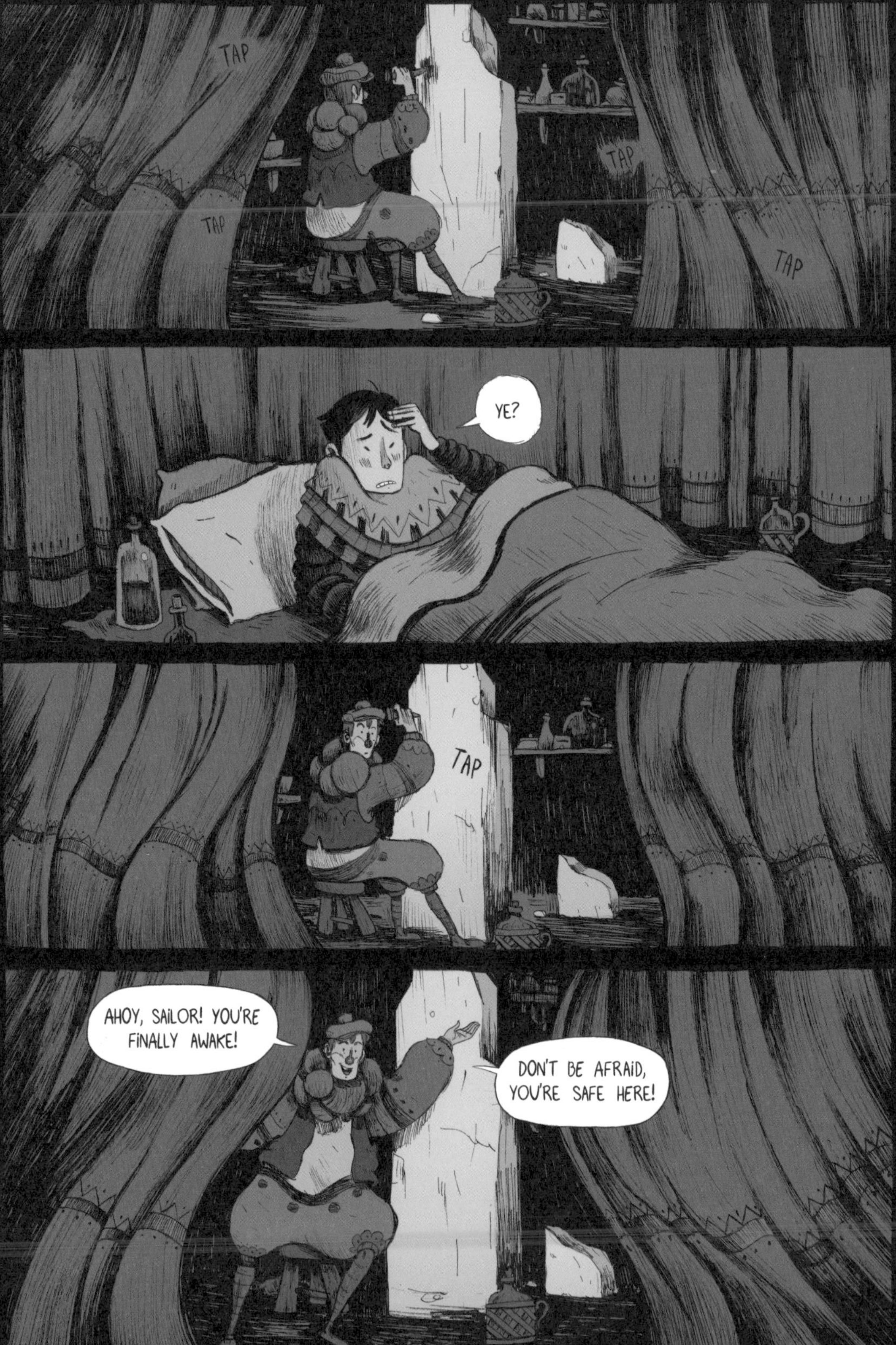
TAP
TAP
TAP
TAP
YE?
TAP
AHOY, SAILOR! YOU'RE FINALLY AWAKE!
DON'T BE AFRAID, YOU'RE SAFE HERE!

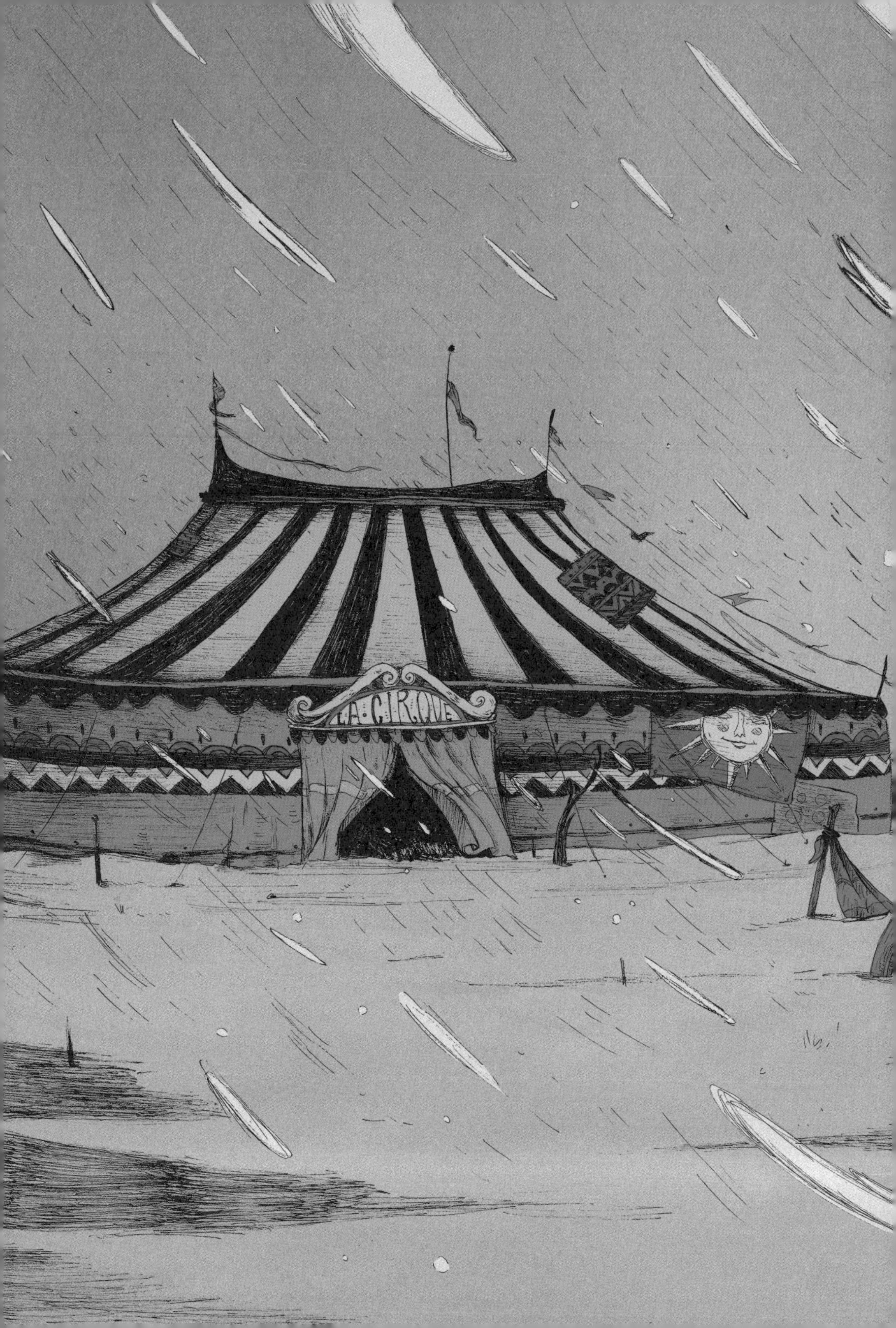
LA CIRQUE

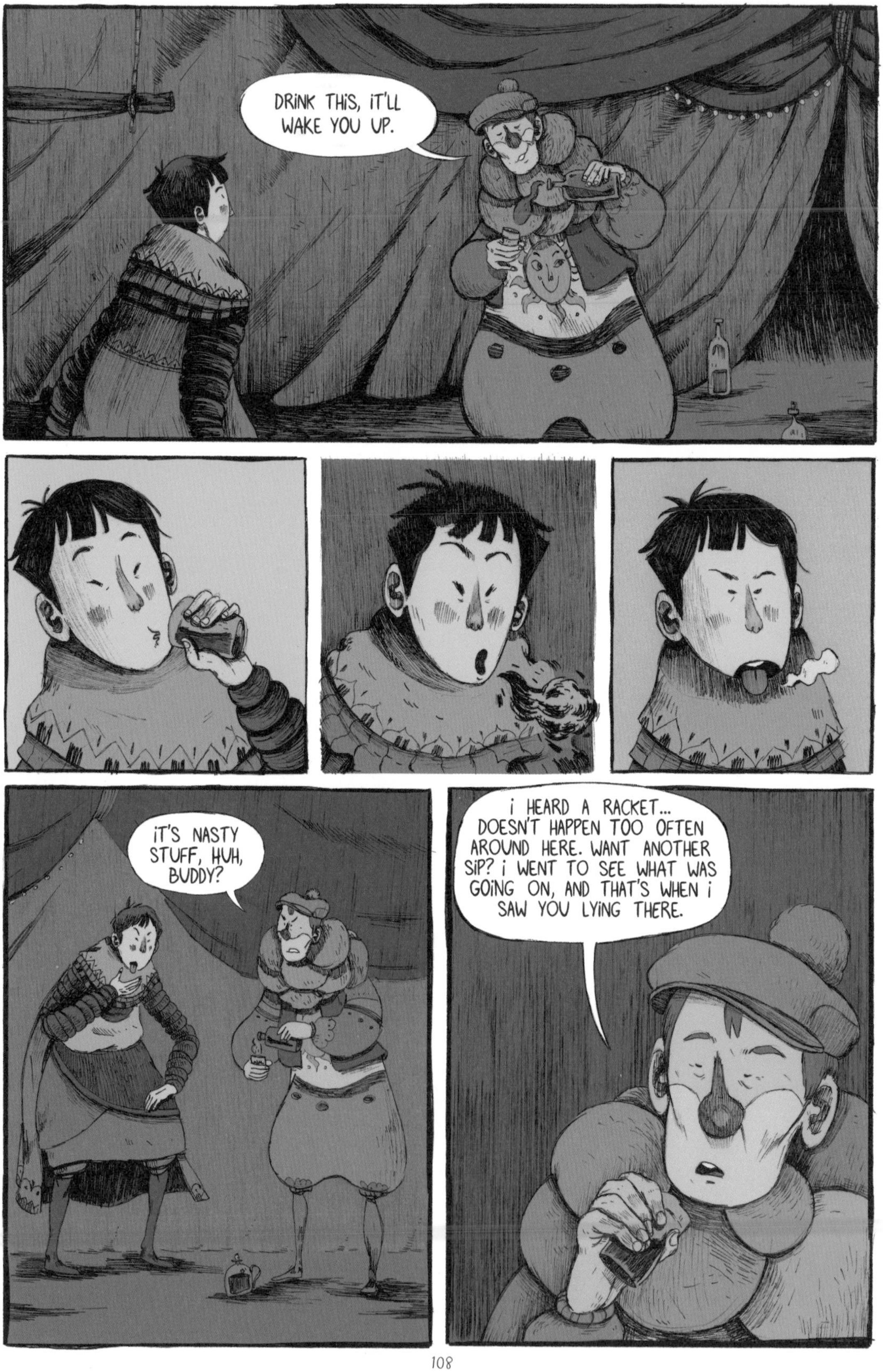
DRINK THIS, IT'LL WAKE YOU UP.
IT'S NASTY STUFF, HUH, BUDDY?
I HEARD A RACKET... DOESN'T HAPPEN TOO OFTEN AROUND HERE. WANT ANOTHER SIP? I WENT TO SEE WHAT WAS GOING ON, AND THAT'S WHEN I SAW YOU LYING THERE.

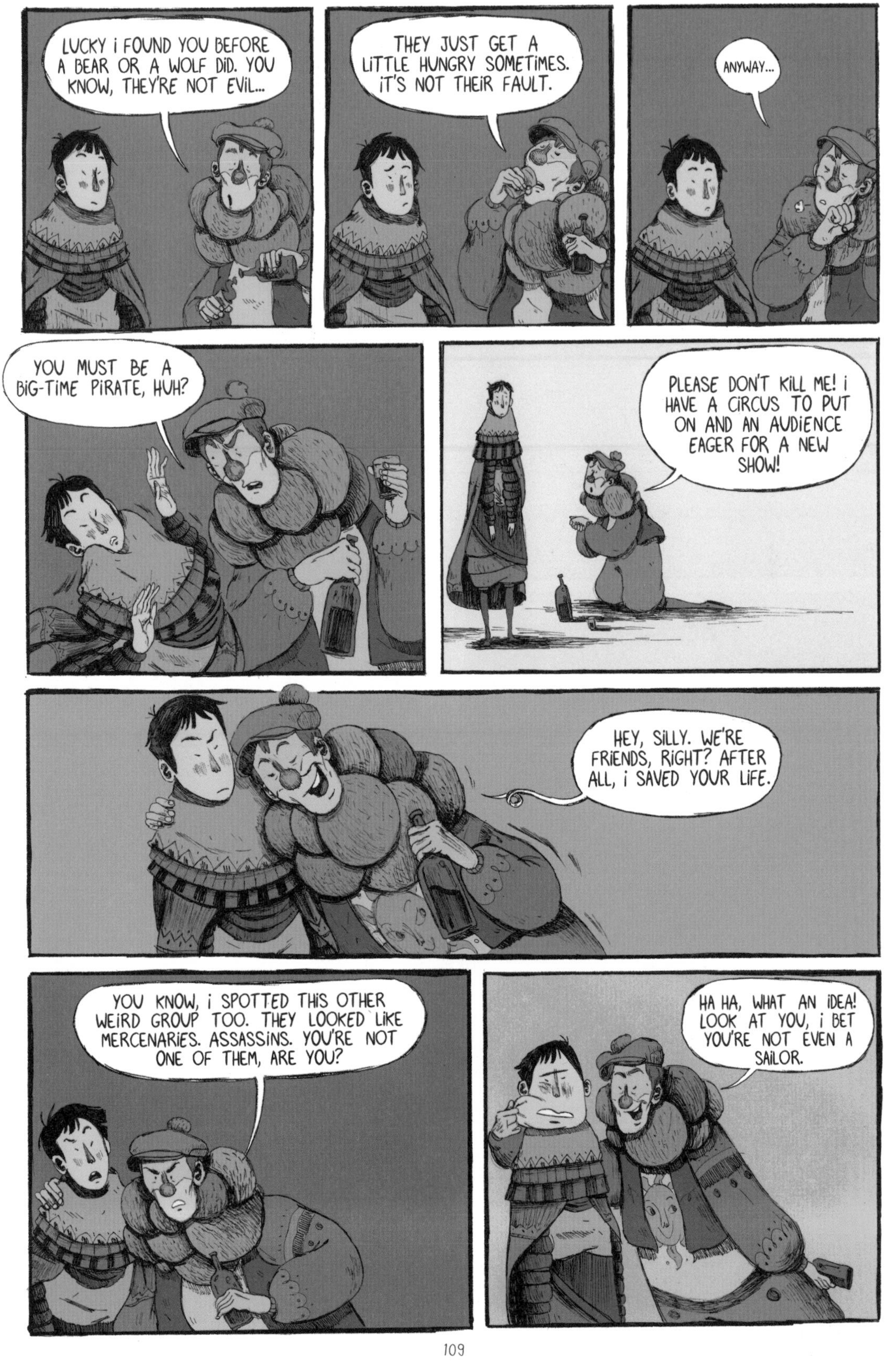
LUCKY i FOUND YOU BEFORE A BEAR OR A WOLF DiD. YOU KNOW, THEY'RE NOT EViL...
THEY JUST GET A LiTTLE HUNGRY SOMETiMES. iT'S NOT THEiR FAULT.
ANYWAY...
YOU MUST BE A BiG-TiME PiRATE, HUH?
PLEASE DON'T KiLL ME! i HAVE A CiRCUS TO PUT ON AND AN AUDiENCE EAGER FOR A NEW SHOW!
HEY, SiLLY. WE'RE FRiENDS, RiGHT? AFTER ALL, i SAVED YOUR LiFE.
YOU KNOW, i SPOTTED THiS OTHER WEiRD GROUP TOO. THEY LOOKED LiKE MERCENARiES. ASSASSiNS. YOU'RE NOT ONE OF THEM, ARE YOU?
HA HA, WHAT AN iDEA! LOOK AT YOU, i BET YOU'RE NOT EVEN A SAiLOR.

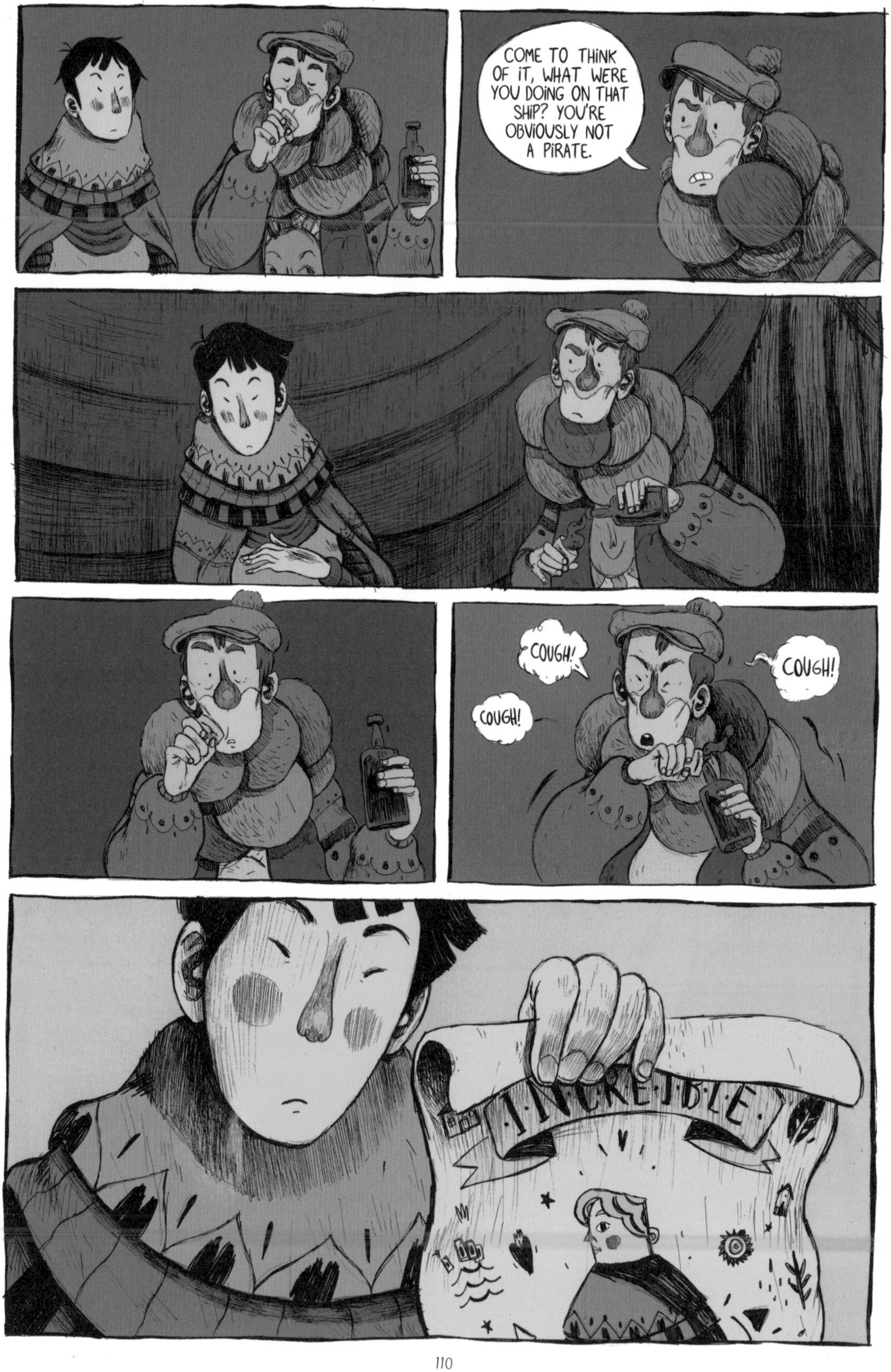
COME TO THINK OF IT, WHAT WERE YOU DOING ON THAT SHIP? YOU'RE OBVIOUSLY NOT A PIRATE.
COUGH!
COUGH!
COUGH!
INCREDIBLE

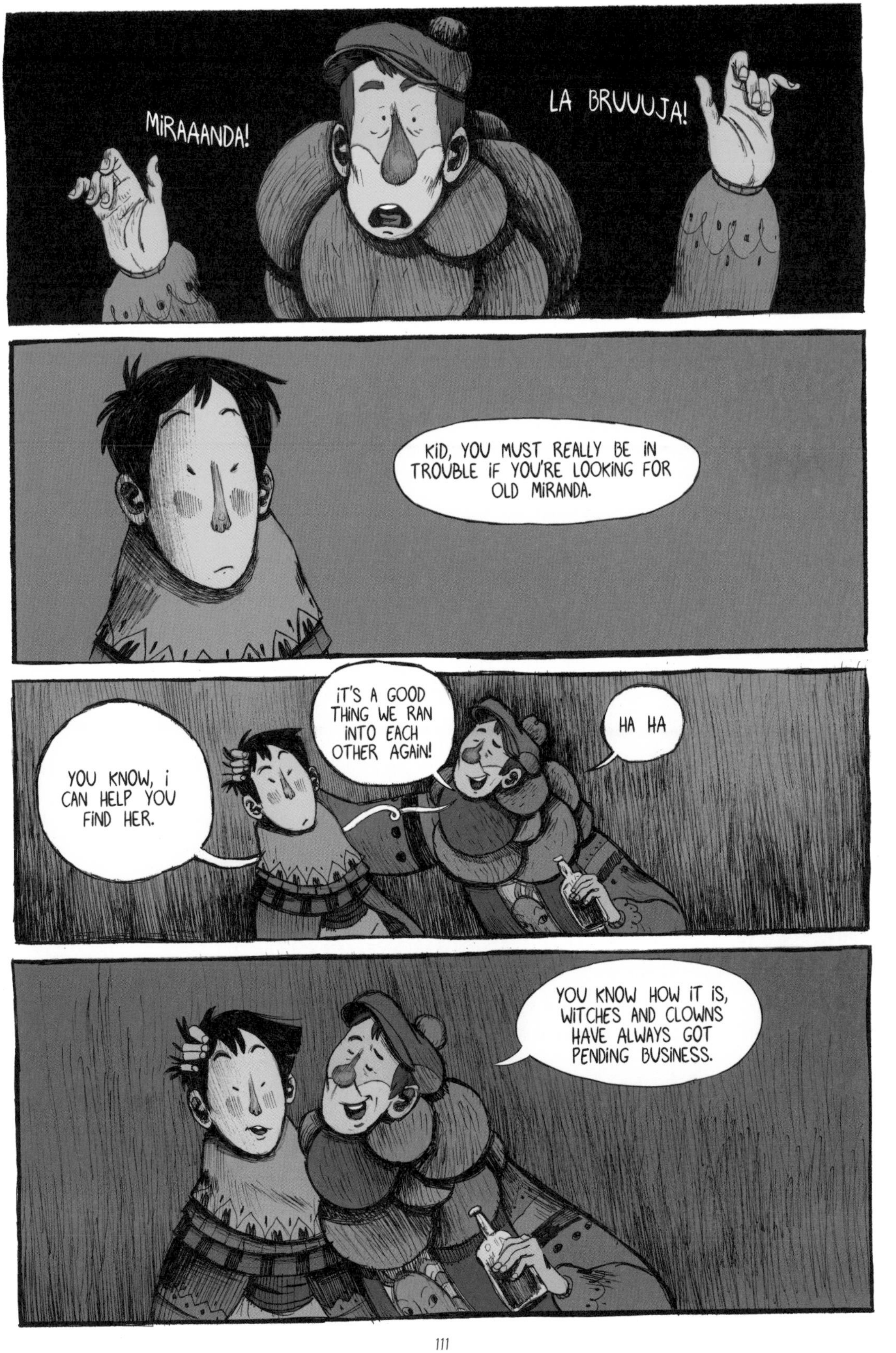
MIRAAANDA!
LA BRUUUJA!
KID, YOU MUST REALLY BE IN TROUBLE IF YOU'RE LOOKING FOR OLD MIRANDA.
YOU KNOW, I CAN HELP YOU FIND HER.
IT'S A GOOD THING WE RAN INTO EACH OTHER AGAIN!
HA HA
YOU KNOW HOW IT IS, WITCHES AND CLOWNS HAVE ALWAYS GOT PENDING BUSINESS.

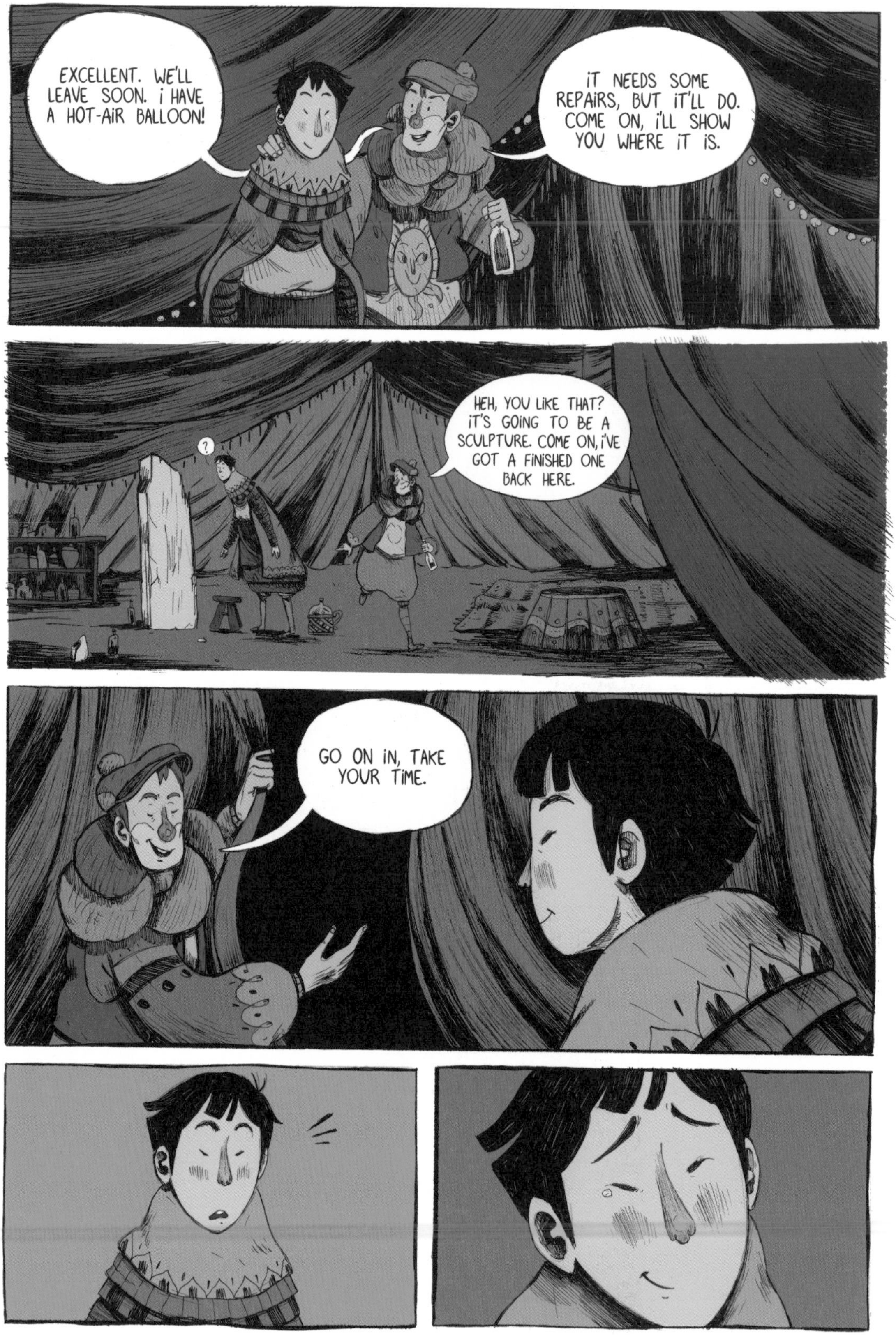
EXCELLENT. WE'LL LEAVE SOON. I HAVE A HOT-AIR BALLOON!
IT NEEDS SOME REPAIRS, BUT IT'LL DO. COME ON, I'LL SHOW YOU WHERE IT IS.
?
HEH, YOU LIKE THAT? IT'S GOING TO BE A SCULPTURE. COME ON, I'VE GOT A FINISHED ONE BACK HERE.
GO ON IN, TAKE YOUR TIME.

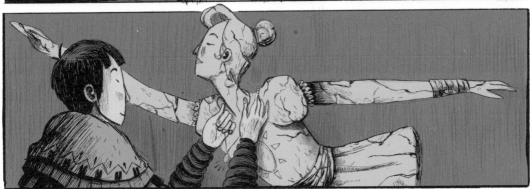

HANDS OFF, KID. SHE'S ALREADY SOMEBODY ELSE'S GIRL.

BUT i THINK SHE LIKED YOU!

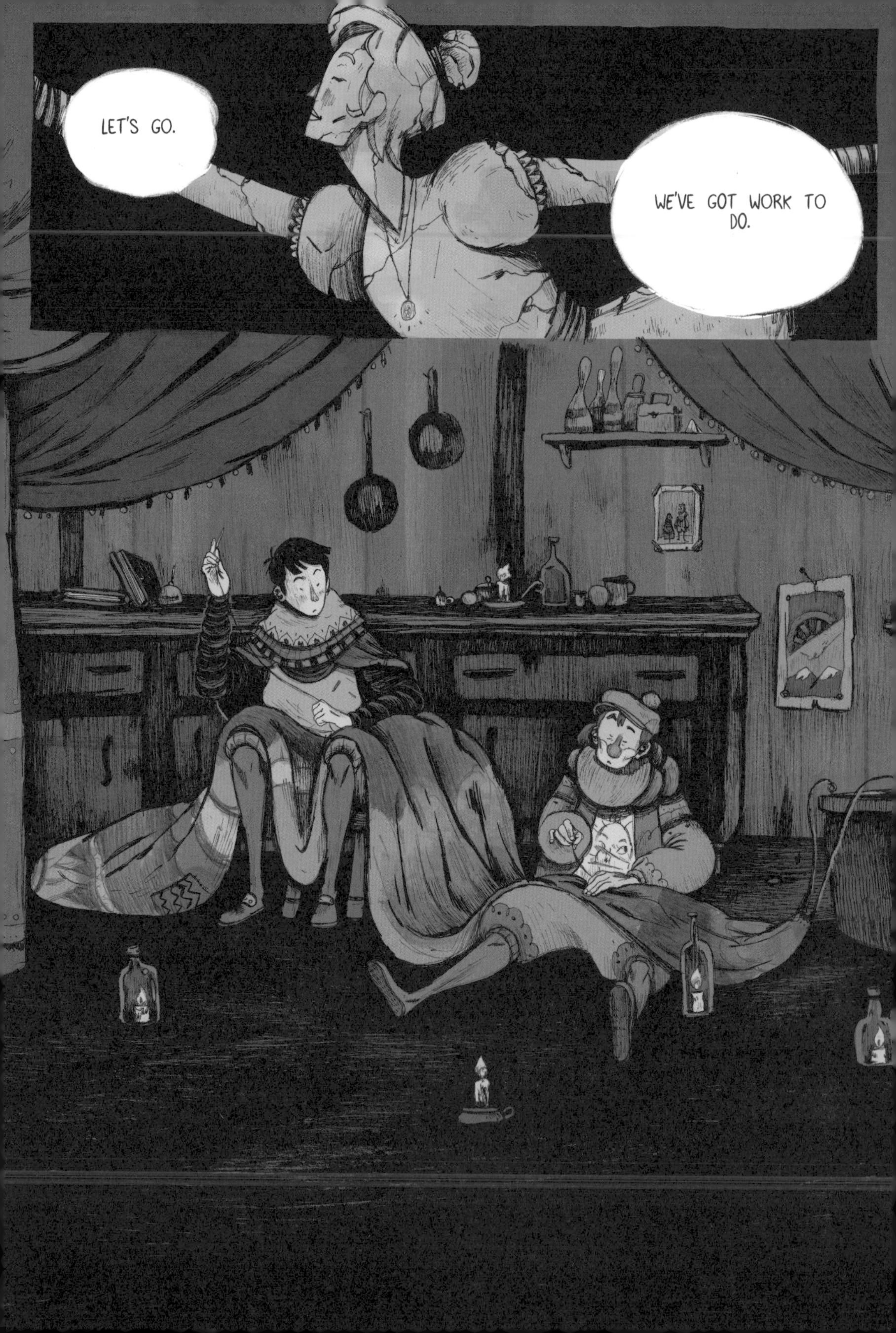
LET'S GO.
WE'VE GOT WORK TO DO.

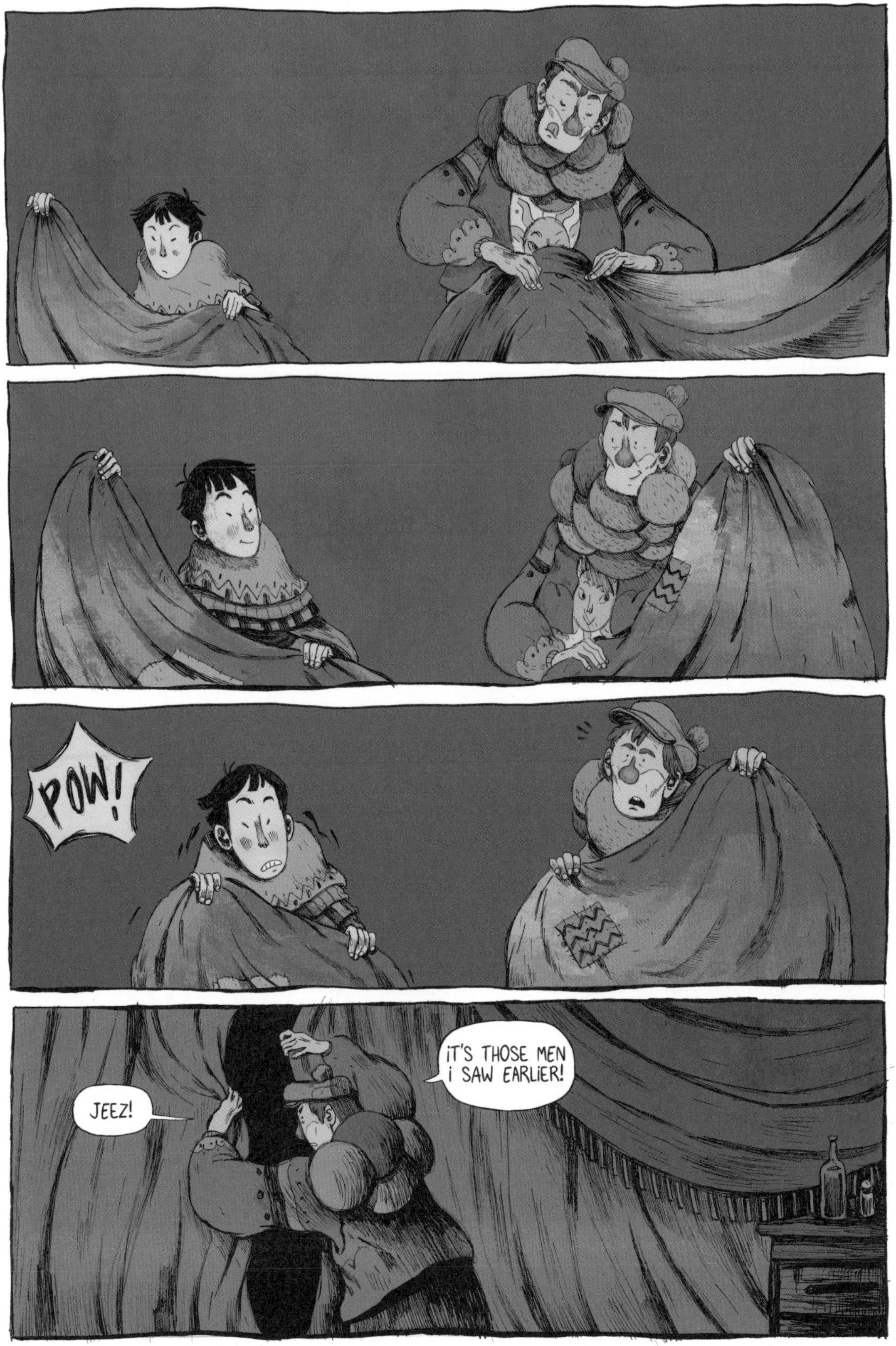
POW!
JEEZ!
IT'S THOSE MEN
I SAW EARLIER!

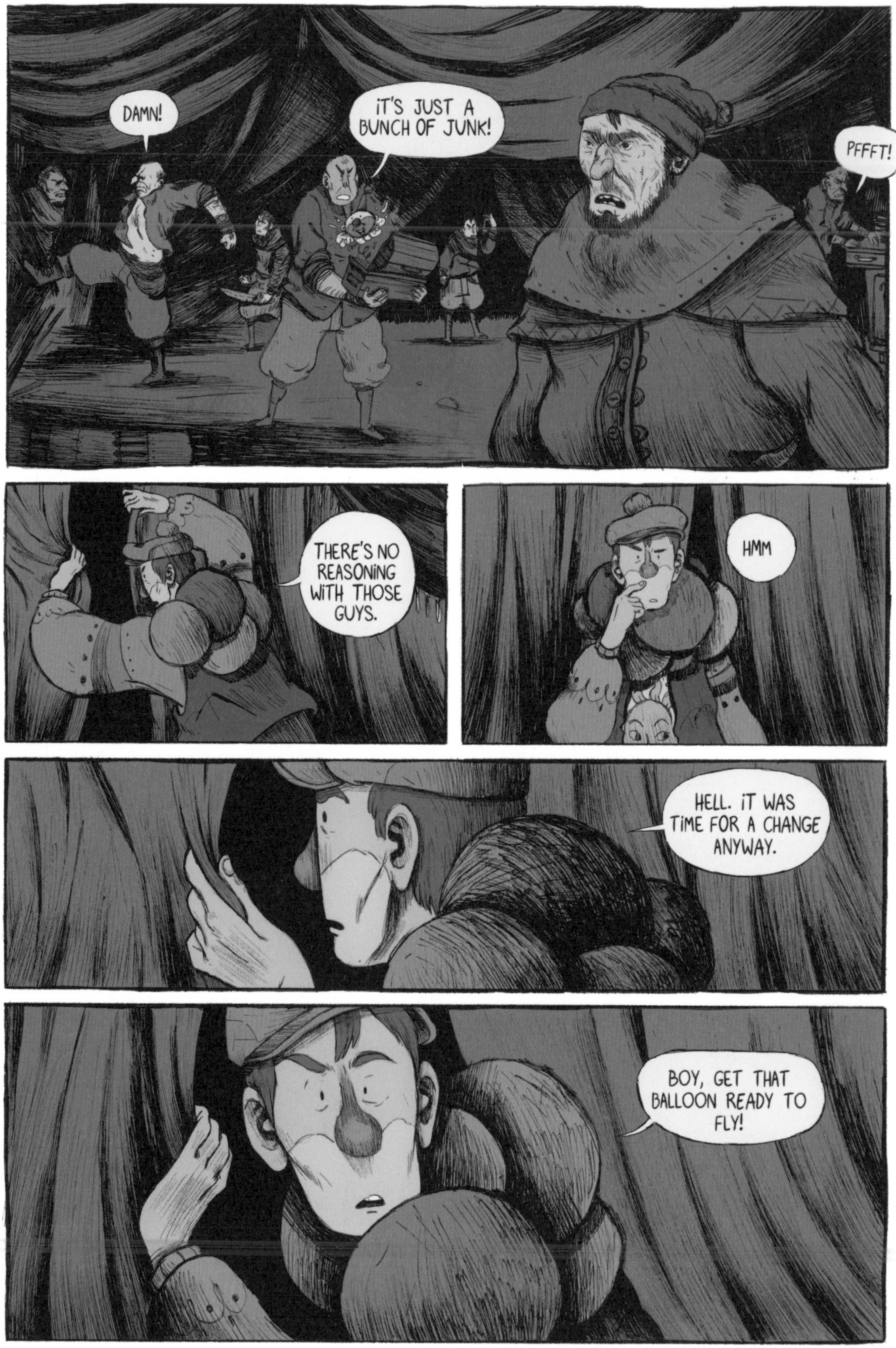
DAMN!
iT'S JUST A BUNCH OF JUNK!
PFFFT!
THERE'S NO REASONiNG WiTH THOSE GUYS.
HMM
HELL. iT WAS TiME FOR A CHANGE ANYWAY.
BOY, GET THAT BALLOON READY TO FLY!

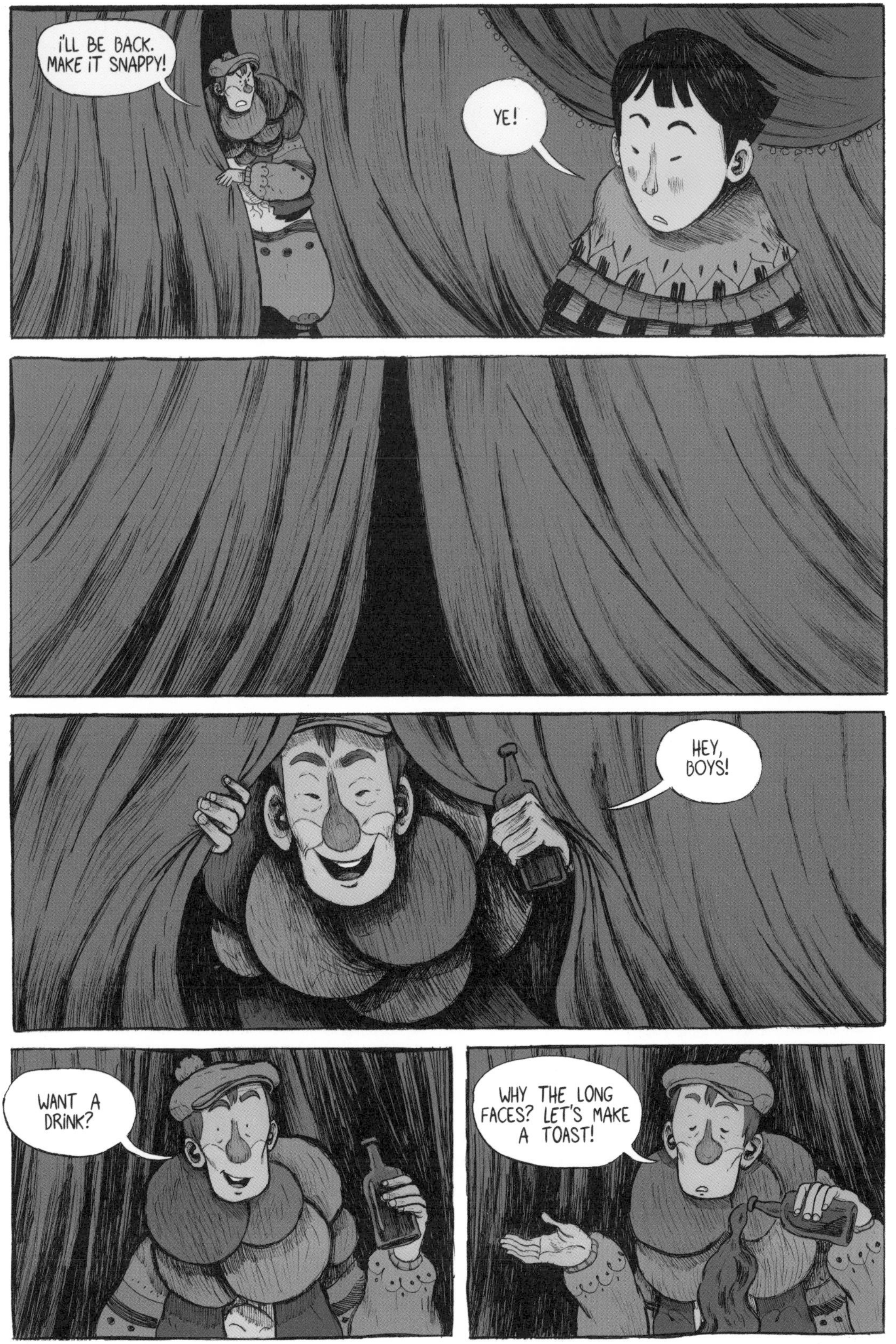
I'LL BE BACK. MAKE IT SNAPPY!
YE!
HEY, BOYS!
WANT A DRINK?
WHY THE LONG FACES? LET'S MAKE A TOAST!

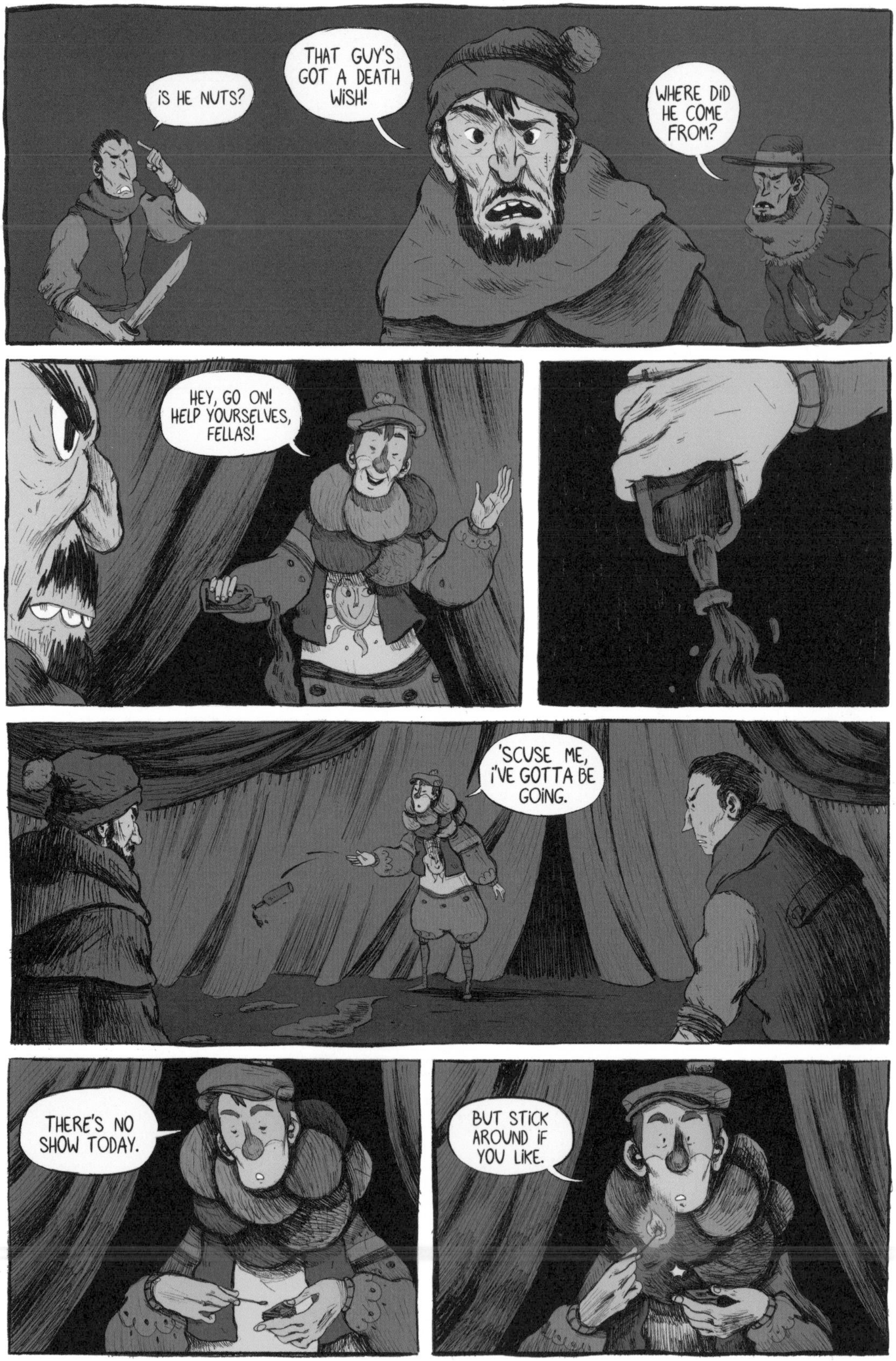
iS HE NUTS?
THAT GUY'S GOT A DEATH WISH!
WHERE DID HE COME FROM?
HEY, GO ON! HELP YOURSELVES, FELLAS!
'SCUSE ME, i'VE GOTTA BE GOiNG.
THERE'S NO SHOW TODAY.
BUT STiCK AROUND iF YOU LiKE.

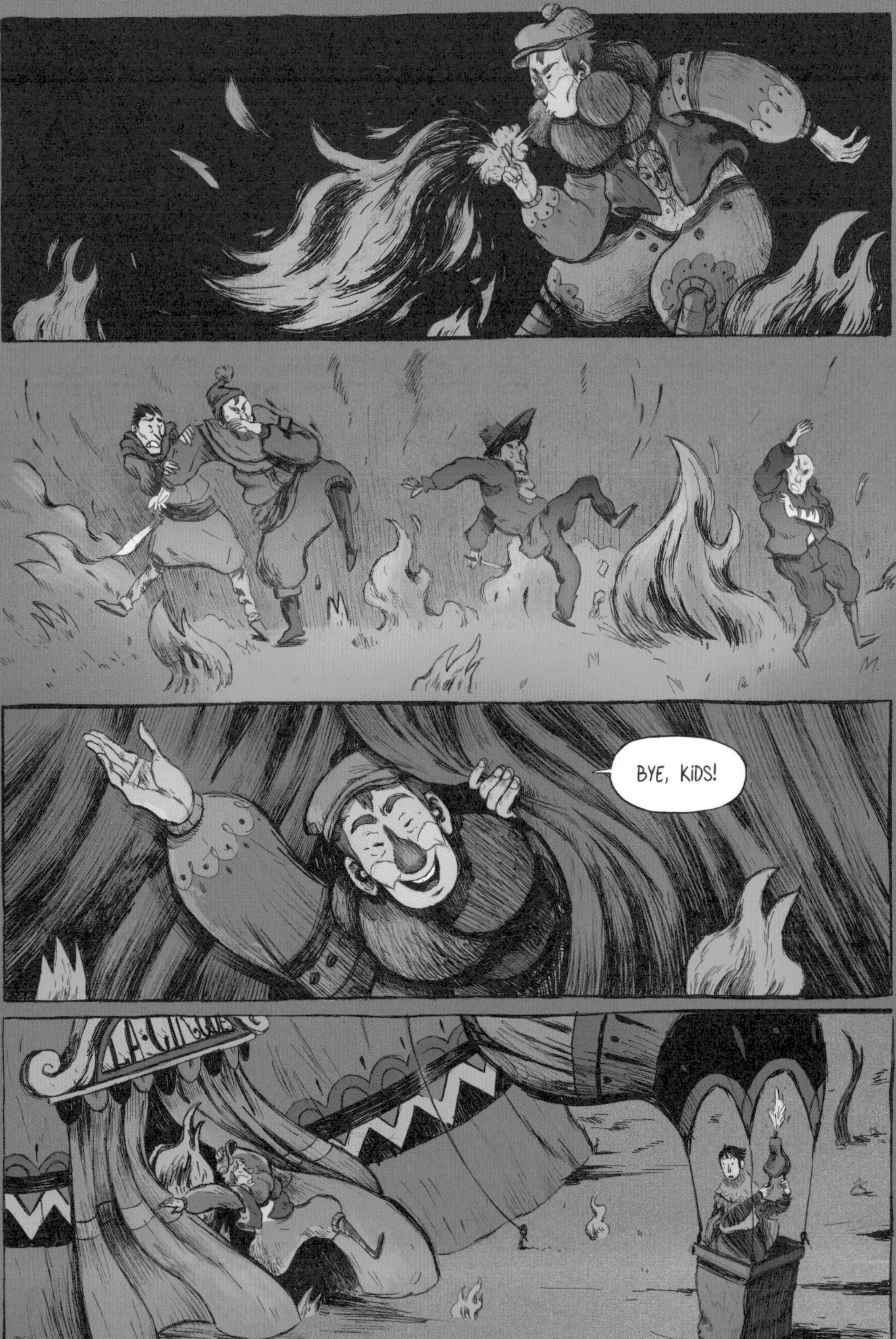
BYE, KIDS!

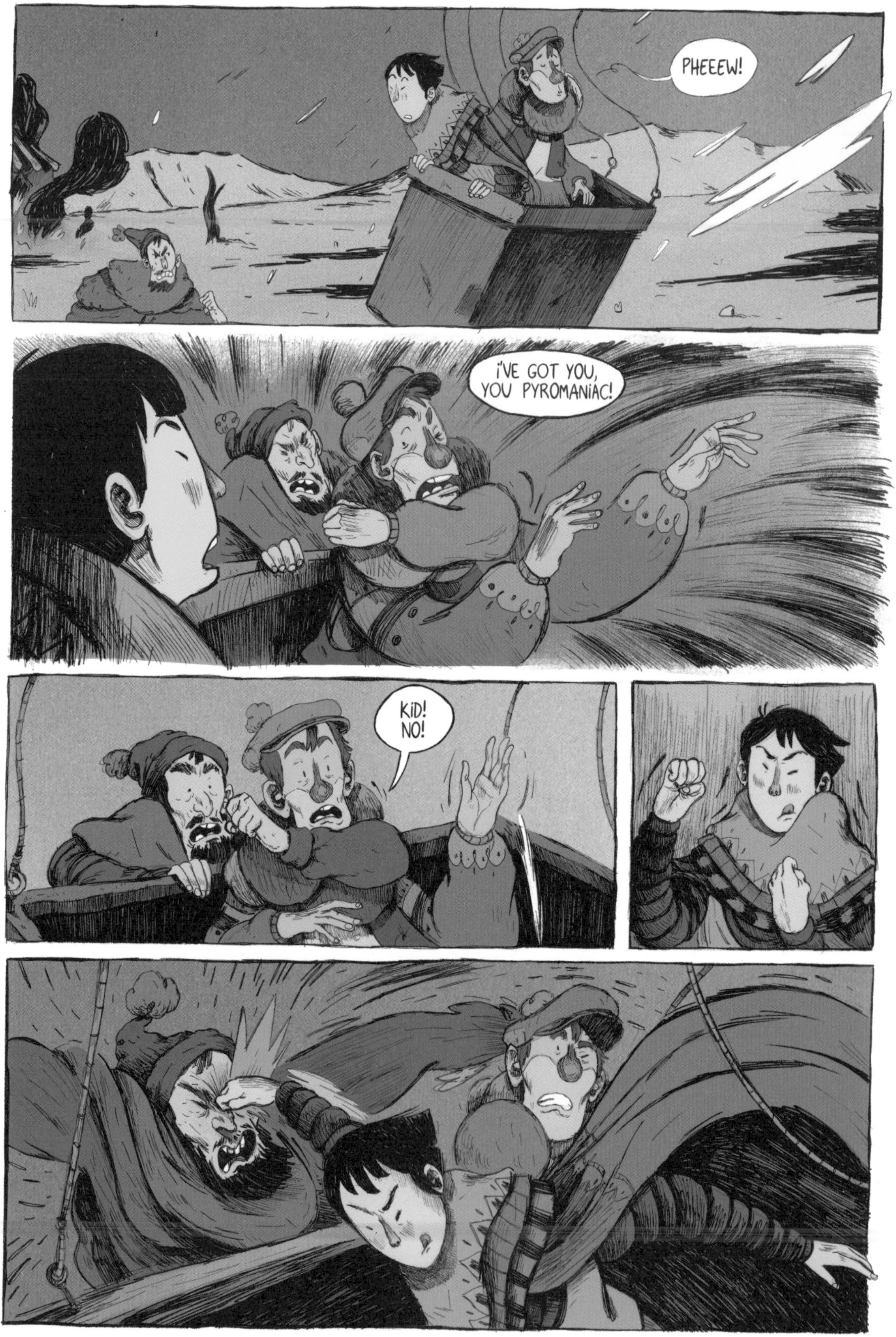
PHEEEW!
i'VE GOT YOU, YOU PYROMANiAC!
KiD! NO!

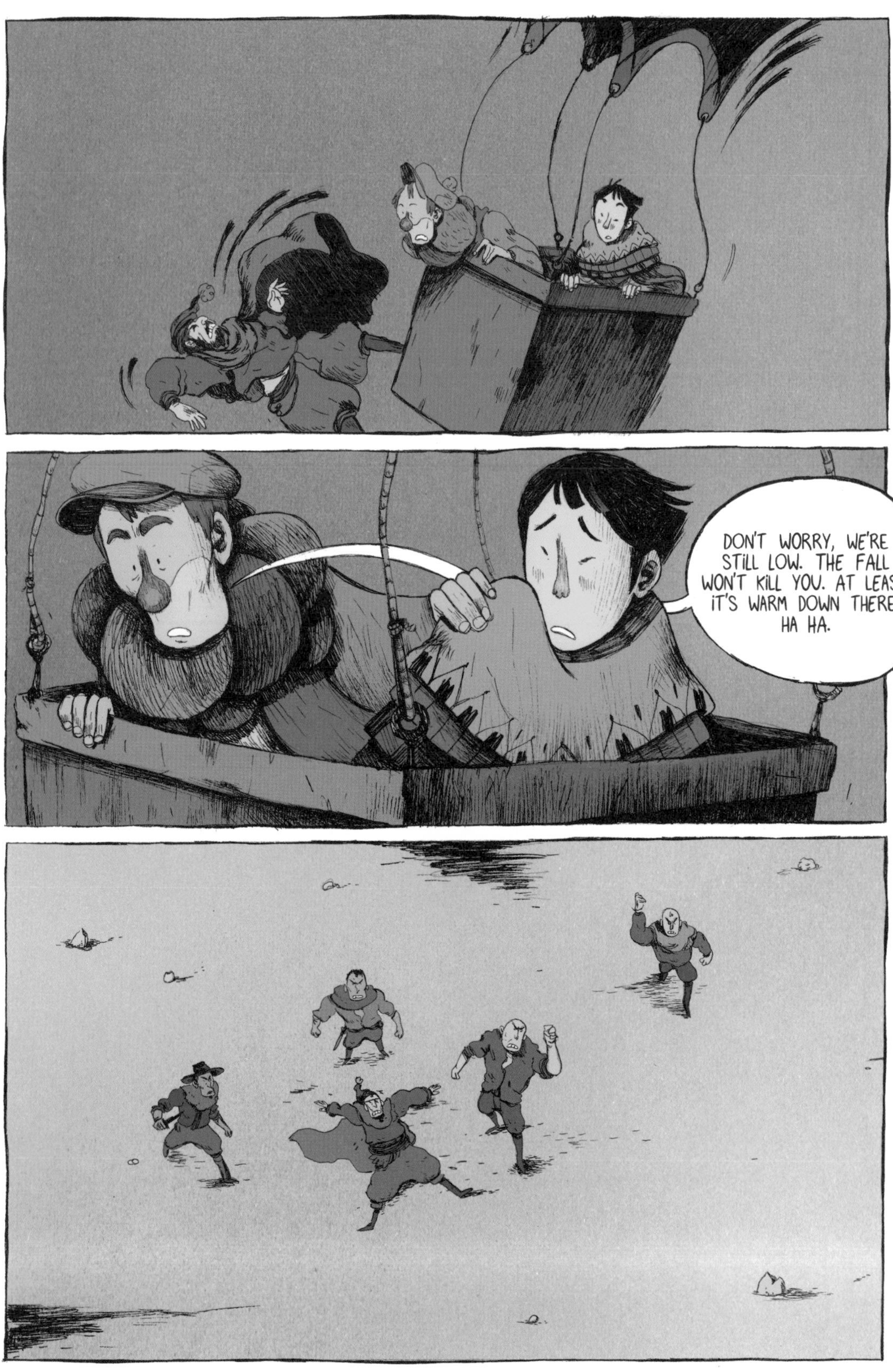
DON'T WORRY, WE'RE STILL LOW. THE FALL WON'T KILL YOU. AT LEAST IT'S WARM DOWN THERE! HA HA.

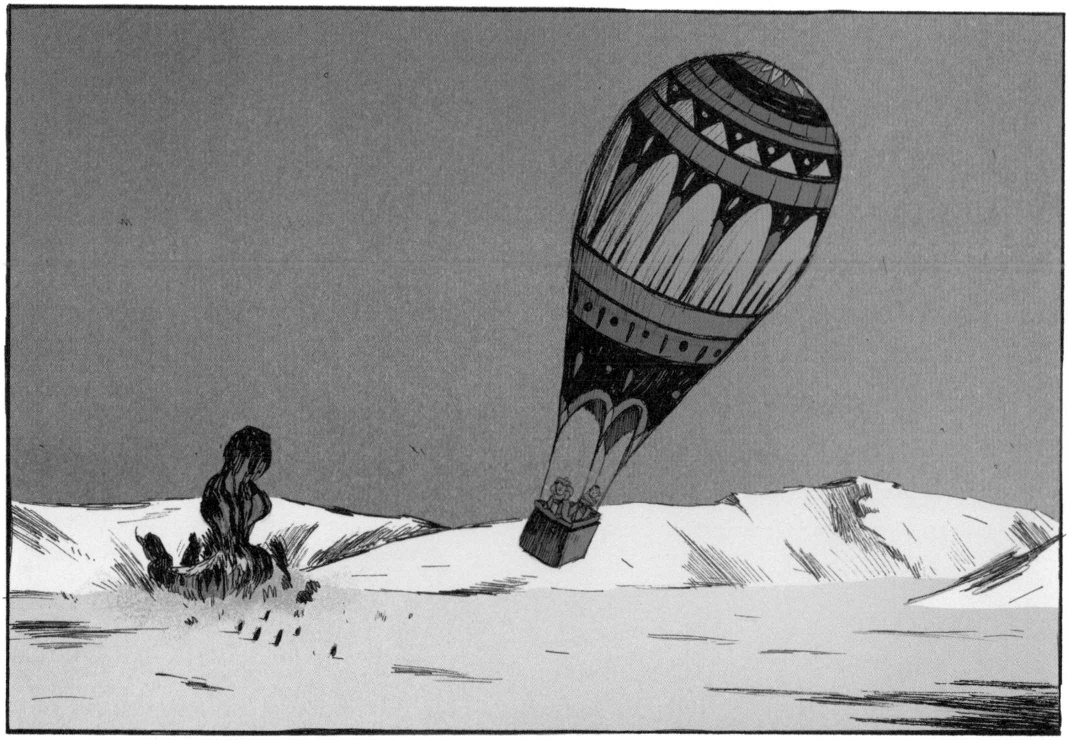

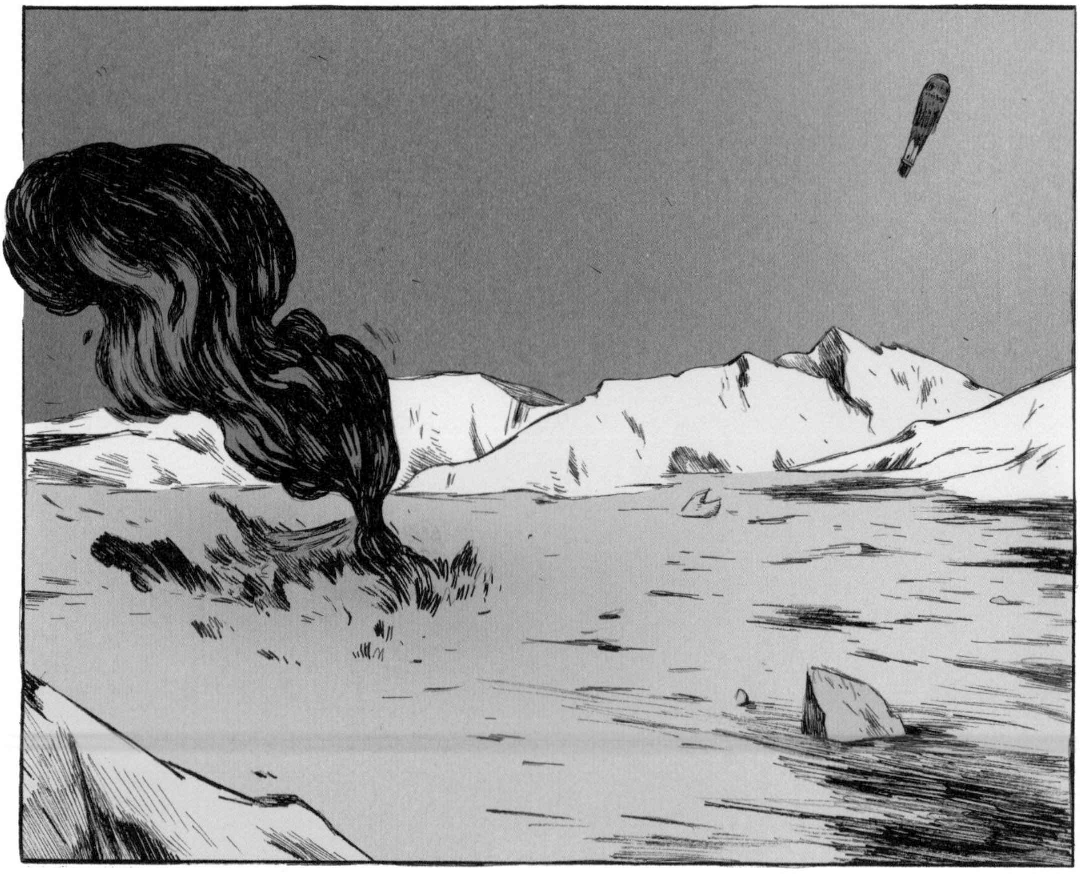

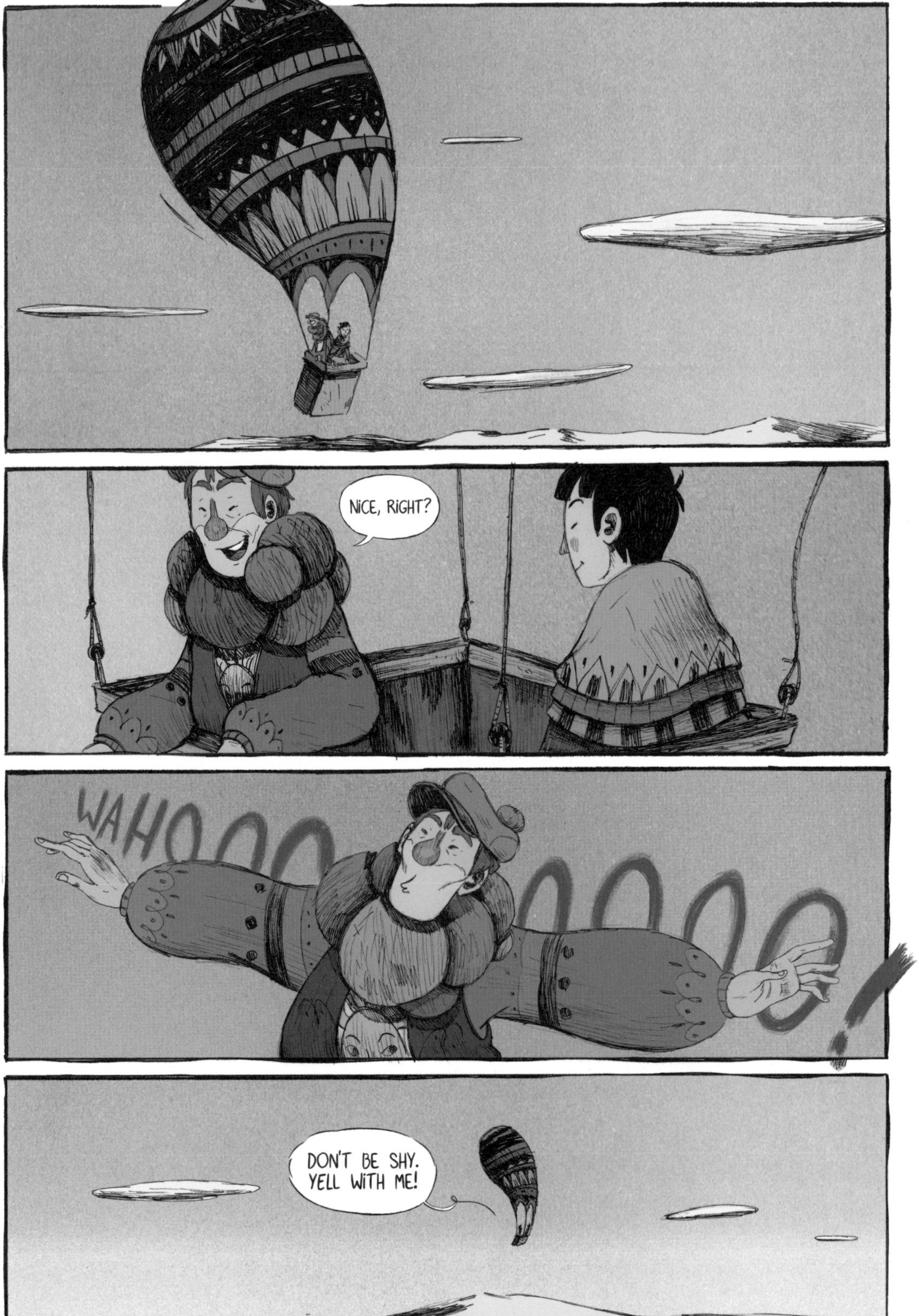
NICE, RIGHT?
WAHOOOOOOOOO!
DON'T BE SHY. YELL WITH ME!

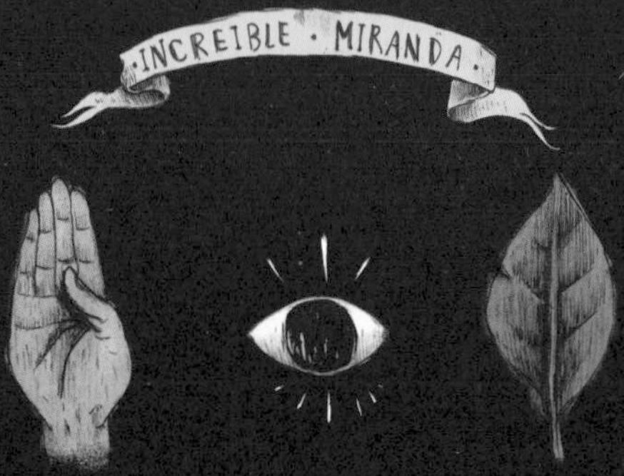
INCREIBLE · MIRANDA

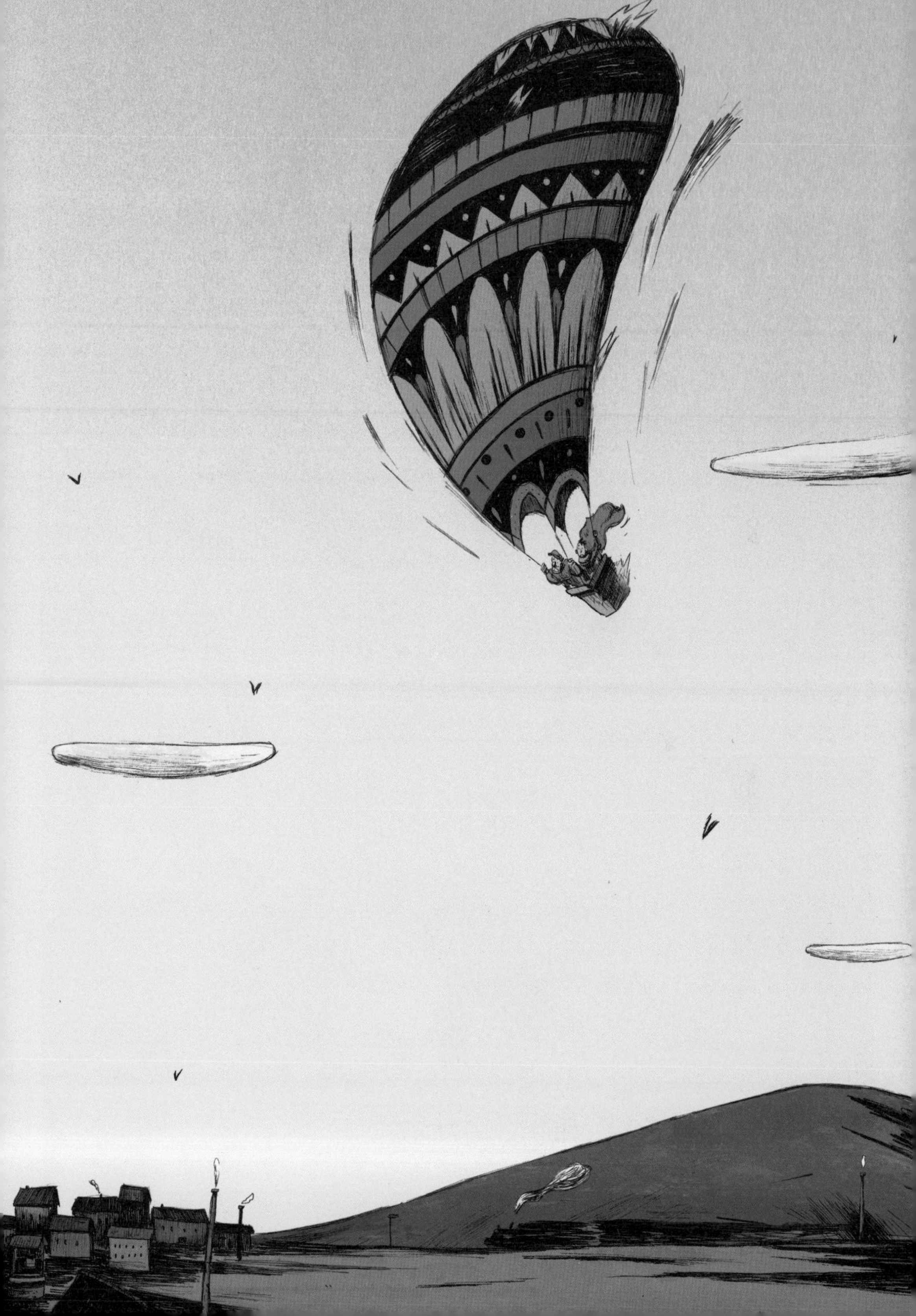

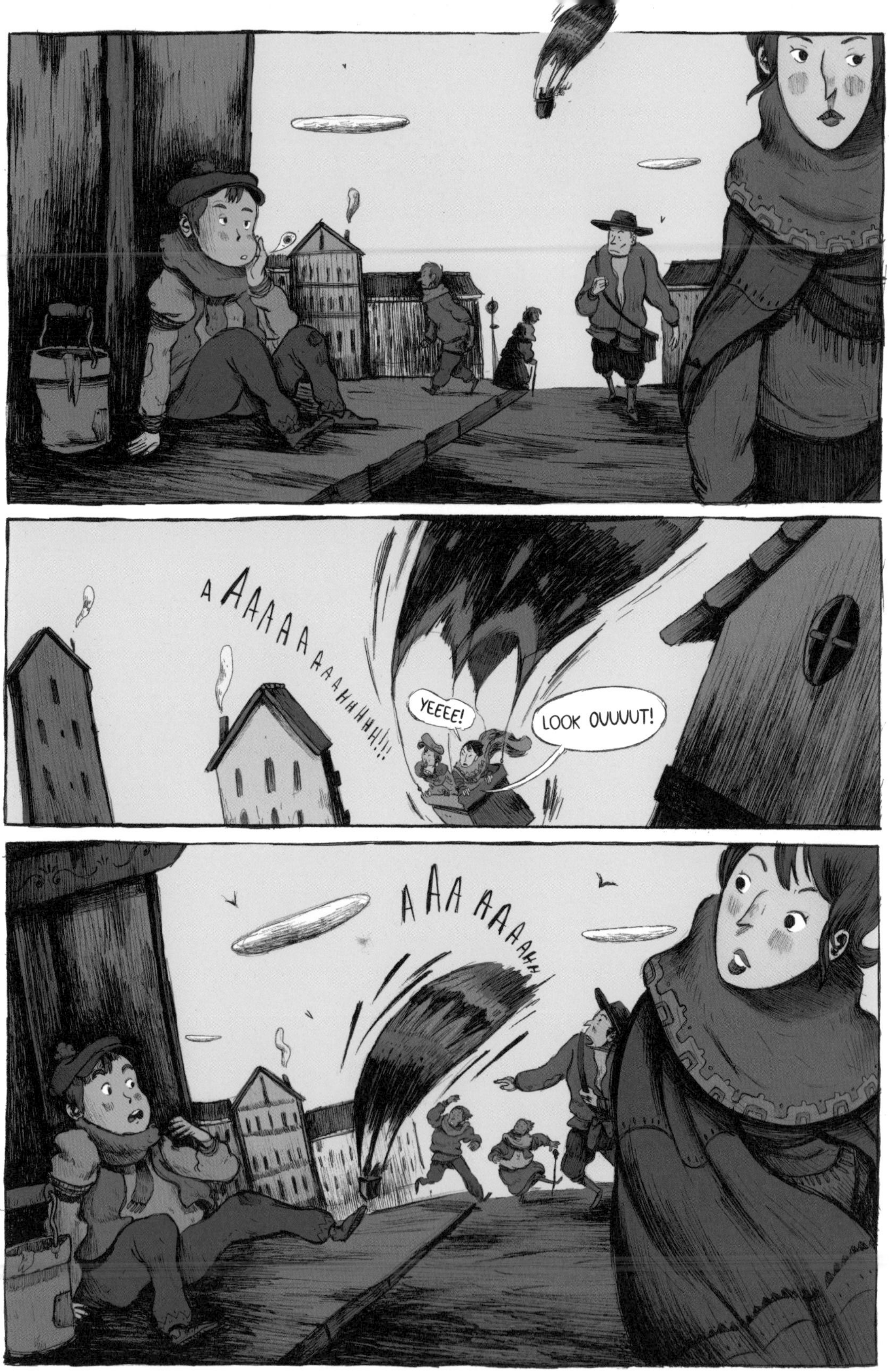
A AAAAAAAAAHHHH!!!!
YEEEE!
LOOK OUUUUT!
AAA AAAAAHH

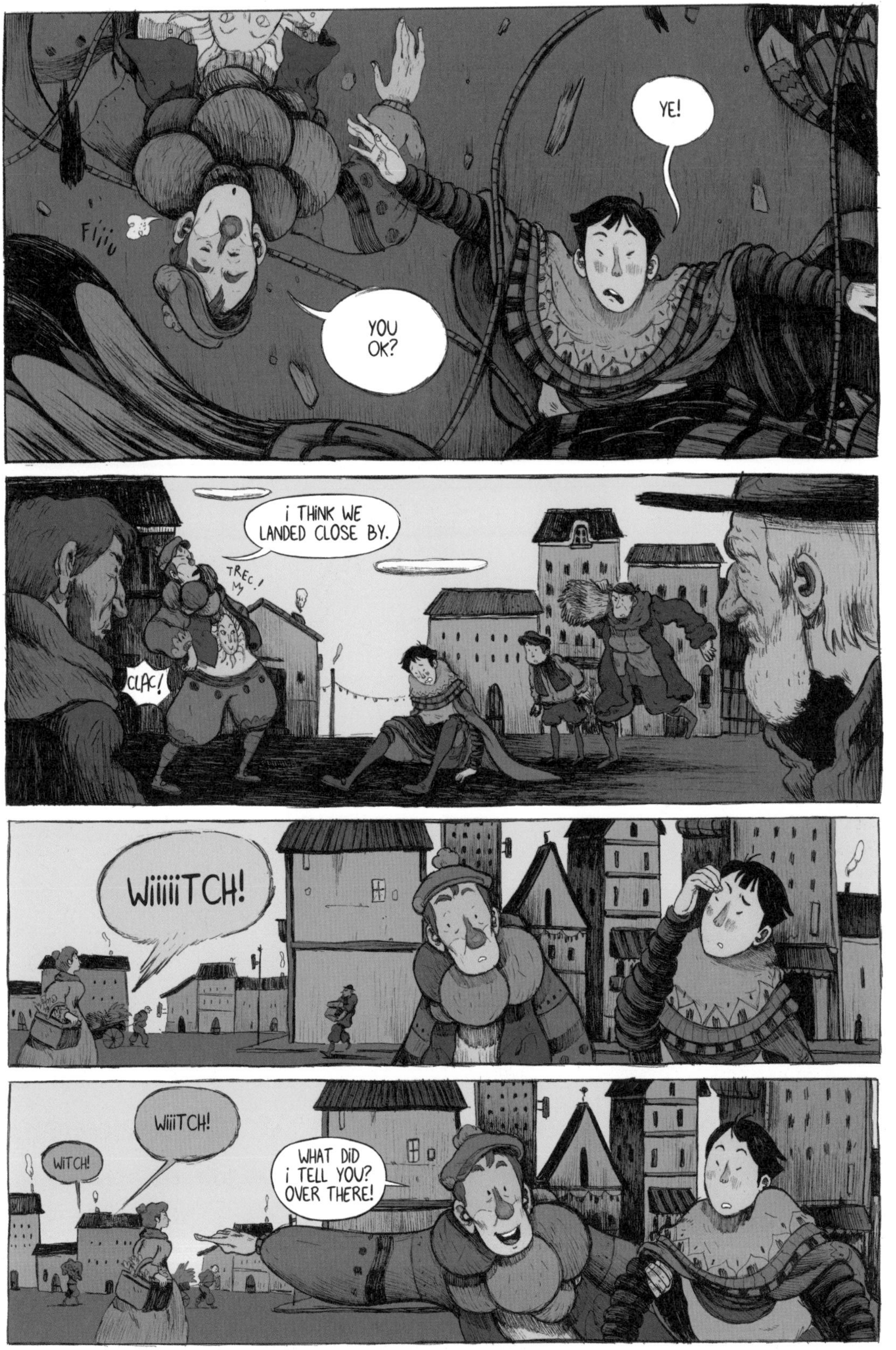
Fiiiu
YOU OK?
YE!
i THINK WE LANDED CLOSE BY.
TREC!
CLAC!
WiiiiiTCH!
WiTCH!
WiiiTCH!
WHAT DID i TELL YOU? OVER THERE!

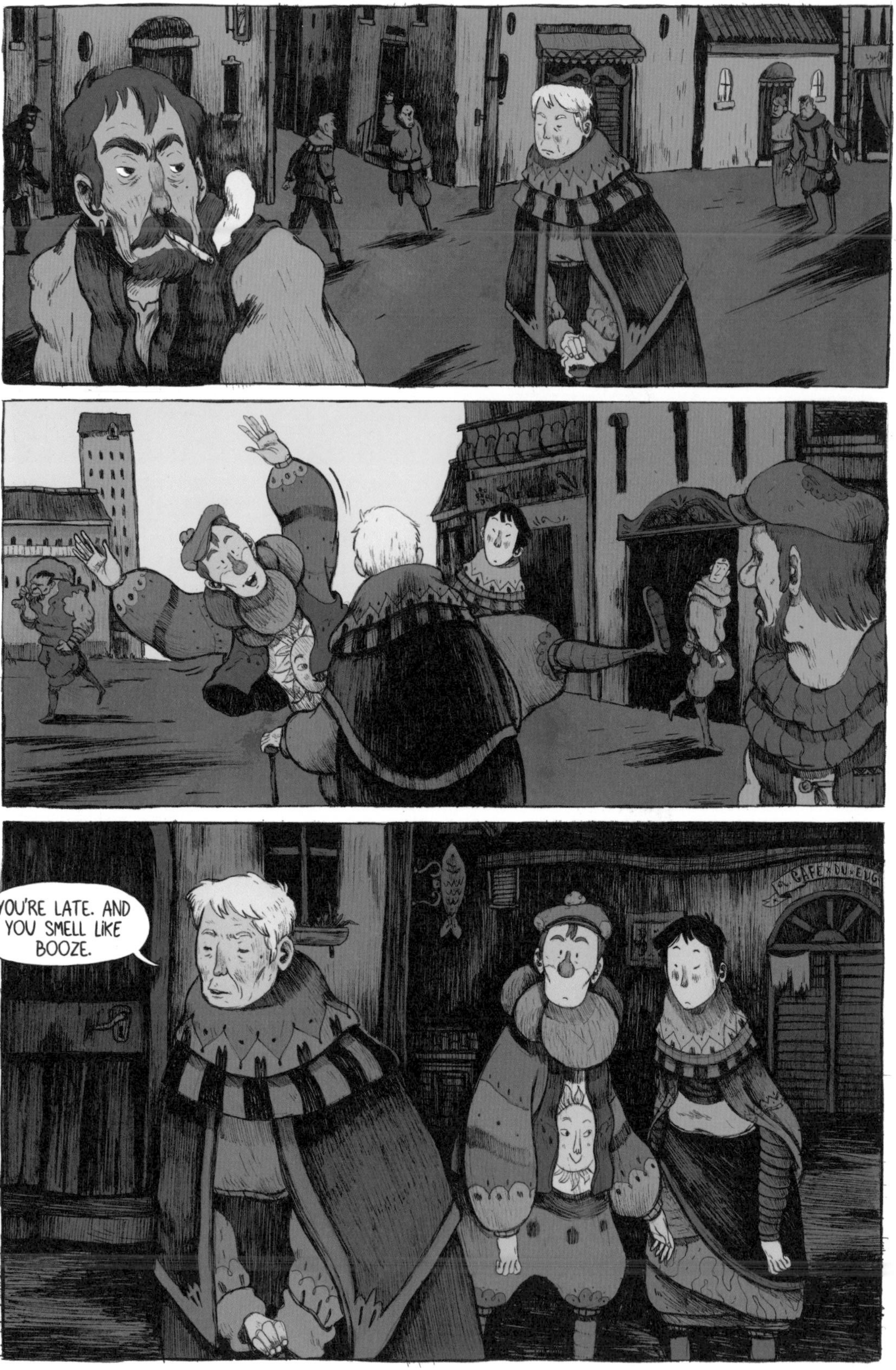
YOU'RE LATE. AND YOU SMELL LIKE BOOZE.

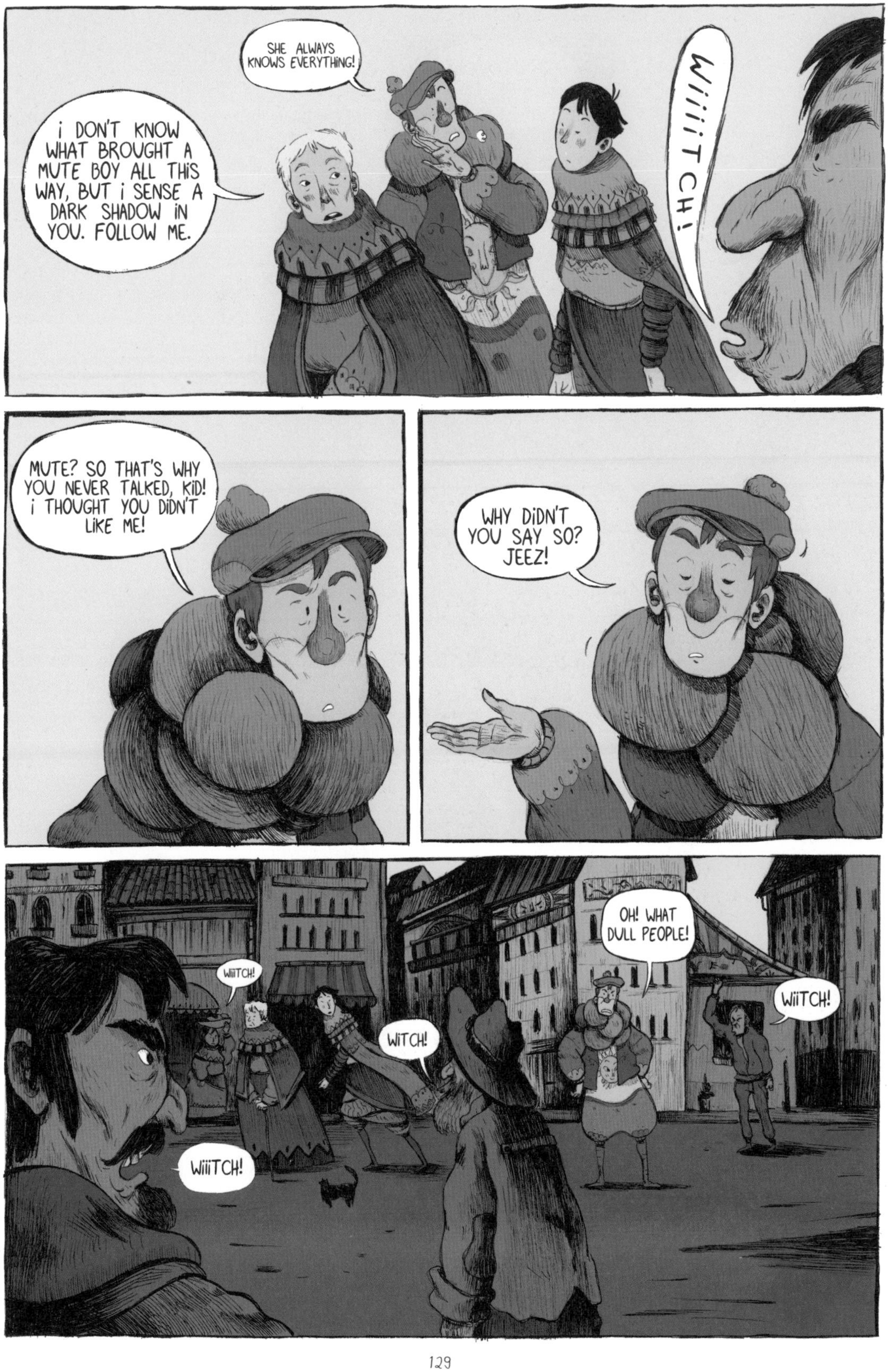
SHE ALWAYS KNOWS EVERYTHING!
I DON'T KNOW WHAT BROUGHT A MUTE BOY ALL THIS WAY, BUT I SENSE A DARK SHADOW IN YOU. FOLLOW ME.
WIIIITCH!
MUTE? SO THAT'S WHY YOU NEVER TALKED, KID! I THOUGHT YOU DIDN'T LIKE ME!
WHY DIDN'T YOU SAY SO? JEEZ!
WIITCH!
WITCH!
WIIITCH!
OH! WHAT DULL PEOPLE!
WIITCH!

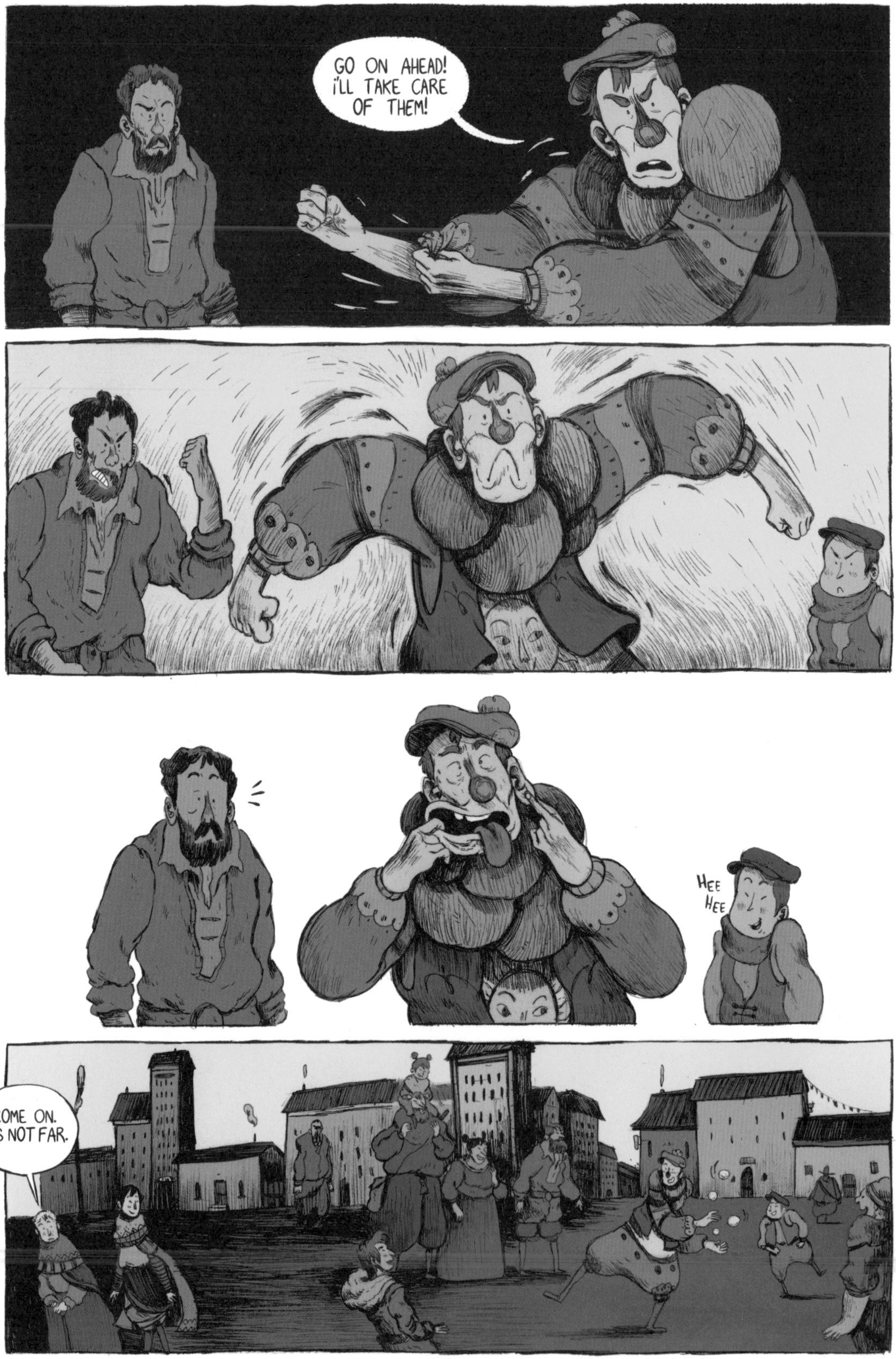
GO ON AHEAD! I'LL TAKE CARE OF THEM!
HEE HEE
COME ON. IT'S NOT FAR.

IT WAS THE WAR THAT MADE THEM THAT WAY. THEY USED TO LIKE ME. THEY'D COME TO MY HOUSE, ASK ME FOR ADVICE, FOR CURES. I TOOK CARE OF THEM.

THE WAR IS OVER, BUT THEY'RE STILL RILED UP. THEY NEED TO VENT THEIR ANGER AT SOMEBODY.

I SEE THE WAR AFFECTED YOU TOO.

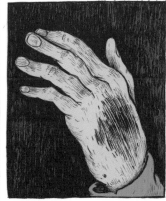

COME ON, THIS IS IT.

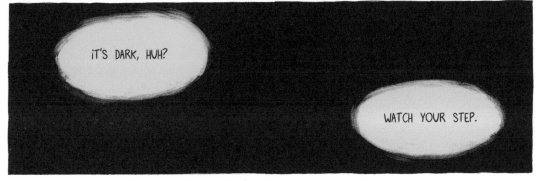

IT'S DARK, HUH?

WATCH YOUR STEP.

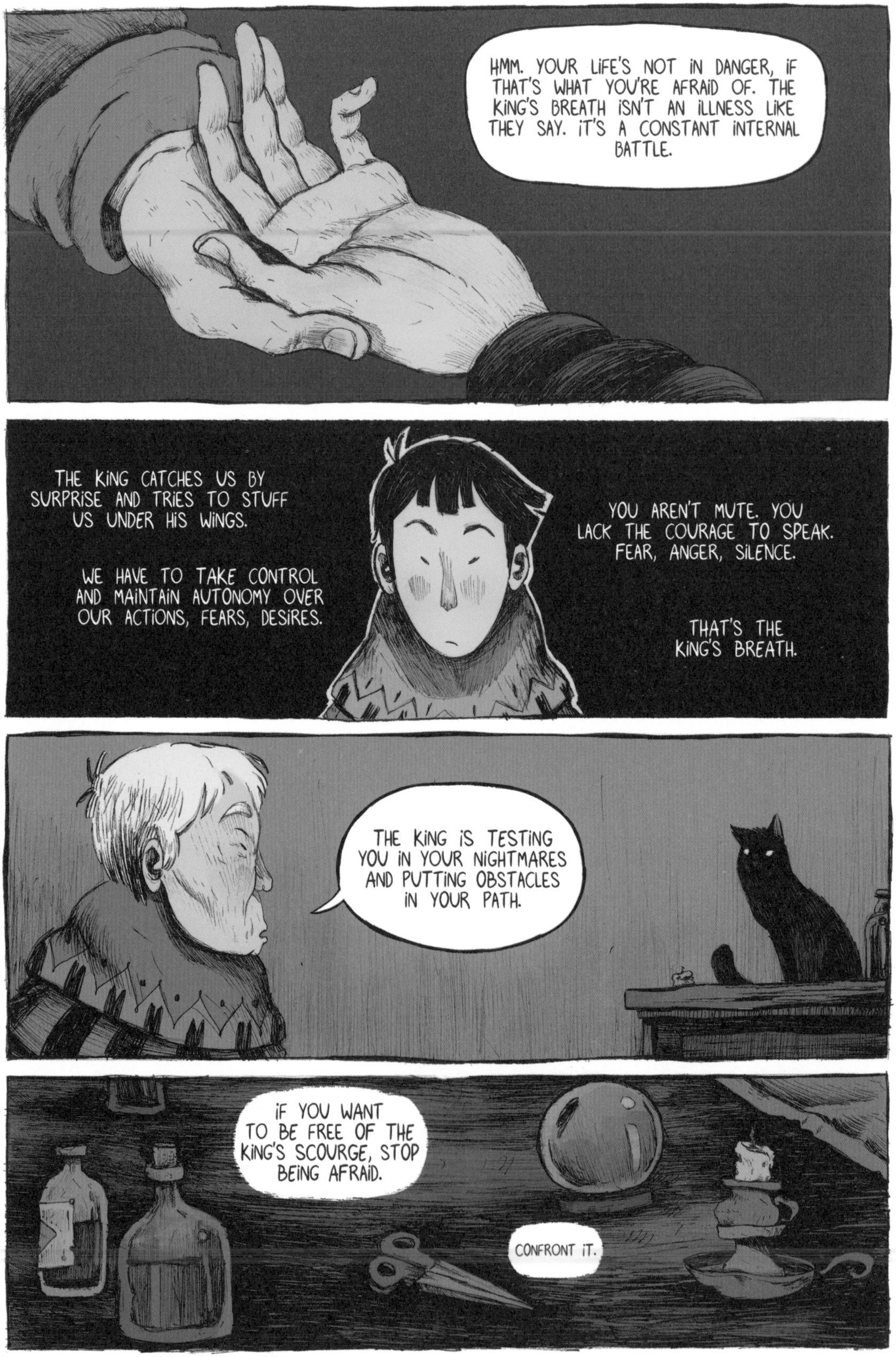
HMM. YOUR LIFE'S NOT IN DANGER, IF THAT'S WHAT YOU'RE AFRAID OF. THE KING'S BREATH ISN'T AN ILLNESS LIKE THEY SAY. IT'S A CONSTANT INTERNAL BATTLE.
THE KING CATCHES US BY SURPRISE AND TRIES TO STUFF US UNDER HIS WINGS.
WE HAVE TO TAKE CONTROL AND MAINTAIN AUTONOMY OVER OUR ACTIONS, FEARS, DESIRES.
YOU AREN'T MUTE. YOU LACK THE COURAGE TO SPEAK. FEAR, ANGER, SILENCE.
THAT'S THE KING'S BREATH.
THE KING IS TESTING YOU IN YOUR NIGHTMARES AND PUTTING OBSTACLES IN YOUR PATH.
IF YOU WANT TO BE FREE OF THE KING'S SCOURGE, STOP BEING AFRAID.
CONFRONT IT.

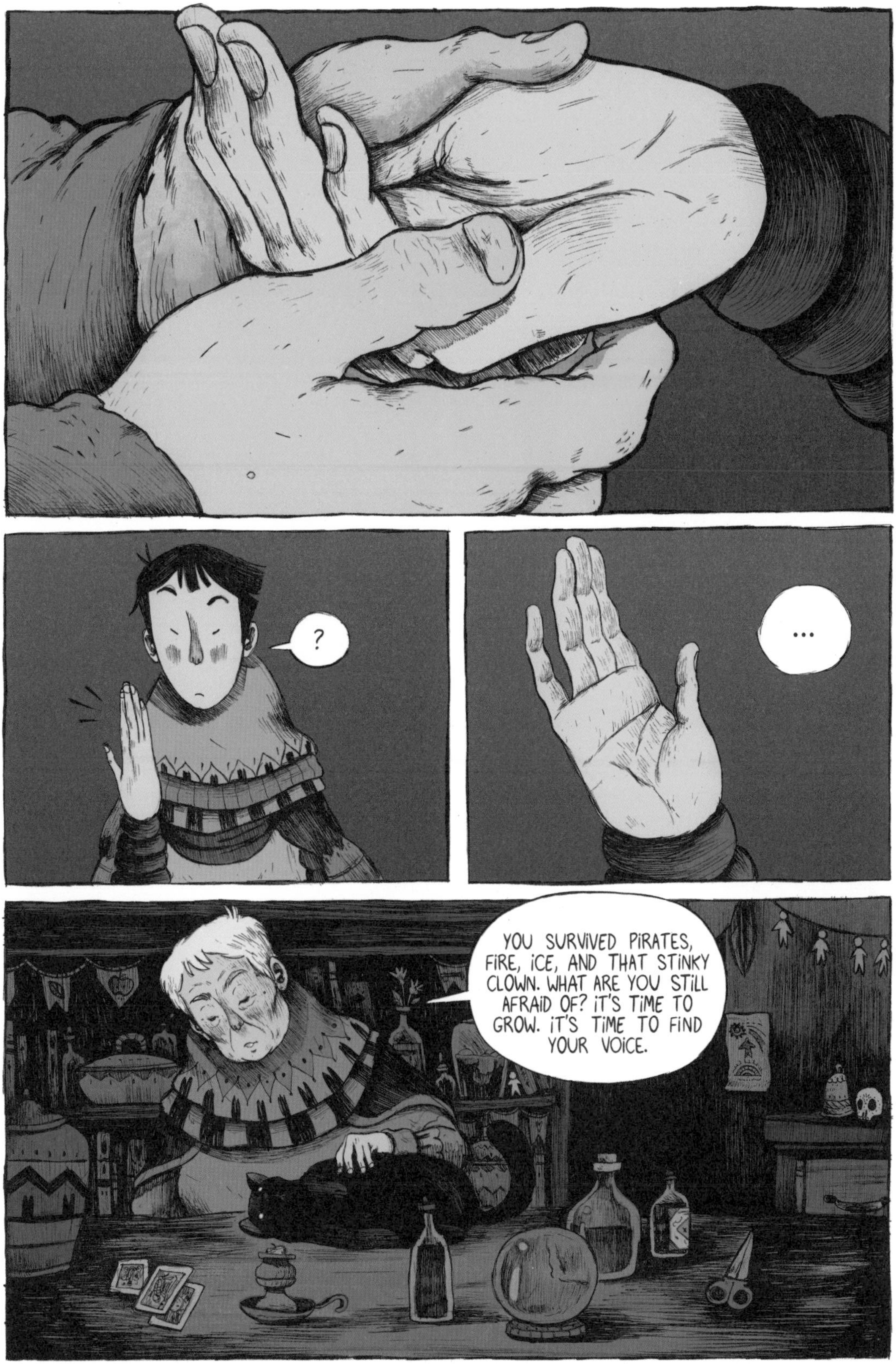
?
...
YOU SURVIVED PIRATES, FIRE, ICE, AND THAT STINKY CLOWN. WHAT ARE YOU STILL AFRAID OF? IT'S TIME TO GROW. IT'S TIME TO FIND YOUR VOICE.

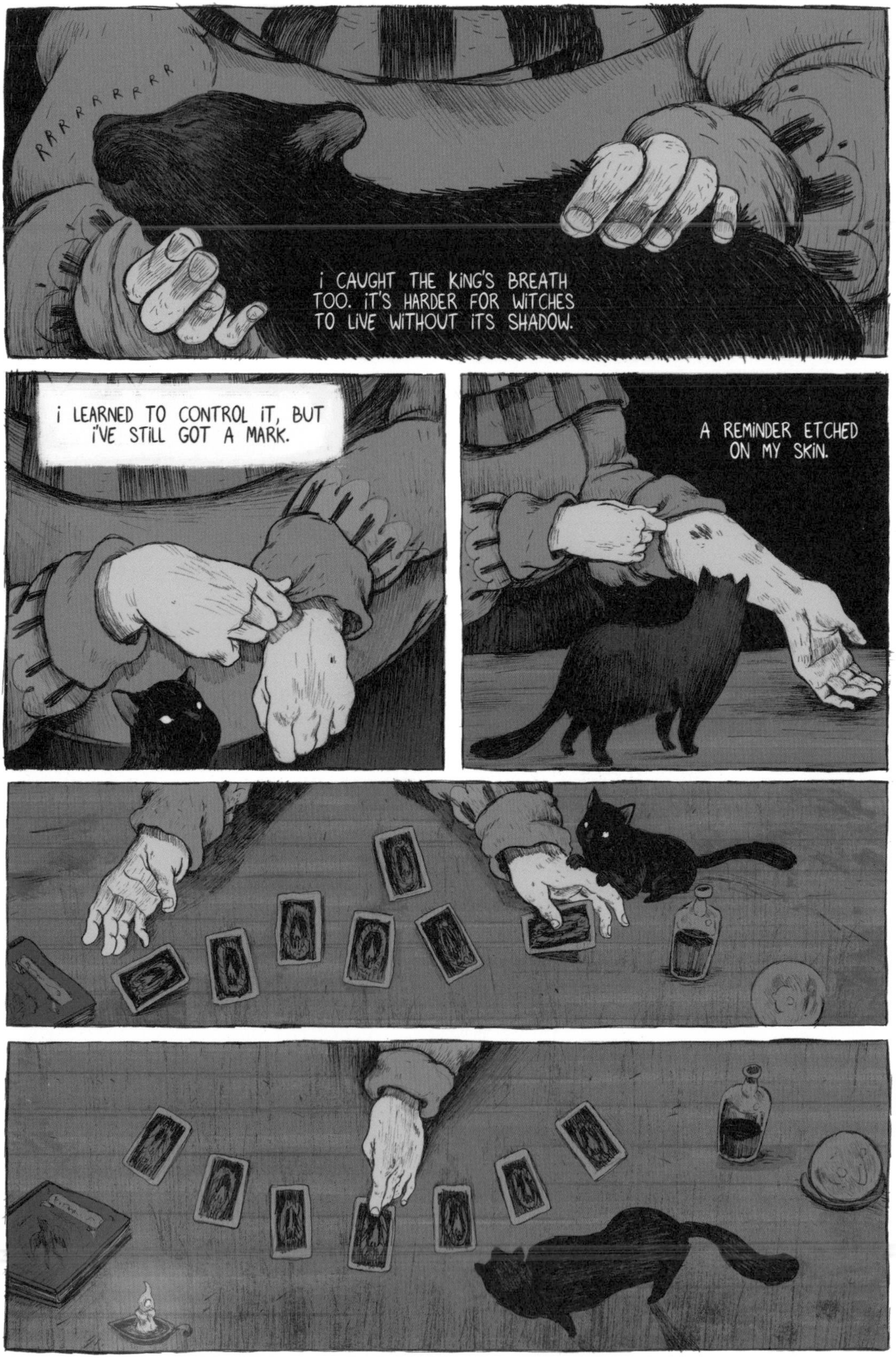
RRRRRRRRR
I CAUGHT THE KING'S BREATH TOO. IT'S HARDER FOR WITCHES TO LIVE WITHOUT ITS SHADOW.
I LEARNED TO CONTROL IT, BUT I'VE STILL GOT A MARK.
A REMINDER ETCHED ON MY SKIN.

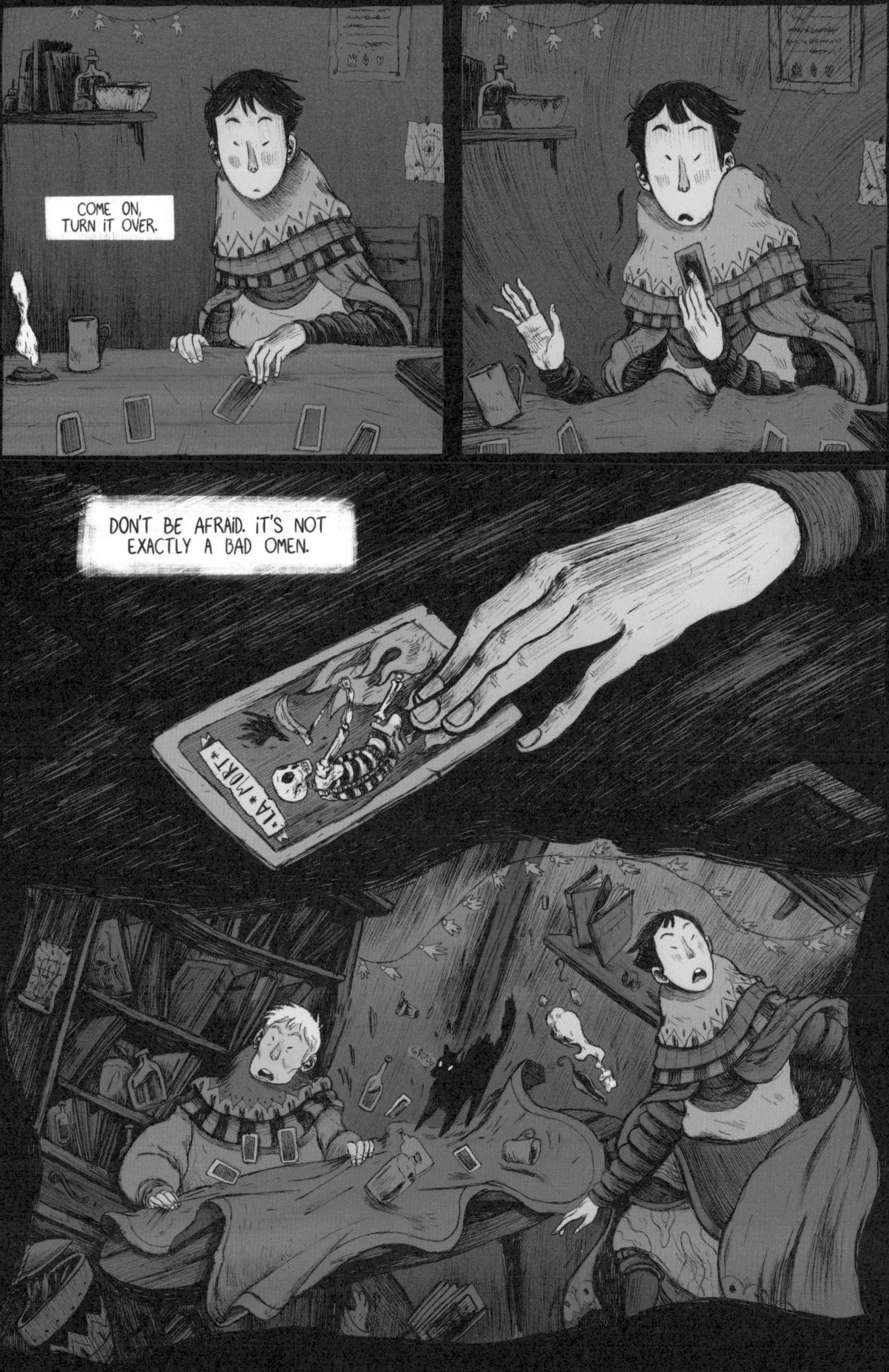
COME ON,
TURN IT OVER.
DON'T BE AFRAID. IT'S NOT
EXACTLY A BAD OMEN.
*LA*MORT*

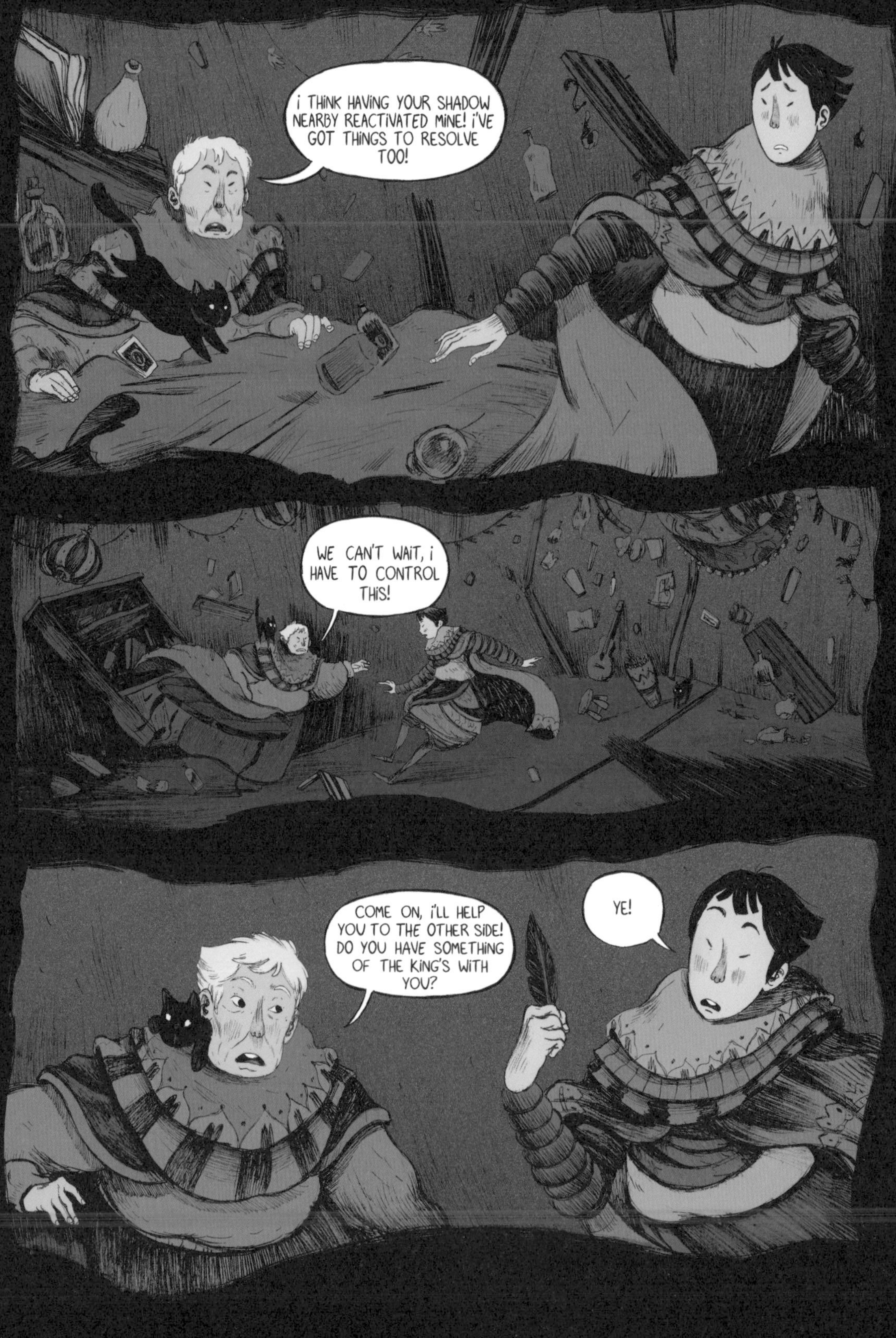
I THINK HAVING YOUR SHADOW NEARBY REACTIVATED MINE! I'VE GOT THINGS TO RESOLVE TOO!
WE CAN'T WAIT, I HAVE TO CONTROL THIS!
COME ON, I'LL HELP YOU TO THE OTHER SIDE! DO YOU HAVE SOMETHING OF THE KING'S WITH YOU?
YE!

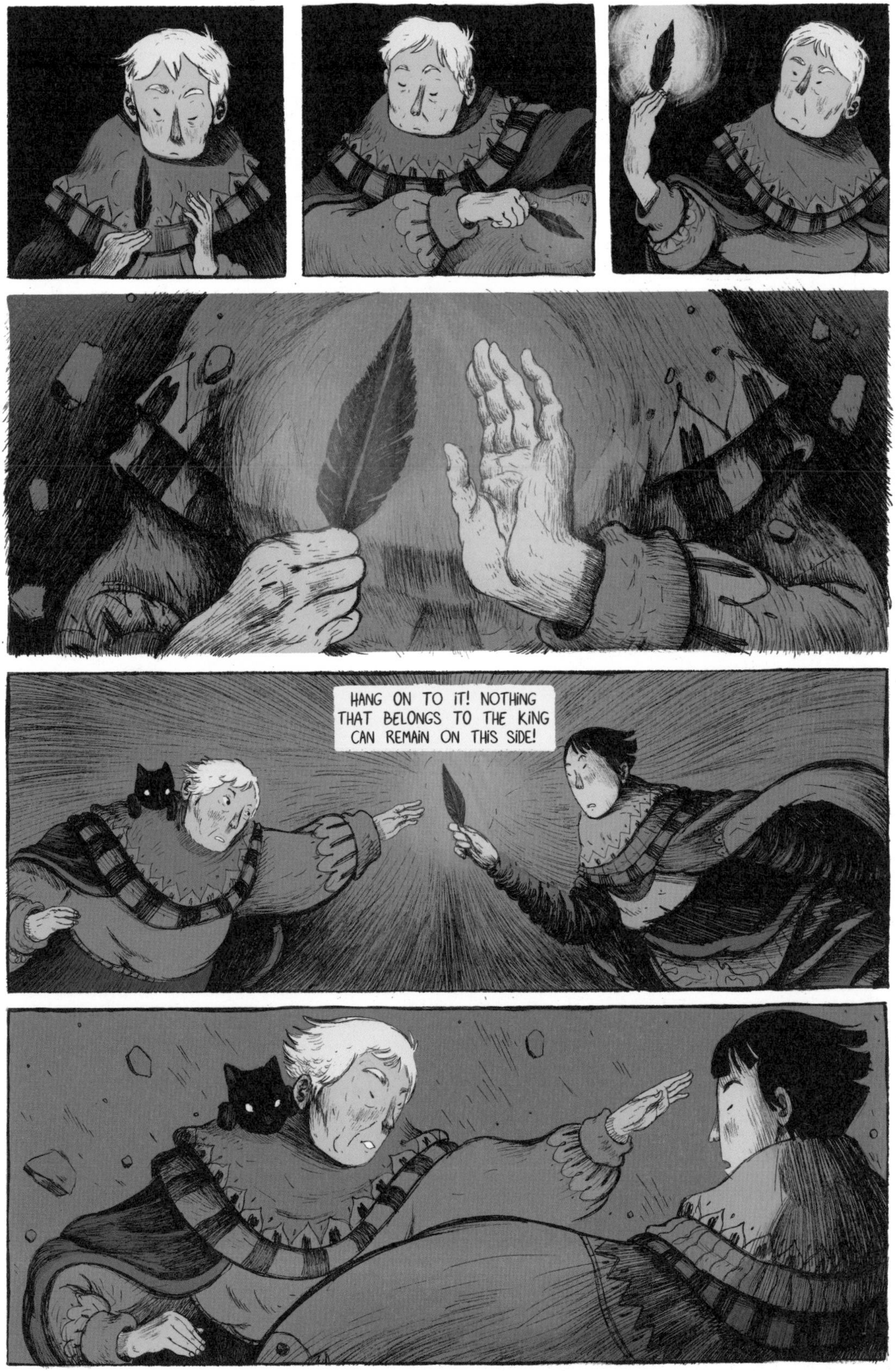
HANG ON TO iT! NOTHiNG THAT BELONGS TO THE KiNG CAN REMAiN ON THIS SiDE!

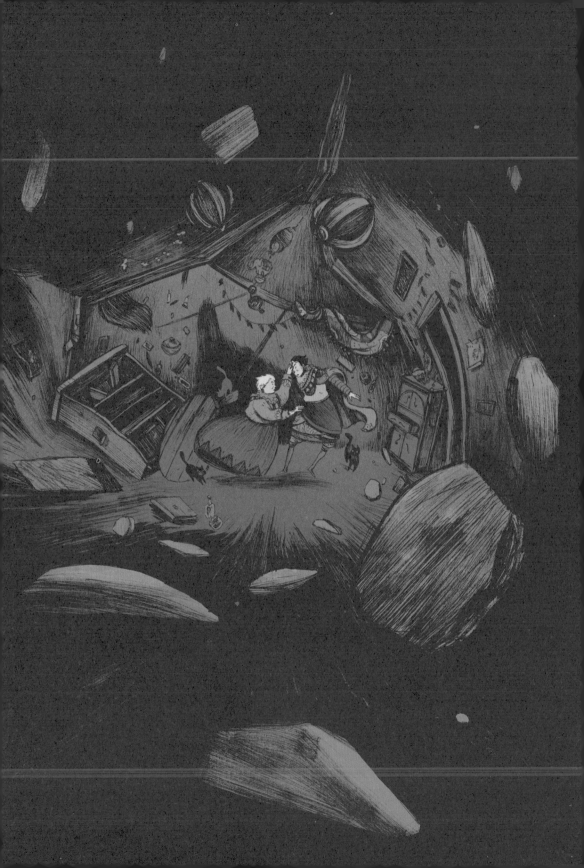

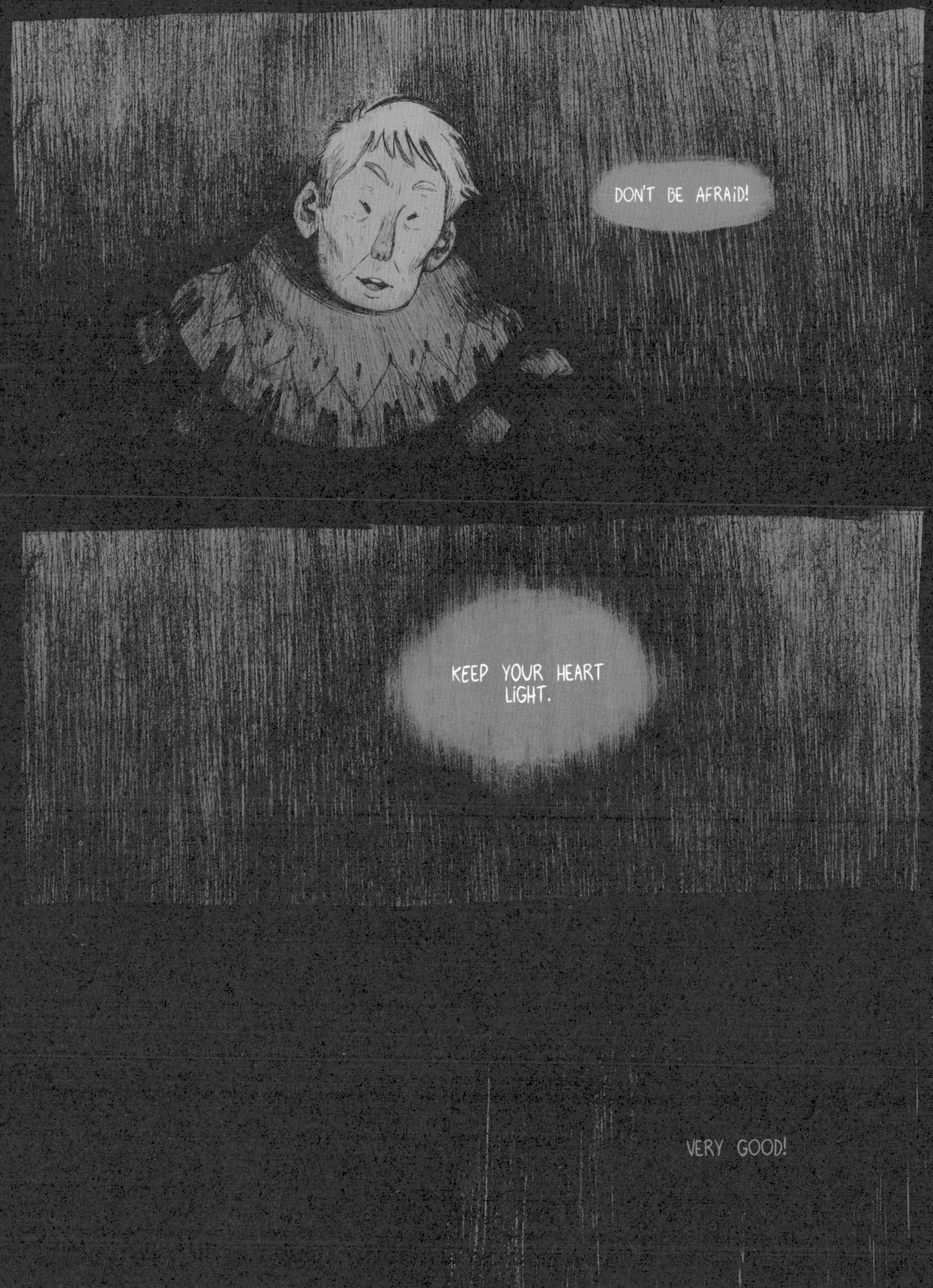
DON'T BE AFRAID!
KEEP YOUR HEART LIGHT.
VERY GOOD!

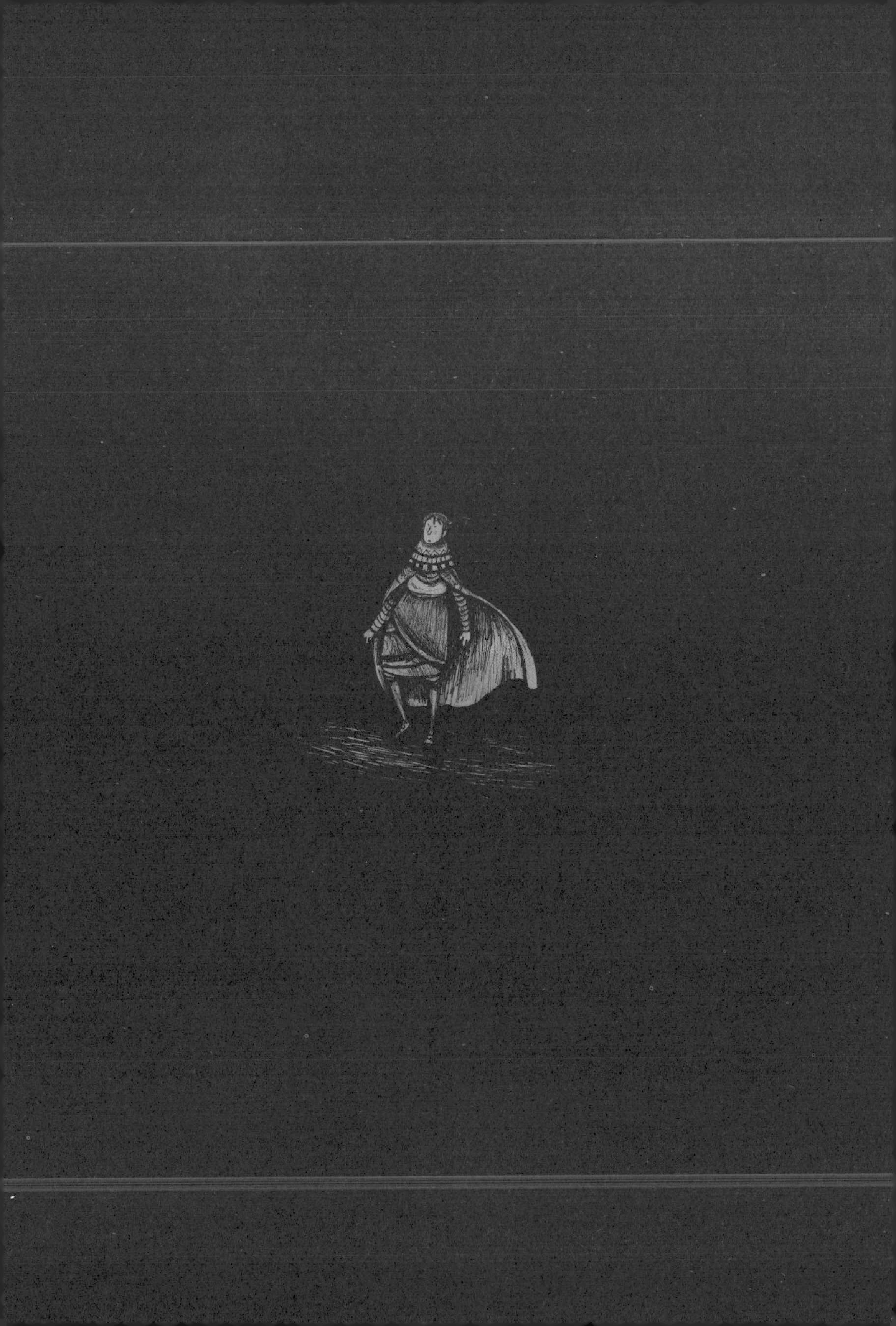

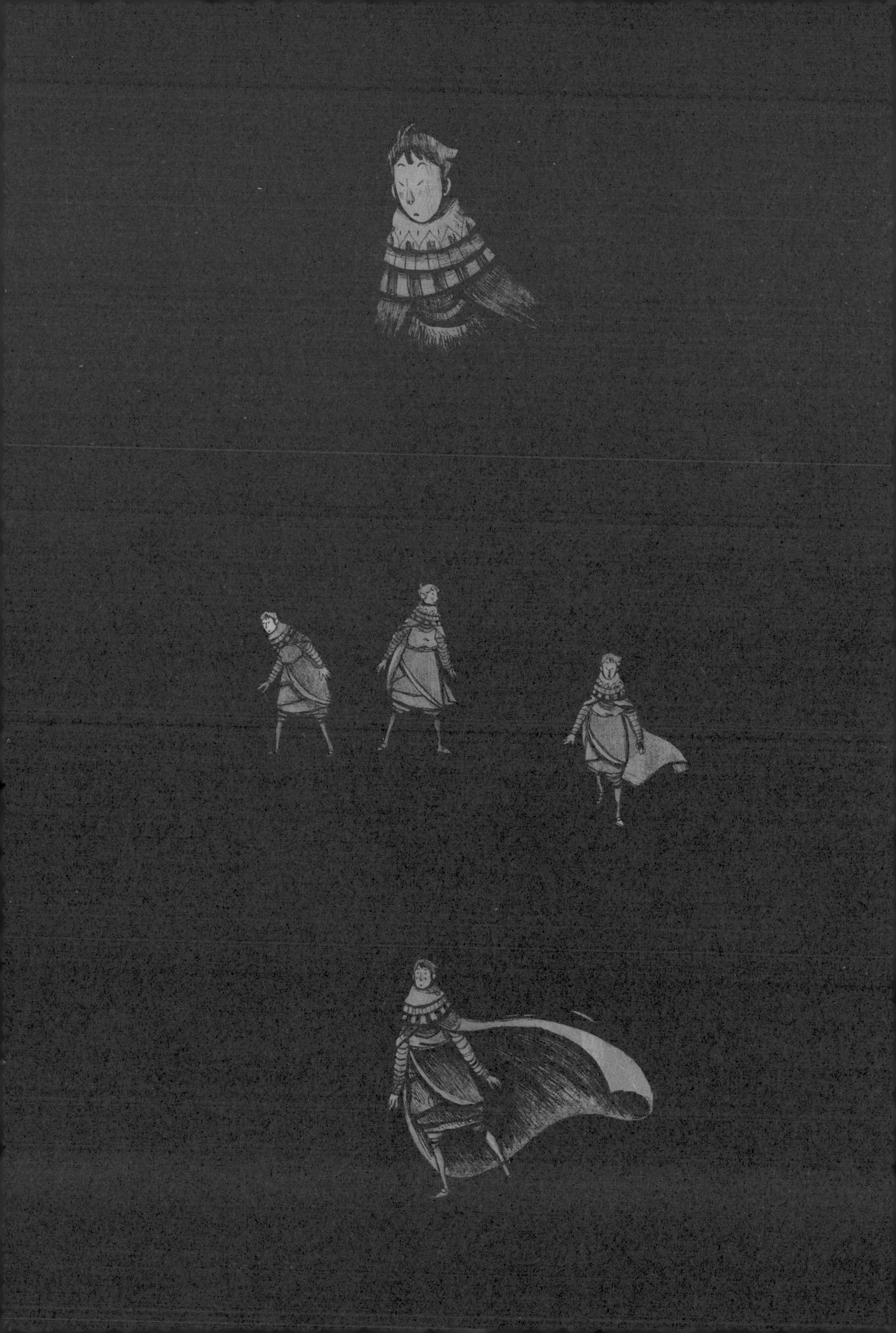

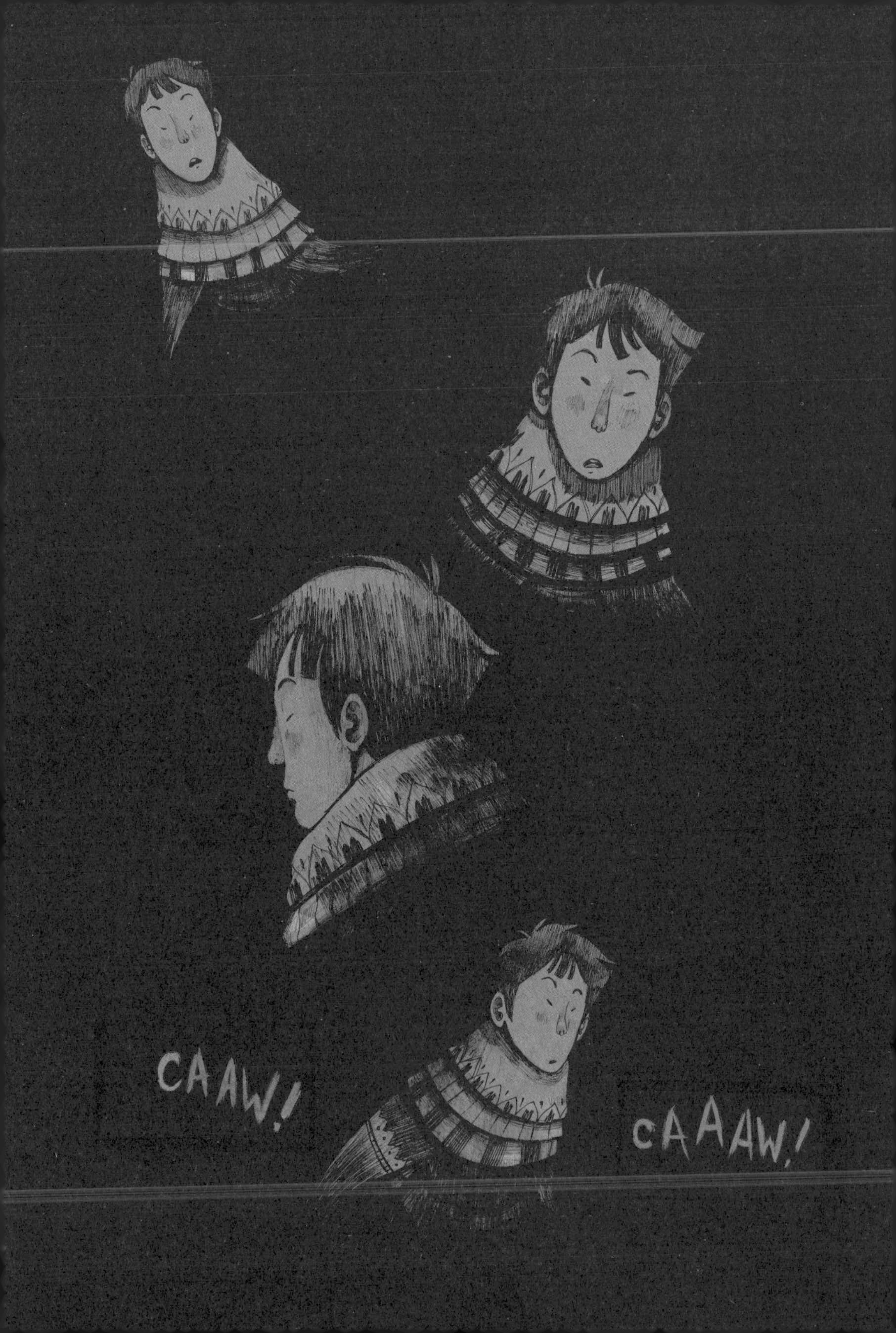
CAAW!
CAAAW!

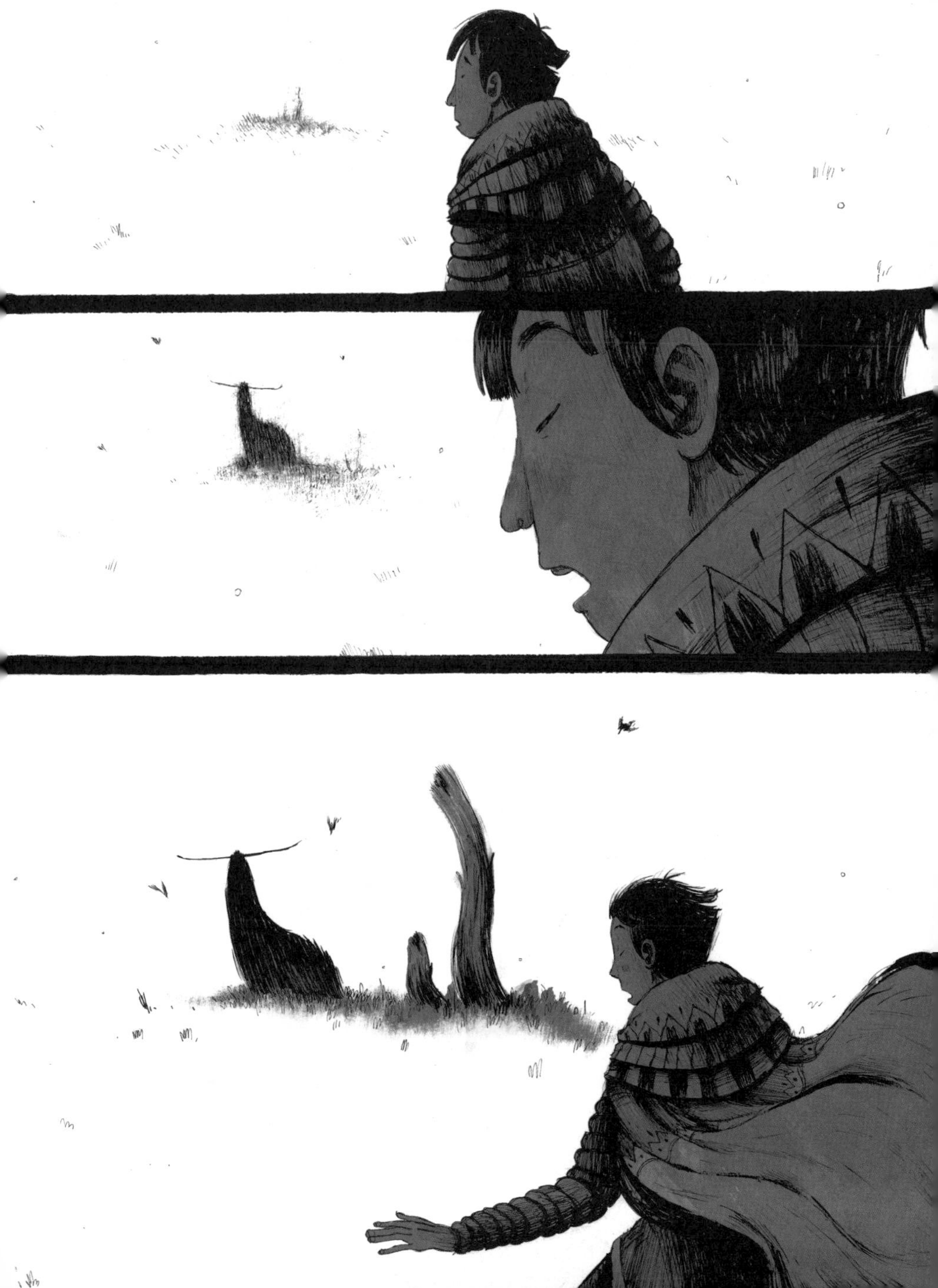

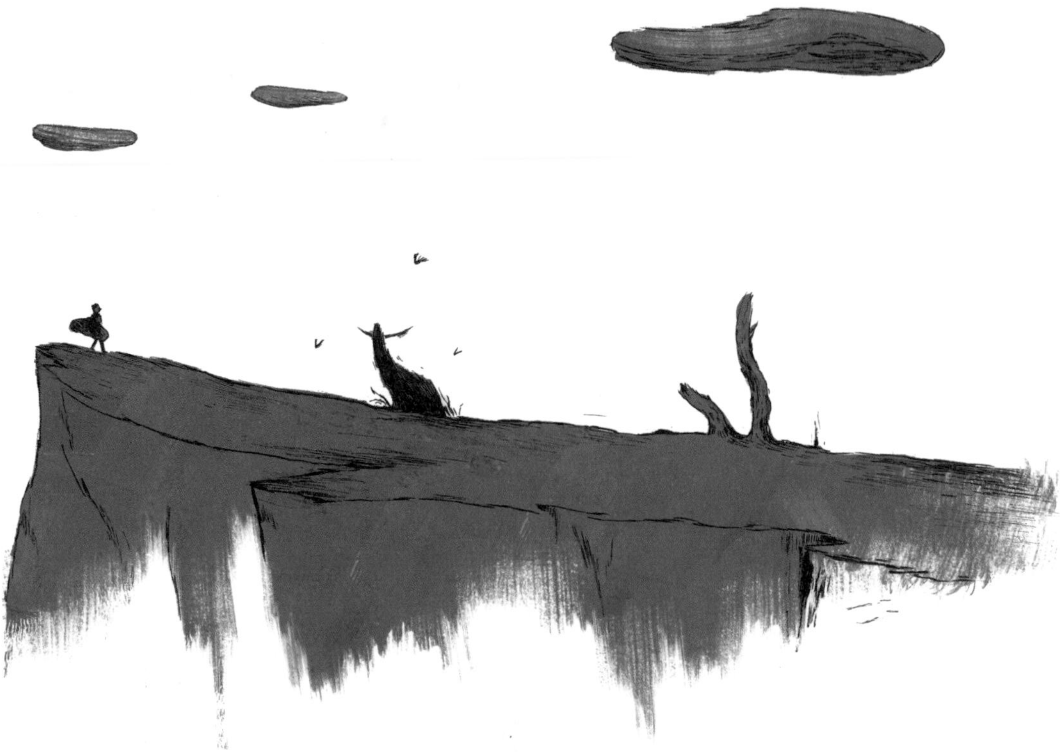

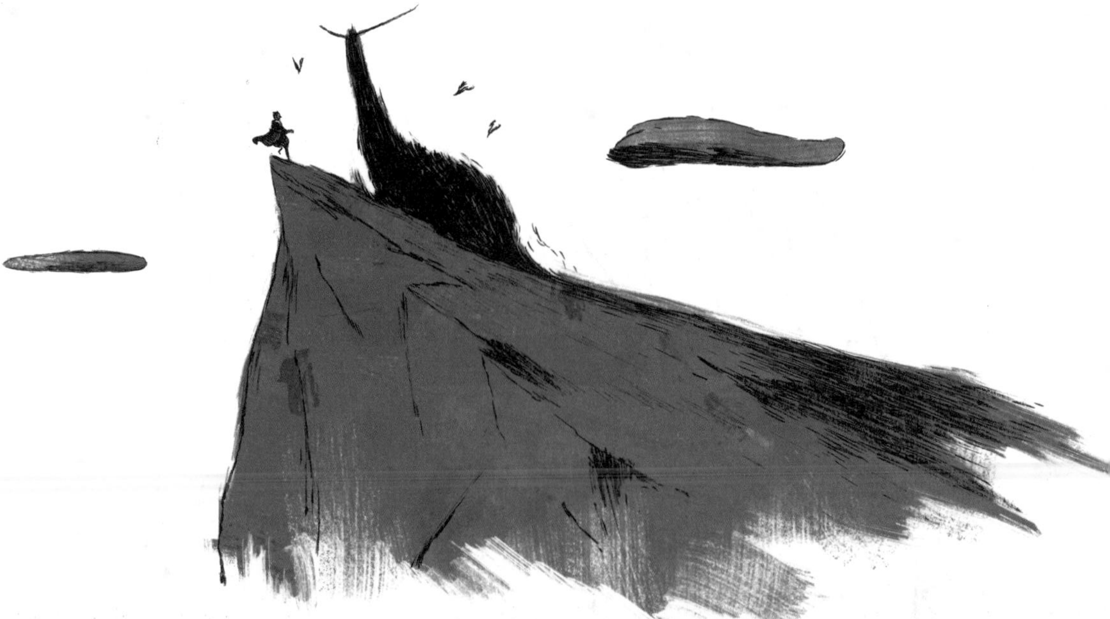

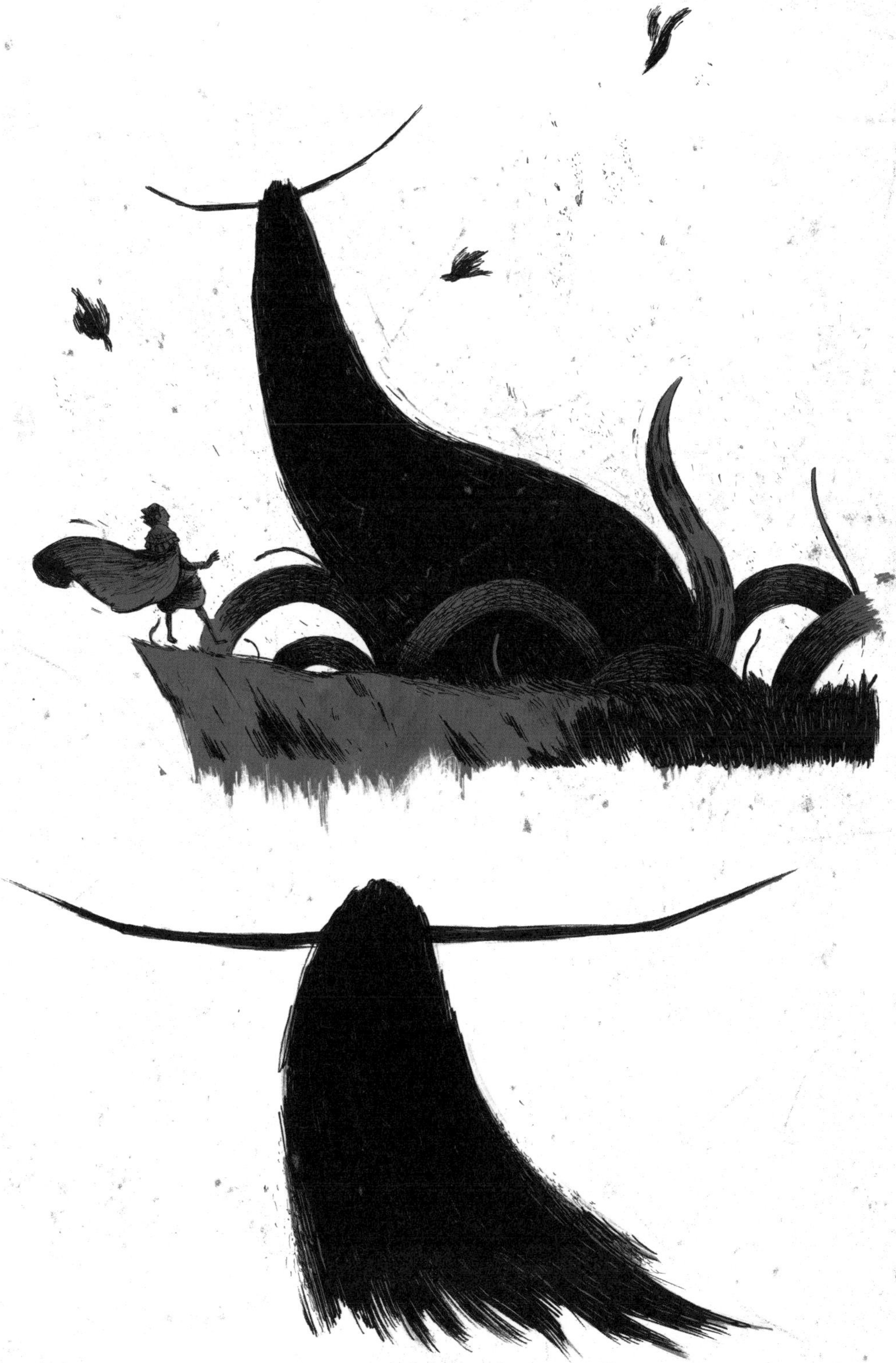

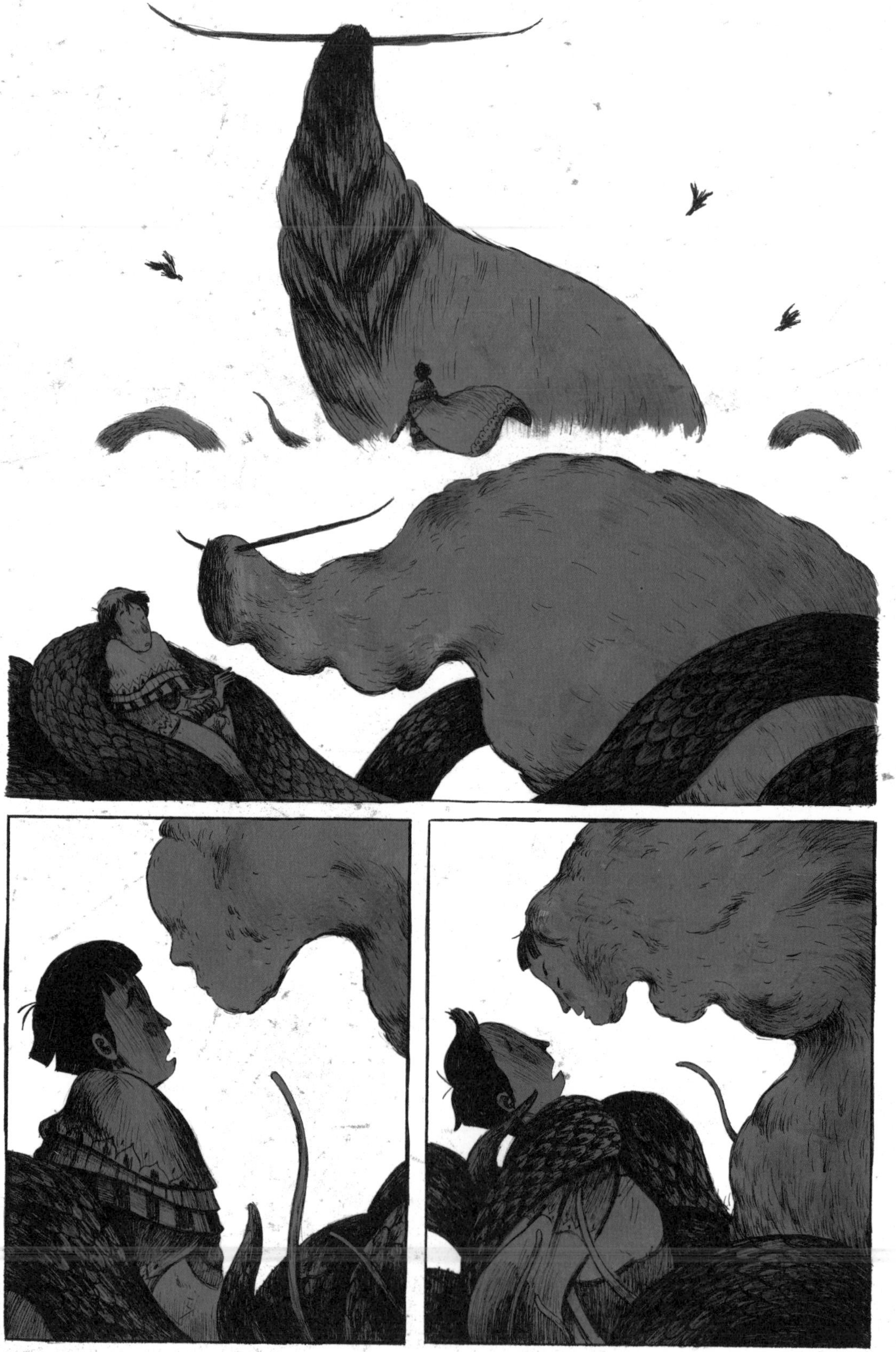

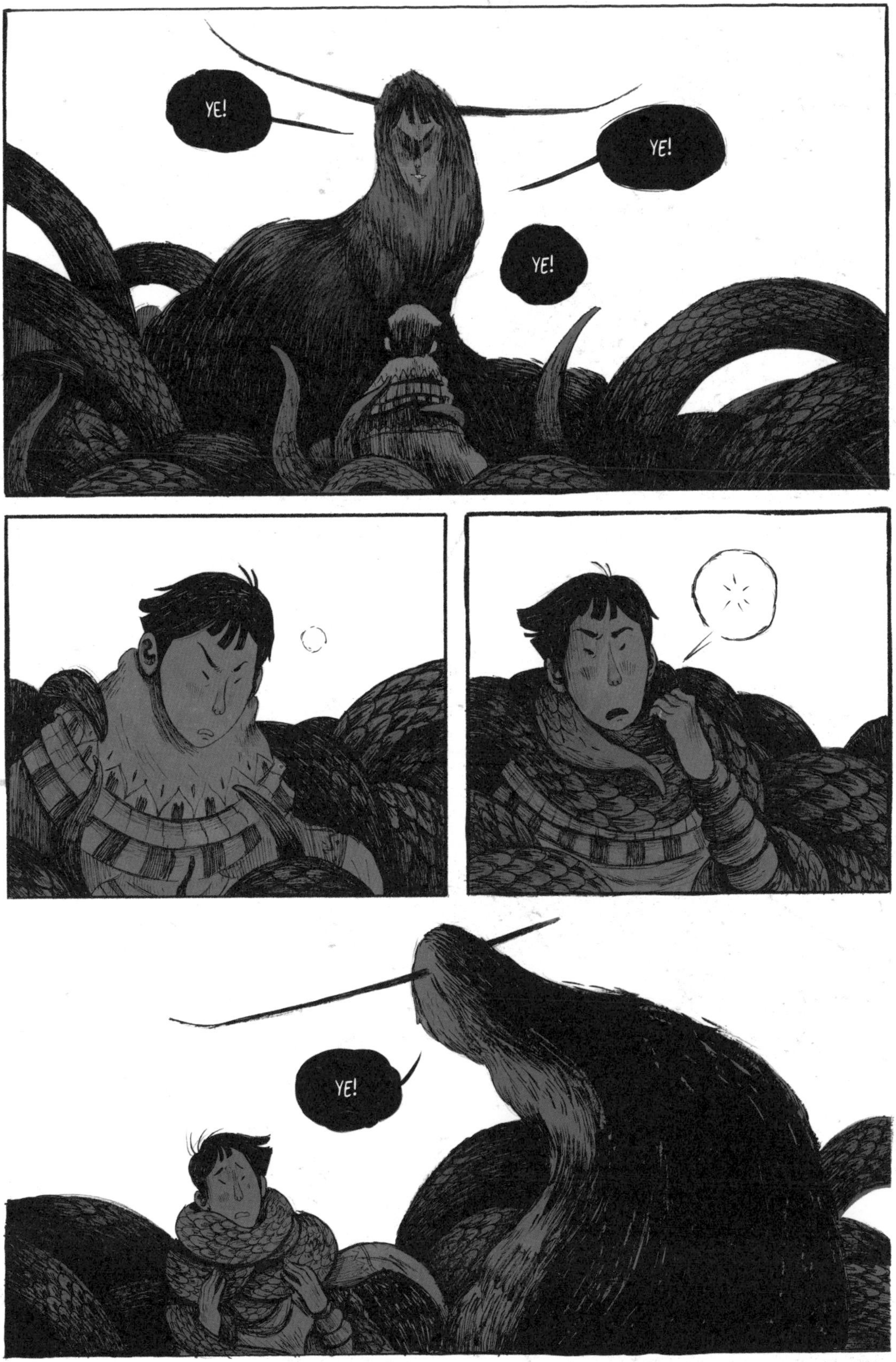
YE!
YE!
YE!
YE!

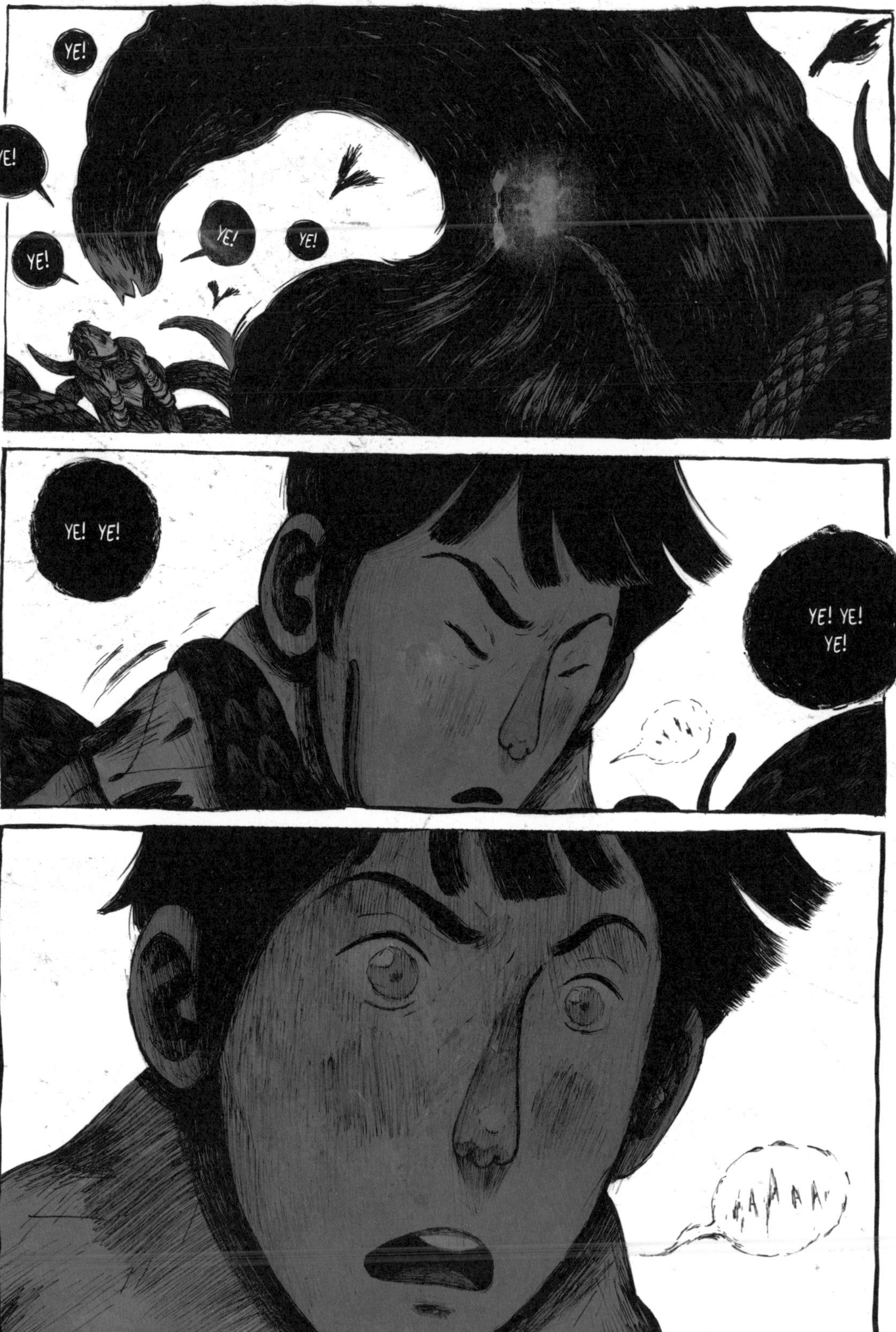
YE!
YE!
YE!
YE!
YE!
YE! YE!
YE! YE!
YE!

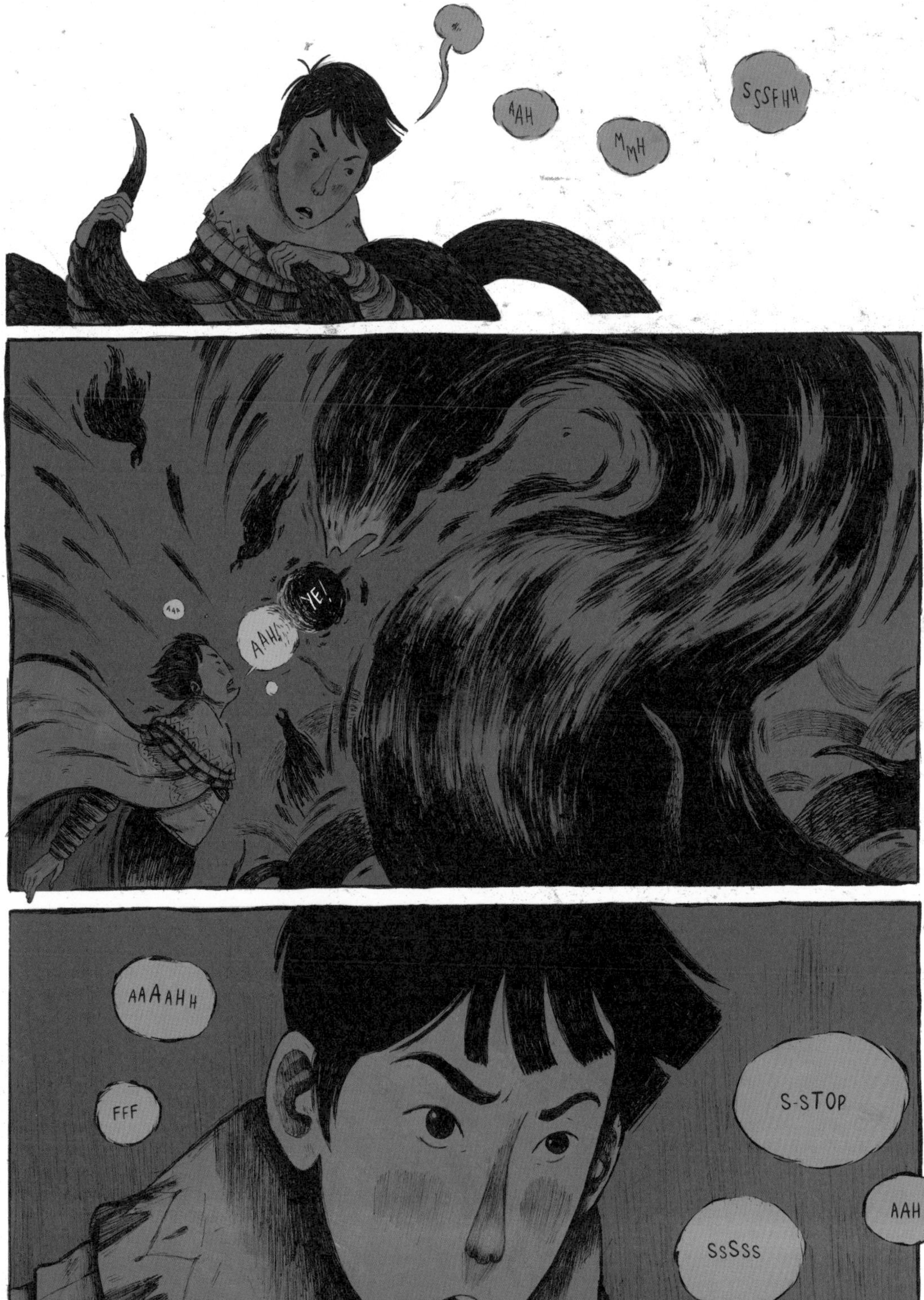
AAH
MMH
SSSFHH
AAH!
YE!
AAAAHH
FFF
S-STOP
SsSSS
AAH

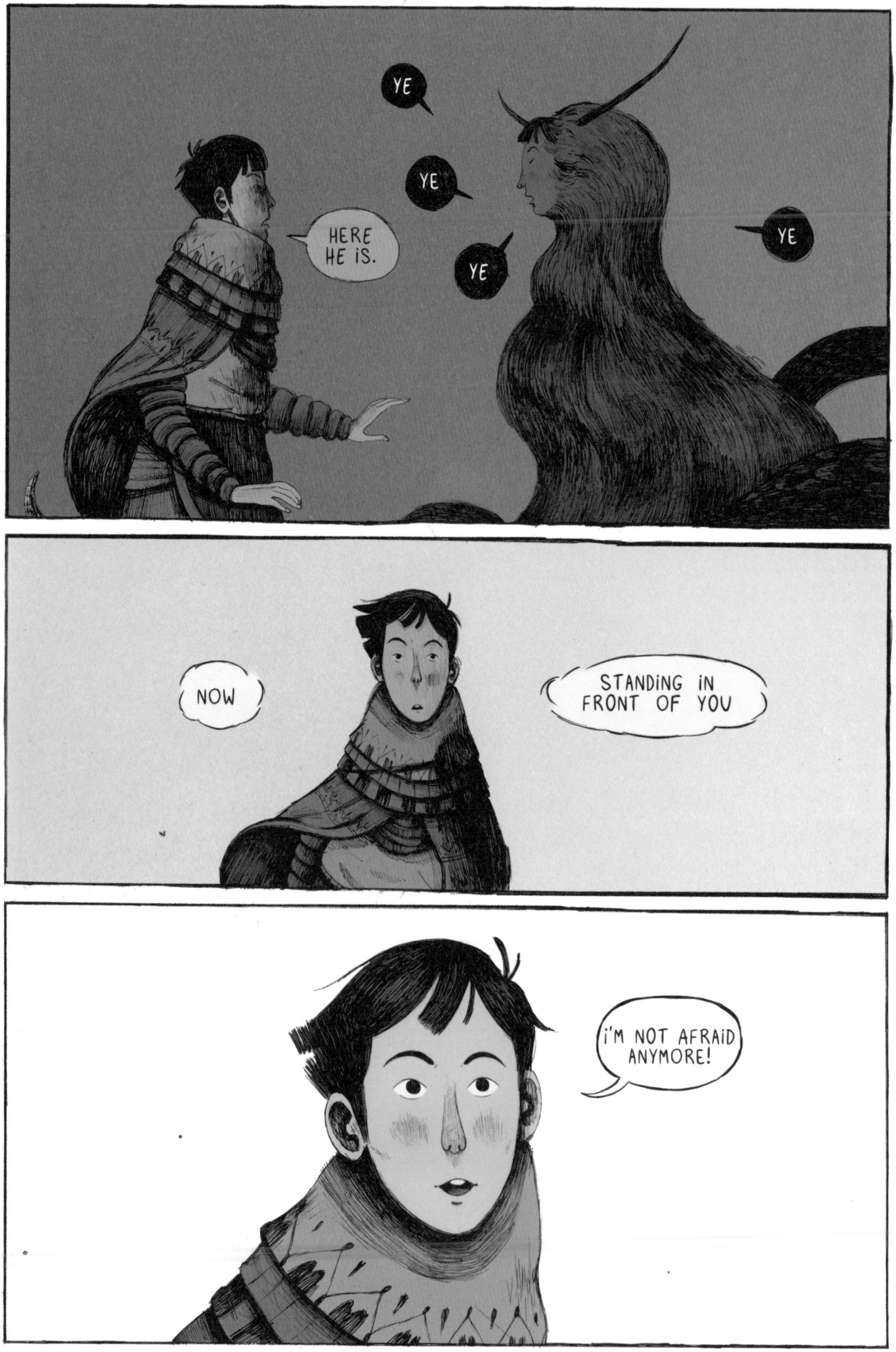
YE
YE
HERE HE IS.
YE
YE
NOW
STANDING IN FRONT OF YOU
i'M NOT AFRAID ANYMORE!

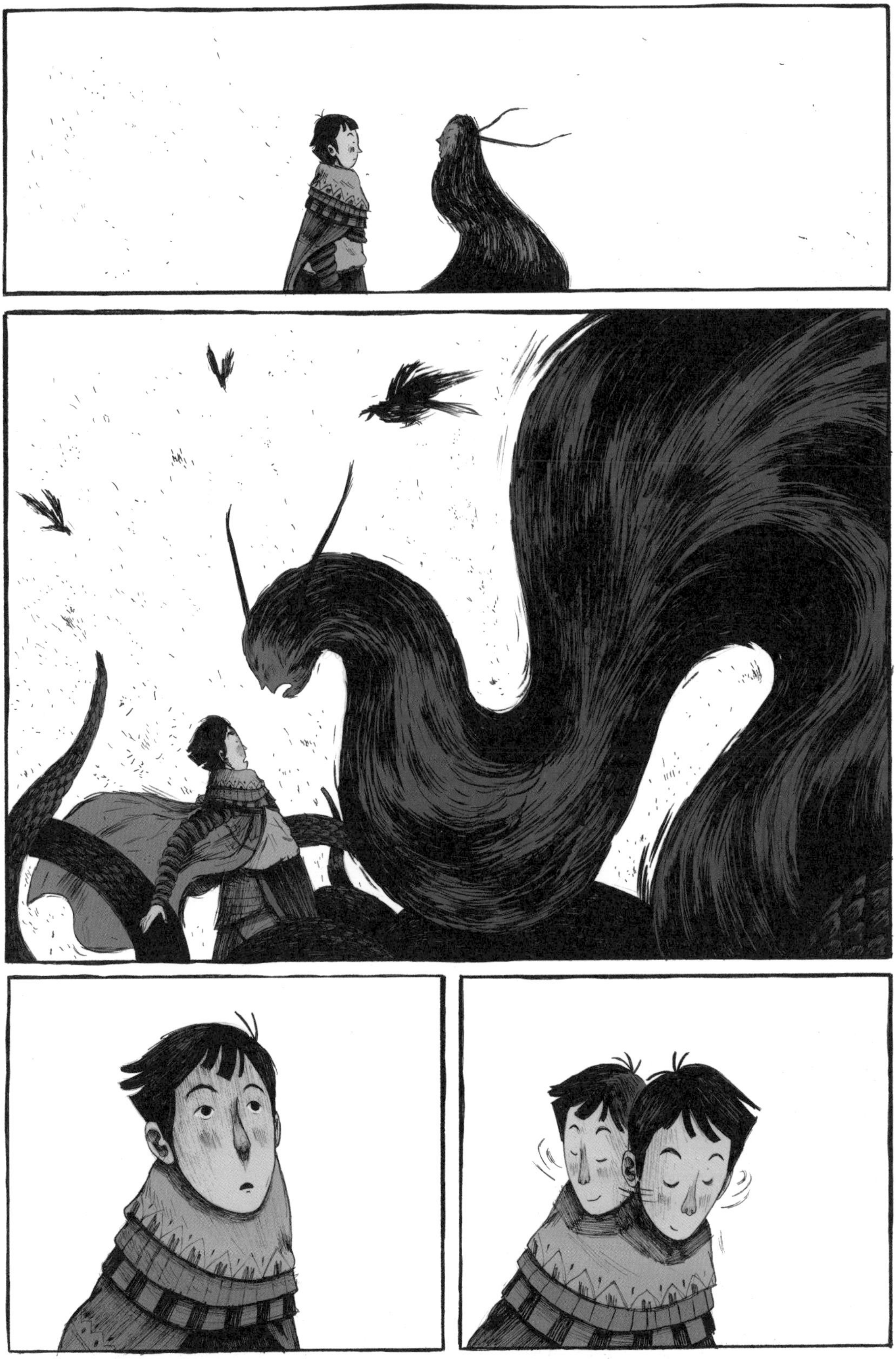

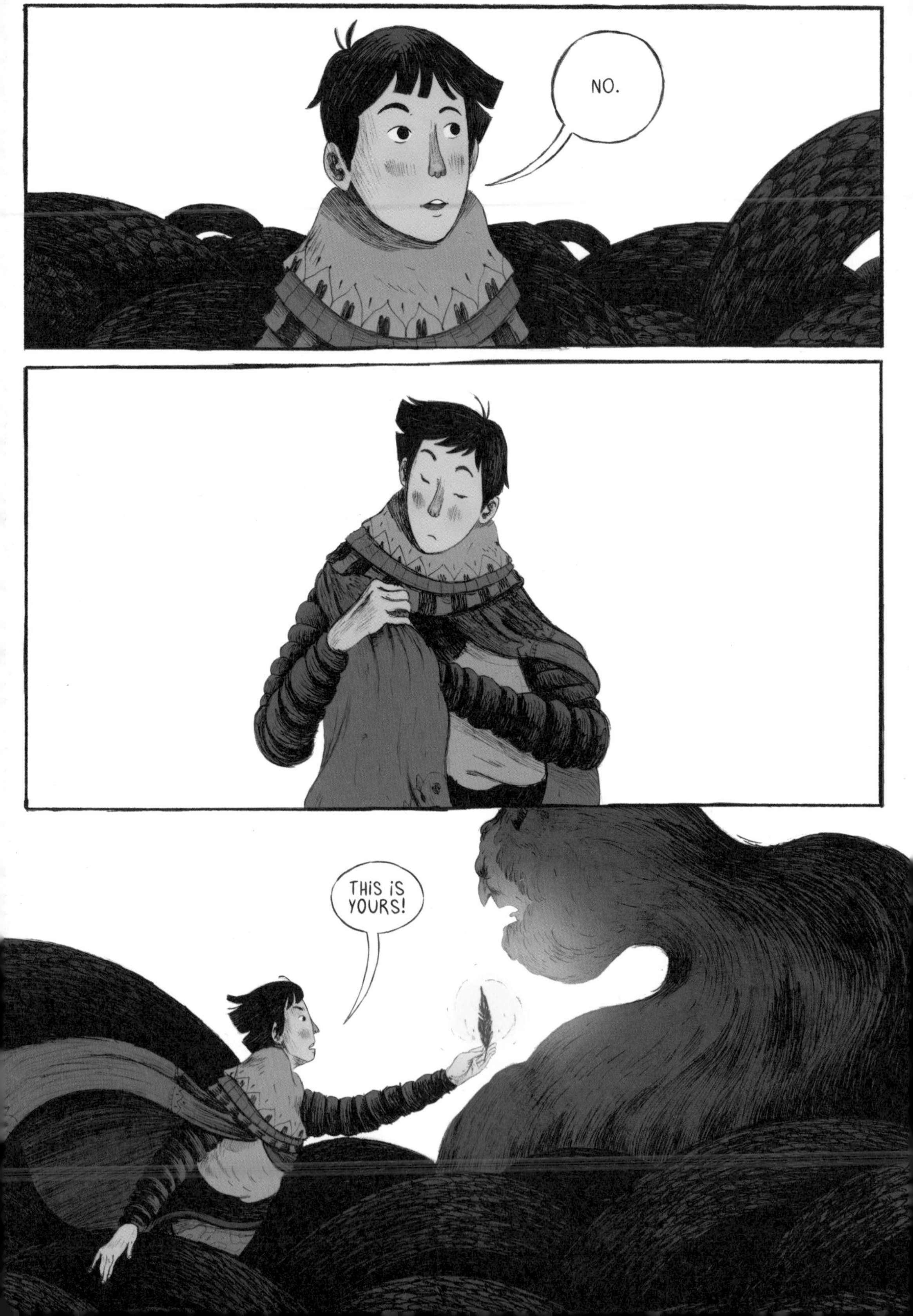
NO.
THIS IS YOURS!

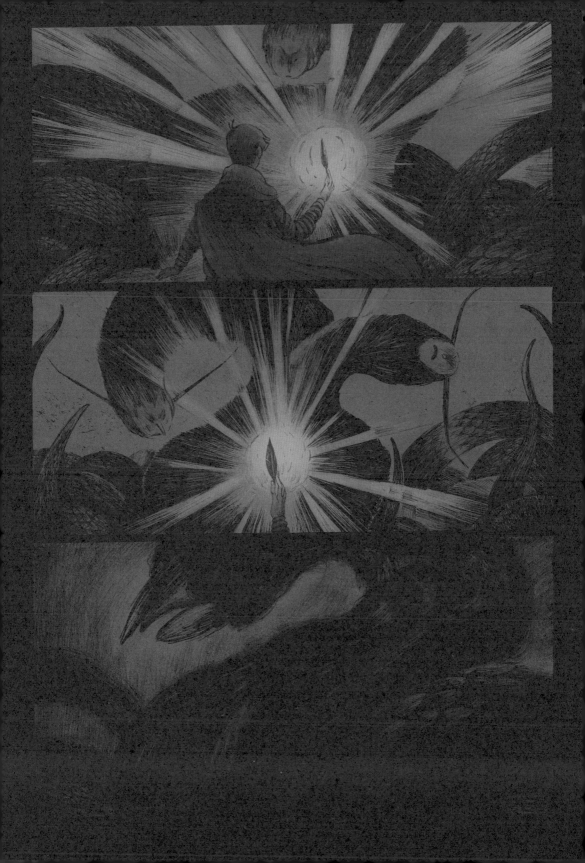

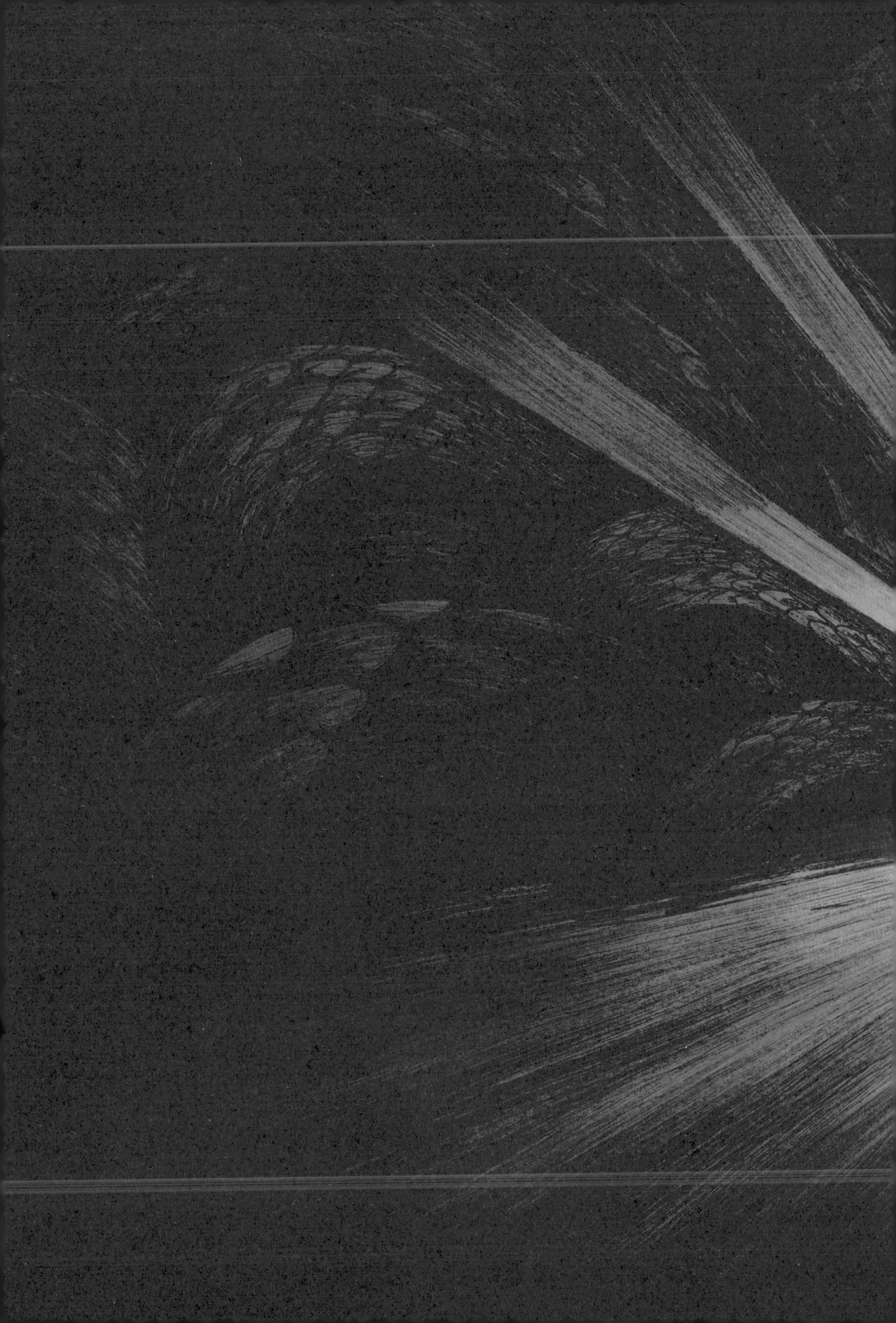

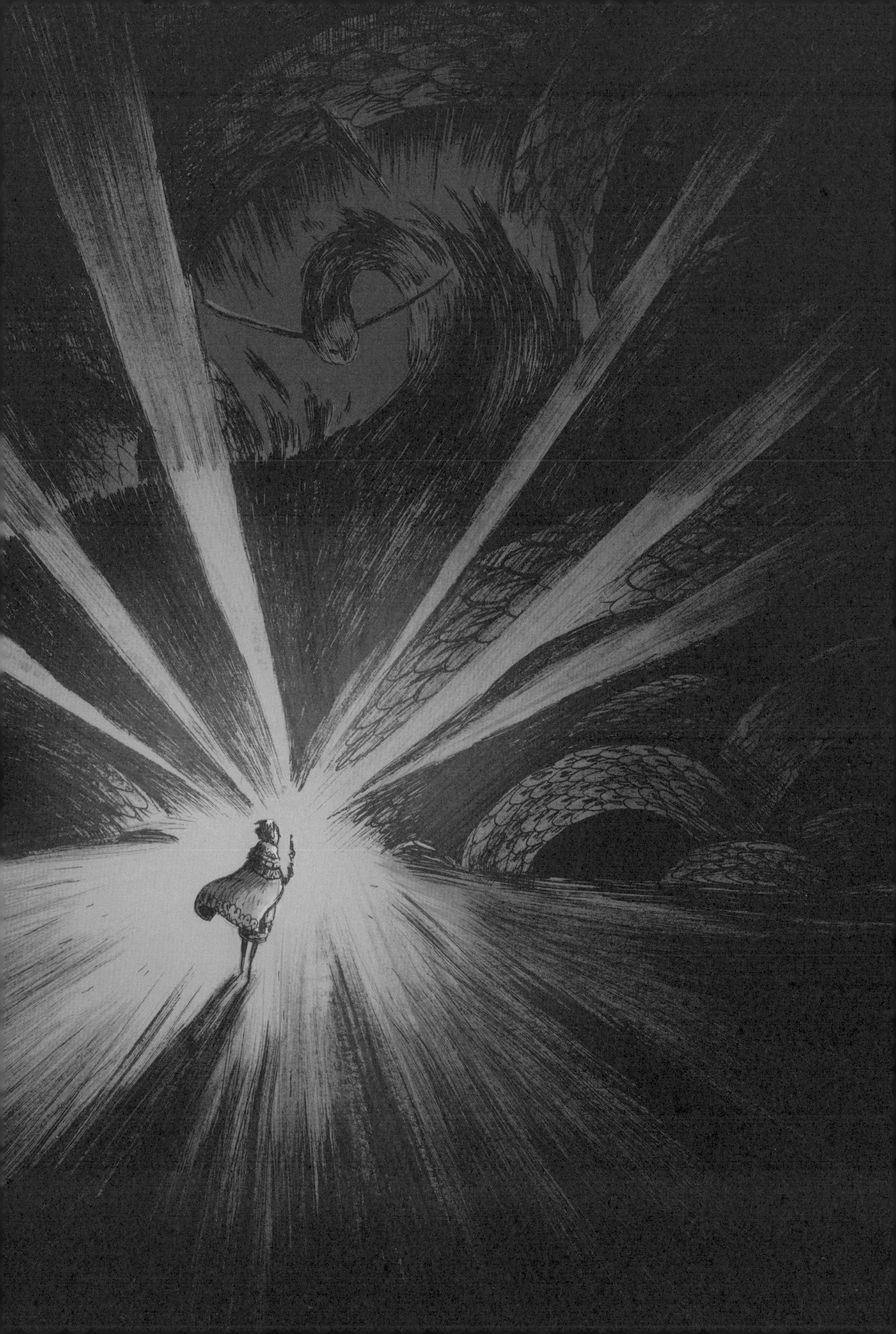

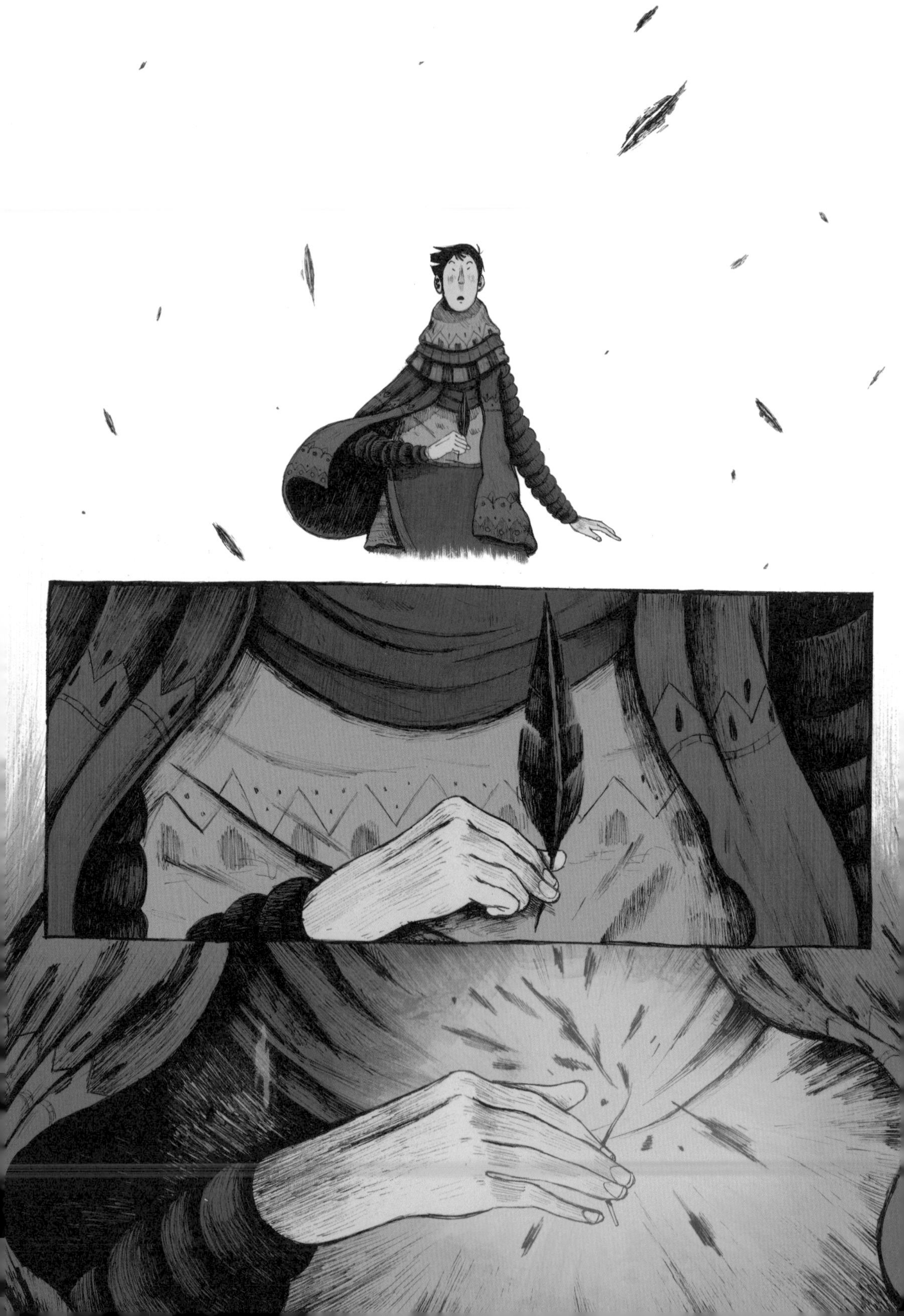

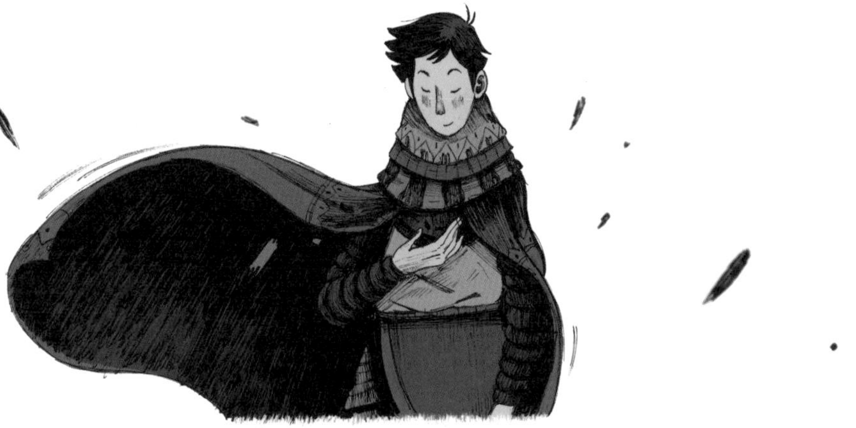
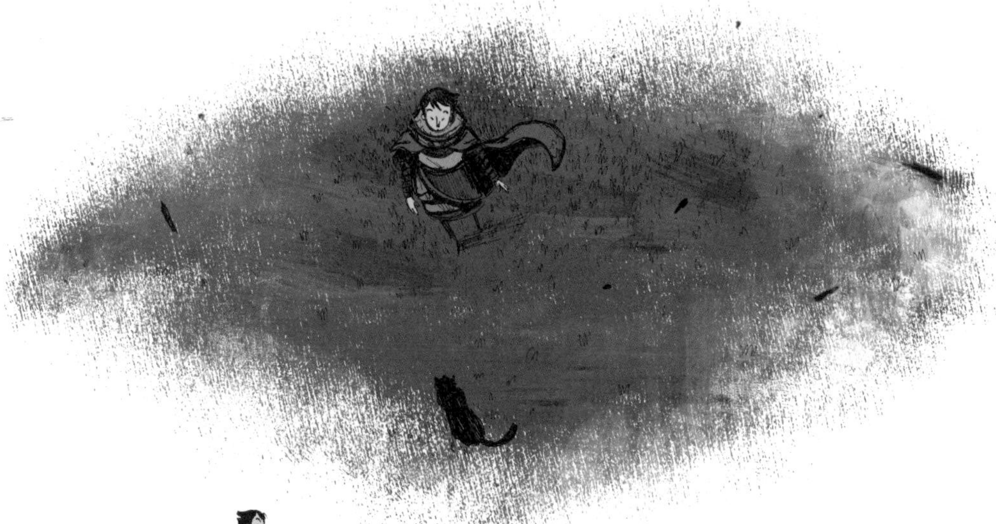
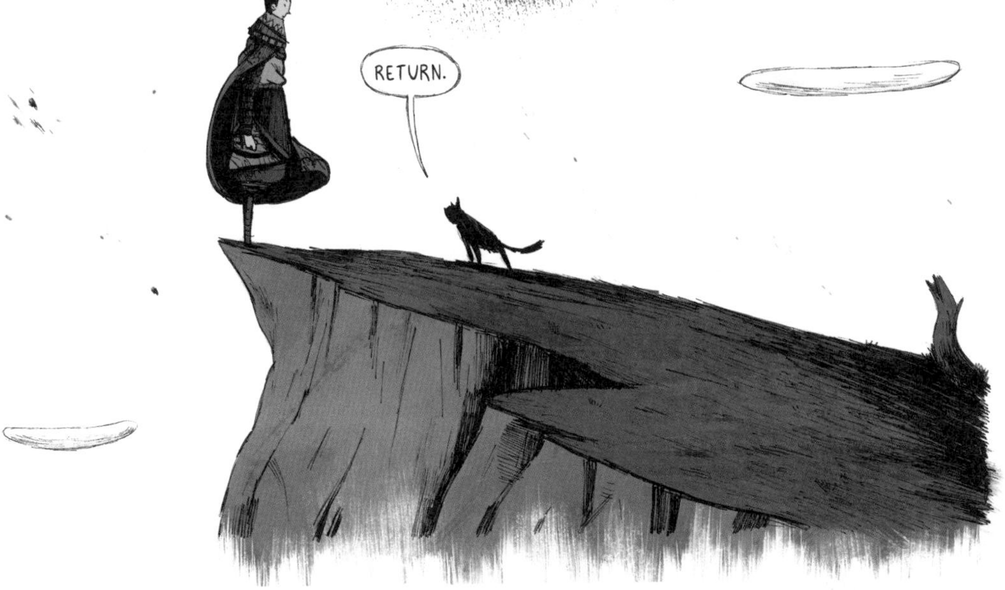
RETURN.

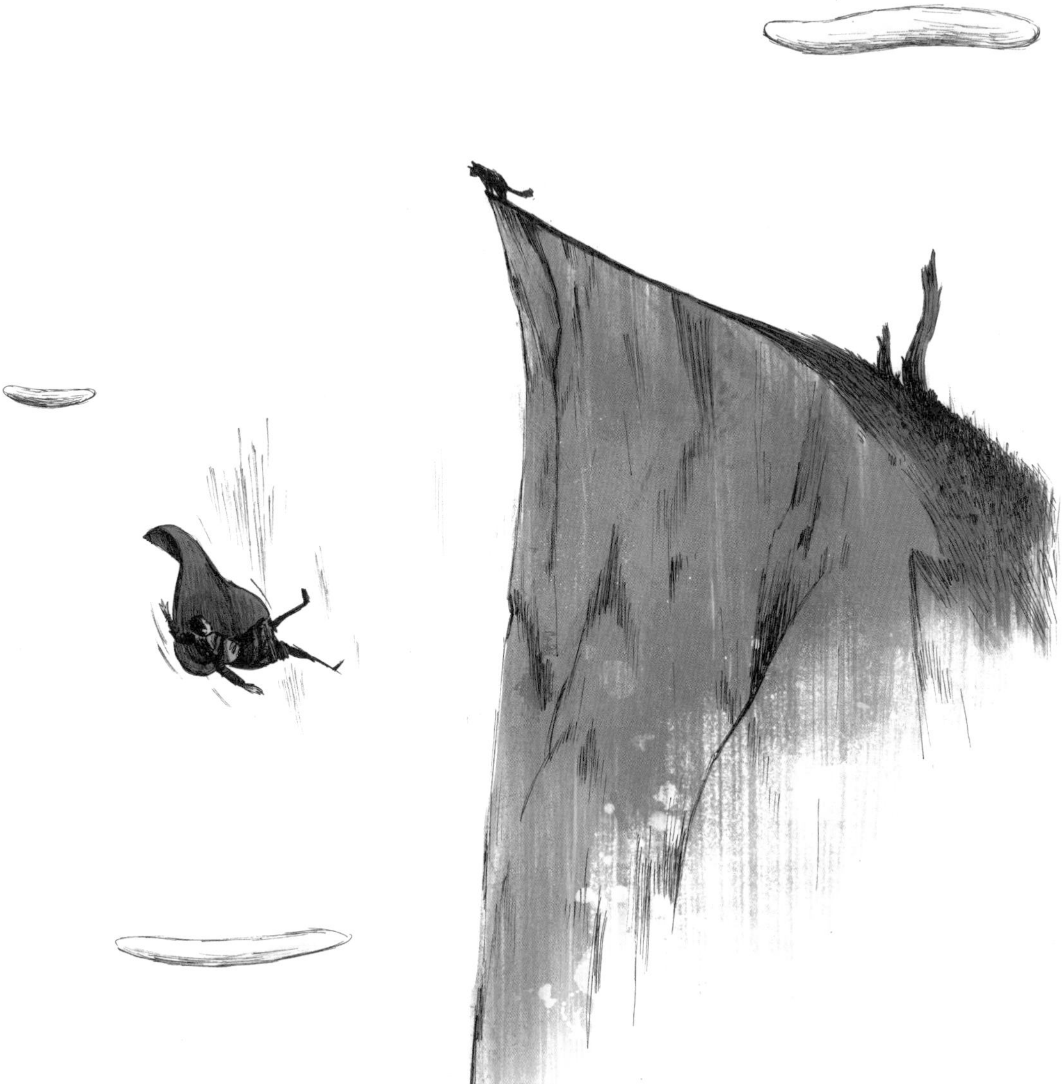

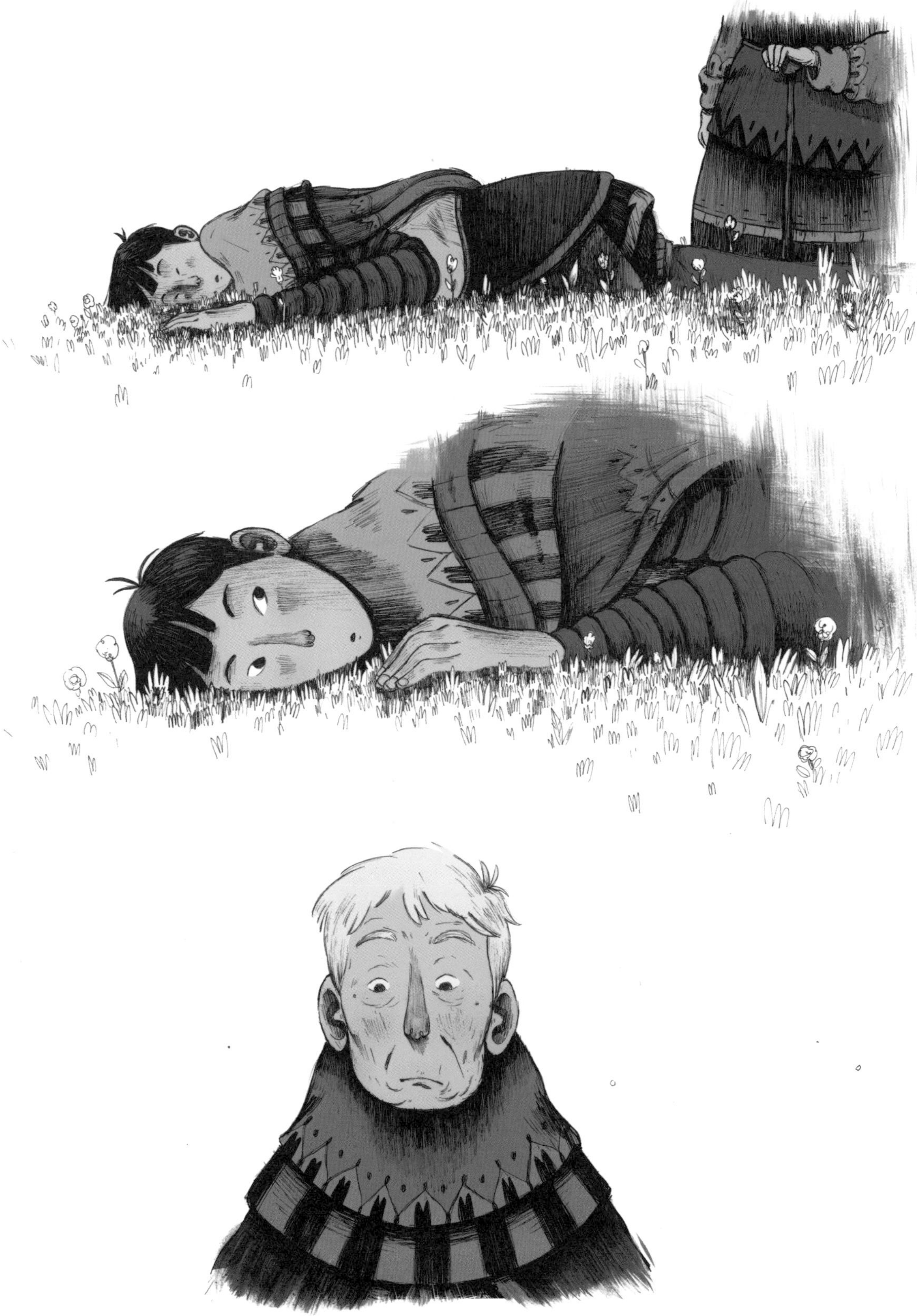

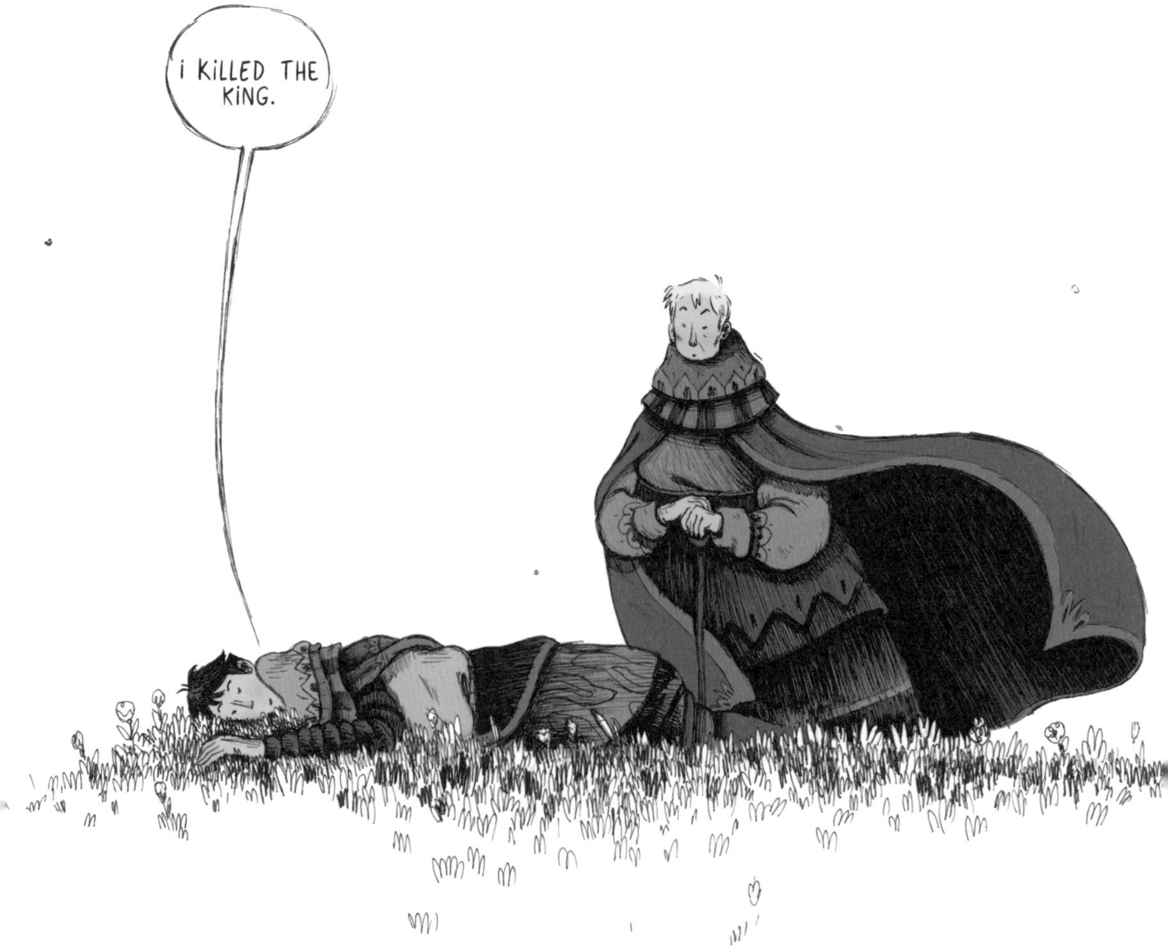
I KILLED THE KING.

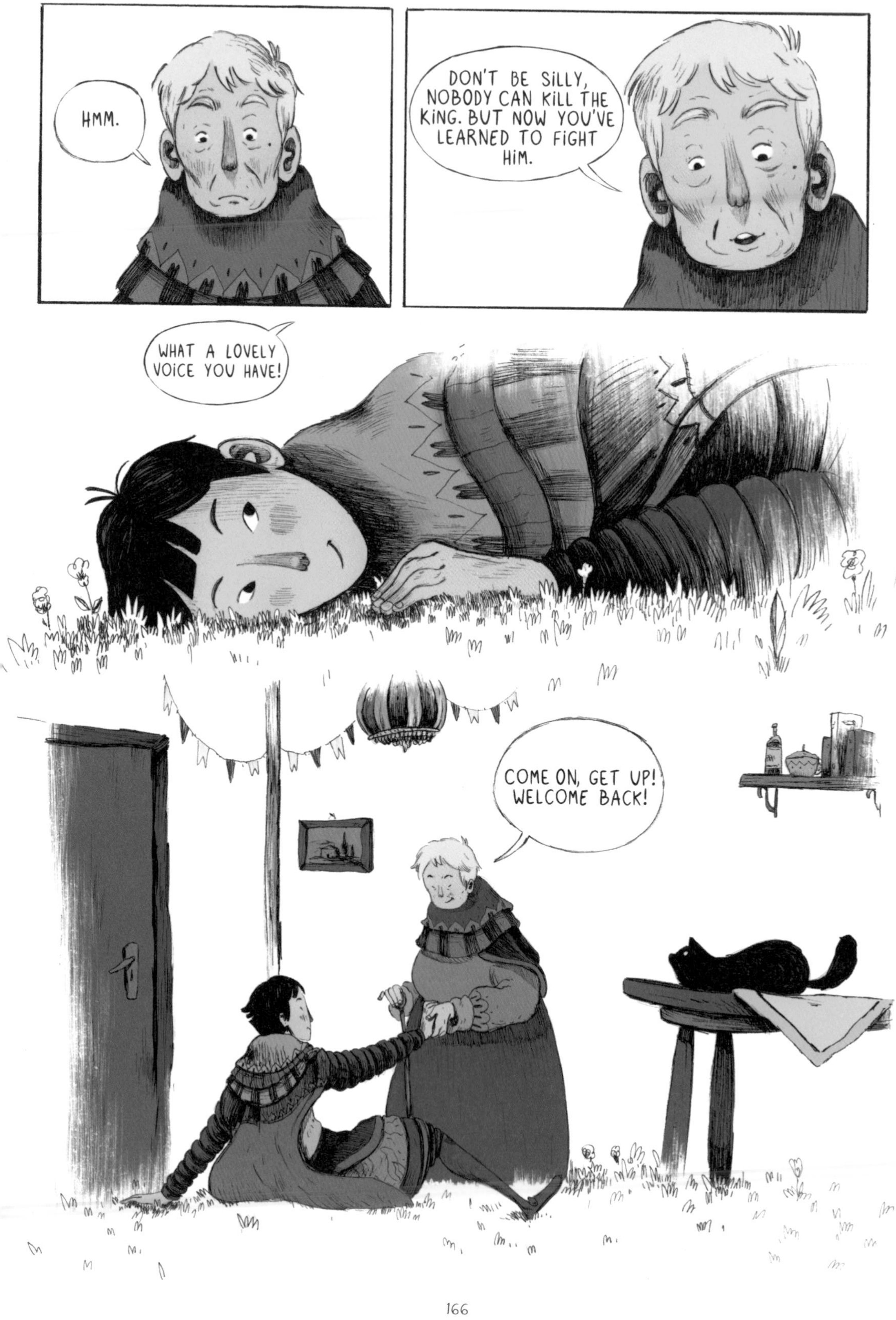
HMM.
DON'T BE SILLY, NOBODY CAN KILL THE KING. BUT NOW YOU'VE LEARNED TO FIGHT HIM.
WHAT A LOVELY VOICE YOU HAVE!
COME ON, GET UP! WELCOME BACK!

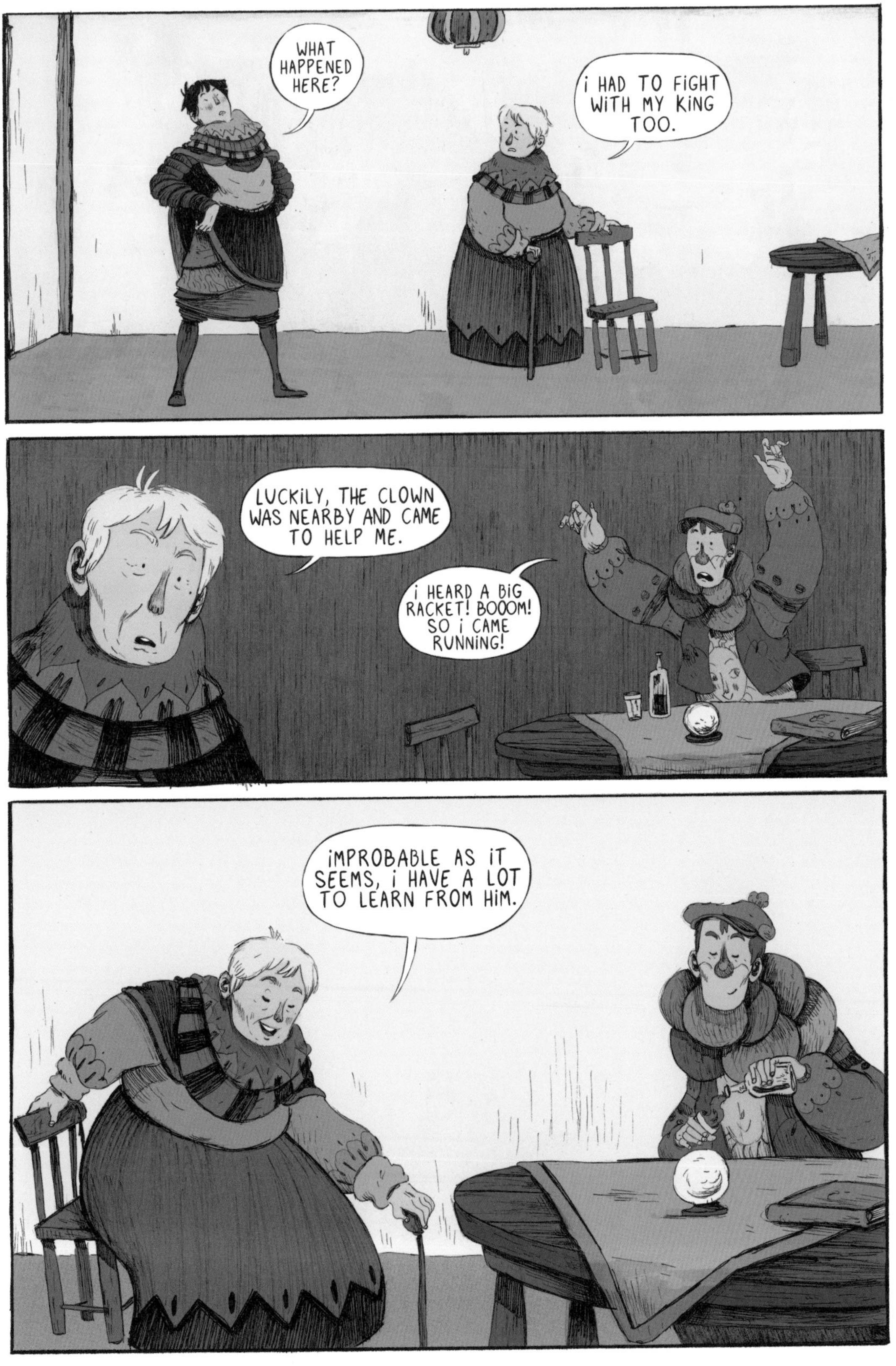
WHAT HAPPENED HERE?
I HAD TO FIGHT WITH MY KING TOO.
LUCKILY, THE CLOWN WAS NEARBY AND CAME TO HELP ME.
I HEARD A BIG RACKET! BOOOM! SO I CAME RUNNING!
IMPROBABLE AS IT SEEMS, I HAVE A LOT TO LEARN FROM HIM.

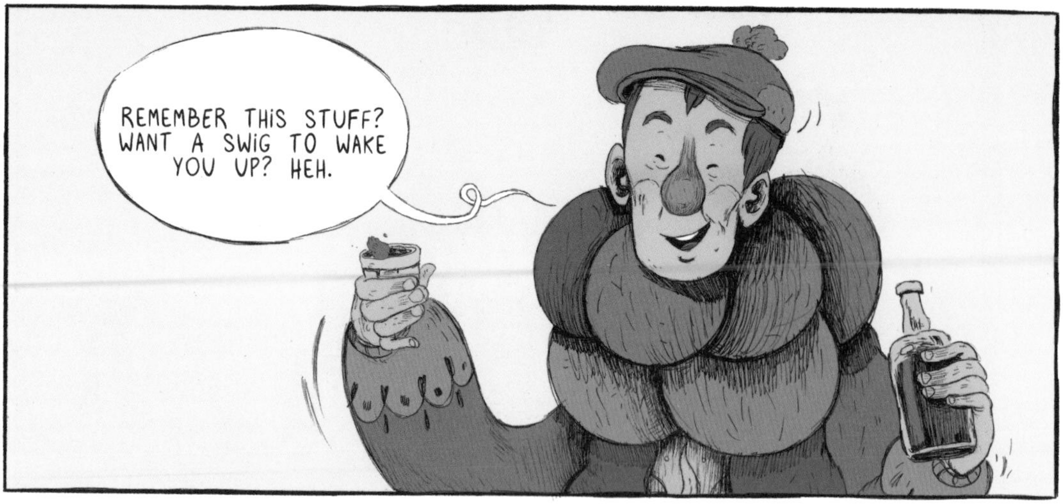
REMEMBER THIS STUFF? WANT A SWIG TO WAKE YOU UP? HEH.

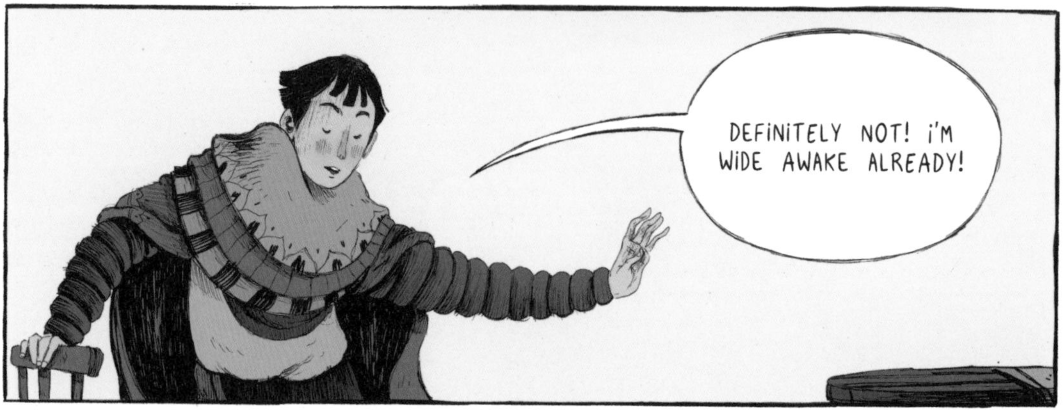
DEFINITELY NOT! I'M WIDE AWAKE ALREADY!

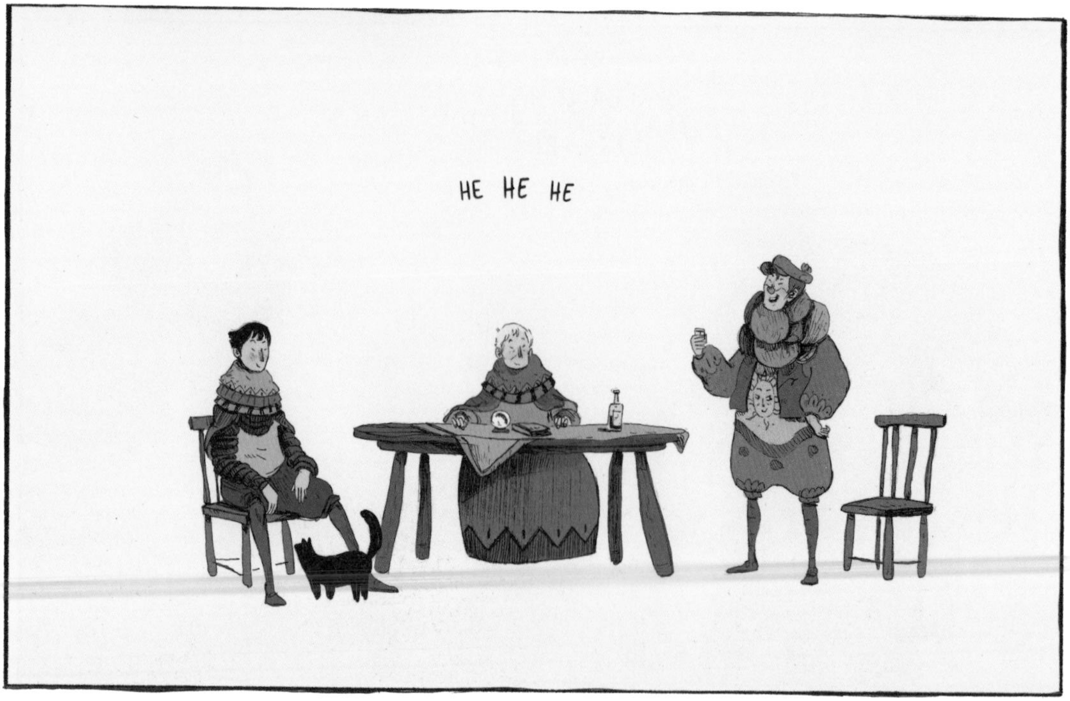
HE HE HE

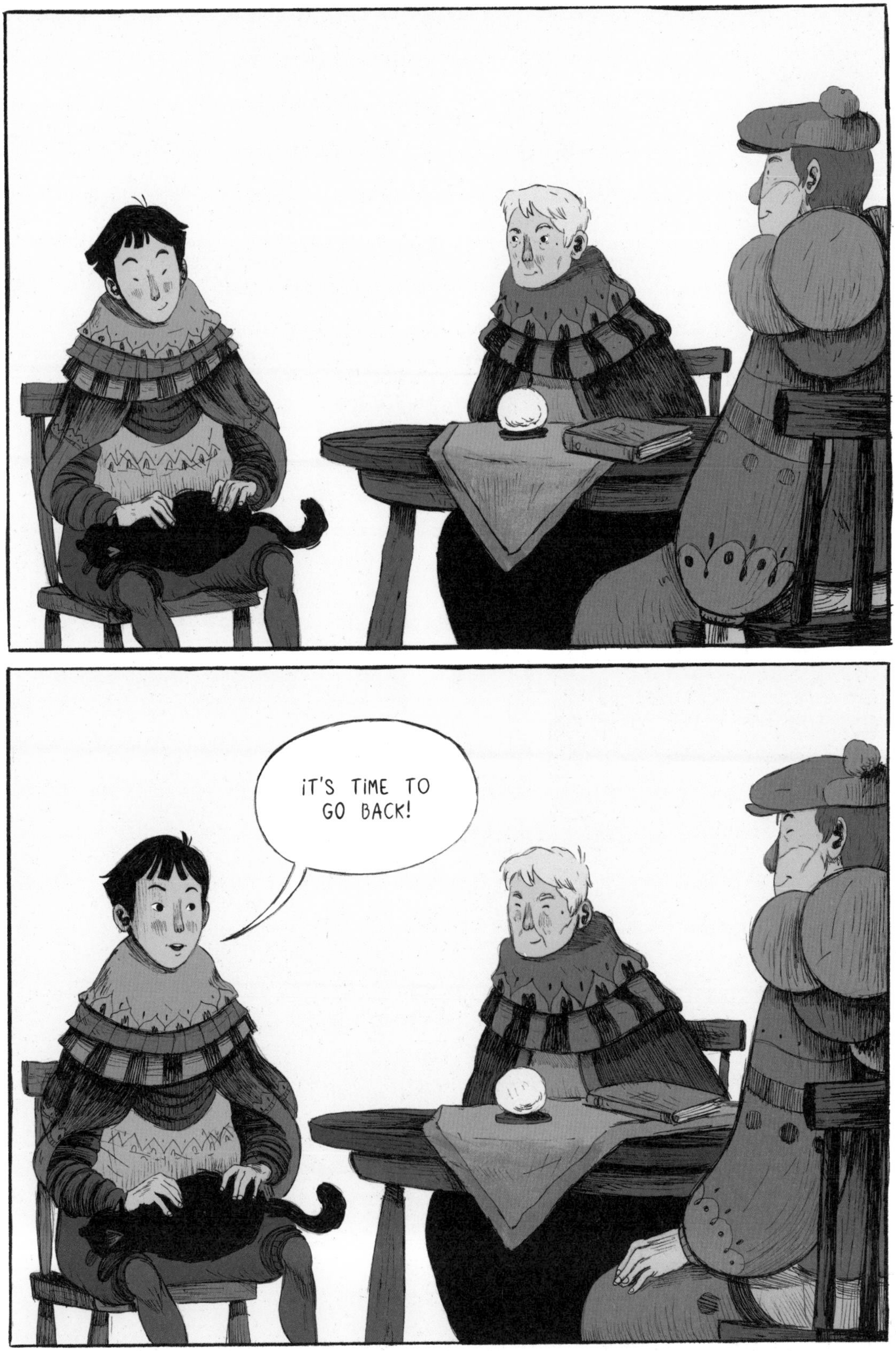
iT'S TiME TO GO BACK!

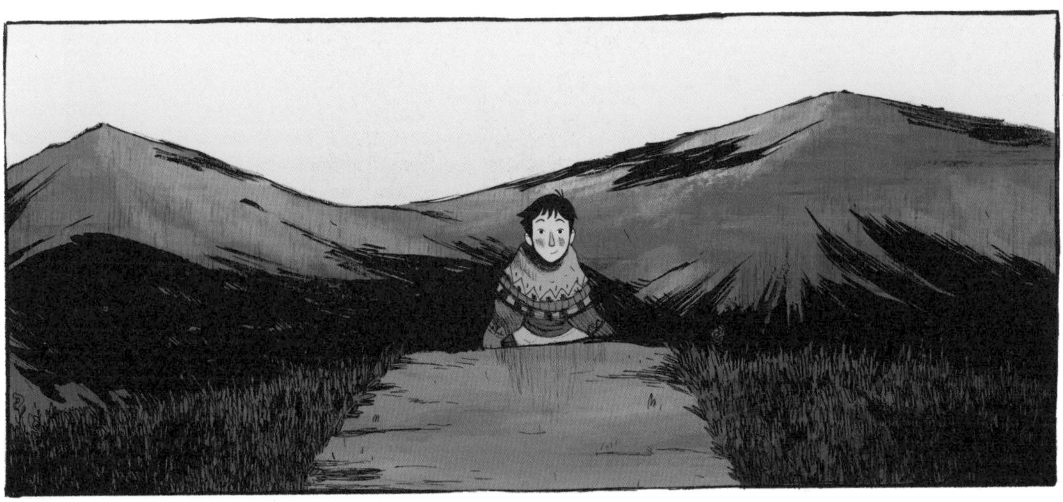

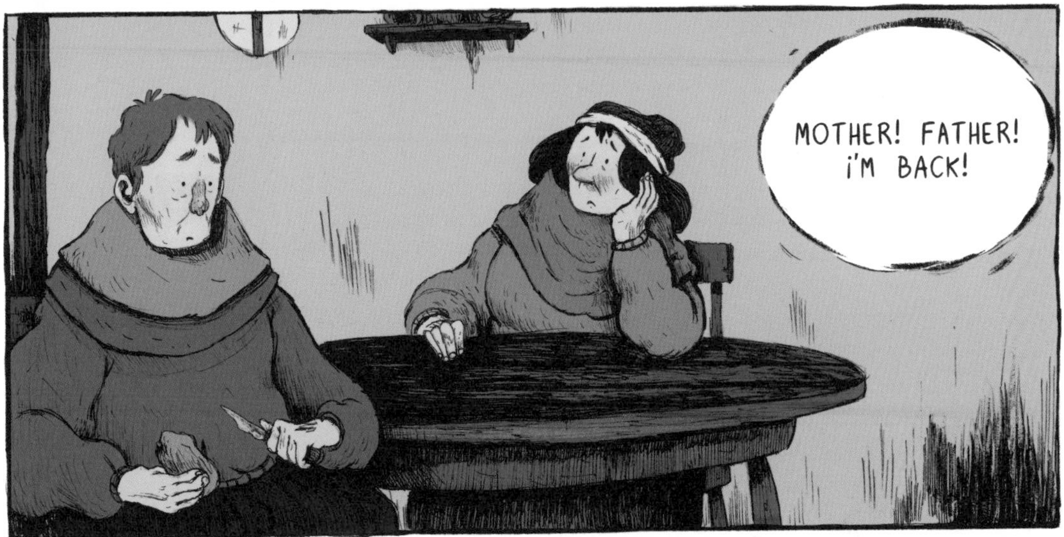
MOTHER! FATHER! i'M BACK!

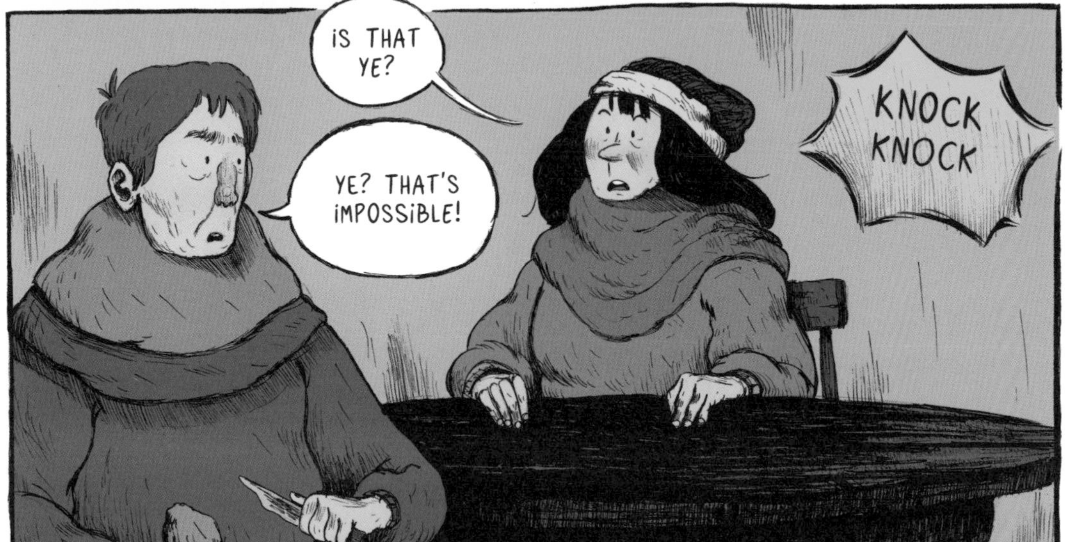
KNOCK KNOCK
iS THAT YE?
YE? THAT'S iMPOSSiBLE!

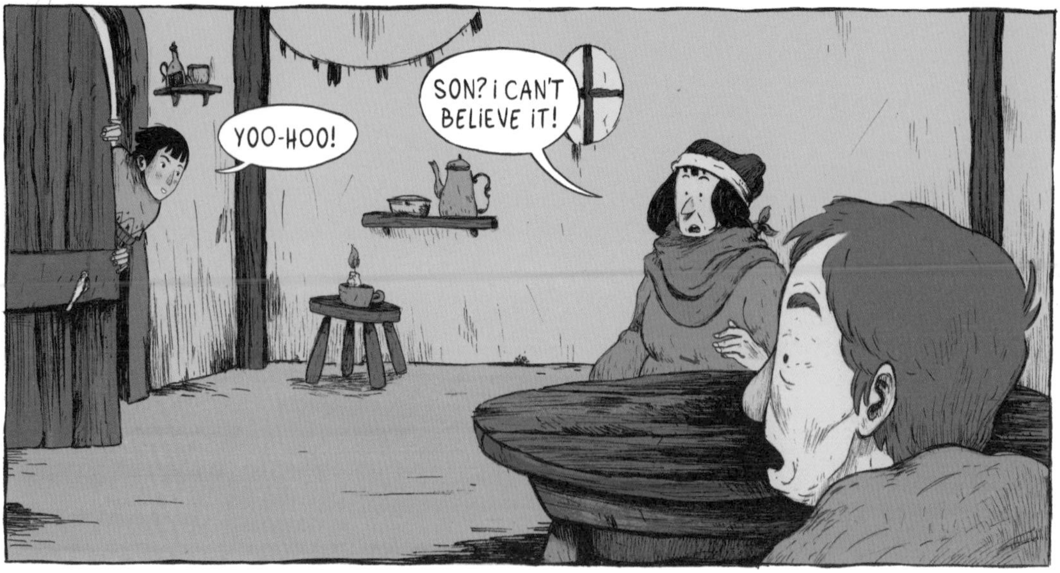
YOO-HOO!
SON? I CAN'T BELIEVE IT!

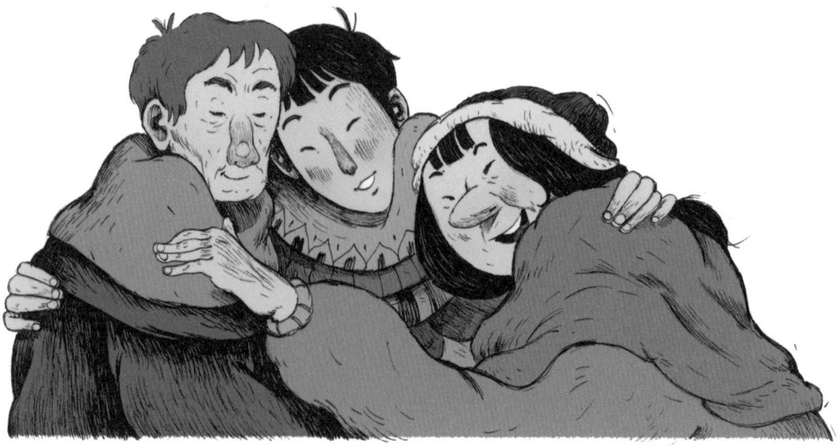

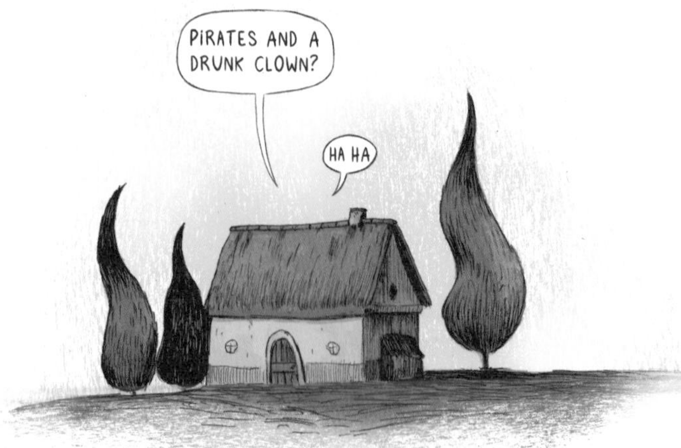
PIRATES AND A DRUNK CLOWN?
HA HA

THE KING'S SHADOW DOESN'T DISAPPEAR ALTOGETHER.
I'VE LEARNED THAT WE ALL LIVE WITH IT, EACH IN OUR OWN WAY.

SOME PEOPLE LIVE HUDDLED UNDER THE KING'S WINGS. I DECIDED TO CONFRONT HIM. SOMETIMES I'M AMAZED. THE ATTACKS SCARE ME, THEY WOUND ME, BUT THEY BRING WITH THEM THE MEMORY OF THE THINGS I'VE LIVED, THE THINGS I'VE LEARNED.

MY WOUND IS ALSO MY CURE.

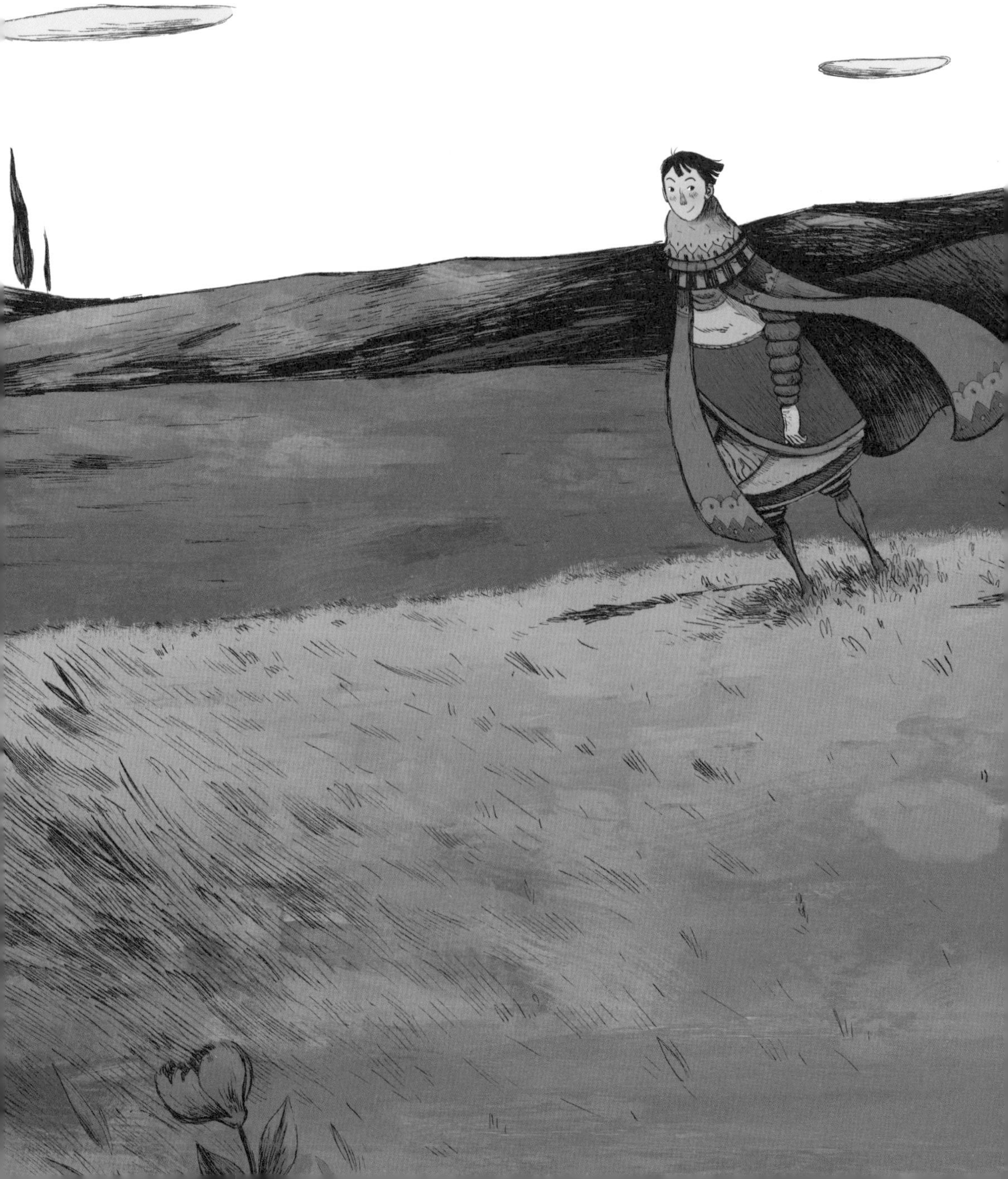

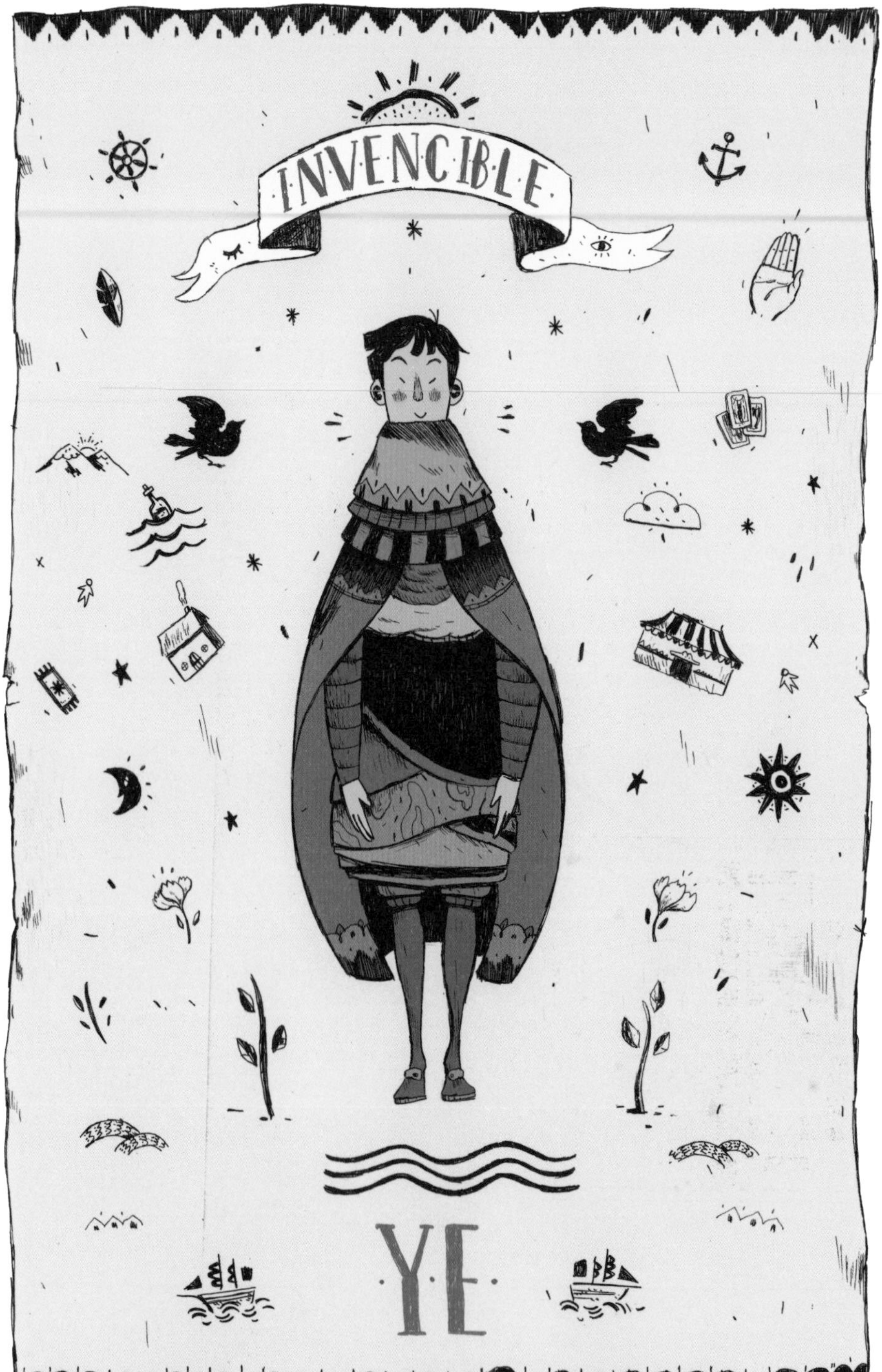
INVENCIBLE
YE